AMY'S

Baby Amy is abandoned on the orphanage steps when her
father runs away to sea. She is all alone in the world except for
her sailor doll, the Captain. She takes him everywhere and tells
him all her secrets. Then one day a strange and wonderful thing
happens. An orphanage is full of searching spirits; dreams and
memories float about . . . it is a place where anything might
happen if you wish for it enough. And suddenly the Captain
comes alive and turns into a real little man. At last Amy has a
real brother.

But for Amy and the Captain there are problems ahead and
even more remarkable things happen before they set off
together on a voyage of discovery . . . to hunt for a treasure
more valuable than gold.

Richard Kennedy is the custodian of the Oregon State University Marine Science Centre. He has also spent some years in
the U.S. Air Force and taught in country schools. He has had
sixteen other books published in the U.S.A. He lives in Oregon
and has two grown-up sons.

Richard Kennedy

AMY'S EYES

PUFFIN BOOKS

PUFFIN BOOKS

Penguin Books Ltd, 27 Wrights Lane, London w8 5tz (Publishing and Editorial)
and Harmondsworth, Middlesex, England (Distribution and Warehouse)
Viking Penguin Inc., 40 West 23rd Street, New York, New York 10010, USA
Penguin Books Australia Ltd, Ringwood, Victoria, Australia
Penguin Books Canada Ltd, 2801 John Street, Markham, Ontario, Canada l3r 1b4
Penguin Books (NZ) Ltd, 182-190 Wairau Road, Auckland 10, New Zealand

First published in the U.S.A. by Harper & Row Junior Books 1985
First published in Great Britain by Julia MacRae Books 1986
Published in Puffin Books 1987

Reproduced, printed and bound in Great Britain by
Hazell Watson & Viney Limited,
Member of the BPCC Group,
Aylesbury, Bucks
Typeset in Sabon

CONTENTS

Acknowledgements

*Thanks to Pat Hayner for Miss Quince's poem,
and thanks to John Chrisman,
his fine judgement and patient ear.
A special thanks to Paul Merrell
and Carol Van Strum for much.*

FOR THE
LEONARD STREET GANG
AND
KATHLEEN GOODMAN

Book One

CHAPTER ONE

The dove says, Coo, coo, what shall I do?
I can scarce maintain two.
Pooh, pooh, says the wren, I have ten,
And keep them all like gentlemen.

 my's eyes were open.
She lay in the basket swinging to and fro,
looking into the bright blue sky. She saw that it
was beautiful, but she would never remember this day
because she was only a baby and not long out of the house.
And now Amy was a poor baby, and she even had no
house. She had no mother, either, for her mother had fallen
ill and died only yesterday. Of course Amy didn't know
this. But Amy's father knew this, and he walked along the
road carrying Amy in the basket. His eyes were fixed in a
stare, as if he were looking into the face of a great grey
stone. The basket swayed to and fro, and Amy lay looking
into the motherly blue sky.

Next to Amy lay her twin brother, wrapped in a towel. A
strange-looking child he was, not blonde and creamy like
Amy, but instead he had a broad, flat face, and his head
came to a point on top. He had no hair at all, and his crusty
brown complexion was covered all over with lines and ruts
and bumps, all wrinkly ... what? Let us look more closely
at this child. No, of course not. This was not a baby – but a
loaf of bread. Amy had no brothers or sisters. Very soon
she was going to be alone in the world entirely, with no

father or mother to remember, nor any other relatives in the world, and no roots to her past.

Yet someone else was also in the basket with Amy and the loaf of bread. He looked rather like a root. He was thin and gangly like a root, dressed in blue trousers and a nice-fitting blue jacket with gold trim and epaulets at the shoulders. He was a Captain in the Navy, if you could tell by his uniform. And he was a doll, was this Captain. He had brass buttons, six in the front and two in the back on the tail of his jacket. He wore a hat pointed at the front and at the back, trimmed with gold (not real gold, of course, but yellow yarn). His insignia was a patch of red silk on his hat. On his belt hung a sword, nicely carved out of a splinter of cedar. You could tell that this doll was meant for important things, that he had a future before him, a mission perhaps, and adventure at least. Yet he also was young. Amy's father, a tailor by trade, had just given the last stitch, bite, and knot to him on the day that Amy was born. And so, being just as young as Amy, he had not yet learned his manners. He lay sprawled at all angles across Amy and the loaf of bread. And the basket swung to and fro.

It was a beautiful day in a poor land. Amy's father was walking towards the sea, for there was no work for a tailor in the country. Many others were without work also, and if you have no work you must save your pennies for bread and take up needle and thread yourself. Why should a sleeve or a pair of trousers be so difficult to fashion, so say you. And you are right. Poverty is a great teacher.

But in a seaport town there might be work for a tailor. Amy's father remembered this again, nodding his head as he walked along. Surely the ships still sail. And a sailing ship needs sails. And what are sails but tailoring done for the wind? A good tailor can sew a nice fit for the wind, tell you that. And then there's netmaking, if the fish still swim. So what's a net but a large sort of embroidery stitch, or maybe crochet?

So. Amy's father was going to the sea.

Perhaps, he thought, he might even be a tattoo artist. Tattoos are done with needles, after all, and needles are a tailor's tool. One night he had come home after an evening at a public house, singing, drinking, and talking with friends, and it had all of a sudden come upon him that the Captain, then unfinished and with no clothing yet, could use a tattoo. It is an old urge among sailors to want a tattoo, and there is probably more to it than the vanity of being decorated. A tattoo is a token of memory and identity, and it is some small comfort after four months at sea, perhaps, to glance at the name of a loved one bordered around with flowers, or in time of trial to remember the tattooed motto "Death Before Dishonour," or when the ship is sinking to think on a graceful script that spells out "Mother," or to contemplate, in bitter moments, the picture of a heart thrust through with a dagger. So Amy's father gave the Captain a tattoo on his right forearm. It looked like this:

It pictured a needle and thread, and touched in red and blue ink gave indelible notice that this was not a mere sailor before the mast, but a doll to take command high upon the poop deck, a doll of some significance.

Amy's father might have been a sailor rather than a

tailor, had the choice been absolutely free to him. When he was young he used to think about the sea, and in books with maps he would trace the tip of his finger across oceans and follow the coasts of continents and buffet a stormy way around Cape Horn and visit peaceful South Sea islands in his mind. He wanted to be a sailor one day. Yet things happened differently. Instead of going to sea, he became a tailor. But now, as he walked along, he smiled to think that he might go to sea at last, and he noticed for the first time that the sky was clear and cloudless. It was only thirty miles to the sea. Amy's father walked faster, even now sniffing the air for the salt of the sea. He raised his face to the sky. High above he saw some white birds flying towards the ocean.

Amy was not going with him. Amy's father was going to leave her behind. When it was dark, he was going to set down the basket and walk away from it. Of course he was going to set it down in a very good place, at the gate of St. Anne's Home for Girls. He planned to return and get her after he had a job, and perhaps another wife to be a mother for Amy. He thought he might return in a year's time.

But here is the truth, and you shall know it now. Amy's father never returned. God only knows what happens to so many people who intend to return, but never do. God only knows what might happen to a good country tailor in a seaport town without a wife to watch over him. There are temptations and dangers in such a place, and a wild chance lurking round about the lanes and alleys such as seafaring men roam at all hours. Or perhaps it is the same wild chance that follows them from the sea, a stormy and haunting wind that blows always about their heads. Indeed, there might be a dozen reasons that Amy's father never came back for her, but not one of them was that he didn't love her more dearly than anything on earth.

It was just dark when they reached St. Anne's Home for Girls. Amy's father sat down under a tree by the road across from the place. A path with trees beside it ran up to the broad stone stairs that entered a great stone building. An iron fence surrounded the place. A dog barked. On the upper floor, lights were lit, moving about in the hands of the Ladies of St. Anne's. They were putting the children to bed.

Amy's father could hear a steady undertone of children's voices, and now and then a squeal, a high scream, or shouting. Then there was the beat of a stick on wood, and all went silent immediately. It was quiet for a minute. Then the last moving light moved out, and it was dark upstairs at St. Anne's. The dog barked again.

Fifteen, maybe twenty minutes passed. Amy's father took a scrap of paper from his pocket. It was too dark to read, but he knew what it said.

> *This is Amy. I love her and will come back for her.*
> *I have gone to the sea. God bless you.*
>
> *Amy's Father*

He pinned the scrap of paper on the Captain's chest, then tucked Amy between the Captain and the loaf of bread. He got up and walked across the roadway and up the path towards St. Anne's. The dog might be a bother, he thought. If it started yowling he would set the basket down outside the gate and run. Some Lady would run out to see the matter of it, and she would find Amy. But a quiet getaway would be best.

And as it happened, the dog was no problem at all. He was a large dog with long legs. He growled when Amy's father was at the gate, but he did not bark. This dog knew the smell of babies, so he knew that this strange man had some proper business with St. Anne's, and he had learned not to bark around babies and small children. Amy's father knelt at the gate. The dog regarded him closely. Putting his head down to his child, Amy's father said, "Good-bye, my dear," and kissed her. He touched the Captain, then, and instructed him. "Take good care of her, Captain." Squeezing the sides of the basket together, he passed it through the iron gate. He then turned his face and walked down the path. He walked all that night towards the seaport town of New Liberty and never came back for Amy.

It was a warm night. Amy awoke now and then and looked at the stars. The big dog with the long legs knew his duty. When it was night-time, it was his duty to guard the property of St. Anne's. Since the basket was inside the iron fence, it seemed to him that Amy was now the property of St. Anne's, so he guarded her.

Now and again he looked into the basket to see that everything was all right. He sniffed about at Amy, the loaf of bread, and the Captain. All seemed well to him. And this was an exceptional dog, for he did not eat the loaf of bread. He did lick at it a bit, however.

CHAPTER TWO

One for anger,
Two for mirth,
Three for a wedding,
Four for a birth,
Five for rich,
Six for poor,
Seven for a witch,
I can tell you no more.

E arly the next morning there came the rapping of a
stick in the upstairs children's dormitory and the
loud, cheerful call of a good Lady of St. Anne's,
"God bless the day! Out of bed with all of you." Only then
did the good watchdog begin barking and running up and
down the stone steps. And then, bundled in greatskirts and
white aprons, from out of the high door of St. Anne's
bustled the High Mistress of the institution, Mrs. Hill.

She ran to the basket, nearly tripping all the while over
the great dog with the long legs. She hesitated a moment
with her fingertips to her cheeks.

"Oohhh," she exclaimed. "Aaahhhh." Mrs. Hill
scooped the basket up to hold to her bosom, returning up
the stairs carefully, murmuring an oath upon a land that
would be so poor that babies are abandoned out of want.
Inside the high door, she was surrounded by the other
Ladies of St. Anne's. They brought the basket inside and set
it on the long oak table in the library.

Amy, the Captain, and the loaf of bread were turned this way and that as every inch of the trio was examined. Mrs. Hill read the note pinned to the Captain. All the Ladies nodded soberly, but approved.

All except for Miss Quince. She had been poking about particularly at the Captain.

"Left by some dirty sailor," said Miss Quince. "It's a sailor doll."

"Nevertheless," said Mrs. Hill.

"Not even wanted, I warrant," said Miss Quince, scowling. "You see by the doll what was wanted was a boy."

"Nevertheless," said Mrs. Hill, handing the loaf of bread to the cook and tucking the blanket around Amy.

"Probably had no proper mother at all," mumbled Miss Quince, and pushing at his coat sleeve she discovered the Captain's tattoo. "And look! A filthy tattoo on him. And a filthy snake it is," she said, mistaking the emblem of needle and thread. "A filthy snake crawling up a filthy ... fence post, I suppose it is."

"Never-the-less!" said Mrs. Hill conclusively. So Amy was taken off to be fed, bathed, and wrapped into a crib.

Miss Quince followed Amy's arrival with a hard eye. She was a woman pinched and thinned by spite, holding her job at St. Anne's chiefly because of an important connection in the world outside. Her small, petty angers could generally be borne, but the arrival of Amy and the Captain was gall to her. For she had known a sailor once, long ago, when she had been young and could still love. But her young sailor had made promises, gone away to sea, and never come back. Miss Quince blamed him for that with a blame so constant and deep that it flooded out of her still. And yet that young sailor might have drowned at sea and been blameless. Miss Quince, however, kept her misery and bitterness after these many years, imagining the very worst of her sailor, alive somewhere, sinning, and breaking promises. So she hated all sailors, and even a sailor doll. She had no love or care for Amy, and wouldn't eat a crumb of that loaf of bread.

When you are raised in an orphanage it is a Rough and Tumble, Catch as Catch Can, the Devil Take the Hindmost and What's in It for Me sort of life. The whole wear and tear of it is written about elsewhere. Our part of the story is only to tell the good news that Amy survived into her fifth year without any terrible damage to her spirit. During those years she had no very great happiness, however, and nothing truly to call her own. During those years the Captain himself was kept in a shoe box on a linen closet shelf. Amy didn't even know he existed. Finally it became obvious to Mrs. Hill and all others that Amy's father would not return, so she took Amy aside and explained to her that her father had been a sailor who had gone away to sea and never come back, but that he loved her and had left a doll with her so that Amy might remember him. Mrs. Hill then presented Amy with the Captain.

Amy carried the Captain with her everywhere she went. Sometimes he was tied around her waist with a ribbon, sometimes slung over her back, sometimes roughly dragged behind. She talked to him constantly, perhaps asking his advice on a matter or explaining to him that she was going to do this or that and didn't care for his opinion.

"Captain," she might say, sitting in the yard with him in her lap, "when Bonnie comes out to play, I'm going to stick this rotten pear down her neck and squash it. Now, I'm not asking your opinion. You *saw* that she knocked my dessert on the floor on purpose." That day, when Bonnie came out to play, she got a rotten pear squashed down her neck, and the Captain was a silent witness.

Amy liked books. When she was six, she could read. She read to the Captain the complete rhymes and riddles out of *Mother Goose*, and, what is more, explained it all.

> "Solomon Grundy,
> Born on a Monday,
> Christened on Tuesday,
> Married on Wednesday,
> Took ill on Thursday,
> Worse on Friday,
> Died on Saturday,
> Buried on Sunday.
> This is the end
> Of Solomon Grundy,"

quoth Amy from *Mother Goose*. "You see, Captain, this is about a man who lived a very fast life. He finally got married, but it was too late for his wife to do anything about him. He never learned to relax, and he drank too much brandy and ate too many rich foods. He died of the gout, I think. Now here's another.

> "We are all in the dumps,
> For diamonds are trumps;
> The kittens are gone to St. Paul's.
> The babies are bit,
> And the moon's in a fit,
> And the houses are built without walls.

"Now, you see, Captain, the first line means that everyone is feeling badly. The second line is to make a rhyme, but it doesn't mean anything. That's called nonsense. Then the story begins. St. Paul ate the kittens and bit the babies, and the moon was angry with him. After that, everybody lived in trees."

Amy looked at the Captain.

"When you are older, dear, you will understand these things. Mother Goose was a very wise woman. See, here is her picture on the cover of her book. She used to fly around the countryside on a great white goose, and when she landed she told poems to the children. Now I shall read you about Mistress Mary.

> *"Mary, Mary, quite contrary,*
> *How does your garden grow?*
> *With silver bells and cockle shells,*
> *And pretty maids all in a row."*

Amy wrinkled her brow at that one.

"What it means ... is that Mary planted seeds that turned into little girls. And bells and seashells." She frowned, looking at him. They rested with their backs against a tree, the Captain gazing into space.

"You mustn't look so stupid. Just because I can't tell you exactly how it happened doesn't mean it *didn't*. It's a mystery, and we must accept it on faith."

The years passed.

Amy was seven, then eight, skinned and bruised, chasing balls and cats, wrestling, kicking and screaming, fighting and kissing, acting ever so sweet and then again not so sweet. But always she was prepared for a mystery, and she had no lack of faith to believe in mysteries or even miracles if they might happen.

Amy had only one real enemy, but she didn't know why that one existed and hardly would have understood the reason. All Amy knew was that Miss Quince watched at her sternly whenever she was about, and was always wanting to catch her breaking a rule. This made Amy quite uncomfortable. If she was running and saw Miss Quince watching her, Amy slowed down, and then walked, carefully gathering the Captain under her arm. If she was playing in a group and saw Miss Quince watching her, Amy stopped playing and stood quietly aside, holding the Captain close, and if someone was needed to take the blame for some act, and the choice was up to Miss Quince, Amy would be blamed. So because of Miss Quince, Amy missed out on many desserts, many recesses, and also some picnics. She knew that Miss Quince liked to punish her, but didn't know why.

It was because Miss Quince hated sailors, also sailor dolls, and also little girls whose fathers had been sailors.

However, Amy also had a good friend among the Ladies of St. Anne's.

This was Miss Eclair.

As often as Miss Quince could find a reason to punish Amy, Miss Eclair could, half the time, save her from it – or at least make the punishment easier. Miss Eclair had given forbidden desserts to Amy, or a toy to make the time go more happily when she was shut up in the dormitory, and once she brought a candle and a book when Amy was imprisoned in a dark cupboard. They shared kisses of joy and sadness, and were the closest of friends.

One of the most lovely afternoons that Amy could remember was when all the others went off for a picnic, but Amy was left behind for punishment, the doing of Miss Quince, of course.

Miss Eclair stayed behind that day also. She sat with Amy and the Captain on the lawn of St. Anne's, and the whole pantry was open to them. They ate buttermilk biscuits spread with marmalade, thick slices of ham, fresh eggs and milk, and apple pie. Miss Eclair took Amy all through St. Anne's, showing her the forbidden rooms in the great stone building. They climbed through a trapdoor into

[22]

a high, small room in the tower. Far, far off they could see all the other children and Ladies of St. Anne's having their picnic in a grove of trees by the river. They shared this grand secret, and other secrets, and Miss Eclair was as much like a mother to Amy as she would ever know.

Amy would occasionally dream about the Captain. When she did, the dreams were most lifelike, and in colour as well. But the dreams were sometimes strange. One night she was dreaming that she was walking with the Captain in the fields. St. Anne's was nowhere in sight, but just the two of them were walking in the sunshine and chatting. Then, turning towards the Captain, she saw a flash of light cross his face, almost as if a mirror were flashed at him. Amy looked around, but could see no one else in the field. Then she looked up. There, above the Captain's head, was hanging a gigantic needle, the thread of which reached into the heavens. It was a flash of light off the steel needle that had touched the Captain. Amy cried out, fearful that the thread would break, and the needle would fall and pierce the Captain. But he only smiled.

"Don't be afraid," he said. *"It's a gift from my father."*

Amy woke up. For a long time she stared at the Captain in the moonlight.

Amy had a private place down by the marsh next to St. Anne's. The girls were warned they must not go down there to play, for there were fish that ate mud down there, and toads, and quicksand, bad smells, and green slime. So the timid girls did not go down there. But Amy did. For there were also lovely furry cat-tails, white lilies that floated, bugs that walked on the glimmering water, beautiful choruses of frog and bird voices, and a lovely green light. There was a dry and soft hollow in the side of a large alder tree. Amy sat in there with the Captain, as if they were at their throne overlooking their forbidden domain.

" 'And they lived happily ever after,' " proclaimed Amy, and laid aside her book. The Captain was propped up against her shoe, staring at her.

"What did my father look like, Captain? Do you remember him? Did he say when he was coming back?"

She took the Captain up, hugged him, and looked closely into his button eyes, trying to see if a reflection of her father might still be there.

"Please try to tell me something, Captain. More than anything, I want him to come back for me. Do you think he ever will?"

And the Captain stared back at her.

"Oh, Captain, can't you help me?"

Amy cried then, and her tears soaked into the Captain's stuffing.

Well, there's lots of crying around an orphanage. Others try to see faces they once knew, or never knew, and the polished hallways when they are deserted and quiet seem almost to be haunted, full of spirits searching, and searched for. Dreams and thin memories float all about, ghosts sit in the waiting room on hard chairs, invisible playmates sleep under the beds, and around any corner might be a fairy godmother or a horse with wings. Wishes are as thick as pollen in the air. Anything might happen.

CHAPTER THREE

Old Mother Twitchett has but one eye,
And a long tail, which she can let fly;
And every time she goes over a gap,
She leaves a bit of her tail in a trap.

(A needle and thread)

ow, when Amy was ten years old, a remarkable thing *did* happen. It changed her life forever.

The Captain had now been dragged about with Amy for six long years, so he looked to be the very grief of a doll. Not only was his sword gone, and all his brass buttons, but also his hat and his coat-tails. His fine blue uniform was scuffed and thin, his seams were split and parting, and his rag stuffing showed in several places. Amy observed this one day with a sort of surprise, for the Captain seemed to her always bright and new and fresh, although he had been through as hard a life as one of Napoleon's foot soldiers. She held him up high and turned him this way and that like a baby, examining the damage. That same afternoon she sat on her bed sewing at the Captain's seams. She was alone. The other girls were outside playing in the sunlight. By and by, when she had zigzag-stitched her way around the Captain's legs, arms, and torso, she studied his shabby head. After stitching in a new straight line for his mouth and stringing some fresh yellow yarn for his hair, she considered his ears.

"Your ears, dear," said Amy, "are falling off. Now we'll

see to that." She took up her scissors. "This won't hurt at all. Here, I'll just carefully snip your ears off and then sew them back on with new thread."

This she did. She held the Captain's ears in her lap and drew the old thread out of them, humming to herself. As she was narrowly concentrating at threading her needle she spoke. "What were my father's ears like, Captain? I've never thought about his ears. I suppose people don't think about ears much, so that's the reason of that. Were they long and like clamshells? No? Were they round and like cauliflowers? No? Maybe tiny like yours and fuzzy all over?" Amy smiled and stuck the thread through the eye of the needle. "But I don't mean to say that your ears aren't beautiful. They are lovely ears. Here, you may look at them." She held them up before the Captain's button eyes.

"Oh, Captain," she said, delighted with an idea. "How many people in the whole world have seen their own ears in front of their eyes? That *is* special, isn't it?"

She knotted her thread and pulled it through one of the Captain's ears. "But of course you can't hear till I get your ears back on your head."

She sewed one on and picked up the other. As she was ready to make the first stitch, she shifted her place on the bed, bumped her elbow on the bedstead, and thrust the needle deep into the Captain's head.

"OUCH!" said the Captain.

Amy dropped the ear on the floor and yanked the needle out of his head. He appeared to blink, but it happened so quickly that she was not sure if she had blinked or if the Captain had. She looked closely.

The Captain's eyes were wet.

Amy touched a finger to one of the buttons, then touched her tongue and tasted. It tasted of salt tears. The

Captain was *alive*, and he was crying from the poke of the needle!

Well, children in orphanages are ready for such wonders. And should it be so surprising, anyway? Suppose you are talked to all the time, as the Captain was, and read to out of books, and hugged and loved constantly, and told the most secret things? Even a bundle of rags might respond to that. Certainly a doll would. And then stick a needle or pin in its head and you might be surprised if it *didn't* yell. Then, with just a little coaxing, you might even start a conversation.

There is, therefore, no doubt about what happened next. In a very short while the Captain and Amy were talking about the remarkable thing that had happened.

After the wonder and joy of it had been expressed by both of them, the Captain considered the case in detail.

"I always *was* alive, in a sort of way, Sis." (The Captain had begun calling Amy "Sis" right off.)

"I could see everything, and hear everything, and when I was caught in a closing door I could feel it, or when dropped from a window I wanted to yell," the Captain said. "But it was different then, in such a way as this. Now I am alive, and right here very close to you and the world. Yet before you stuck the needle in my head, I was just as alive, but it seemed like I was a thousand miles away. It was the poke with the needle that brought me to this place. Can you understand that?"

Amy tried to understand, and she thought she understood it well enough. Anyway, since the Captain always *had* been alive, even in that other sort of way, Amy and he had much to talk about, since everything was in common to them, the Captain having been seldom away from Amy's touch. But as for the first four years in the shoe box, the Captain remembered nothing – nothing of a social nature, anyway.

[27]

"I blame no one for that," the Captain said, "and it gave me time to think, and I thought about the sea and ships, and studied what I was thinking. Then I thought about the stars and how they go across the sky, and how the sun moves and the seasons change, and how you can find your way about the sea by knowing these things. And I thought about the wind and sea currents, and clouds and weather, and seabirds, and turtles that swim a thousand miles without stopping. And I thought about the many different kinds of fish there are, and about sails and ropes and brass fittings, and the North Star and the Southern Cross.... Oh, there was a lot to think about, Sis, for you see, I was learning my trade. I sailed all around the world in my mind, along the coasts of continents, across great oceans, and I visited South Sea islands. I don't doubt at all that I could take a ship to sea right now and sail it around the world if I'd a mind to."

The Captain grew thoughtful. "But from where I remembered all these things I don't know." He smiled. "But I wasn't so very lonely even in the shoe box, Sis. I dreamed about you, and I dreamed I saw you growing up and running about St. Anne's."

"I dreamed about you, too, Captain. Sometimes I dreamed about you standing on a sailing ship."

"Now, that's just exactly a dream I had many times," said the Captain. "Well, we *are* twins, you know, both of us finished up on the very same day. Yes, even that I can remember, and I heard your first crying out. We came into the world together, and it might be that we can have the same dreams."

"And you say you remember our father?"

"Clearly. Do you want to hear about him again?"

Amy nodded.

"A straight and honest man. Hair like straw and a happy

face. Bright eyes, like young hazelnuts. Not a big man, but not small. Very sure hands, delicate fingers like a musician, but of course you know he was a tailor, and tailors have a nice touch. He held you up in the air and loved you like the sunshine, Sis."

"And then ... our mother ..."

The Captain looked at the floor sadly. "I never knew her. She was very sick in those days. I remember there was a beautiful blue dress on a hanger near her bedroom door, with pearl blue buttons down the front. There were flowers in the window she had picked. Your father kept a lamp lit all night long. Then one day the flowers were gone." He sat silent for a moment. "But enough of that. The next thing was that we were swinging to and fro in a basket, and you may be sure that our mother was watching over us." He paused. "I hear a mouse."

"A mouse?"

"A mouse. I hear a mouse walking. Quiet. Yes, it's a mouse. There! Now I hear it sniffing."

"But there's no mouse," said Amy. "Just the two of us. Are you feeling all right, Captain?"

"It's on the floor. I hear its toenails clicking."

Amy looked over the side of the bed. There, on the floor, next to the Captain's fallen ear, was a mouse. It dashed to the wall and scampered away when Amy moved. She picked up the ear and began sewing it back on the Captain's head.

"What a very strange thing," said Amy. "Now, does this hurt?"

"Not those little stitches. But that stab in the head is something I wouldn't like to happen again."

"How curious – that your ear could hear when it was on the floor."

"Most anything could be expected now, I suppose. And I

[29]

wouldn't think it was a piece of thread that connects the ears with hearing, anyway. Hmmmm. Yes, I suppose you could leave me here and carry my ears around in your pocket and I could hear everything that happened no matter where you went."

"That's an awful thing to say, Captain! What would happen if I lost them when I was playing, and ... a bird flew off with them to line her nest. Then you'd hear nothing the rest of your life except the peeping of chicks."

The Captain then told about the first night inside the gate of St. Anne's, and about the big dog with the long legs, and how the Ladies took Amy in. Next came the four years in the shoe box, the Captain learning his trade and Amy learning to walk and talk. After that they were together again, and now they talked, laughed, and remembered things all afternoon.

When another child would now and then come into the dormitory, Amy hummed, and the Captain was silent. When at last the girls gathered together awaiting the call to clean up for supper, Amy sat on the edge of her bed with the Captain in her lap, turning his head this way and that so he might not miss any of the more interesting trouble or fights. You can always find a fight in an orphanage, or some small tragedy off in a corner.

From wash up time to bedtime there was no more chance to talk with the Captain. Amy dared only to wish him a single good night.

"Good night, Captain."

"Good night, Sis."

And they slept. Amy had dreams that all happened under a bright blue sky filled with white birds, and a sun that sang with light and warmth over the great rolling ocean.

CHAPTER FOUR

Follow my Bangalorey Man;
Follow my Bangalorey Man;
I'll do all that ever I can,
To follow my Bangalorey Man.
We'll borrow a horse, and steal a gig,
And round the world we'll do a jig,
And I'll do all that ever I can
To follow my Bangalorey Man.

Not only this, in the wonder of things — not only this, that the Captain was alive and could talk, but in less than a day's time he began to change into a real flesh-and-blood person.

It happened so quickly, his button eyes turning into real eyes, his ears into real ears, his hair into real hair, and his skin into real skin, that Amy knew he must be hidden from sight or he would be discovered. It must be done right away. Therefore she got busy at once sewing scraps of cloth to make a bag to carry the Captain in. When she was finished, she didn't have to pop him into the bag like a limp doll. The Captain could move by himself. He furled the edge of the bag like a sailcloth and stepped inside.

"It'll do for now, Sis," he said, "but it won't do for even a week, I'm afraid. I'm growing, you know. And I'm hungry as well."

"I'll think of something," said Amy, closing the bag over his head.

But she could think of nothing, and dared not tell even Miss Eclair of her problem. In the next two days, the Captain grew three inches. Amy saved bread from her own meals, a scrap of meat perhaps, half a potato, a handful of peas. She also made him a new jacket and a pair of pants. During the day she let him peek over the top of the bag to get some fresh air, but even that was a risk. Sometimes, when other children were about, the Captain shifted his position inside the bag. When this was noticed, it was hard for Amy to explain. Always she was on the lookout for Miss Quince, and stayed away from any of her paths of business.

The Captain continued growing. Each day he needed more food, so that Amy's health might be in danger if she continued to carry away so much of her own dinner from the table. Clearly, it was impossible that Amy should keep the Captain. He was nearly half as tall as Amy now, and less than a week had passed since Amy had brought him out of his trance with her needle. Now he must double in two like a jackknife to fit into the bag, which was most uncomfortable for him. Anyone with half an eye would soon discover how it was with the Captain. But Amy, thinking perhaps that some miracle as neat and quick as a pinprick might set things wonderfully to rights, let the deception bloom, although the situation would soon be as obvious as the coming of spring.

It was a Sunday afternoon. Amy and the Captain were down at the marsh. Amy had been reading to him about the albatross.

"Did you hear, Captain? The albatross is the largest bird in the world. Some of them are twelve feet from wing tip to wing tip, and white as clouds. Now, you should remember this, Captain, for if you ever sail on the ocean you'll likely see one of them, and you mustn't think it's an angel, because it's angels that come and take us to heaven when we die. So you mustn't be afraid. It's only a very big bird, and they are said to be friendly with sailors and ships. Sometimes they even land on a ship's deck."

But the Captain seemed not to be listening. Amy frowned and closed her book. The Captain was mumbling some latitudes and longitudes to himself. Amy sighed and lay back into the alcove of her tree. She half closed her eyes and whisked dreamily at the long grasses with a twig. After a while the Captain ceased reciting, for he had found a vacant place in his memory. After puzzling to himself for a few minutes, he spoke aloud.

"Tasmania," said the Captain.

"I beg your pardon."

"Tasmania, Sis. It's an island below the line – or in the southern hemisphere, as you would say. But confound it if I can remember if it's south of Australia or off the Cape of Good Hope at the tip of Africa. It's a large island, further-more, and that's what makes it so bothersome. It's ship-wrecks I'm worried about."

"Why should a large island be so bothersome, more so than a small one? Less bothersome, I should think, especially if you were shipwrecked on it."

"No, Sis, it's not the *size* of it I'm worried about. It's *where* it is that's got me troubled."

"Does it matter, really?" said Amy, languidly touching her nose with her twig.

The reply prompted the Captain to his feet. This made him as tall as Amy was sitting down, so he could look her level in the eye.

"Does it *matter*? I should *say* it matters!"

The Captain was in quite an anxious state. He proposed a case to Amy to indicate how serious the problem was.

"Let us propose the case that I was master of a ship

outward bound from Cape Hope, Africa, bearing for Tasmania. Now propose the case that I thought the island lay directly south. But let us propose that I was wrong. Propose the case instead that the island of Tasmania lay directly south of Australia. There, you see? Sailing before a good wind, confident that we would raise sight of Tasmania at last, and Tasmania being on the other side of the world almost, where would I be with my ship and my crew?"

"I don't know, dear. Where would you be?"

"Why, *lost!* We would sail directly into the South Polar Seas and be crushed between ice floes, there to freeze to death for lack of proper clothing and provisions. Dead to the last man jack of us, and our ship crushed to splinters. And it would be my fault alone."

The Captain sat down again and sank his head on his chest in desperate concentration, covering his eyes with his hands the better to search his memory. Amy plucked at her lip to see the Captain so disturbed. She had never heard of the island of Tasmania, much less did she know where it was. But she had the answer.

"Would it help to see a map?"

The Captain looked up, hope in his eyes.

"Into the bag, Captain," she said smartly. "We'll sneak into the Ladies' library. I've been in there with Miss Eclair. They've got big books in there, lots of them."

"Books with maps? Books with charts? An atlas?"

"That's what I think," said Amy. "Into the bag!"

CHAPTER FIVE

Bobby Shaftoe's gone to sea,
Silver buckles at his knee;
He'll come back and marry me,
Pretty Bobby Shaftoe!
Bobby Shaftoe's fat and fair,
Combing down his yellow hair;
He's my love for evermore,
Pretty Bobby Shaftoe.

S
till it is Sunday. It will be Sunday for some
while yet. What a slow day it is, the Sabbath,
God's day of rest. And if God rests, what much
can happen? God rests, and it is difficult to get up from
one place and go to another. The sun in the sky hardly
moves. It is noontime for hours. Afternoons last a week.
The children play slower and chew their food slower, and
if a child has reason to beat someone, it is a slower beating,
so that a beating you might endure for three minutes on a
Wednesday, for example, you would have to suffer for a
half hour on a Sunday. The Ladies of St. Anne's were
caught up in this backwater of time also. They turned their
heads slower towards a commotion, and then they saw less
of it, for they blinked slower and they heard slower also.
And they had long, slow thoughts about when they were
young.

The children of St. Anne's did not suspect that the Ladies
had thoughts about their youth. The Ladies were generally

thought to have been brand-newly hatched at middle age.
Thirty-five years old forever.

So it was the perfect day to sneak into the Ladies'
library. Amy slung the bag over her shoulder and crouched
under the weight. A quick-witted, wide-awake girl has the
advantage on a Sunday afternoon, and her heels might trip
around a corner before one of the Ladies could see. On any
other day Amy would hardly have dared to sneak into the
Ladies' library. It lay directly off to the left of the front
door of St. Anne's. Across the hall was the office, and next
to the library was the Ladies' parlour.

Amy passed around the side of the stone building,
stooping close against it. She paused behind a stone pillar
at the bottom of the front steps. The great front door was
open. Amy planned a quick run up the stairs and then a
dodge into the library. If she were to be caught, there was
no major punishment for it, perhaps no playtime after
supper. And she *did* worry about the crew of that ship, all
frozen and lying about ice-bound and starving just
because the Captain didn't know exactly where Tasmania
was.

Amy took a deep breath, and was just about to run up
the steps. But she had waited too long. There was a bark
behind her. It was the big dog with the long legs, older
now, but just as wise as ever. He lowered his head as he
approached, and growled, then touched his nose to Amy's
bag. Men sometimes came to St. Anne's. The postrider
came almost every day of the week, so the dog knew the
smell of a man. In his long life this was new to him, and he
knew it was bad. It would have been worse if he'd come
upon a man carrying *Amy* in a bag, but this was bad
enough.

"Shoo!" Amy said. But the dog caught the bag in his
teeth and began shaking his head back and forth, growling

more deeply and louder now, and he and Amy were in a tug of war.

"Let go, let go!" Amy commanded him, but he backed with his hind legs and worried and tugged all the more. The Captain cried out to know what was happening.

"The dog, the dog!" Amy cried.

"Take me out! Run!" cried the Captain. It was the best plan, for the dog would never let go of the bag. It was ripping now, and soon the dog would be at him. Undoing the top, Amy grabbed the Captain by an arm and dashed up the front stairs. She ducked through the front door, and in a few steps down the polished wooden floor she slipped inside the library.

Amy and the Captain sat side by side at the closed door, listening to the dog outside. He was tearing the bag into slobbery strips. Discovering that the quarry had escaped, he left the shreds and began barking, then went sniffing about to find the vanished man.

Amy caught her breath, took her ear from the door, and looked about the room. It was a wonderful library. Three of the walls were lined with books all made with great care and love, leather-bound books with pages like fine cream, with each individual letter of every word pressed into the page. Some were bound in supple Morocco leather, some in sheepskin, with reinforced corners and ribs across the spine. Many were painted with gold all around the edges of the pages. Tight and sturdy books, all of them, with their titles all stamped in gold, and the titles a treasure of study in themselves. Amy and the Captain surveyed all this wealth, and the Captain saw at once what was needed.

"Up there," he said. "See, up there, those very tall books. Those would be atlases and books with charts. You'll need a chair to reach them, Sis."

In the middle of the room was the oak table with six

chairs along the sides, heavy chairs with plush velvet seats. Amy and the Captain pulled one of them over to set beneath the tall books.

Amy hopped up on the chair and was reaching for one of the books when they heard voices right outside the library door. Amy jumped off the chair. She and the Captain tumbled over the back of a couch and huddled next to the wall below a window, listening.

"What was all that racket outside about?" said Mrs. Hill. She had grasped the doorknob, but paused.

"The dog was bothering something," said Miss Quince. She was now the Secondmost High Lady at St. Anne's. Miss Eclair was there also, she was now the Thirdmost High Lady at St. Anne's. The three Ladies entered the library. Noticing at once that one chair was out of place, set over against a wall of books, they all three went to inspect.

"Footprints," said Miss Quince, touching the dusty print on the plush velvet. "One of the ten-year-olds I should say, by the size of it."

"Never mind," said Mrs. Hill, brushing the print away and turning toward the table. "We've more important business at hand."

Positioning the chair in its proper place at the long table, the three High Ladies sat themselves down, all with their hands folded atop the polished wood. These three Ladies, by virtue of their longevity, had the power of law in all matters within the iron fence and stone walls of St. Anne's. Mrs. Hill, being the highest of the High Ladies, established her authority by keeping a silence for a few moments, looking at her clasped hands. The other two Ladies waited in silence. With a deep sigh, Mrs. Hill raised her head and spoke.

"We have a problem at St. Anne's, a unique situation

that calls upon our deliberation and wisdom. It's about Amy."

"More precisely about the Captain," said Miss Quince.

"About Amy *and* the Captain, to be more precise," said Mrs. Hill. "And we are grateful to Miss Quince for noticing how it is with the Captain."

"He wouldn't likely fool me," said Miss Quince, fidgeting with her clasped hands and smiling tightly.

"Perhaps it will go no further than it has," said Miss Eclair, making her plea towards Mrs. Hill.

"I should say it's gone quite far enough already," said Miss Quince. "I caught another glimpse of him this morning."

"But he is only a doll," said Miss Eclair.

"There is very little of the doll in him anymore," said Miss Quince. "I tell you he is as real as a person, half as big as Amy is already, and growing each day."

"But he is such a *little* man," said Miss Eclair.

"There! That is the whole matter of it. You say it yourself. He is a man!"

"Ladies, ladies," said Mrs. Hill, with a quieting gesture to each of them. "Miss Eclair is only thinking of Amy's feelings, of that I'm sure. And although a defence in the Captain's favour is good-hearted, I think we all agree that something must be done."

Miss Eclair lowered her head. That was beyond doubt. Mrs. Hill continued.

"It is only a question of *what* must be done."

"I say put him in a bread box," said Miss Quince.

Miss Eclair raised her head and was about to make protest, but Mrs. Hill held up her hand.

"That is one of the choices we have," she said. "Miss Quince has assured me that he will fit nicely into a bread box, whereupon he might be kept on the pantry shelf."

"Oh, please," said Miss Eclair plaintively. "Not the bread box. It would break Amy's heart. He is such a little man, after all, and no harm. Only a week ago he was a doll, and perhaps he'll change back again."

"If we could depend on that, there would be no problem," said Mrs. Hill. "But there is ample reason to believe that as long as the Captain is under Amy's influence, he will continue to grow. And we cannot confine the problem alone to a consideration of Amy's feelings. There are . . ." Mrs. Hill cleared her throat. "There are the older girls to consider."

"And he is . . ." Miss Quince put in, and then she began the sentence again for added emphasis. "He *is*, after all, a sailor."

There was no argument about that. There was a silence for a moment devoted to imagining the peril that a sailor represented to the older girls. These were, at least, the perilous imaginings of Mrs. Hill and Miss Quince. Miss Eclair cherished this silence for other memories. She spoke next in a voice that surprised the other two Ladies by its wistfulness.

"I knew a sailor once," said Miss Eclair, gazing towards the window.

The other two Ladies looked at Miss Eclair with a curiosity that had not been freshened for many years. Unclasping her hands and laying them palms down on the table, Miss Eclair gazed through a mist of time as she moved one index finger to touch the other. She said again, this time with a voice full of resignation and longing:

"I knew a sailor once."

No one made reply. Mrs. Hill cleared her throat and spoke again, gently.

"Of course, the bread box may not be the perfect solution. We might take the Captain from Amy and send

[40]

him to the Boys' Home."

"I say put him in the bread box," said Miss Quince.

There followed a discussion on the merits of either course of action. Mrs. Hill, who was basically of a freedom-loving disposition, found it difficult to agree that the Captain should be confined in a bread box. But then again, as she considered it, the Captain might then change back into a doll. This might serve Amy best. The Captain could remain at St. Anne's kept safely for all concerned, until the time came that Amy was eighteen years old and would go out into the world. Then she could take the Captain with her. Whereas, if the Captain were given over to the Boys' Home, the grief of this very real loss might badly affect Amy, for it was doubtful she would ever see him again.

Miss Quince did not look so deeply into the problem. One drawer in her classroom desk was filled with balls and tops and such treasures that a teacher may gain from a classroom full of children. And she never gave back a thing. Neither did she inspect her trove, nor did she take any pleasure in it, nor did she have any use for it. But year after year that deep drawer filled up, all the merriment in it fallen to silence, until at last the deepest treasures in it were forgotten even by the children who had supposed that a part of their heart had been taken from them. And so, aside from her misery towards sailors, it was Miss Quince's nature to want to put the Captain in a bread box.

But Mrs. Hill could not decide. She considered also the added danger of sending the Captain to the Boys' Home, for Amy might then run away. Now and then, being grievously set against the world in their minds, girls *had* run away from St. Anne's, which was a scandal and the poorest sort of example to the other girls.

"Ohhhh," moaned Mrs. Hill, bowing to the doubt and

pressure of the decision. "Oh, to know what is best, the bread box or the Boys' Home."

Miss Eclair had for some time been away in her memories. She was now looking out of the window directly at the back of the couch behind which lay Amy and the Captain. Out that way was the sea. Now Miss Eclair spoke again, this time more slowly and longingly than ever as she expanded on her theme.

"I knew a sailor once. I was sixteen, and he was a midshipman. He sailed away to the southern seas."

Mrs. Hill could not help but be touched by the poignancy of Miss Eclair's voice. She looked up.

"And did he never come back?" she asked sympathetically.

"Never," said Miss Eclair. "Never."

"There you are!" cried Miss Quince. "I should say that settles it. Put him in a bread box!"

And so it was, pushed so relentlessly in this direction, and with this last exchange falling so definitely to the side of Miss Quince, Mrs. Hill at last decided that the Captain should be taken from Amy that very evening after supper and put into a bread box.

The business of the meeting thus disastrously concluded, two of the High Ladies returned to their duties. Miss Eclair remained awhile at the table. She drifted over to the window and stood silently in front of the couch. Gazing out towards the sea, Miss Eclair several times sighed. Presently she was raised to poetry by her memories, and she recited a rhapsody for her lost midshipman who never came back, her face as soft as the moon behind a cloud.

> *"Full fathom five thy father lies;*
> *Of his bones are coral made;*
> *Those are pearls that were his eyes:*

Nothing of him that doth fade,
But doth suffer a sea-change
Into something rich and strange..."

At this place Miss Eclair heard a sob, and she spied Amy's blonde hair behind the couch.

"Amy!" she said, putting a knee on the couch.

"Oh, Miss Eclair," cried Amy, raising her tearful face from behind the couch. "Don't let them, oh, please don't let them!"

Miss Eclair ran to close the door of the library. She returned and sat on the couch holding Amy closely and comforting her. As for the Captain, he was ready to leap out of a window and run, except for fear of the dog. He had calculated that if he were to lie in a bread box until Amy was eighteen, it would be eight more whole years of darkness, and the smell of stale bread besides. Even though he might remember exactly where Tasmania was in that time, the knowledge seemed not worth it. He decided to make a run for the door. But Miss Eclair caught his eye as he emerged around the corner of the couch and the Captain saw a look that promised him no harm, so he stayed. Perhaps Miss Eclair was not newly hatched at middle age each day.

CHAPTER SIX

How many miles to Babylon?
Threescore miles and ten.
Can I get there by candle-light?
Yes, and back again.
If your heels are nimble and light,
You may get there by candle-light.

T he island of Tasmania lies directly south of
Melbourne, Australia. The Captain and Amy
found the information in an atlas after Miss
Eclair left them alone again in the library. So the Captain
was not likely ever to sail unwarily into the South Polar
Seas in search of the place. The danger of the day was a
closer threat, for the Captain might yet end it imprisoned
in a bread box. The answer to that threat was in no book,
but depended on the wits of Miss Eclair.

Sitting on the couch, the three of them decided that the
Captain must escape from St. Anne's, and the escape must
be done quickly. Miss Eclair went to the door and listened,
holding her finger to her lips. Amy and the Captain sat
quietly. Miss Eclair stood perfectly still for a minute, then
opened the door and was gone. Outside, she hurried down
the hallway to arrange certain things to make clear the way
for the Captain's flight. This must take place before supper,
be it remembered that the Captain was to be taken from
Amy and stuck in the bread box right after supper.

Now, satisfied that his imaginary ship and its crew were

safely harboured in a gentle bay in Tasmania, the Captain sat with Amy on the couch, her hand in his two smaller ones.

"Have no fear of my going," said the Captain to Amy. "I know my profession, Sis, and I am certain to acquit myself smartly. I'll find a berth as a cabin boy on some coastal ship. In a month's time I should be fully the size of a man, and with money in my pocket. Then I'll return and take you away with me. They *must* let me take my very own sister away from here. Then we'll go to the sea again and find some way of life. Now, what do you suppose has happened to Miss Eclair?"

The Captain looked anxiously towards the door. As best she could be, Amy was comforted. There was really no other answer to the problem but that the Captain must take to the road.

"You *will* come back, Captain?" Amy asked.

"Have no fear. How could you suppose I would not? And in a month's time, no longer. If events fall that I cannot be at the door of St. Anne's in that time, you will be sure to have a letter from me. And if I fail my promise in that, you may just as soon think I am dead."

"Oh, Captain." Amy began to cry.

"But I won't be dead. I will be here or you'll know exactly of my fortunes. What matters is that I must be of a size to face off Mrs. Hill and Miss Quince upon my return. They surely must give you into my charge when they see I am a full-grown man. Now, where is Miss Eclair?"

"Oh, Captain, I will miss you so," said Amy, hugging him close. The Captain patted her hand.

A bell sounded throughout St. Anne's. It was the call to wash for supper. Before it had ceased, Miss Eclair slipped inside the library door. She presented the Captain with an ample leather bag, such as a lady going out a-riding might carry.

"Here is food for the road," she said. "There is no time to waste."

As the Captain slung the bag over his shoulder, Miss Eclair went to one of the front windows and peeked through a curtain. She returned quickly and held out a hand. A half-dozen silver coins lay in her palm.

"You'll need money. Take this. You can repay me when you return for Amy. How soon do you think that will be?"

"A month's time," said the Captain. "Or a letter will come. No longer. Count me as dead if I fail."

Miss Eclair went to the front window again. "All right, be ready. Get to the door. Have you made your goodbyes?"

"Oh, Captain," cried Amy, and she began wailing.

But the Captain gently thrust away her reaching arms, kissed her quickly, and hopped over to the library door.

"The cook will call the dog away at any minute," Miss Eclair explained. "Usually he has his bowls outside, but tonight his bowls will be inside and the door closed after him. I've arranged it with the cook."

Miss Eclair stood looking out of the window, watching for the dog. The Captain stood ready at the door, one hand placed firmly over the leather bag.

Miss Eclair said, "There he goes!" She raised her hand and counted aloud from ten down to one. Then she said, "Go! And God go with you."

The Captain swung open the library door and leaped into the hallway. He slipped on the polished floor, regained his balance, and rushed for the front door. He grasped the large brass handle and pulled. The door was locked. Above the Captain's head, and out of reach, a brass bolt was shot into place. This had been Miss Quince's work. Already she

[46]

had been about locking up against the Captain's escape – if he tried to run when they came to put him in the bread box after supper.

Unharnessing himself of the leather bag, the Captain swung it wildly at the bolt. Voices and footsteps were coming down the hallway. The Captain could not slip the bolt with his wild swings. On either side of the great front door, cut-glass windows ran vertically down each side of the heavy jambs. The leather bag had weight, for apples were inside it. The Captain swung the bag desperately into a side window. Glass broke and scattered on the floor. He kicked his foot at the window and broke more glass. There was room enough to climb through. Miss Quince came stomping down the hallway. She was screaming, "Stop! Thief! Liar! Traitor! Lothario!" The Captain squeezed through the opening. His jacket caught. He could not move. Miss Quince reached out a hand to grab his leg. "You'll never get away. Never!" she shrieked. But just as she touched his boot, the Captain wrenched himself free, and tumbled across the porch landing and down the stairs. He recovered himself and ran to the iron gate. Just then the great dog with long legs bounded around the corner of the building. No door had been closed behind him at all – the cook had not understood Miss Eclair's instructions. Swinging the leather bag around his head like a battle-axe, the Captain held the dog at bay and got a foot through the gate. Mrs. Hill and Miss Quince were in the front of the charge down the front steps. Children came pouring out of the front door. Others of the Ladies of St. Anne's attempted futilely to herd them. Amy was among those who witnessed the heroic efforts of the Captain, flailing at the great dog with the leather bag, yelling, "Down, you cur, down!" The dog's gnashing teeth tore at the bag and snapped at the Captain, and it seemed that the Captain might at any moment be caught and torn to pieces on the spot. But he slipped his body through the iron gate and was off and running up the tree-lined path towards the roadway.

Miss Quince was first at the gate. She put her hand on the iron latch to open it so that the dog might give chase. But Mrs. Hill was there, also, only a breath later. She clamped her broad hand over Miss Quince's hand and held it still.

"Let the dog have him!" cried Miss Quince. "Oh, let the dog have him!"

Mrs. Hill set her jaw firmly and said nothing, holding Miss Quince's hand pinned and unmoving at the latch. Miss Quince let out a wail and then a pitiful whimper, "Oh, let the dog have him." She struggled to free her hand, but Mrs. Hill was the stronger, and she held. Meanwhile the Captain ran. He turned out of sight down the roadway before Mrs. Hill let Miss Quince slip her hand out from under her own.

The throng and clamour had allowed Amy and Miss Eclair to leave the library without being noticed. They joined the crowd of children and Ladies and even found the heart to play-act at being astonished. They were not suspected to be partners in the escapade. Supper was all a-babbling that evening. Amy was a great attraction. But Miss Eclair caught her eye and nodded gravely at her, and Amy declined to expand or expound on what had taken place at the gate, or to detail at all any information on how the Captain had come to be alive, and why he had escaped. But the children had patched together a fair version of the story by bedtime, and they stared with awe at Amy, and with fear at Miss Quince. All through dinner Miss Quince glared at her plate and stabbed at every one of her peas individually, and chewed each to extinction with terrible

[48]

method. Mrs. Hill sat benignly and silently at the head of the Ladies' table, giving scant attention to the hubbub all about. With a great stolid authority she seemed to be drawing some mantle of concluded history over the whole afternoon's adventure. She was content with the outcome.

The children went to bed with their imaginations in the highest realm of wonder. Amy was pestered for information, but remained silent. In the dark dormitory that night there was the sound of murmuring like a sea as a score of girls hugged and coaxed a number of dolls, toy rabbits and teddy bears to come alive, searching for the words and the caress to make it be so.

CHAPTER SEVEN

As I walked by myself,
And talked to myself,
Myself said unto me,
Look to thyself,
Take care of thyself,
For nobody cares for thee.

O n the following days, Amy became as quiet and
withdrawn as an undiscovered island. When she
was not absolutely required to be elsewhere, she
sat on her bed and stared out of her window towards the
sea. And in some private and nether space inside herself
that did not include a single other person or piece of furni-
ture in the dormitory, she waited and worried. Her mind
was on the Captain, and on the quick and unexpected
dangers that might befall a very little man gone alone into
the wonderful and terrible world. He might already have
been trampled by a horse, or destroyed by the next dog
down the roadway.

But Amy did not cry for him. There would have been no
one to comfort her, in any case. Miss Eclair was no longer
at St. Anne's. She had been dismissed from service. Miss
Quince was the cause. In bitter diligence, Miss Quince had
searched the ground near the gate where the Captain had
done battle with the dog, and had found an iron clasp torn
from the leather bag when the Captain had made his heroic
stand. The clasp was fashioned in the shape of a mono-

gram, and the letters that lay against one another were Miss Eclair's initials. Also, Miss Quince found more evidence in the library. A chair was out of place again. And the dusty footprints on the plush velvet exactly matched the size and pattern of Amy's shoes. It was remembered that Miss Eclair had stayed alone in the library when Mrs. Hill and Miss Quince had left.

The evidence was circumstantial, but when Miss Eclair was confronted by it, she confessed her part in the Captain's escape. She argued with Miss Quince and pleaded with Mrs. Hill that what had come about was best. It was a better conclusion, so she said, than either the Boys' Home or the bread box. "For after all, he might return when he is grown up," she said.

"Return? A sailor? Not likely!" said Miss Quince.

Mrs. Hill was in sympathy with Amy and the Captain. But there were such rules of conduct applied to the Ladies of St. Anne's that there was nothing for Mrs. Hill to do but dismiss Miss Eclair from service, as much as she regretted having to do so. And so Miss Eclair had to leave behind the child she loved most.

When Miss Eclair came to say good-bye to Amy, it was to Amy one emptiness falling into another, and she could not even raise a tear. It was as if Miss Quince's hands were choking off her life deep inside. So, even though Amy loved Miss Eclair very much, she could make only a listless good-bye and brush an almost indifferent kiss to Miss Eclair's cheek. Miss Eclair promised to write soon. Amy nodded and looked away vacantly. Then Miss Eclair left her sitting alone on her bed. Amy ate little and played not at all in these days after the Captain had escaped and Miss Eclair had been fired. Although the other girls wanted much more information concerning the Captain and how he came to be, Amy gave them nothing, neither could she be drawn into any talk about the battle at the gate. As yet the other girls were having no luck with their own dolls, though many of them had been coddled and kissed nearly to threads. Amy only shrugged at their questions and moved away to stand or sit apart, and to wait and worry about the Captain.

Then, three weeks after the Captain had made his escape from St. Anne's, the postrider brought two letters for Amy. One was from the Captain, and one was from Miss Eclair. Now, it was Miss Quince who always seemed to be on hand and nearby to answer the postrider's whistle at the front gate. It was a duty that she was not properly charged with, but that she undertook out of nosiness. This day, as she sorted through the letters, she found the Captain's letter to Amy. The return address read: "The Captain, General Delivery, New Liberty." New Liberty was the nearby seaport town. A nicely drawn sailing ship decorated a corner of the envelope. Miss Quince's hands were all over the Captain's letter before she stuck it inside the bosom of her apron. She also found the letter from Miss Eclair, and it followed the Captain's letter out of sight. Miss Quince left the rest of the letters off at the office, then snuck the two hidden letters up to her room. There she ripped them both open, read them, and gloated over them.

CHAPTER EIGHT

Tom, he was a piper's son,
He learned to play when he was young,
And all the tune that he could play
Was, "Over the hills and far away".
Over the hills and a great way off,
And the wind shall blow my top-knot off.

he Captain's letter was a thick packet, and told all the news, and told of adventures and fortunes worth copying out in full. This is what it said:

Ahoy, Sister!

The great ocean rolls beneath me, therefore excuse my penmanship. I have a berth aboard the *Ariel*, a frigate merchantman that trades between the Northern Coasts and the Southern Islands. In the three weeks since we parted, I have nearly cracked my head open, have almost drowned, and have been shipwrecked, yet each seemingly disastrous event has only raised my station. I have been befriended by a fine man, very like a father to me. I am now the second mate of the *Ariel*, and have been promised the captaincy of the ship in due time.

Omitting the very particular details of my adventures thus far (there will be leisure time to tell you everything), here is the gist of what has occurred since my escape from St. Anne's.

After fighting that cursed dog at the gate, I walked

steadily towards the sea all that evening and night, and arrived in New Liberty early in the morning. Going directly to the docks, I walked about freely, to all casual eyes no more than a boy who was romancing alongside the ships that lay tied up there. Finding myself near a party of sailors who were working casks of water up a gangplank, I ventured to ask the nearest if he might direct me to a coastal trader. In answer, I received first a curse, and then, as the man's foot gave slip on the gangplank, a double curse. Then I saw that the water cask was free and rumbling down the gangplank directly to crush me in its path.

In my attempt to leap aside, I stumbled and pitched headlong off the dock and into the water, knocking myself unconscious on a piling. Had the sailors at hand waited for me to surface they would be waiting still, but one of them leaped immediately into the water, dived, and grasped the sling of Miss Eclair's leather bag and drew me to the surface. Captain Clarence Kimberly, master and owner of the ship, and indeed it was the frigate *Ariel*, had come on deck to oversee the commotion. I was carried to his cabin. There it was that I was prevailed upon to breathe again by dint of whacking and pumping upon my body. (All this, of course, was later told me by the Captain.) Recovering both colour and breath, I lay for two days unconscious by reason of the concussion suffered to my brains, recovering under the eye and care of good Captain Kimberly.

Well, one might suppose that I could not have begun my career with worse fortune, but the very contrary applies; I count my good fortune to have begun when I tumbled off that gangplank.

Captain Kimberly's patience and single-handed care

brought me around to the light in two days' time. First off, he thought me to be a boy, as did the other sailors. But in caring for me alone, taking close notice of me during the course of my recovery, pouring warm broth between my lips and replacing cool cloths upon my head, he naturally perceived that I was not a boy at all, but was fully a man, yet very small.

Captain Kimberly is an old man, a full three score and ten, yet his years rest easily upon him. Having been burdened with much hard life and work, his head and back are yet straight, and having seen much of danger and loss, his eyes are still merry, and having shouted much, his voice is still hearty. And he has understanding. Most particularly, as regards my case, having thought much and considered many wonders, he is yet willing to think again and consider the world anew. Thus, it was without undue dismay that he observed me to grow four inches in two days' time, the exact mark of which he kept by measuring me against his folding telescope every few hours.

When at last I recovered and had been made acquainted with my accident and condition, and how I came to be aboard the *Ariel*, Captain Kimberly very frankly broached the subject of the curiosity of my size and my unnaturally rapid growth. I trusted him at once, and told him all, even unto the telling of the entire story of St. Anne's and how I came to be, and of yourself, dear sister. I told him that I must work for a month on a coastal trader, by which time I would be up to full size. Then I must return to take you from St. Anne's. Captain Kimberly listened carefully, smoked his pipe, and studied me.

Presently he got up from the chair at my bedside and strolled around the cabin for a while. Then he sat down again and told me something of his life. He had never married, he said, being too busy in the ways of the sea, but had always wanted a son. And now, he being seventy years old, it was too late, and even in such a remarkable case he was too old to enjoy watching a son grow up. But in the past two days, he confessed, it was almost as if I were a boy, growing up very rapidly. He said he felt like a father observing it, and caring for me. And he said he had feelings he had never felt before, and . . .But perhaps I am saying too much of this matter, it being so close to his heart.

Never mind, then. The *Ariel* was not a coastal trader, but carried in its hold goods from the Southern Islands—tobacco, indigo, Spanish brandy. . . The Captain had laid up at New Liberty these past two days because of a fever on board thought to be due to bad water. The second mate had died, and the *Ariel* was taking on fresh water. Now, the fever having passed, Captain Kimberly was making sail for the ports farther north, where the exotic goods we carried would be sold. Then the *Ariel* would return to the Southern Islands with luxuries from the Northern Ports to profit the ship and crew.

And so Captain Kimberly said that if I would sail north with the *Ariel*, on our return passage I could be put aboard the pilot ship off New Liberty and return to St. Anne's, as was my plan. Furthermore, if I would take residence in New Liberty, Captain Kimberly promised me a berth as second mate when again the *Ariel* returned to that port. It was a handsome offer, and I accepted, of course. Meanwhile, said the Captain, he would watch me grow, and I would learn things of the sea. So it was concluded, and I was most happy indeed. Yet an adventure followed that changed this plan entirely.

Three days out of New Liberty we were thwarted by the wind and thrust upon a rocky shelf a mile from shore. We were in grievous danger of sinking, since the bow of the ship was caught between two great rocks and split below the waterline. So it seemed that the *Ariel* must surely sink when the rising tide released us from that grip of stone.

Now, Captain Kimberly had thought it best that my particular condition be held in secret for the while, and I had been seldom observed on deck the *Ariel*. I had grown another inch or two, which, in any ordinary aspect, is a bit unaccountable, and Captain Kimberly wished not to alarm the crew. But many secrets come to light aboard a sinking ship. The general assessment of our situation argued that a repair to our hull must be undertaken from the outside, our hold being too crowded for access to the wound from within. Furthermore, the agreement was unanimous that there was not space between those grinding rocks that a full-grown man might expect to enter into the sea on a rope's end and be retrieved alive, so shifting and treacherous were the conditions down there. There was, perhaps, room for a boy, but it was not a boy's job, hanging over the rail and being dashed in the face by the churning waters, in imminent danger of being crushed. But it was a job a little *man* might undertake.

And so I perceived it, standing there on the heaving deck, hanging on to a ratline in the howling wind. Then all at once I sailed my hat into the water and – this is very strange to me – I began calling out commands. Captain Kimberly was as much surprised as the other men, but he nevertheless seconded my every word with a nod and a gruff order to back me up, and the men who stood about gaping in wonder, in a sort of trance, turned to their duty.

Forthwith, then, following my commands, I was weighted with a ballast stone, secured to the end of a rope, and lowered overboard. Likewise, a large weighted basket of tar and oakum was lowered within my reach. Taking a deep breath, I waved a hand and was let into the water between the crushing rocks.

I confess to you that, because of my recent experience with near-drowning and the blow to my head, I was much in dread down there in that narrow, shifting space. Yet I did the job. Having somewhat shored the rent in our hull with the oakum, I then called for boards, sledge, and spikes. After considerable effort I managed to spike some boards fairly enough in place that, after all was retrieved and the tide hove us free from the rocks, we floated and gained safe water. We at last made our way to our destined port and unburdened ourselves of our cargo. We then laid up in dry dock for the repair of the *Ariel*'s hull.

In a week's time we were seaworthy again. We filled our hold with goods for the Southern Islands and sailed on a booming tide, myself now dressed in a new blue uniform and standing close to Captain Kimberly on the afterdeck, surveying the widening fortunes that lay before me.

Captain Kimberly shared his cabin with me, and in the evenings, over our pipes (mine recently purchased) and wine, we discussed my singular case. However much the Captain might question me concerning nautical affairs and the various details of navigation, sailing, and the general command of a ship, I had the answer quickly to mind and tongue. We pondered how this should be so, since I had never been schooled in such a wealth of information. At last we concluded that it was only the most perfectly natural outcome that could be expected. Such as, had I been created as a carpenter doll, then I would know everything a carpenter should know. Or if I had been created a tailor doll, then I would know everything a tailor should know. And the application of the rule would no doubt apply if I had been created as a farmer doll, a blacksmith doll, a baker doll, and so forth. So, having been created a seafaring Captain, then the whole business of seafaring I rightly knew, and we found no mystery in it after all.

We smoked our pipes and sipped our wine with great satisfaction, then, and Captain Kimberly looked at me with the pride of a father. At length the Captain told me that for some time he had been of the desire to quit the sea. Therefore, he offered to me that if I would stay aboard the *Ariel* with him and be instructed in the ways of a merchantman (I have little knowledge of business, having been created a naval officer), then this would be his final voyage and he would retire to the land and would make me master of the *Ariel*.

Now, believe me, dear Amy, I could not have accepted this most generous offer but for one thing alone. Believe me, if I were given the promise of a fleet of ships under my command, I would not have failed to return to you in this month's time, but for one thing alone, and it is this. I am not growing nearly as fast as I did while I was with you, nor as fast as I did when I lay unconscious in the Captain's cabin those first two days aboard the *Ariel*. My growth has slowed in your absence, and it will take me longer to reach the full height of a man than we had supposed. At the moment I write this, I am to the top of my head the height of your shoulder, perhaps. At this size I would as yet be subject to the intimidation of the dog and the Ladies of St. Anne's. If I came to get you while at this size, I think I could not expect to take you away with me. I still grow, but slowly. In three months' time, growing at this slow rate, I estimate that I will be fully grown, and futhermore master of the *Ariel*.

Therefore, I have accepted Captain Kimberly's offer. We will sail to the Southern Islands and return to New Liberty in three months' time. At this moment we are off New Liberty, and I hear the channel buoys clanging. The pilot ship will be alongside soon and I must give this letter to its keeping. Quickly, then, I fold and seal these pages with love to you and in hope that you may find joy and patience these next three months. Be assured that you will be on my mind, and that I will perform my duties in such a manner that will reflect honour upon my dearest sister. Remindful always of your care and gentle love, I remain,

> *Your loving brother,*
> *The Captain*

P.S. Please give my compliments to Miss Eclair.
P.P.S. I have made a little drawing of the *Ariel* on the envelope.

After reading once through the Captain's long letter to Amy, Miss Quince narrowed her eyes and thumbed through the pages a second time to set the facts in her memory. She then consigned the pages to her tin wastepaper basket and touched a flame to the papers, all the while nodding to herself and smirking with mischief. As the fire burned low, she remembered the letter from Miss Eclair to Amy. She ripped it open. It was a much shorter letter, and read thus:

My dearest Amy,

I have secured a position at Mother Helen's House for Disappointed Girls, which is but a few miles' journey from St. Anne's. It is in fact visited by the same postrider that will deliver this letter to you. I think of you every day. For several weeks I must be on probation in my position, and I may not leave the grounds. But I will visit you the first Sunday I have free. I know that it must be difficult and lonely for you with the Captain gone, but keep your spirits up. Remember that you have a friend in Mrs. Hill. Also, be wary of Miss Quince, for the harm she intends toward the happiness of yourself and the Captain may not have reached its depths. Within a fortnight, God willing, the Captain will return as he promised. Have courage and patience. At any rate, please write and tell me what news there is. You have my address on this envelope. My anticipation is to see the Captain and you, my dear, coming up the road to visit me as you set out on your new life.

My fondest love,
Miss Eclair

Miss Quince cackled out a little laugh and dumped this letter into the dying fire in the tin wastepaper basket. When it had burned completely out, she poked a ruler into the ashes and stirred them about as if she wished she might further disturb the peace of Amy, the Captain, and Miss Eclair. Then Miss Quince leaned back in her chair, clenched the arms of it, and stared out towards the sea, grinding her teeth. As has been said, she also had lost a sailor to the sea, the same as Miss Eclair. She also knew a poem to remind her of that sailor, and of his going away and never coming back. In her poem, however, there was no hope, no love, no resignation. Aloud, now, she declared it, a curse towards the sea, towards the past, and towards all sailors:

> "Once I loved a sailor,
> Who said he loved but me,
> He promised marriage also,
> Then sailed away to sea.

> "Once I loved a sailor,
> Who loved me by and by,
> Oh, rack his bones with scuttling crabs,
> Oh, drown and damn his eyes."

Then she spat into the ashes in the wastepaper basket and thumped her fists on the arms of the chair in a fury she could not at the moment spend otherwise.

CHAPTER NINE

Oh, dear! What can the matter be?
Dear, dear! What can the matter be?
Oh, dear! What can the matter be?
Johnny's so long at the fair.

T*he loss of the letter* from the Captain was of serious consequence to Amy and gave unexpected results. When two weeks more were past, and a whole month well gone since the Captain left, Amy believed that surely the Captain was dead. That was his very prophecy. He had told Amy that if she didn't hear from him in a month, then she might count him dead. Amy now entered a decline that was marked and hurried. She lay abed all day, hardly stirring, staring at the ceiling. Thrice now she had been deserted: by her father, by Miss Eclair, and now by the Captain. Why let life be a further burden? Why endure it? So Amy might have thought, and she lay in her bed quietly, hardly breathing. And then, in the sixth week of the Captain's absence, a wonderful thing happened.

Amy had not been rising up with the other girls at daybreak, but Mrs. Hill was holding close to the idea that time would cure her and soon she would be up and off playing again. The doctor came around and said, "It's a loss of heart." So Amy was not forced to leave her bed. One of the Ladies came around every morning with a tray of breakfast, which was set at Amy's bedside. But in recent days the outlay had gone cold. Neither did Amy eat any other meal, and she drank only water. But on the particular morning we are examining for its wonder, the breakfast tray was not set nicely on the small table at Amy's bedside. Instead, the good Lady who brought it dropped it on the floor, which made a clatter of broken dish and glass that was not quite as loud as the good Lady's cry of dismay when she beheld Amy that day. And other Ladies, and children, came running, and all voices entered into the clamour and cries of astonishment.

For behold! – Amy had changed into a doll!

Her face was now of cloth and her hair was yellow yarn. She lay staring at the ceiling with her blue button eyes, and the thread of her mouth was a stitching of red. The transformation happened overnight – as quickly as that, and she was no bigger than the Captain had been when he was a doll.

Miss Quince wedged through the crowd around Amy's bed. Her voice cut through the rest.

"Tear her up! Make rags out of her!"

Mrs. Hill would have none of that. In truth, she was becoming quite distressed at Miss Quince's miserable outlook on the world. Amy, of course, would not be torn into rags. Mrs. Hill took her gently up and away to her room. She found a shoe box and laid Amy inside it, speaking as she did so.

"My dear, I believe in your Captain. I've had delays myself. Nothing is proved by absence. He lay in a shoe box four long years when you were very young, waiting in the dark to see you again. And now, even though it be four whole years again, certainly he will return to you one day. Meanwhile, you shall wait on a shelf in the fresh linen closet. It is dry and quiet there, and you must comfort yourself with the happy memories of your days together."

Mrs. Hill looked at Amy for a long time. Then she put the lid on the box and placed it on a high shelf in the fresh linen closet, and left her alone. No one else knew she was there.

So now Amy was a thousand miles away in some place that was absolutely dark and totally empty. Whether she was infinitely small inside her doll body or infinitely large outside of it she could not tell. She had heard Mrs. Hill speak to her, and she might have thanked her for her care, but everything seemed so utterly far away that she could not cross the distance even to blink an eye or move a lip. But then, she thought to herself, since she was a doll, she must have button eyes and a stitched line for a mouth. So what might she have done after all? She lay in the dark, in the immense distance away as a doll is in its awareness, and for a while she thought no more. When next she had a thought, it was a day later, though it seemed to her only a few seconds. She thought about the Captain, and wondered if he was truly dead. When Amy had been a girl, and not a doll, she was sure that the Captain was dead. This was all the cause of her grief, and the cause of her changing into a doll. Yet now, being a doll, she was not so sure.

Dolls have a great patience also. Dolls know how to wait, and how to keep love. A world-hardened weary man in his middle years might one day come across a stuffed bear he loved as a child and be surprised, and his hardness broken for a minute as he feels a tug in his breast as if a line immensely long and thin were still attached between his heart and this scuffed and forgotten friend. But the bear never doubted.

So Amy lay quietly, and in the serenity of the shoe box she passed several weeks remembering the happy times when she and the Captain had been together.

Then, on a certain day, Miss Quince opened the closet

door wherein Amy lay. She loaded some sheets over her arm, reached to close the door, and her glance fell upon the shoe box on the top shelf. She put the sheets down and on tiptoe reached up for the box. Letting her heels fall to the floor, she opened the shoe box and discovered Amy. "Aha!" she said. "So I've found your hiding place. And now won't you make a fine kitchen mop." But then, feeling a presence behind her, she turned and beheld Mrs. Hill. A look was cast between them that caused Miss Quince's ears to grow red and hot as she dropped the shoe box and hurried away. Mrs. Hill then took the shoe box to her own room. And there Amy would stay in a bottom dresser drawer until the Captain returned, if he returned.

Miss Quince's only relief from this humiliation was to contemplate what she *might* have done to Amy if only she had got away with the shoe box. She had no great fear that the Captain would really return. Her experience in the matter, proven so harshly as to be the very code of her soul, was that sailors, no matter what they promise, do *not* return. Miss Quince sat stiffly in her chair, improving on this conceit as if it were a pet reptile. Sailors do not return, and that's all there is to that. Still, she had a lingering doubt about the Captain. After all, Amy was not the Captain's sweetheart, but his sister. That's how he had addressed her in the letter, "Ahoy, Sister!" And that is a different sort of love. Miss Quince clawed at the arm of her chair and considered this. If the Captain did *not* drown, as she dearly hoped he would, then he *might* return. Yes, it would be best to have Amy torn to kitchen rags, stopping up rat holes and mopping up filth. Miss Quince smiled to think of it. Yet she had failed in that. She thought and wondered how else she might accomplish the ruin of this relationship between Amy and the Captain.

Each day Miss Quince listened for the postrider's

whistle. This is a cheerful sound for most persons, a bright and airy clarion, the announcement of a great magic being performed, that mere marks on a paper can so convey the cast of a loved one's mind, and the warmth of the heart, that these sketches of a few drops of ink are kept as a treasure forever, tied perhaps in a dusty ribboned bundle and handled with caresses. But to Miss Quince that whistle was a shrill call that moved her to hope for tragic news. She hurried to receive the letters, thrilling to think that maybe the Captain was dead.

CHAPTER TEN

Little Polly Flinders
Sat among the cinders,
Warming her pretty little toes;
Her mother came and caught her,
And whipped her little daughter
For spoiling her nice new clothes.

A t last came another letter from the Captain to Amy. She had been a doll for six weeks now. Reaching down from his horse, the postrider passed through the iron gate a small bundle of letters into the hands of Miss Quince. She turned, and while walking up the stone steps, shuffled through the mail. Finding the letter from the Captain to Amy, she glanced up and about quickly, then stuffed the letter into her apron and hurried up the steps and inside. So absorbed was she in her low practice that she did not notice that the postrider still sat on his horse, watching her. Miss Quince took the purloined letter directly to her room, where she sat and read.

After Miss Quince had disappeared into St. Anne's, the postrider called out to one of the girls playing outside the building. He tossed her a penny and asked her to fetch Mrs. Hill, as he had a private message for her.

Upstairs, sitting in her room, with the tin wastepaper basket close by, Miss Quince tore open the envelope and read the Captain's letter.

My Dear Sister,

This letter I give into the hands of Captain Peixotto, master of a Portuguese frigate bound for New Liberty, God save his passage and speed this epistle to you.

The melancholy news is this: Captain Kimberly is dead. He died only yesterday and was buried this sunrise in the rich earth of this beautiful island. The sickness he suffered came on suddenly, and was of a striking virulence. In thirty hours his fever rose and subsided three times, I at his bedside the entire time administering to him as best I could, but his age had so diluted the strength of his humours that he at last surrendered to the thick and morbid airs one sometimes encounters in these latitudes.

During these last hours, Captain Kimberly drew up a legal document setting me forth as his heir. He was under no shade of delirium, and the document was duly witnessed by the first mate, Mister Cloud, and it is in all correct accord with the legal statutes bearing thereon. Thus, as it stands, I am the owner and master of the frigate *Ariel*, the last and sole possession of Captain Kimberly. But my heart finds no cheer in that at the moment. The *Ariel* is a sad ship, but time is the best friend of those who grieve, and our sorrow will pass. Then again the *Ariel* will sail with glad hearts.

As for myself, I am in good health and nearly up to my full height, so far as I can judge, lacking perhaps another inch or two of growth. I stand well to the front of any man, and my bearing of command has only increased by the example of Captain Kimberly. The men answer to my authority, and I am fully confident that I can perform my duties to the advantage of us all, lacking nothing in seamanship, and having gained greatly in the understanding of the play and ploy of a good merchantman. Only somewhat do I have a small doubt, and that is to the disposition of the first mate, Mister Cloud, who, so I suspect, harbours some jealousy towards my good fortune. He has for some several years sailed with Captain Kimberly, and might have expected to measure more greatly in his bequest than myself. But that problem can be dealt with, I believe, with understanding and firmness.

You may expect my return within six weeks – thereabouts. We will discharge our island goods on the Northern coasts, refit and supply the ship, and will soon thereafter be riding at anchor in New Liberty, at which time I will come directly to St. Anne's and take you forever beyond those iron gates. There is, I must admit it, the single dark fear in my life that I shall change again into a doll. The examination of this whole mystery has brought me little relief. Who knows but that even a pinprick or a slight cut, or some vagrant thought, or a dream, might change me back into a doll. Sometimes I am overcome with the dreadful fear that I will wake up as someone else. But then again, to support my spirits, there comes a feeling that this shall *not* happen, but that I have a destiny as a man. It is like a beacon that shines within me, and whether it draws me to safe harbour or to wreck, I will pursue that destiny, and with a cheerful heart no matter the outcome.

Now I will risk a secret, since it is hand to hand that this letter goes with Captain Peixotto, who is to be trusted entirely if my knowledge of human nature is to be relied on at all. Amy, there is a gold treasure to be got. A pirate ship loaded with gold lies sunken in a place I know of. Captain Kimberly, as he lay close to his last act and breath, disclosed to me a hidden cabinet in his quarters, out of which I extracted a map of the place where this treasure lies. The sunken ship belonged to Captain Cowl the pirate, quite infamous in his day, who terrified these sea-lanes several years ago. Captain Kimberly found this map in a bottle on his very last voyage. He had intended to search for and find the treasure to finance his retirement from the sea, a retirement that, judging by the estimate of the treasure, would have enabled him to live like several kings. No more of this for now.

Farewell, then, dear sister. Have patience still in this last forfeit to time of our joy and fortune together. We will be together soon, and then we sail for pirate treasure!

Your loving brother,
The Captain

P.S. Again, my compliments to Miss Eclair.

Miss Quince frowned to herself, crumpled the pages of the letter into a ball, and tossed it into the tin wastepaper basket. She set a candle flame to it and watched it burn. The information widened her interest in the Captain's affairs. Brooding upon ways she might cause him unhappiness, she had thus far concluded that the changing of Amy into a doll might be a good clinging grief for him. But now there was gold treasure to think about. Although gold cannot overcome grief, it might soften the fierce edge of his despair. She wanted the Captain to have a full measure of misery. She wanted the Captain to be sad, *and* poor, without Amy, without any treasure, and, if only she could think how to accomplish it, without the ship as well. Miss Quince smiled ruefully. Yes, and who knows, perhaps she might even find how to change him back into a doll. And then — what a joy it was for her to think of it — she could throw him to a pack of dogs for a plaything. Miss Quince smiled a peculiar lopsided smile, one side of her mouth mocking the other side, and she watched the letter burn in the tin wastepaper basket.

Now — below stairs, out by the gate, Mrs. Hill had been fetched to the postrider.

"Yes, what is it, man?"

Without a word, he handed down to her an envelope that had been put into his own hands by Miss Eclair. On the envelope was written these words: "Mrs. Hill. For her eyes only, into her hands only." Mrs. Hill opened it on the spot. This is what it said:

Dear Mrs. Hill,

The caution I have taken to get this letter to you is unnecessary, I hope. I have once before written to Amy, but have received no answer. This is not like Amy. My best hope is that the Captain has returned and taken her away. Yet I also fear for her health. Whatever the events that have transpired since I left St. Anne's, please let me know, for there is no child I have loved as much. If all is well with her and I have merely suffered the understandable neglect of a child, please excuse the subterfuge that has got this note to you. (Yet I do remember that Miss Quince has the first possession of the post.)

Sincerely yours,
Miss Eclair

The postrider had been sitting quietly on his horse, chewing on the end of the rein. Miss Eclair had instructed him to wait for a reply from Mrs. Hill. Seeing that Mrs.

Hill had finished the letter, he spat out some juice, and spoke:

"Miss Eclair said wait for an answer."

Mrs. Hill turned the letter over, back to front, looked into the envelope, then stuffed the letter back in its case.

"Was there anything else?" she asked.

"For you? No ma'am."

"Several weeks ago – was there a letter for Amy?"

The postrider rubbed his cheek with the wet end of the rein and cast his eyes upwards, remembering.

"Weeks ago ... yes ... yes. Hard to remember, but I do, because there was two letters on the same day. Not often one of your girls gets letters at all, and none ever did get two on the same day before. Yes, I remember that. Two on the same day."

"One from Miss Eclair?" prompted Mrs. Hill.

"That's right, that's right."

"And the other?"

"Long time ago," the postrider said. "Not any of my business, you know, reading who letters come from. All I know is who they go to."

"Yes, yes, of course...."

"Seems I remember something about the Navy or something ..." said the postrider, screwing the end of rein into his ear and twisting it thoughtfully.

"From a sailor," said Mrs. Hill, "maybe mailed from New Liberty?"

"That's it," said the postrider, taking the rein from his ear and pointing it at Mrs. Hill. "That's what it was. It had a drawing of a ship on the envelope. See, I don't pry into things, but I'd remember that – a drawing of a ship on the envelope."

"Did Miss Quince take the letters that day?"

"Does most every day, don't she?"

"And were there other letters for Amy?"

The postrider was getting impatient. He rubbed the end of the rein alongside his nose. He had letters to deliver. If Mrs. Hill held him there much longer, he'd stick the end of it in his nose and wiggle it around. It was a way he'd found to end a conversation without being too impolite.

"Can't remember that far back," he said. "Today, now, that's easy. One letter for Amy from that Captain fellow. It came off a ship at New Liberty. I gave it to Miss Quince."

"Oh, you stupid man!" said Mrs. Hill, bending to grasp up her skirt. "Don't you see the intrigue in this?"

"Huh?" said the postrider, and just before Mrs. Hill turned to hurry up the stairs, he stuck the end of the reign in his nose and said, "Well, if I'd wanted to be a spy, I'd 'a joined the Army," and he left the scene in as much indignation as Mrs. Hill.

Miss Quince had stared too long into the tin wastepaper basket, drawn off by her plotting of what to do about the Captain and Amy. For Mrs. Hill arrived at her door and boldly inserted her skeleton key into the keyhole. With a single clack she turned the bolt and swung open the door. Blue smoke was curling out of the wastepaper basket. Without a word, Mrs. Hill went directly to the washstand, took up the bowl resting there, stepped smartly to the smoking tin wastepaper basket, and dashed half a bowl of water into it. Then she stood before Miss Quince, who had jumped out of the chair, splashed with some of the water, and spoke in a tone of magnificent righteousness.

"You may pack your belongings, madam. I will wait here until you are gone from this room for the last time. Your service at St. Anne's is ended."

Oh, the wretched creature, how she skulked and burned with shame, how she creeped and cringed in mortification, humiliated to the bone, the miserable wretch. Held sternly under the glance of Mrs. Hill, fretful and shamed, Miss Quince packed two large bags and took one last look about the room. Mrs. Hill stood aside from the open door. Without a word, Miss Quince walked down the stairs, through the hallway, and directly on out of the front door and down the steps of St. Anne's. She set down one bag to lift the latch of the iron gate. Then she turned and looked up at Mrs. Hill, who was standing at the top of the steps. Miss Quince attempted to direct a last offence toward the High Mistress of St. Anne's. She parted her lips, her teeth clenched, as if she were going to say a final scathing word and a curse, but no word came, only a seething sound from between her teeth, a snake-like hissing. Mrs. Hill stood broadly at the top of the stone steps, in aspect as sturdy and virtuous as a protecting goddess, and Miss Quince, that vile product, bowed her head, opened the gate, and left St. Anne's forever.

After securing the gate, Mrs. Hill went again to Miss Quince's room. The Captain's letter to Amy was almost totally burned away, but Miss Quince had knotted the ball of it tightly so that some inner parts of the pages had not yet been touched by the flames. Legible still was the mention of a Captain Kimberly, who had apparently died, and news that the Captain, Amy's Captain, was nearly full grown. Also something about a pirate. But most important were the words: "... expect my return [a space burned away here] ... six weeks..." It was enough.

Mrs. Hill went directly to her room, stretched a clothesline and pinned the scraps of paper up to dry. Then, getting out pen and paper, she sat at her desk and wrote a letter to Miss Eclair, telling her of the treachery of Miss Quince. She said that the Captain would return in about six weeks' time to get Amy, but dared not tell her that Amy had turned into a doll, not wanting to alarm her, thinking that Amy might turn back into a real girl under the Captain's influence. The outcome of it all, prayed Mrs. Hill, might well be placed in the gentle hands of their good patron, St. Anne.

She left the envelope unsealed. Next day, when the burned scraps of the Captain's letter had been entered also into the envelope, Mrs. Hill sealed it. She was waiting for the postrider when he rode up to the gate. He handed her some letters, and she handed him the letter for Miss Eclair. They said not a word to each other. But what a peculiar man, thought Mrs. Hill, as she walked up the steps, riding about the countryside with the end of a rein stuck up his nose.

CHAPTER ELEVEN

Trip and go, heave and ho,
Up and down, to and fro,
From the town to the grove
Two and two, let us rove;
A-Maying, a-playing;
Love hath no gainsaying;
So merrily trip and go,
So merrily trip and go.

I t was May the first. The children were singing and dancing around a maypole in the sunny yard of St. Anne's. The coloured streamers twined around the pole as the children wove and laughed and bumped into one another until finally they came all together at the bottom of the pole and churned about like piglets seeking their dinners. The High Ladies sat on blankets nibbling out of baskets, for this was a picnic. All were gathered to be gay and to play, and to partake of cheese, biscuits, chicken, spiced meat, cold delicious lemonade, and juicy apples and oranges. Then at once, perfectly fitted to the gaiety on the lawn, a fine carriage with many fixtures of sparkling brass came up the roadway. It was pulled by two chestnut horses that gleamed like shoe leather, all with new harness set here and about with silver buckles and studs. A handsome affair indeed, and sitting atop the box was a coachman all attired in black, wearing a top hat and showing off glimpses of a startlingly bright red waistcoat as he snapped his whip high above the horses' heads to urge them to pick up their feet more smartly now that there was an audience.

The girls and the High Ladies turned to watch the grand vehicle with its prancing horses. And all were surprised when the carriage did not go down the roadway, but instead turned in at St. Anne's and stopped in front of the iron gate. The horses blew out of their noses while the coachman, now acting as a footman, swung to the ground and pulled out two folding steps from under the carriage. He stuck his hat under his arm and opened the door. Out stepped the Captain.

A fine figure of a man he was, dressed in a brand-new blue uniform, trimmed with real gold braid now, and with a real sword at his side, not just a splinter of cedar, upon the pommel of which he lightly rested his hand. He stood smiling upon the crowd of children who had run to the gate, and his eyes darted among them, looking for Amy. But he could not find her, and he raised a curious eyebrow as Mrs. Hill approached the gate. She had recognised him immediately, even though the Captain now had side-whiskers nicely cut to a point along his jawline.

"Make clear, make clear!" cried Mrs. Hill as she pushed through the crowd of children who *must* get closer to the fine carriage and the horses. The other High Ladies herded the children aside, snatching at sleeves, braids, and ears. A small way was made clear. The Captain swept his hat from his head when Mrs. Hill opened the gate for him to enter, and he executed a bow. But not having acquired his land legs yet, he tottered a bit. Seeing this, Mrs. Hill wondered if he had taken to drink. But when the Captain embraced her, she was sure he had not, for he smelled only of the freshness of the sea.

"Oh, my dear Captain," said Mrs. Hill, "how good it is to see you. Now, *won't* you children make *way* for the Captain!"

Taking him by the arm, she pressed through the girls, all of them reaching out hands towards the Captain. He smiled widely and touched them on their heads as he passed through and up the steps in tow of Mrs. Hill. Then the girls, all in a great cry and fuss, went to goggle at the horses and the carriage.

"But where is Amy?" asked the Captain as Mrs. Hill closed the front door. He glanced at the side window, now repaired, that he had broken to make his escape from St. Anne's many weeks ago.

"Several things have happened," said Mrs. Hill, leading the way into the library. The Captain followed, and both sat at the oak table.

"She's not ill?" asked the Captain.

"No, not ill," said Mrs. Hill. "I wouldn't say that exactly. It isn't so much that, as . . ." She paused. "Let me tell you from the beginning."

"Please do." The Captain set his hat aboard the table and looked keenly at Mrs. Hill.

"You wrote to Amy . . . how many times?"

"Well, twice," said the Captain. "First, to tell her why I could not return as soon as I had promised –"

"Ah, you promised to return at a certain time."

"In one month's time from when I left. It was a vow. I would return or write to her. Otherwise she might as well consider me dead."

"Then that was it," mused Mrs. Hill, touching her lower lip. "She thought you were dead."

"But I wrote to her to tell her I'd be delayed."

"She did not receive the letter."

"She ran away!" said the Captain with a start. He stood up and took his hat in his hand, throwing a glance at the door.

"No, no." Mrs. Hill put a hand on the Captain's arm. "She didn't run away."

The Captain sat down again.

"Do you remember Miss Quince?" asked Mrs. Hill.

The Captain narrowed his eyes. "I have had bad dreams about her."

"She has since been dismissed from service at St. Anne's, but I'm afraid she intercepted both of your letters and burned them. Amy had had no news of you these several weeks you've been gone."

"Then she's here?" exclaimed the Captain.

"She is."

"Quickly, then. Let us see her!" He was rising from his chair, but Mrs. Hill touched his arm again.

"Please sit down, Captain, and prepare yourself for this."

The Captain set his mouth grimly and stared intently at Mrs. Hill. She could find no better way to pass on the news than to say it straight out. "My dear Captain, Amy has changed into a doll. She is now keeping her time in one of my dresser drawers."

Mrs. Hill had expected this information to purge all colour, joy, and starch out of the Captain. So it was to her great surprise that, after raising his eyebrows in a moment's astonishment, he frowned a second, then smiled slightly, then grinned widely, then chuckled, and at last threw his head back and laughed, causing Mrs. Hill considerable dismay. For half a minute the Captain laughed, and with such gusto that he had to wipe his eyes.

"Good heavens, Captain!" Mrs. Hill cried. She had been sitting back with her brow vexed and crossed by the Captain's outburst.

The Captain held both hands up to settle Mrs. Hill's alarm, and his laugh died to a chuckle again.

"Why, Mrs. Hill, it's wonderful, believe me. Why this means that almost anything could happen. Oh, my dear Mrs. Hill, the whole world is open to us now. I thought, perhaps, being a human being and all, that there might be certain limits. But this is wonderful. Anything at all might happen, and we might be in need of all the luck we can get, even if it comes about a bit strangely. As to Amy, have no fears. I was a doll once myself, you know, and there are worse beginnings, and worse endings, I daresay. It's not what you think at all, Mrs. Hill. Amy will be herself again soon, I promise. And now I would like to see her immediately."

Saying this, the Captain stood up, so then did Mrs. Hill, and they left the library. They walked down the polished hallway to the polished stairway in admirable procession, the High Mistress of St. Anne's and the brightly uniformed Captain, and they marched up the stairs and into Mrs. Hill's room. By the time they got there, Mrs. Hill had come to believe that Amy *would* be herself again, now that she would be in the Captain's care. She expressed herself to be much relieved as she drew the shoe box from her lower dresser drawer.

"I supposed she might be gone forever, Captain – into being a doll, I mean."

"Not at all," said the Captain. "Don't you know I've had experience in this? Why, it's wonderful, not what you think at all."

Mrs. Hill set the box on top of the dresser and removed the lid. The Captain looked in on Amy. He reached in, lifted her out, and cradled her in his arms somewhat awkwardly.

"Dear Sister," he said, studying her for a moment, then turned to Mrs. Hill. "She looks just fine. I would know her among a thousand dolls. It's in the eyes, you know. And

[81]

soon she'll be herself again, now that we're together. All it needs is that she have some company and someone to read to her, and then ..."

Yet the Captain thought perhaps it was best not to reveal how the resurrection of Amy was finally to be accomplished – that is, by poking her in the head with a needle. Certain magical things, be they too widely known, are thereby shed of their full potency, and the Captain declined the risk of telling all to Mrs. Hill. "And then," he continued, vaguely waving a hand, "then she will be herself again, just as she was."

"Oh my, what a relief," said Mrs. Hill. "I supposed she might be a doll forever."

"Say no more," said the Captain. "She hears, you know, hears every word we're saying." The Captain replaced the lid and stuck the box under his arm. Reaching into his waistcoat pocket, he extracted several gold coins and handed them towards Mrs. Hill. She shied from the offering, but the Captain found her hand and pressed the coins into her palm.

"This, for your care and love. Perhaps a part of it may buy a doll for some child who has none. And now, if I may pay my respects to Miss Eclair, Amy and I will be on our way."

"Oh, but didn't I say? Miss Eclair isn't here anymore either."

"Something of Miss Quince's doing, I suppose?"

"Something of that sort."

"Does she know of Amy's condition?"

"I thought it best not to tell her."

"Just so," said the Captain. Mrs. Hill then wrote down Miss Eclair's address for the Captain. The Captain studied the address for a moment, frowning to himself. "Hmmmm. Certainly Amy would like to see her again, but do you agree, Mrs. Hill, that the meeting might be a bit of a shock to Miss Eclair? Yes. No doubt it would be best to wait until Amy comes to herself again. Yes, of course, and she'll have some interesting stories to tell after a few weeks at sea." They went out of the room and proceeded down the stairway, the Captain commenting over his shoulder as they descended.

"And we sail tomorrow, Mrs. Hill. Did you say that nobody at all saw those letters but Miss Quince? Well, in that case let me tell you that I am doing quite well, as you see. I have my own ship and reason to believe that a happy and prosperous future waits for me. Amy, of course, will always be provided for."

"And you both go with my blessing," said Mrs. Hill. Down the hall they went, out the front door, and into the sunshine.

The girls at the gate were making smooching sounds and whistling at the horses. Some were offering apples to the horses. The coachman was on his box, trying to keep the horses' heads forward. Now and then he grunted and turned with a sour look towards the children. "Keep away, there! Mind your own business, won't you. Go goggle somewhere else. How'd you like to be goggled at half the day?"

The children drew away from the carriage as the Captain and Mrs. Hill approached. The coachman jumped down from his box. The Captain gripped Mrs. Hill's hand, kissed it, put on his hat, and mounted into the carriage. The coachman shut the door and climbed to his seat. All being made ready, the coachman cracked his whip and wheeled the horses tightly on the roadway. The Captain waved a last good-bye. Mrs. Hill blew a kiss toward them, and off they went towards the sea as the children shouted and cheered.

A bird flying through the air on this lovely May day might have flown over St. Anne's and, observing all these fine and bright things, the bird might have thought that all was happiness and festivity on these few acres of earth. Looking down, a bird might have thought that no trouble at all diminished or darkened the day, at least not in this place. But if that bird had flown low and flown into the small forest across from St. Anne's, he might have landed on a branch and observed something that would have made him think differently. For there in the forest in a dark spot, looking outwards into the light, stood a dun horse with a rider dressed all in brown, in a dark cloak with a hood pulled well forward on the head. This rider had come along the road shortly after the Captain's carriage arrived at St. Anne's gate. This rider had entered the forest then, and stood out of sight, watching intently all that happened. This rider had followed the Captain ever since he had docked the frigate *Ariel* in New Liberty. And now this rider cautiously urged the dun horse out of the shadows and loped along some distance behind the Captain's carriage.

CHAPTER TWELVE

There was an old woman who rode on a broom,
With a high gee ho, gee humble;
And she took her old cat behind for a groom,
With a bimble, bamble, bumble.

R umbling *away in the carriage,* the Captain cradled Amy in his arms. He settled back with a contented smile. His thoughts chased ahead towards the sea, the wind, the waves, the clear nights with stars thrown across the sky, glittering nights when he and Amy might sit on a hatch cover, sipping tea perhaps and plotting adventure. He smiled down at her. Amy's button eyes stared up at him.

"Have you noticed my gold earring, Sis?" the Captain asked. He turned his head sideways to her. At the lobe of his left ear a golden earring dangled and glinted in the May sunshine. "Maybe you'll want one yourself. There's a promise for you. Aye, maybe one for each ear, as you'll be a lady of the sea. But us sailor men need only one. It's a superstition, Sis, wearing a golden earring is. You see, there's a King of the Sea, and his name is King Neptune. He's in command of all that happens on top of the water and down below, and if a sailor's not lucky, he'll meet him face to face. I mean to say, if your ship sinks and you drown, you go down to where his kingdom is under the sea. Aye, there's many men that go down with their ships to King Neptune's shining halls deep under the sea. And all plump from drowning, those sailors float into his palace, which is made up of shells and bones and fish scales and undersea flowers, with the walls and pillars and floors set about with gold pieces and precious jewels, all the riches that King Neptune has taken off the wrecked treasure ships that the fishes find, because King Neptune, he's the King of all the fishes as well.

"Mermaids are there, too, as beautiful as the pictures show them, sitting around combing their long hair with the ribs of fishes, just wearing the smallest bits of wet seaweed for clothes and such. Aye, Sis, it's the sort of place a drowned sailor wishes for after a hard and lonesome life. But you see, King Neptune wants his payment if you're going to enter his kingdom, and it's got to be paid in gold. Then he lets you stay there and get acquainted with the mermaids, but you've got to pay him his gold first."

The Captain flicked his earring with a finger.

"So suppose your ship sinks in the middle of the night, and you run up on deck without any trousers on? I mean, if you had a gold coin in your pocket that was meant for payment to King Neptune? Suppose then a great wave throws you off the ship, and down you go. So there you are at King Neptune's palace without your trousers on and no gold to give him. So King Neptune turns you out, and the sharks and crabs have you for dinner. Aye, the sharks and crabs ask no payment to enter *their* palaces."

The Captain laughed, and the coachman, at last heeding to the Captain's voice, opened a small sliding door that looked into the carriage from his driving box.

"Begging the gentleman's pardon, sir, but was ye talking to me?"

"Not at all, my good man, only talking to myself. And what's that to you?"

The coachman had suspected as much.

[86]

"Indeed, sir, what is that to me? Often I says to myself, what is that to me? Compared with going barmy, if I may say so, sir."

With that remark, the little door slid shut. The Captain mused for a moment if he had been insulted or merely instructed. He shrugged and smiled at Amy again.

"So if a sailor drowns or gets buried at sea, he wants to have his gold payment for King Neptune. Well, it's a superstition, Sis, but a sailor's got to believe in something, and doesn't everyone want to believe he'll end in a happy way?" Saying this, the Captain took on a puzzled expression. After a few moments he shook his head as if trying to rid himself of a thought. He smiled at Amy.

The Captain then told her of all that had happened to him, and of all the news contained in the letters that Amy had never seen, about his adventure when he saved the ship, and about the death of Captain Kimberly, and about the treasure map the Captain had given him. Now and then he glanced out of the window through the dust of the carriage at the road behind them. At last he spoke of those backward glances.

"We're being followed, Sis. Shortly after I left the ship I noticed him. Clever fellow, whoever he is. I tried to waylay him in New Liberty, but he kept his distance."

He held Amy up and pointed her face out the back window.

"See, Sis? See that rising of dust way back there? See him? Dressed darkly, wearing a hood, riding alone."

He sat Amy on his lap again.

"I expect he'll come close tonight, either to state his business or to do his dirty work. But I'll be ready for him."

The Captain turned his coat aside and patted a pistol stuck in his wide belt. "There's no worry now, Sis, but I'll be ready for him." He laid his head back then, set Amy aside, and closed his eyes. In a little while he mumbled, "A long day, Sis. Might as well get some sleep." And in a few moments his head lolled to the side. Amy slumped in the seat next to him, and the carriage rocked and creaked as they rolled along towards New Liberty.

The Captain slept without dreaming. Now and then the driver snapped his whip and shouted at the horses. Once or twice the Captain woke and made a mental note of the time, seeing the shadows lengthen across the fields that sped past. He turned his head to look out of the window, and in the distance still was the cloud of dust and the single rider. There would be business soon enough with the fellow, so the Captain took his opportunity again and rested his head as comfortably as he could and slept some more. The carriage rocked, and the horses, being well matched, clopped in a steady unison on the roadway. In his gauzy state of mind just before sleep, the rhythm of their hooves seemed to make words in the Captain's head: "To the sea, to the sea, Amy's free, Amy's free." With these apparitions of words playing through his head, the Captain fell asleep again.

Late in the afternoon the Captain awoke with a bang. One wheel of the carriage had run off the roadway and the Captain was thrown across the coach. "Hi! Hi! Hey!" the coachman was yelling at the horses. The Captain grabbed the roadside window frame and pulled himself up. All was dust and thunder outside. "Hi! Hi!" yelled the coachman. "Give room, give room, are you crazy? Pull off, pull off!" And through the dust the Captain was looking at a crazed woman half standing in a cart and whipping at a charging draught horse. The wheels of the two vehicles clashed and screeched together as the coachman yelled and tried to hold the road. The woman also was yelling at her great horse. Then she turned her head to look in at the Captain.

She was dressed entirely in black, and a black mourning veil was blown against her face. Then this madwoman screamed violently at the Captain.

"Murderer!" she cried. "Killer! Damned villain! Assassin! You killed him! You murdered my brother, damn you! Strangler, murderer!"

She then took a large rock from her cloak and hurled it at the Captain's head. He ducked it, and when again he put his head to the window she was pulling ahead, still crying out murder and mayhem. In the next moment her juggernaut of a wagon burst into greater speed and passed the carriage. The coachman put all his skill to work and regained the centre of the roadway. Then he slowly brought his team to a halt.

He swung down from his box. The Captain was out on the road a second later. In the fog of the whirling dust they stood looking up the roadway at that raging wagon growing small in the distance. And having barely escaped a bad crash into the ditch, they now barely escaped being trampled into the ground. For now the single rider in the brown cloak and hood whom the Captain had spied out the back window came abreast of the carriage and charged past, narrowly avoiding a collision with the Captain and the coachman. But this rider threw no curse or rock at the Captain, and in a few seconds was also lost out of sight in a billow of dust.

They stood there as the dust cleared and the coachman settled his horses. The Captain came around to help calm the beasts. At the same time he also tried to calm the coachman, who was demanding what in the name of the Almighty was that? Finding that two spokes of a wheel were broken and an axle cracked, he was also threatening the law and the courts. The Captain soothed him with a gold coin and answered to the outrage as best he could, all the while having more questions about it than the coachman and no one to ask for an explanation.

"Screaming about murder, she was!" said the coachman.

"A madwoman of some kind," the Captain assured him. "Can we ride on that wheel? A madwoman. I've never seen her before."

The coachman smoothed the neck of the horse he was attending as the Captain smoothed its muzzle. The horses at last blew themselves out and stood firm. The coachman inspected the injured wheel once again.

"We might make it," he said, coming out from under the carriage. "Maybe, if we go slow, if we walk the horses in. Might be in New Liberty by dark. If we don't get ambushed and murdered. That's what she was yelling. I heard her. She was yelling murder all the time she was passing."

"Some mistake," the Captain said. "No need to think further on it, my good man. I'm a sailor, clean from the sea, no need to say anything about it to anyone. Here, take this," giving the coachman another gold coin. "Nothing more to say on it. All a mistake. Just some madwoman. Bad luck to talk about such things."

So with grunting and grumbling, but sticking the gold coin deep in a pocket, the coachman mounted his box again. The Captain took his place and they continued, very slowly, on towards the sea.

The Captain was greatly puzzled by the event. He propped Amy up on the seat, and stroked his chin, thinking. The slow and sly approach of the figure in the brown cloak, who had followed him since he had docked at New Liberty, was evidently only the shadow of the vicious woman in black, a soft shadow of some more outraged insanity. His foot touched the rock that she had thrown at his head, and he picked it up. A closely folded piece of paper was tied to it. The Captain slipped the note from under the string binding, unfolded it, and read. This is what is said:

Murderer! You killed my brother Captain Clarence Kimberly, master of the *Ariel*. You smothered him in his bed. I have proof of it. A witness will swear to it before the law. You also forged his will and stole his ship. The *Ariel* is rightly mine, and I will have it and see you hanged for murder. Meet me tonight at the Riptide Tavern and you might save your life.

Captain Kimberly's Sister

The Captain stared out of the window. Here was an evil turn indeed. So – Captain Kimberly had a sister, and a crazy one. That was reason enough the good captain had not spoken of her. This was bad. She had invented a lie of murder, perhaps true to her in her twisted mind, or out of her cunning. And could she find someone who would back her in her story? She mentioned a witness to this imaginary act of murder. The Captain thought of the first mate, Mister Cloud. There might be some jealousy there – Mister Cloud might have expected to be master of the ship. Perhaps. An image of the hooded figure that had followed him crossed the Captain's mind. No, thought the Captain, Cloud was a larger man than that. Maybe, then, it was a conspiracy of three, maybe even more. The Captain folded the note and put it in an inner pocket. So now it seemed that his fortune, which he had thought to be at flood tide, was at low ebb instead. It seemed he was in danger of being hanged, or at least of losing the ship.

"Amy," the Captain said, sitting her on his lap, "we're in

trouble. It seems that Captain Kimberly had a sister, and ..."

The little door slid open and the coachman put his face to it and spoke to the Captain.

"I wouldn't be talking to myself anymore, sir, if it's all the same to you. I mean, we wouldn't want to *attract* any crazy women, would we, sir?"

Slowly, limping as it were on the broken wheel, they proceeded on towards New Liberty. It was late dusk when they arrived.

CHAPTER THIRTEEN

Hinx, minx, the old witch winks,
The fat begins to fry,
Nobody at home but Jumping Joan,
Father, Mother, and I.
Stick, stock, stone dead,
Blind man can't see;
Every knave will have a slave,
You or I must be he.

T he *Riptide Tavern* was directly on the waterfront. Only a wide-boarded walkway separated the building from the docks. More than one deep-water sailor who had made safe passage around Cape Horn a dozen times had gone beam end over and off that boardwalk after reeling out of the Riptide Tavern, never to surface in the black water.

The Captain paid off the coachman at a gravelled street that dead-ended at the boardwalk, giving him extra and saying again he knew nothing about the woman who had nearly driven them off the road, which of course the driver did not believe. He mumbled something as he climbed onto his box again.

"I beg your pardon?" said the Captain.

"Just talking to myself, sir, if it's all the same to you."

Sticking Amy inside his coat, the Captain found the establishment he sought, pushed open the door of the Riptide Tavern and walked up to the bar. The place was loud with singing, shouting, the rattling of glasses, the pounding of fists on tables, and the stomping of feet.

"Aye, mate?" said the bartender, raking an eye over the Captain. He was a great trunk of a man with a sweating bald head. He swiped at the bar with a dirty rag, then dragged it over his head, back to front.

"Port," said the Captain. It was served up in a glass mug. The Captain squeezed in behind a small table next to a window looking out onto the boardwalk. He took a drink of his wine. At the farther end of the room, a sailor with a broken leg propped up on a stool was playing the concertina, and some others were helping him sing a song about the charms and inclinations of a woman named Molly Stouter, the Innkeeper's Daughter. When the refrain came around, the Captain reached inside his coat and pinched his thumb and forefinger over Amy's ears. Then, when the song about Molly was done, the sailors laughed, called for drinks, and started on another ditty about a woman of much the same temperament and character, a delight to sailors of all ages and everywhere. The Captain removed his fingers from Amy's ears. He would get a cramp in his hand trying to save her innocence in this place, and she would be among sailors on a ship at sea soon enough, so what was the use anyway? He took another drink of his port and looked out of the window.

Someone bumped into his table.

"Evening, Captain."

The Captain looked up. It was the old carpenter of the *Ariel*. Wisps of grey hair floated before his bleary eyes.

"Good evening, Ned," said the Captain.

"Aye, it is," said Ned. "And a salute to ye, Captain." With this he tilted his mug in a sloppy toast. The Captain raised his glass and took a sip. Old Ned guzzled his ale.

The Captain then set a small polite smile on his face, nodded, and turned his head towards the window again.

Old Ned belched, saw that he was being ignored, shrugged, waved a hand in farewell – but hesitated, staring at the Captain's midsection. Something almost like sobriety came into his eyes for a moment. The Captain followed Ned's gaze to his coat front. Amy's head was hanging out and she was staring back at the old carpenter. The Captain poked it inside his coat again, folded his arms, and returned Ned's astonished stare with a look of stern command. Ned's eyes fogged over; he stumbled and returned down the bar to a table where his shipmates were gathered. Had the Captain not turned his attention out of the window again, he would have seen all eyes at that table directed at him very soon. Ned was gurgling out something about a doll inside the Captain's coat.

The Captain himself was admiring the lines of a handsome three-masted fore-and-aft schooner that was tied up directly across from the Riptide. Down at the farther end of the Riptide an insult was passed from one sailor to another, and from out of the gloom a bottle was hurled the full length of the bar. It smashed against the wall near the Captain's head. He immediately ducked into a corner and put a hand over Amy. Two men were grappling in the gutter of the bar. Two more were upright, thrashing about, knocking over tables and chairs. It looked about to become a general riot when the bartender bounded over the top of the bar with a belaying pin in his hand. A xylophone player could not have played more sweetly than did that bald bartender on the noggins of the four fighting men. There was almost a tune and rhythm to it, and the four men were knocked out cold on the floor. A lovely orchestration, and something of the ballet in it as well with the bartender's leap over the bar. He then stuck the belaying pin in his belt, took the four men by their collars, and dragged them outside, where he laid them side by side on the boardwalk.

Then he returned to his station behind the bar, mopped his head with the bar rag, and it was business as usual again.

The Captain watched this little play with interest. He loked out of the window at the heap of bodies laid out so neatly, and wondered if it would help or hinder business. Then he saw Captain Kimberly's sister approaching along the boardwalk.

She was wearing a black mourning veil that entirely obscured her features, and was dressed all in black, as befitted a grieving woman. She came along in a jerky sort of gait, as if she were stabbing her feet into the ground at each stride. Now it was getting dark. But several yards behind her the Captain could see the hooded figure. Captain Kimberly's sister paused at the entrance of the Riptide, tossed a disgusted glance at the bodies lying outside the door, and entered. The Captain rose from his seat, leaned out to pick up a chair that had been knocked over in the fight, and set it at his table. The woman saw him and gave a jerk of her head and sat down across from him at the small table. As she did so, the hooded figure entered, got a mug of ale from the bar, and leaned up against a post nearby the Captain's table, facing the other way. This was close enough, however, to overhear the conversation. The woman in black noticed this, turning her head to look at the hooded figure, then spoke to the Captain.

"The trouble with spies," she said, "is they get fat like fleas from sucking up so much information, and it slows 'em down. You ever squashed a fat flea, Captain? Messy, ain't it?"

The Captain squinted his eyes, peering at the black veil, making nothing of this enigmatic comment. He wondered if the woman could see out of the darkness. He could not penetrate the veil at all. She might as well have been wearing a pot on her head.

"Squinty drunk already," she said to him.

"Not at all, madam. A gentleman may drink without getting drunk. And a lady also. May I order for you?"

"None of your swill for me."

"Just as well. I believe we have some very sober business to discuss." The Captain reached inside his coat, drew out the note and unfolded it, looking hard at the impenetrable black veil. "Now, you say you are Captain Kimberly's sister. May I address you as Miss Kimberly?"

She chuckled. "Take me for an old maid, eh? Well, maybe it ain't as ugly this side of the veil as your own side, if you think the looks of yourself is so grand. But never mind that. I came to talk about how things are, not how things look. Let's talk about how murder is, Captain, and how it might feel to hang by the neck until you're dead."

The woman jerked her head around at a shout from the farther end of the tavern. The concertina player struck up another song.

"Brutes," she said, turning toward the Captain. "You take live pigs aboard ships, don't you sometimes? Aye, you do. What I wonder is how you can tell them from the sailors. Heh, heh."

She enjoyed her joke for a moment, then spoke again.

"Tell you what, just call me Captain Kimberly's Bad Sister. My dear brother, my dear dead brother, hah, that's what he thought about it. No, you'd never hear him tell about me, no, not about his Bad Sister. Uh-uh, it wouldn't be like my dear dead Clarence to ever mention his poor sister. He was too good a man for that, wasn't he, Captain? Oh, yes, a fine man, and here I am, his only blood relative in the whole world, lying up on land like a dead mackerel while he goes off deserting all my needs, never caring or thinking about me, having rich trade and a good ship while I myself, his baby sister, have to make do in the hard ways.

Aye, his Bad Sister, who might not have been so bad if she wasn't left without any help — lying on the beach like a gasping fish sucking at pennies."

The woman was fairly trembling with her spite, the root of which was no doubt a great hurt, imagined or not, for the Captain could not cast Captain Kimberly in the role the Bad Sister was making for him.

"Aye, his Bad Sister, and now I wish he was alive just to see how I can live up to that name, almost like he was calling me to the job himself. 'Cause blood is thicker than water, mind you, Captain, and it's allowed to me by all the rights of kinship that the *Ariel* should have come under my hand when my brother died, and not be given to some upstart boy sailor — "

And there she stopped abruptly, seeing that the heat of her passion had led her to say too much.

"Exactly!" said the Captain. "Now you have said the truth exactly as it is. Your brother *did* give the ship to me. You have just confessed it out of your own mouth. You know it to be true, and you know your accusations to be lies, damned lies."

Now the Captain's blood was rising. He shook the note at the Bad Sister, taking his turn of passion.

"You say I murdered your brother. That is a damned lie! I loved your brother. He took me aboard his ship as a mere cabin-boy and treated me like a son. He schooled me and took pride in me, and I became a capable master under his tutelage. You say I forged his will. That also is a damned lie! When your brother was ready to die, it was only natural that this generous-hearted man should will his ship to me. I had not the slightest calculation of that outcome, and my grief at Captain Kimberly's passing far outweighed any material gain that could have come of it."

The Captain continued in a quieter voice. The Bad Sister sat silently.

"Surely, if you have spoken to any of the crew, you would know the truth of this. But I do recognise obligations of blood relationships. And such relationships touch upon the honour and decency of a man, no matter your differences or alienation from your brother. Say no more of that. My proposal to you would be this: that so long as I am owner and master of the *Ariel*, you shall enjoy a profit from its voyages. The value of this, which accumulates for no other reason than that you and Captain Kimberly were born of the same mother, I place at ... well, let us say ten percent, and I count that to be quite fair."

At this point, the Bad Sister began shaking her head slowly back and forth, but the Captain continued speaking.

"I will initiate this obligation by forwarding you a sum of money which should see you over until our next voyage is concluded. Thereafter, you will have ten percent of all the *Ariel*'s profit. A woman of modest means might do ... quite nicely ... considering ... " But he could not go on. "Why do you shake your head, madam?"

The Bad Sister placed her hands on the table. They were clad in fine black leather gloves. She folded them before herself in almost a prayerful manner.

"Now, Captain, if you've blown yourself out with all that slop, hear my little speech. I have accused you of murder and forgery. You say I'm lying, but there's lies that get to the truth finally, Captain, and the truth is that I've been scratching poor for a long time while my dear brother was stuffing up a pig crew and socking plenty away for himself, I can bet you. But let's forget the past, Captain. Let's talk about the future, and your hanging."

The Bad Sister let the burden of that statement rest on

the Captain for a moment. The hooded figure at the post leaned closer.

"I have a witness," continued the Bad Sister, "who will swear and testify before God in a court-room that you killed my brother, and that you were seen doing it, smothering him in his bed. Also, this witness will swear that you forged the will that gave you the ship, directing my poor brother's dying hand to sign it. Think now – what could you say to escape hanging?" She paused. "No? Nothing?" She paused again. "Yes, nothing. There were some strange things that happened aboard that ship, Captain – things that would give an honest jury suspicions even if I didn't have a witness."

"More lies yet?" said the Captain feebly, looking at the table. There seemed to him no way out of the Bad Sister's plot. He saw in his mind's eye the *Ariel* sailing away without him, and he and Amy on the roadway, walking off to God knows where.

"Oh, we needn't worry about telling the truth, you and me, Captain. If we wanted to tell the truth, we might tell about other things, mightn't we? Aye, some strange sorts of truths about how you came aboard, just a wee lad, and how you grew so sudden, and where might you have come from to begin with, and other things if we wanted to get into the truth of things, Captain. Who knows what might come of it if a good searching out was done on you to find out who you are and what rights you might have to anything?"

The Captain looked up and studied the black veil. Now the threat seemed to touch on Amy as well, and his rights as a guardian. The Captain decided at that moment to sign the ship over to the Bad Sister and be done with the madwoman. Somehow the Bad Sister must have found out about his past, and about Amy, but yet when she spoke again she seemed to deny that.

"Oh, not that I know anything special about you or your affairs, Captain, or even want to. But you know how courts of law are, always wanting to be messing about with your background. Sailors like to gossip, and who knows what might turn up if we got to looking into history.

"But never mind all that. I'd as soon kill the past as think on it. It's the future I'm always thinking of, Captain. That's what we've got between us, Captain, the future – and a certain map."

The Captain smiled wanly.

"So you know about the map?"

"Ah," said the Bad Sister, clapping her hands together. "A regular model of honesty you are, Captain. You ought to be teaching little children to tell the truth. I thought you'd lie to me and I'd have to squeeze it out of you. Yes, Captain, the map is what I'm talking about, the map to the gold treasure. That's my chief concern, Captain. Gold. And when we find that treasure, you'll want to know how much of the gold I'll want for my share. Don't let the question trouble you at all, Captain. You needn't do any fancy arithmetic, because I want exactly one half of it."

The Captain nodded. "Yes, I suppose you would. And then what percentage of the ship and her profits?"

"No, Captain, you're wrong about me. I ain't no merchant. After we get the gold treasure you may scuttle your stinking ship for all of my concern and go pigs and all to the bottom with it. All I want, Captain, is the gold, and then we're quits and I'll see you in hell."

"Hell cannot be so bad as all that, madam. But otherwise I accept your proposal. As to the map, however – and you may not know this – it is quite crude. There's no telling if we can even find the treasure."

"Aye, I'd expect you'd say that. I'd expect you'd say we was right now sitting in a queen's bedchamber if you thought I'd believe it. But nothing like that is going to work, Captain, because when we cast off from this place I'm going to be aboard the *Ariel* to look after my concerns."

The Captain half rose in his seat to object to that demand, but the Bad Sister was up on her feet even faster.

"It's that or hanging, Captain. Tomorrow morning bright I'll be alongside the *Ariel*. You just pipe me on board and we'll talk things over with that map between us."

With that, the Bad Sister swept out of the door. A moment afterwards the figure in the cloak and hood followed her.

The Captain watched them out of the window. The Bad Sister stopped a little way down the boardwalk. She looked behind her at the hooded figure. Then, shadow following shadow, they walked down the boardwalk.

One man in the stack of bodies outside the tavern stirred, stood up, and, seemingly nonplussed at the violence of the tide that had ripped him out of the place, he unsteadily floated forwards, bounced both shoulders off the jambs of the door and entered with a smile complacent as a clam. At the back of the tavern, old Ned the carpenter took hold of a shipmate's collar and pulled him around to look up the length of the bar, saying, "Mark it, Turvey — d'ye see it? There! A doll's head sticking out of the Captain's coat, a little girl's doll, Turvey, like I said. And wasn't that a witch talking with him? Like friends they was, up to some business, and now what d'ye think we're in for?"

The Captain rested a hand on Amy's head and stared into the darkness towards the *Ariel*.

CHAPTER FOURTEEN

The cock doth crow
To let you know:
If you be wise
'Tis time to rise.

T he sun cleared the horizon and the *Ariel* heaved
slowly in the long morning swells. The Captain
swung his legs out of his bunk, pulled on his
trousers, and looked towards where Amy lay on the chart
table. Tucking in his shirt, and heading for the washbasin,
he propped Amy up against a lantern as he passed.

"Good morning, Sis. A beautiful day. Ah, if only you
could breathe that air." This said while latching open a
window. Standing there, he beat his chest a couple of
times, held a long breath and let it out noisily. "A day to
celebrate, Sis. Aye, and yesterday, too. Out of St. Anne's
and away to the sea, full sail and off to adventure and
treasure." The Captain had further praises for the day, but
the memory of the night came back to him. He walked to
the basin and dashed some water in his face.
"Hmmmmm," he said, taking a towel and rubbing at an
ear as he spoke. "Nearly forgot about the Bad Sister. And
she's not likely to fade in the sunshine. Oh well, breakfast
first. Time enough to worry about her when she shows up.
But first off, Sis, there's something we've got to discuss."
He pulled up a chair to the chart table and sat down.
"Now, here's the situation, Sis . . ."

Just then came a knock at the cabin door.

"Aye, Cookie, that's you?"

The cook entered carrying a tray with the Captain's breakfast, hot and steaming from the galley, ham and eggs, fresh milk and butter, biscuits and jam, and coffee.

"Morning, Captain," said the cook. He was a small man with a dirty apron. He laid eyes on Amy suspiciously as he set the tray down.

"Lovely morning, Cookie," said the Captain. He touched Amy's foot. "Here, now, Cookie, I'd like you to meet my ..."

"Aye, Captain?" said Cookie, for he was most curious about Amy. Old Ned had passed some words about the Captain as he had seen him in the Riptide, cuddling a doll. For his own part, the Captain thought that he could explain everything about Amy to the crew, but just now he decided it might be better to wait until they got to sea, for certain reasons that he had been going to explain to Amy when the cook had knocked.

"Never mind, Cookie. Nothing at all. No. Nothing else for the moment, Cookie. Thank you."

Cookie left. The Captain sliced some ham. "There it is, Sis, almost gave you away, and now isn't the time for it. Last night before going to sleep I was thinking it over. It's about your becoming real again."

The Captain took a drink of coffee, sprinkled salt and pepper on his eggs, stuffed his mouth with a load of ham, eggs, and a big bite of biscuit.

"Mfff. Good." He washed the mouthful down with a gulp of milk. "Sorry you can't have breakfast, Sis. Aye, you don't eat this well at sea. But here's the problem, as I was going to tell you. The way I figure is this. All that's needed is a pinprick in the head to start you coming back to yourself. I just don't have any doubt about that, having gone through it all myself. But I think it's best to be out to sea before we do that."

This was said between bites and drinks of coffee and milk. As he chewed, the Captain nodded his head slowly, continuing to think it over.

"We don't want to bring you back to yourself while there's the chance of any high-situation ladies or gentlemen around. You see how they'd think? What's a small girl like yourself doing skipping around a rough old crew of a three-master like this instead of being at school or in the care of some nurse? Aye, that's what they'd wonder, watching us as we're tied up here. You see what I mean, Sis? I speak of the authorities. What I might have done is got a paper from Mrs. Hill, somehow saying you belonged to me and everything was all right. But what could such a paper say, anyway? The way that you're my sister isn't written up in any book of law. See, if I said you were my sister because we had the same father and were twins, then they'd say why aren't we the same age? And what's my answer to that?"

Amy stared at the Captain. He looked into her pearly blue button eyes and thought he saw understanding there. From a thousand miles away Amy heard everything and saw everything, and understood, and was not very concerned, as it was all so remote. The morning sunlight now and then sparkled in her button eyes. The violent adventure on the road, the Riptide Tavern, the Bad Sister – all was like a dream, not even as real as the sunlight playing across her and the gentle rocking of the ship. She was content. Dolls have calm and simple pleasures and a spherical patience. They can spend weeks propped up nicely on a shelf and not feel very much neglected. They can enjoy watching the slow changing of the light and shadows moving on the wall. There is time enough to be real. And if it never happens, that can be all right, too.

"If you were a boy, that would be different," said the Captain, finishing up his breakfast. "Some cabin boys aren't any older than yourself. But a girl . . . ?" The Captain shook his head. "So that's how it is," he said, shoving his tray aside. "And there's also the Bad Sister. No telling what sort of danger she may be. Best you stay a doll until we're out at sea. Then, if there's any complaints from the crew or that witch, it's mutiny, and all sailors fear a mutiny. If you go against a Captain when you're out at sea you'd best take a good grip on your gold earring. So we'll sail first, then I'll make you real again."

The Captain got up, slipped into his coat, stuck his hat on his head, and tucked Amy under his arm.

"But right now we'll take a stroll around the ship so you'll have an idea of your new home, Sis."

And out they went. The sun was up, the day was fresh, and the docks were busy with carts and horses and men. The ships both fore and aft of the *Ariel* were working their crews, one loading grain sacks, the other heaving large heavy boxes into the hold. But the *Ariel* was quiet, all hands tumbled into the fo'c'sle or soon to be staggering aboard, fallen out of some strange bed or swept out of some bay-front establishment. But the salt wind was blowing and all soon would be revived and ready to sail.

"Up there, that stagelike place, Sis, that's the poop deck, or call it the afterdeck. That brass box in front of the wheel, that's the binnacle. Inside that is something most important, Sis, for that's the home of the compass, and without a compass a ship is hardly better than blind."

The Captain cradled Amy and faced the front of the ship.

"Now we're looking forward, Sis. The back end of the ship is aft. That mast there, tall and straight as a tree, is the mainmast, and way up there is the foremast. That's the mizzenmast there. That little ladderway there goes down to the fo'c'sle, where the crew lives, and forward of that, that low, houselike place is the galley, or kitchen. Now we'll stroll along here, this being the port side of the ship, the left side, and the other side is called the starboard side.

"Everything has a name, Sis, and all things have a proper place on a ship." The Captain reached out and touched ropes and rigging as he walked along. "These ropes are shrouds, and these are sheets, here's a deadeye, lanyards, these, and those are called the ratlines, and set all along here are belaying pins. Now look above. Those little platforms are the crosstrees, and where you see all the sails bunched up, those are the yards. All the sails have names, Sis."

Being amidships now, the Captain was in a good place to point out and name the various sails, but a man came out of the galley carrying a steaming cup of coffee.

"Ah, Skivvy," said the Captain, greeting him with a wave of his hand.

The man did not appear to be a sailor at first glance, for he hadn't the colour or the deep lining in his face that the open sea paints and traces on a sailor. Then you might look at his hands. They were not the scarred and rough instruments that give their strength and grip to work a ship across an ocean. But upon looking closer at this man, looking him in the eyes, no deepwater seven-seas sailor would doubt that this man belonged to the sea, for he had the look of great distances, the faraway look of a man just down from watch at the masthead, the searching look of a man intent on some far landfall or a star.

"Morning, Captain," said the man.

"Skivvy," said the Captain, throwing a quick glance around to see that no one else was about. "I'd like you to meet my sister. Amy, this is Skivvy, my second mate. As you can see, Skivvy, my sister is at the moment a doll."

"Pleased to meet you, miss," said Skivvy politely, "and I hope you'll be yourself again soon. I was a pair of long underwear myself, once, begging your pardon and no offence intended, miss."

"And none taken, Skivvy," said the Captain. "Are all hands aboard?"

"Nearly so," said Skivvy. "Not much fit for the day, Captain. 'They are out of the way through strong drink; they err in vision, they stumble in judgment.' Isaiah 28:7, if I may mention it, sir, and also First Corinthians 6:18, begging the lady's pardon again, sir."

"Quite all right, Skivvy, and I'll make a note of it. As to now, we'll soon be expecting a visitor. Turn the men out. There's business to settle they must know of, and we sail on the evening tide."

"Aye, sir," said Skivvy, going towards the fo'c'sle.

"A strange case, Skivvy," whispered the Captain to Amy, and he moved a few more paces along the railing. "That's the mainsail, Sis, furled up to the yard, the largest and most glorious to see when she's working."

Again the Captain dropped his voice to a confidential whisper.

"Speaking of Skivvy again, Sis. You might wonder why I didn't mind introducing him to you, but he's got a special story. When Captain Kimberly died, I took his cabin, you understand. And being fond of reading, naturally as I might be since you read to me so much, I looked about the cabin and couldn't find anything of interest. Oh, there were books on navigation and such, mostly columns of figures and diagrams, but no real books of poetry or stories, you know, and that's what was wanted so as to pass the time at night."

The Captain glanced up as two men stumbled out of the fo'c'sle. "And there's the fore lower topsail, fore upper topsail, and fore royal up there highest of all."

The two sailors, both looking a little sick, nodded as they passed the Captain. They entered the galley. One paused at the door and looked back at the Captain. He seemed to have a dim recollection that Captains of sailing ships didn't often walk about cradling dolls and talking to themselves. But hot black coffee was more on this man's mind. He shrugged and entered the galley. The Captain walked farther forward.

"And those sails farthest forward are the jibs, Sis: the flying jib, outer jib, and inner jib."

He looked towards the galley door for a moment.

"But as I say, Sis, there wasn't anything to read. Except for just one thing. The Bible. And since I had some grief on my mind, the good Captain being dead and all, I set to reading it to find some comfort. I started out at the beginning. And right away, Sis, the Bible talks about how God created the world. That's how it all begins, you know. 'In the beginning God created the heaven and the earth.' Then very soon it talks about how God created man. So right off it had me thinking. I laid the Bible aside and thought about creation."

The Captain sat down on the capstan.

"Out there is the very point of the ship, Sis. It's called the bowsprit."

The Captain stood up and walked forward, leaned on a rail, and held Amy in an outstretched hand over the side of the ship.

"There, Sis, that's our figurehead. Can you get a look at it? A sea spirit she is, and quite a nice carving. Now we'll just walk back a way here and sit down and rest. Ah, a lovely day, Amy. I'm sure you'll like the sea. This is the capstan I'm sitting on. A winch it is, and hauls up the anchors and does other heavy work that's needed. Each of those large timbers sticking out from the bow are called catheads. The anchors swing from them, hauling up or down."

For a while the Captain sat silently, watching the loading activity aboard the ship in front of them. At last he spoke.

"So I was reading the Bible, and it's difficult, Sis, having to think about creation when you've been just a doll before. And I thought that it was a great wonder how that happened, how God created man, and man created dolls, and then how a doll could come to life. I got to thinking very deep on it, and wondered if a doll who came to be a man could create another man out of a doll. See, I wondered if I read out of that Bible to a doll, for example, and then stuck it in the head with a needle, would it come alive? Because you see, Sis, it seemed to me that it was the reading that does it, being read to by someone who cares, like you did with me, for that's a way to know you're loved. After you started reading to me, I was ready to come to life most any time. 'In the beginning was the word,' or something like that, perhaps. Then all it took was the stick of that needle in my head to get me started. So I determined to try it out myself. But I hadn't a doll to read to, so here's what I did. I took a pair of long underwear, stuffed it with laundry, bunched up a towel for a head, and tacked it all up on the wall and started reading the Bible to it."

Some of the men were on deck now. A couple more came lurching up the gangway. Sitting about, drinking coffee in the sun, they were stealing glances at the Captain, who, having forgotten himself in the telling of his story, had set Amy on his knee and was speaking to her quite as plainly and loudly as if she were a real little girl. Now the Captain saw that he was being observed. He turned away and mumbled a concluding remark to Amy.

"Making it short, Sis, I read the Bible clear through to that pair of long underwear. Then I stuck it in the head with a sailmaker's needle, and there's Skivvy for you. 'What hath God wrought?' Those were his first words, and he's still wondering about it. Aye. Worries a lot about his soul, does Skivvy."

Then, just as the Captain tucked Amy under his arm and turned around to face off anyone left staring at him, there came a shrill yell from dockside.

"Ahoy there, Captain, or whatever your stupid word is for getting some attention. If you've got a sailor on board who can stand on his feet this morning, send him to give me a hand up this plank like the fine gentleman you are."

It was the Bad Sister, standing at the end of the gangway with a large bag on either side of herself.

CHAPTER FIFTEEN

The hart he loves the high wood,
The hare she loves the hill;
The knight he loves his bright sword,
The lady loves her will.

T he Bad Sister wore no veil in the morning light.
She frowned and pouted as she was led up the
gangway on the arm of one of the sailors, which
she thrust aside like a piece of garbage as soon as she had a
safe foot aboard the *Ariel*. As the Captain approached her,
he searched her features to find a likeness to her brother. But
if there was a likeness, it was hidden under a heavy base of
pancake make-up, upon which, layer by layer, the Bad Sister
had built a grotesque cosmetic mask. Her eyelids were of a
purple hue, befitting her mourning state perhaps. On her
cheeks were two nearly symmetrical circles of a bright,
blood red rouge. Her lips were painted unevenly on their
contours, so that her mouth seemed to dip lopsidedly, and
all was powdered over with a heavy flesh-coloured dust. She
seemed almost to be painted for the stage, or for some
fiction that takes place at a distance, as in a play, and not
meant to be too closely examined. Even as she spoke, her
expression seemed over-animated and artificial, almost
deliberately contorted. The total impression was quite ugly.

"Careful with that bag, goat legs," she commanded a
sailor as her belongings were handed aboard. "There's
breakables in there."

As her face was made up in layers, so also was she dressed in layers, She wore a heavy long skirt, under which must have been several petticoats, and a worsted jacket, over all of which was thrown a cape large enough to serve as a blanket. She had on a flat black hat with yellowing lace around its border. It was evident that her hair was a black wig.

The old carpenter, Ned, who had handled one of her bags, nudged a shipmate and whispered a couple of words to him, who in turn passed the word along. Here she was in broad daylight, the Captain's confidante of the night before in the Riptide. "That's her," the word was whispered around. "That's the witch!"

The Captain removed his hat and made a small bow, attempting to keep his face void of disgust.

"Welcome aboard, madam."

To which she replied, "Pigsty," and pointed her nose around at the group of sailors, saying, "Is this a working ship or does everyone stand around all day like jackasses?"

"Lay to, men," said the Captain. As the sailors began to disperse towards the fo'c'sle, he called to Skivvy. "Please come with Mister Cloud to my cabin."

"He's ashore, Captain. There was some commotion down the way. He went off to take a look at it."

The Captain nodded and frowned. Of course. If the Bad Sister and Mister Cloud were against him in this plot, they must have found some time on shore to make their final plans.

"When he returns, then, Skivvy. And now, madam, will you accompany me." Leading the way, the Captain descended with the Bad Sister to his cabin. It was not so very small a room, or so very dim, but the Bad Sister made the most of its shortcomings. She looked about.

"Creepy little place, ain't it?" she commented. "Stuffy and stinking."

The Captain reached up and propped open the skylight. "Aye, madam, and there are smaller places yet on board the ship, and they seem to get smaller the longer you're at sea. Confined, that's the feeling you get, like you're in a trap, and you just have to put up with the bad smells, excusing me for mentioning it, madam. No, there's not much comfort aboard a sailing ship this size. It's a place that's hardly fit for a lady to live."

"Oh, Captain, don't you worry about my comfort," said the Bad Sister, sitting down at the chart table. "It's gold that's going to be my comfort, Captain. Gold or a hanging. It soothes my mind to think on it. I could sleep in a coffin and think comforting thoughts about gold, so I can tolerate your stinking little boat, don't you worry."

The Captain went to a window and latched it open. Ah, and there he saw Mister Cloud approaching the ship. The first mate swung onto the gangway, and the Captain heard Skivvy call out to him. The Captain took a deep breath and pulled his head inside. The Bad Sister had taken his attention out of the window to be for another reason.

"Are you looking for someone else to come along behind me, Captain? A sort of shadow, maybe, wearing a hood, maybe? Never mind it, Captain. Sometimes it's best to keep your shadow to yourself. They can be packed tight into small places, and slid under doors, don't you know. But if I decide to throw my shadow onto something, don't think I can't find it. But let's not talk about dark things right now, Captain. Let's talk about gold, and treasure maps."

At just this moment there was a rap on the cabin door.

"Exactly," said the Captain, "now we talk about gold."

He opened the door. Mister Cloud and Skivvy entered.

Down in the fo'c'sle several sailors were talking, gathered around their tin cups.

"So what d'ye think, Ned?"

"Blasted strange is what I think."

"Who is she?"

"His mother?"

"God save us!"

"His wife?"

"God save us twice!"

"A witch is what she is, and no doubt about it. Maybe Mother Carey, the mother of the witches, and *her* old man's Davy Jones, don't you know."

The cook poked his head up out of the hatch, standing there with one foot on the ladder.

"The mates are in on it, whatever it is. They just went in, Cloud and Skivvy."

"That Skivvy!"

"I ain't sailing with anything that looks like her."

"Aye, and we sail on the evening tide."

"You seen him talking with that little girl doll?"

"God save us!"

"Here now, just hand me my seabag. The *Gloria* needs another couple of hands."

"What's the day?"

"Friday."

"That's worse yet."

"Who's Master of the *Gloria*?"

"Whatever, he don't talk to dolls, and there ain't no witch on board."

"Blasted strange is what I think."

"It never began right. The way the Captain grew up like that all of a sudden. And then there's that Skivvy."

"A man made out of rags!"

"Ye don't believe that?"

"Carl saw it. Hanging up on the wall."

"Don't say a thing like that. You'll bring down judgment on all of us."

"It's blasphemy! Touch a Bible!"

"God save us!"

Mister Cloud might have had better reasons to complain of small places and low ceilings than the Bad Sister, for he was a big man. He had to duck his head to enter the cabin, Skivvy following him. The first mate was sixty years old or thereabouts, with a great bush of a beard. His face was darkly tanned and deeply grooved with lines of expression that accommodated both a forbidding scowl and a smile, for he smiled with his mouth turned down, as some men of hard authority do. His eyes were clear, and the colour of the sea beneath an overcast. His features were like a map of many close-fought campaigns with the elements, and he carried himself with the uprightness of an old survivor of a noble war. He had sailed with Captain Kimberly for more than twenty years. He had gone to sea when he was only ten years old. For half a century he had stood off from the land, and he took contentment in being apart from the world. He thus tended to stand off from his fellow men, as if they were landfalls to be avoided. But this very aloofness gives a man the sort of staunch demeanour that commands respect, and because of his size and the cold authority with which he gave orders, his humour was not broached. He was a good first mate.

"Morning, Captain," Mister Cloud said. Then he looked at the Bad Sister.

The Captain had been anticipating the moment. He tried to catch in this first glance the proof of their conspiracy. But he saw no recognition pass between them. Indeed, they almost seemed to be sizing each other up. Yet, thought the Captain, if you are acting a part for a gold treasure, your dramatic efforts may be brought up to an unusual competence. Introductions were made, and the two mates of the *Ariel* took chairs at the chart table.

"Have you spent the night ashore, Mister Cloud?" the Captain asked.

"No. There was talk of a drowning down the way. I went off to have a look..."

"Let us consider it a happy omen, Captain, of my coming aboard," the Bad Sister interrupted. "A day can't be all bad that begins with a drowned sailor."

Skivvy grunted and said, "Revelation 20:13."

"Eh?" said the Bad Sister.

"Captain Kimberly's sister?" asked Mister Cloud. "His half sister?"

"His blood sister," she said. "But don't look for no likeness between us. When my brother laughed, I cried, and when he cried, I laughed, and it came to make us look like strangers. But it's blood that counts, and it's blood that brings me on board this ship to get my rights, and I give the floor to the good Captain to set all that out before you."

"Indeed," said the Captain. He propped Amy up against the brass lantern and stood with the tips of his fingers touching the top of the table. He explained to the mates how, the Bad Sister being a relative of Captain Kimberly's and in need as well, and these facts touching both upon his honour and decency, not to say how the courts might decide the issue, and so forth and so on – never mentioning, of course, that the Bad Sister had plans to get him hanged otherwise – that the Bad Sister would sail with them and take a proper profit from the voyage. Both Skivvy and Mister Cloud lowered their heads and made

faces to hear this, but looked up smartly when the Captain
finished his speech with these words:

"And we sail for gold treasure."

CHAPTER SIXTEEN

If ifs and ands
Were pots and pans,
There would be no need for tinkers!

T he *Bad Sister* rubbed her hands together. The
Captain went to the chart cabinet, as he did so
briefly sketching the history of the treasure map,
how Captain Kimberly had found it in a bottle half buried
in the sand on a lonely beach. Mister Cloud took out his
pipe, nodding slowly to himself. He poked his tobacco
down, his face in deep concentration, the picture of a man
trying to put a puzzle together without all the pieces.
Skivvy was shaking his head, doing his own meditation. He
muttered to himself, "'How much better it is to get
wisdom than gold.' Proverbs 16:16."

No one replied.

Amy's thoughts continued to float. She thought the
Captain's reasons for not bringing her immediately to
herself were good reasons. Let the other world care for
itself. It was far beyond her. The trouble was with the Bad
Sister, all of it. A *Mother Goose* rhyme floated up in her
head.

For every evil under the sun,
There is a remedy or there is none.
If there be one, try and find it;
If there be none, never mind it.

She would have smiled, but the stitched line of her mouth prevented it.

"And this is the treasure map," said the Captain. He carefully smoothed out a large scrap of paper. Both mates and the Bad Sister leaned their heads close to it.

It seemed to be the poorest sort of map to go treasure-hunting with. Any man with an eye for a map would say so. The paper was apparently torn from a large ledger book. The edges of it were brown and crumbled. It was water-stained, spotted, and toasted with age. The markings on it were extremely faint, not in ink, nor yet even in pencil, but it appeared as if the drawing on it was done by the sharp end of a charcoal stick taken from a fire. At the top of the page were written the words:

Gold Treasure

The map pictured the outline of an island of undistinguished aspect, shaped more or less like a squash. If any geographical features had once been drawn onto the island itself, they were now lost as smudges. But the gold treasure was not on the island itself. A little way off the small end of this squash-like outline was marked an X in the water. Beneath that marking was the legend: "Captain Cowl all hands."

"Cowl," said the first mate, touching a finger below the legend. "A bloody pirate. Raided the sea-lanes down south. Disappeared, he did, must have been ten years ago. Some say he retired to Spain. Goldnose took up his old haunts."

"Goldnose?" the Captain said.

"Same thing as Cowl. A bloody pirate. Lucky if you

don't meet up with him. Got his nose cut off, or bit off, or it dwindled away or something. Anyway, now he wears one made out of gold."

"I see. And Cowl in Spain?"

"That's what's said. Nobody knows."

"Then this could be right," said the Captain, tapping the map with his forefinger. "I read it to mean that Cowl's ship went down here with all hands, loaded with gold – ten years ago."

"Not all hands," said the Bad Sister. "One of the scum floated up, or how would the map be done?"

"Now, that's right," agreed Skivvy.

"It is and it isn't," said the Captain. "I've had more time to think on it than you. Suppose it's like this. Suppose some pirate who knew about Cowl put out this map in a bottle after he got marooned on this island. So suppose it's got nothing to do with Cowl at all. Perhaps it's just some marooned pirate on an island far out of the way, trying to lure himself a rescue. Or suppose this. Suppose some pirates live on that island. They send out hundreds of these bottles with maps in them to get ships like us to come treasure-hunting. Then we get hunted instead."

"True," said Skivvy. "There's ships that just disappear."

Cloud leaned closer to the map. "No. If it was some trick to get somebody to go there, this is no map to make it work. See here, no latitude, no longitude. North not even marked. But I suppose anyone knows north is at the top."

"Could be the map maker was a prisoner," said Skivvy. "Maybe he didn't know where he was when the ship went down."

"Anyway," said Mister Cloud, waving a dismissing hand at the scrap of paper. "You might as well close your eyes and go off sailing as try to find that place." Then, turning to the Bad Sister, "Madam, if this gold treasure is your interest in sailing with us, I'd recommend you get some geese and chase 'em on dry land. You'd spare yourself short rations, hard sleeping, danger of drowning, and gold-nosed pirates."

"Aye," said Skivvy. "It ain't no kind of a map to find any treasure. And just as well. 'For the love of money is the root of all evil.' First Timothy 6:10."

"Amen," said the Captain, by which he meant amen to the Bible reference, not amen to agreeing that the venture was impossible. But the Bad Sister took the remark differently and was stirred.

"And amen to you all," she said, standing straight up, and throwing her cape back on her shoulders. "I see the scheme you're putting up. Maybe I'm ignorant about how a map should look, but I'm not so ignorant I don't see how your eyes light up looking at it. You'd have me off the ship and all the gold to yourselves, that's your plan! But I'll sail with you, and I'll have half that gold when we raise it. That's my blood share in my brother's business. Say it ain't and we'll see what comes of that to please you. There's a better day than what begins with a drowned sailor, and that's a day what ends with a hanging one." She glanced at the mates, put her eye on the Captain and pointed a finger at him. "And there might be more than two of us here that knows what is meant by that little saying."

"Be pacified, madam," said the Captain. "No one is trying to cheat you of your share in this. What the mates say is true. No ship could set a course by this map. But your brother pursued a study of this scrap of paper. If the island exists at all, he may have located it."

He reached for a large rolled-up chart he had set to the side of the table.

"I say he *may* have found the island, be clear on that. He must have had doubts in his own mind, so therefore never turned the ship to the effort to search out the island. But for what it is worth, here is his work on paper."

The Captain rolled out the chart and set the lantern on one end and his pistol on the other. The chart encompassed within its borders several thousand square miles of ocean, with the very edge of a continental land mass showing at the northwest corner. There were several small islands indicated, some of them with names, the largest of which was pictured no larger than a pea. Near the centre of the chart was a group of islands. One of these islands, no larger than a whole peppercorn, was circled in red. It was named Vulcan Island. Alongside this island, in Captain Kimberly's handwriting, was the word "Cowl." Below that was a red arrow pointing northwest.

Again the heads huddled over the table. The Captain spoke.

"Your brother must have gone over many charts to find this particular one, madam. This was his conclusion at last, but still, as I say, there is much doubt if anything has been found at all."

Skivvy slid the treasure map alongside to compare it with the indicated island on the chart. "Neither island makes up any shape you could say much about. You couldn't say it was the same island."

"I agree," said the Captain. "Which leads me to think that Captain Kimberly must have had some other clue to go on. Perhaps he took some information from the tides or winds at the time and place he found the bottle. Look – he circled this island with vigour. Vulcan Island. On all his charts there are hundreds of other little specks like this, but none are circled, just this one. And look, one more thing, this red arrow underneath Vulcan Island. You'll notice that it points northwest, to the continent.

"And here's something you missed. Look again at the

treasure map. See, this arrow below the island, pointing northwest as well. My opinion, and it must have been Captain Kimberly's, is that the maker of the map meant to indicate the nearest continent as he best knew it. So this circled island could well be the island on the map. Vulcan Island." The Captain rapped the map with his knuckles.

"A smudge," said the first mate.

"It's not much of an arrow," said Skivvy.

"Imagination," said the first mate, leaning back into his chair. "Mind, I've nothing to say against Captain Kimberly as a sailor, but this is an old man's dream. He never told me about any of this at all, and I was close to him. It's unseamanlike, all of it. He must have been ashamed to mention it to me. Well, I see why. This is some dream, and dreams and fantasies have got no place aboard a trading ship."

"Do you have anything more in mind by that remark, Mister Cloud?" said the Captain. He was well aware that this belittling talk of fantasy might fit his own situation, and Skivvy's as well. But the first mate slapped the back of his hand on the chart.

"This is what I mean, Captain, no other thing. The map's no better than an old rumour, a boy's trick maybe, or less than that." Mister Cloud turned to the Bad Sister. "Madam, I'd have gone to hot places for your brother, but I'd say this was a folly if he was standing here in the room with us. I'd say there wasn't anything left of your brother's affairs of any worth except this ship, and his soul, God save us both."

Skivvy, of course, said "Amen" to that.

"And amen again," said the Bad Sister hotly. "Amen and do unto others as you think you might get away with it, eh? You'd like to put me off and go for the treasure yourselves. But not much of that for me, thank you. Where's my cabin, Captain? And amen to you all again. I'm going off to sing a hymn or two about how much nicer an ocean voyage is than getting hanged for murder. Maybe the good Captain can hum you the tune to it."

She stomped to the door. The Captain nodded to Skivvy to show her the way to her quarters. When she was gone, the Captain stood for a minute looking vacantly at the chart table.

"Tell the crew, Mister Cloud, that Captain Kimberley's sister sails with us. Tell the crew we sail for gold treasure on the evening tide."

"Aye, Captain." He stood for a minute tugging at his beard and biting his lip at the map, then went out.

The Captain watched him go. What was he to make of this first scene between him and the Bad Sister? It *seemed* as if Mister Cloud was trying to discourage the Bad Sister in this voyage, and would gladly have had her off the ship. Well, tricks upon tricks, thought the Captain. Out at sea, things would come clear. The breath of the honest ocean sometimes forced the most deceitful to speak the truth. The Captain picked up Amy.

"I'll read to you tonight, Sis. I'm going to need some company these coming days."

CHAPTER SEVENTEEN

There was an old woman tossed up in a basket,
Seventeen times as high as the moon;
Where she was going I couldn't but ask it,
For in her hand she carried a broom.

"Old woman, old woman, old woman," quoth I,
"Where are you going to up so high?"
"To brush the cobwebs off the sky!"
"May I go with you?" "Ay, by-and-by."

N ow, it has long been known to sailing men that a voyage should never under any account be started on a Friday. Doing so brings on the worst sort of bad luck. Good men otherwise, honest and true to their duty, sober and robust, have refused to throw off lines on a Friday, or have jumped overboard and swum to shore like rats rather than set sail on that day of the week. This is an old wisdom – or superstition you may call it – so old that memory of the reason of it is forgotten. No one knows why so much grief is raised aboard a ship that sets sail on that unlucky day. But a seagoing man knows it to be true. Sail on a Friday and you risk scurvy aboard ship, stove-in hatches, drownings, spoiled meat, mutiny and bad water, calms that last for days or entire destruction in a storm. Why it should be so, no man knows. The connecting reason between these sorts of hazards and sailing on a Friday drifts as insubstantially as fog, but is just as dangerous to a ship. And this was a Friday.

There is another superstition, also. Never sail with a woman on board. This is a great danger. And the more beautiful she is, the more dangerous is the voyage. Strong men fall from the rigging when a beautiful woman is on deck. Men get into fights about nothing in particular, they neglect their duties, and they are disobedient to the officers. No one knows why. The mystery is as great as beauty itself. As for the Bad Sister, she was an ugly brute — no danger in that respect at all. Yet word had got around that she was some sort of witch, and that condition is considered to be as dangerous as beauty.

So when the first mate returned to the Captain's cabin, after informing the crew that the Bad Sister would sail with them, the whole of the crew was right then stuffing seabags and hauling sea chests onto the deck. They had seen the Bad Sister and would not sail with her. Also, it was a Friday, as noted. The mate passed this information on to the Captain.

"Do they know we sail for gold treasure?"

"Aye, but they say she's a witch, Captain, and this being a Friday as well." He sank his fingers into his great white beard. The Captain had been doing some small chores about the cabin, with Amy still tucked under an arm. "There's more talk, too, Captain." The mate scraped a foot on the deck, and let his report dangle.

"Well? Out with it, Mister Cloud."

"It's the doll, Captain."

The Captain took Amy from under his arm and set her down on the table. He turned his back on the first mate and walked to the window looking out on the sea, wondering what tack to take now.

"Will you sail, Mister Cloud, with a witch on a Friday, the doll and all?"

[127]

"Aye, Captain."

"Of course. Then let me tell you something concerning this doll, at least. If you sail, you'll see things more fantastic aboard this ship than you've ever seen before."

"I expected this to be a strange voyage, Captain. I can't say I much like it, but I'll sail, for I have my reason."

"Aye, gold is a good enough reason for many things," the Captain mumbled, and then in a louder voice, "Very well, then. Pay the crew off and round up another."

"Aye, Captain, but if I can do that I fear they'll all be deaf, dumb, and blind." Opening the door, the first mate paused and put in a final word. "As for my reason for sailing, Captain, I wouldn't want you to be mistaken. The word isn't gold, Captain. It's loyalty."

"What was that?" said the Captain. "Loyalty?" But the first mate was out of the door.

Men yelled and seagulls screeched. The last of the crew was hauling up his seabag out of the fo'c'sle. Mister Cloud paid them all off. They trundled down the gangway, some towards the *Gloria* and some towards strong drink. Seamen from other ships were standing about on the dock, gazing with interest at the *Ariel*. Word was out on her, and they stood about as if they had paid admission, for they heard it was a witch's ship, and that there was a man on board made out of rags. The first mate saw there was no collecting a crew out of this crowd. When he came down the gangway they turned their backs and formed groups, looking over their shoulders and making room for him to pass. Deep in his thoughts, Mister Cloud walked towards the brightly lit roofs of New Liberty.

But the news was just as bad in town. Word was going around the taverns about the *Ariel* that was worse yet. This part of it wasn't said aloud. Men were glancing to left and right, lowering their voices to a whisper, and saying with a strange mixture of wonder, fear, derision, humour, and embarrassment that the Captain of the *Ariel* had got himself a little girl doll. He was carrying it around with him on deck and talking to it, cradling it, and smoothing its yarn hair. There was a laugh that went around when this was told. But some more reflective souls settled back and drew deeply on their pipes and thought to themselves, "There but for the grace of God go I," coming to some sort of repose amidst their brutish and brawling thoughts. They took the next tot of rum double large. Sobering, yes. Life is long, the ocean is wide, and the mind is deep.

Yet more. There were stories of how the Captain of the *Ariel* was no more than a yard high when he came aboard and had grown to full size in a matter of weeks. The ship was marked. Painted black with black sails, it would have stood no more cursed. But it was said that the *Ariel* was sailing for gold treasure. Shouldn't that rouse a man to clamour for a berth aboard her? Not so. Nothing could redeem the mark on the *Ariel*. She was a cursed and doomed ship, and so said all, a floating coffin, so never mind the gold that was promised.

Soon enough the first mate found this out. Not a man jack in town would sail on the *Ariel*. There was even some talk of cutting her loose to drift if she was still tied up after dark.

CHAPTER EIGHTEEN

To market, to market, to buy a fat pig,
Home again, home again, jiggety-jig;

To market, to market, to buy a fat hog,
Home again, home again, jiggety-jog.

efore returning to the ship, having failed to collect any men at the Riptide, the Galley Ho, the Anchor, the Uptown, the Sandbar, Kidd's, Alice's, the Barge Inn, the Pub, Moby Dick's, Danny's, or the Whale's Tale, Mister Cloud made one last attempt to enlist a crew in a tavern called the Bay Haven. The mate entered, called attention to himself, and in the dim, smoky place, raised his voice and made his business known. But his business was known already by almost every seaman in town. Rough, scarred, bearded faces turned to the mate, then turned again to drink. Some guarded hoots and jeers played amidst the clanking of mugs and tinkling of glasses. The mate would have liked to put his eye for sure on one of the catcallers and break his head, his ire having steadily risen over the insults he had received in the last couple of hours. But he was left clenching his fists, standing silently when he had finished his say. There was nothing to do but turn and go.

"I'd sail with ye, mate, if I wasn't a sick man."

The voice came out of the dark, a little nook to the side of the room. The mate strode over to the table. An old sea dog was sitting there over a noggin of rum, wearing a broad hat pinned front to crown with the skull of a long-beaked seabird of some sort. He wore a heavy greatcoat of the old cut, and he rested a hand on a large silver buckle that crowned his mountainous belly. He watched the mate with shrewd eyes that were given all the more expression because his whole face otherwise was draped in a red and white spotted bandanna.

"Aye, mate, when ye says 'gold', then here's a man for ye, but the sawbones has got me landlocked. Aye, blast all that scuttlebutt I been hearing, I'd sail with ye, but a doctor what's got regular university schooling says the taste of salt air will kill me. I got to wear this rag on my face and breathe through it or he says, that sawbones does, that me lungs'll luff in like a flapping sail, and I'll die coughing up salt water."

The mate, casting an eye over the old sea dog, saw that it was no great loss to sail without this fellow. He turned to go, giving only a grunt of acknowledgement to the man.

"But there's men I know that may sail with ye," said the fellow. The mate turned again. "Aye, a stout crew might be raised – but it's more information that's wanted, thinking of this crew I've got to mind. There ain't no fools among 'em, and they'd want to know more about this gold treasure you're going at, for example, such as do ye have a decent map to find it. Aye? And some says it's the very treasure of Cowl, but we all took him to be retired like a gentleman. Aye, so it is Cowl's, eh? Ah, now, they'd be happy to hear it, this crew I got to mind. I think I know where I can find 'em convenient, and I'll tell 'em how it stands."

"There's a gold piece for signing on," said the mate, "tell 'em that." He expected nothing to come of this. He took the old sea dog for some rummy dreamer who liked to make himself important with talk. Again he turned towards the door. The fat old dog saluted his departure with the promise that he'd surely pass the word along.

"And I hates it I can't sign up with ye, but that sawbones says I'm a dead man in a sea breeze."

He lifted the lower edge of his bandanna then, shot down the noggin of rum and called for another as if he had no intention of leaving the place that day, and no one to share any news with except the cockroach that just then crawled up to his table. The only news the old dog gave it was oblivion – smashing it with his empty cup.

Returning to the ship, Mister Cloud made his report to the Captain that no crew was to be had in New Liberty. Also that he had heard some black talk about cutting the *Ariel* loose that night. The Captain dismissed him. He stood at the stern window with his hands clasped behind his back. Presently his thoughts were interrupted by the sound of stiff-shoed stepping on the deck above him. The Bad Sister out for a stroll. Some seamen at dockside called out to her. The Captain caught the word "broomstick" in a string of words. Then the Bad Sister yelled back a curse that had the words "sea slugs" in it. The seamen laughed and called out again. The Captain moved to the starboard window in time to hear one of the salts ask her if she changed into a bat at night. She paid him off with a comment about his mother and an offer to change him into a choirboy if he'd like to come aboard for it. This got another laugh.

Then the Captain had an inspiration. "Skivvy!" he yelled, even before he had the cabin door open. Then again, "Skivvy!" Skivvy came hopping down the steps.

"Listen, Skivvy – I've a wonderful idea. Mister Cloud can't find us a new crew, so we'll get a crew the same way you were got, the same way I was got." Skivvy laid his head to one side quizzically. "Dolls, Skivvy, don't you see? You'll go to town and buy up all the sailor dolls you can find and bring them here. We'll anchor out in the bay. I'll read to them until they're ready, then stick them each in the head with a needle." The Captain opened his hands in gesture. "Then there it is, a crew that you couldn't find more loyalty in. And all of them born sailors."

Skivvy traced a finger on the table and turned his mouth down in dejection. "Well, Skivvy? It's a wonderful idea, don't you think? Skivvy? Is there something the matter?"

"It's only this, Captain," said Skivvy. "I thought I was doing my duty in a proper way, putting aside that I wasn't a born sailor like yourself, and like this crew you're thinking about."

"Why, so you are, Skivvy, I've not had a fault to put to you."

"I expected to hear the others run me down, Captain, the old crew. I took it charitable as I could, knowing it was just prejudice and they couldn't help it, since they was put up hard to understand how I came about anyway." Skivvy increased the pressure of his finger-rubbing along a groove in the table. His voice rose as he next spoke. "But dammit, Captain, God forgive me for swearing," said the mate, now looking the Captain in the eye, "if it ain't good enough to come from a family background of long underwear, maybe I'd just as soon not go on the voyage with you after all."

"Ohhhh," said the Captain heavily, for he now saw what Skivvy's grievance was. "Oh, now, Skivvy, I didn't mean at all to suggest ..."

Skivvy, almost at the point of tears, responded. "So if it ain't good enough to get a crew out of a few pairs of long underwear, being as you prefer sailor dolls, maybe I ain't good enough for a mate. Maybe I ought just to do this last duty for you and stay ashore when you sail."

For the next few minutes the Captain made apologies and reassurances. At last Skivvy was convinced of the esteem the Captain held him in, and that the Captain truly had no prejudice in the matter. The Captain said that he found Skivvy to be excellent company and a good friend. He would not think of his leaving the ship. The conversation at last came around so smoothly and brotherly that the two men clasped hands, vowing to one another the truest part of their affection, man to man, shipmate to shipmate, and sailor doll to long underwear if ever it came to that. Skivvy nodded sympathetically when the Captain laid out his only real objection to having a crew made up of long underwear.

"You know how I read the Bible to you, front to back? And right now I'm having memories of the dark nights with you tacked up on the wall, Skivvy, just lit by a candle, billowing out into the room when the ship rolled, like a ghost floating in the air. And moonlit nights I remember when the light of the moon swayed back and forth across you. Now and then an arm would pull out a tack, and the arm would swing down at me and touch my cheek in the silence and dangle there, fluttering. It gets spooky, Skivvy, if you'll excuse me for saying so. It gets spooky along about Deuteronomy. There's more than one time I shut the Bible on Revelation. Imagine it. Just me alone in here and you hanging up on the wall like a ghost. Whoosh! It gets spooky, Skivvy. I think it might affect a man's brains to keep up a schedule like that more than once."

So it was concluded. Skivvy would immediately set off for town. After returning with the dolls, the mates would put out the ship's boat, fasten to the *Ariel*, and pull her into the bay with the help of the outgoing tide. There they would anchor, safe from the taunting seamen at dockside and whatever mischief they might be planning. And there the Captain would begin his reading to the sailor dolls, the next smart crew of the *Ariel*. The Captain had a last piece of instruction for Skivvy.

"Don't forget to get a book for me to read. Now, I was always fond of *Mother Goose*, as Amy used to read it to me when I was a doll. You might find a copy of it handily enough."

"Aye, Captain." Out he went, and down the gangplank in the midst of jeers, such as wouldn't the Captain come out and play hopscotch, and he'd best look to it the witch didn't change him into a black cat, but Skivvy remained admirably impassive and marched towards town on his business.

Business was bad. Skivvy lost his good disposition before an hour was up. He also had a little adventure, the end of it being that he was brought back to the *Ariel* by a policeman. He had a black eye and bruises on his face. Here's what happened.

Skivvy visited all the likely places trying to buy up little man dolls, but couldn't find even one. He couldn't be interested in little girl dolls. When he had come to the end of places to market at, he leaned against a storefront window wondering what to do now. Inside the window of the establishment was a rubber duck on display among some other dolls and toys. Skivvy found himself staring at it. Why not, thought he, if a pair of long underwear can be a second mate, why not a rubber duck an ordinary seaman? He went in and bought the rubber duck, along with two monkeys made out of stuffed stockings. Then he went backwards on his marketing route. He bought up a felt chicken, a couple of stuffed rabbits, a donkey, a pig, a goat, and some other assorted toy animals, dropping them all together into a large bag. At the last place, he picked up two satin cats. There he found a copy of *Mother Goose* as well. This is where he had the trouble.

It was a general sort of store, stocked with dry goods, hardware, tinned meat and biscuits, fishing tackle, household items, and a few things for children as well. A grumpy red-faced man took Skivvy's money for the satin cats and the copy of *Mother Goose*. He was the owner, and with an owner's liberty had been drinking beer for lunch. He had heard the talk going around about the *Ariel*. As he was about to give Skivvy his change, he realized that he was dealing with one of the principals of the stories. He looked into Skivvy's bag as the mate opened it to drop in the cats and the book with the other animals. The owner of the store withheld the few coins of change in his hand and took some sport.

"Ah, some few little girls having a birthday, I'm thinking?"

"No," said Skivvy, settling the contents of the bag.

"Let me guess something," said the owner. "By the looks of yourself I'd say you was a seaman. If I've got eyes, that's the truth, yes? And I wouldn't doubt I could name your ship, just throwing out a guess, mind you. Wouldn't that ship be the *Ariel*?"

Skivvy, reflecting nothing, nodded and drew the neck of the bag closed. He held out his hand for his change. But the owner clenched his hand on the coins, smiling gleefully. He was something of a bully anyway if he could find a suitable object for the offence. Skivvy seemed to be the size to absorb some taunting. So the owner, regretting there was no one else in the store to enjoy the scene, but delighting to think how he would later act it out again in the tavern, dropped into a mincing and disgusting little performance.

"Oh, yes, the *Ariel*. Toys and dollies for the pretty little ship with the pretty little Captain. My, my, oh yes, for the itsy bitsy pretty little Captain and his pretty little dolly. Hah, hah, hah!"

Skivvy, seeing he was being put upon, hoisted the bag on his shoulder. It was small change, anyway. He'd go.

"Oh, Mother Goosey, be nice to the cutesy Captain and his little girlies, oh my."

Skivvy had turned to go, but the owner was in a regular fit of inspiration. He pranced after Skivvy and chanted like a bothersome uncle. "Mother Goosey, and a pretty little pussy for the Captain and his crewsy. Oh, yes, for the sissy little sailors on the sissy little ship, with their pretty little dollies — "

That was when Skivvy turned and hit him.

So shortly after that, having taken the worse part of the fight, Skivvy was hauled by a policeman up to the gangplank of the *Ariel*, his bag in one hand, the other turned up behind his back by the officer. The Captain came at the officer's shout and accepted Skivvy aboard. The policeman's last word was a threat that there would be no law to abide over the safety of anyone else who came ashore from the *Ariel*. The crowd of seamen standing about cheered to justify the threat, while the Bad Sister stood at the rail and made an obscene gesture at them. Mister Cloud stood with clenched fists, wishing he could be down among them breaking heads.

Skivvy slumped in a chair, touching his jawbone gently and licking the inside of his mouth. The Captain dumped the contents of the bag on the table. He looked silently at the crowd of toy animals, clearly disappointed.

"There were no sailor dolls, Captain. No boy dolls at all."

The Captain nodded. Presently he was left alone to ponder the situation. It was clear that they must take the outgoing tide and anchor in the bay. They were as good as prisoners aboard the ship, and they risked vandalism if they stayed tied up at the dock. The Captain took up the copy of *Mother Goose*, happy to see that at least. He sat on his bunk with Amy by his side. It was a large book with wonderful coloured pictures in it. The Captain opened it at random and held it before Amy's face, then he read from the page.

> *"See a pin and pick it up;*
> *All the day you'll have good luck;*
> *See a pin and let it lay,*
> *Bad luck you'll have all the day."*

On the opposite page of that poem was a picture of a sailing ship manned by mice. The Captain was a duck. The Captain pulled at his side-whiskers and looked at the toy animals on the table.

The ship's boat was put into the water as it was growing dusk, lines were slipped, and the mates Cloud and Skivvy, side by side at their oars in the little boat, turned the *Ariel*'s bow to the open sea. With the advantage of the tide working for them, they pulled the *Ariel* out into the wide bay. Securing the boat, they climbed aboard the *Ariel* and dropped anchor. And there they rested in the bay. The undersides of the clouds blossomed like roses in the setting sun. A few first lights twinkled in New Liberty across the water. All provisions for a voyage were aboard. They were ready to sail for gold treasure if only they had a crew.

Below deck in his cabin, the Captain had set all the toy animals upright on his bunk alongside the bulkhead. He pulled up a chair in front of them. With Amy on his knee and *Mother Goose* open in front of him, he began to read to the little group as if he were a schoolteacher. They looked back at him with whatever expression had been set on their faces by their makers, and they listened. The Captain read a rhyme from the book.

> *"Smiling girls, rosy boys,*
> *Come and buy my little toys —*
> *Monkeys made of gingerbread,*
> *And sugar horses painted red."*

A stoutish, full-rigged ship named the *Locust* was tied up at the last dock on the waterfront. The fat master of that ship stood, feet braced solidly apart, looking through his brass telescope at the *Ariel* riding gently at anchor. After a minute he shot the telescope closed with a thump of his open palm. He spoke to his quartermaster.

"If she hauls anchor or lays on a yard of sail, make quick legs and call me out. Set the watch here."

Handing the quartermaster the telescope, he lumbered down the poop-deck ladder, then down again into his cabin. The stern window had a view of the *Ariel*. Lighting a small oil lamp, he sat down at the table and opened the ship's logbook. Taking up a quill pen, he looked up at the ceiling, pinching his lower lip in concentration, for he had a difficult time getting the day's most ordinary business into words. Noticing that he was still wearing the red and white spotted bandanna over his face, he pulled it down about his neck. Then he pinched his lips some more, thinking, for sometimes he found it dreadfully hard just to think of a first word to set down. Ah — at last he had it. He grunted, dipped his quill into the ink pot, and put the word down in a scrawly hand.

The

Whereupon he looked to the ceiling again, pinching his lip some more, hoping that the second word would come easier. And his gold nose shone brightly in the small flame light.

CHAPTER NINETEEN

There were two birds sat on a stone,
Fa, la, la la lal de,
One flew away, and then there was one,
Fa la, la la lal de,
The other flew after, and then there was none,
Fa, la, la la lal de,
And so the poor stone was left all alone,
Fa, la, la la lal de.

Midnight. The Captain took up his long-stemmed clay pipe and ascended the companionway to the deck of the *Ariel*. For three hours he had been reading to the toy animals out of *Mother Goose*. He stretched, breathed deeply of the shore breeze, studied the sky for weather signs, then walked towards the bow of the ship, drawing on his pipe. Coming to the prow of the ship, he leaned over the starboard railing.

"Skivvy?"

"Aye, Captain."

Skivvy was sitting astride the timber cathead, his back against the ship's side. It was a station he often took at night when at sea, his refuge from the late-night gabble of the seamen, and his place of meditation. Or rather, his place of brooding, for Skivvy found much to brood about. As the Captain had put it to Amy, "He worries a lot about his soul, does Skivvy." The Captain set his elbows on the railing, puffed at his pipe, and gazed off towards New Liberty. In this way, the two mates often passed an hour or more in close company. They often said not another word to each other after their greeting. And finally, each wrapped in mystery, wonder, or foreboding, listening to the hum of the universe, watching one by one the stars extinguished by the dark horizon, they would part with no more comment than "Good night, Skivvy," and "Good night, Captain."

And what could they say? Any ordinary seaman, in such a setting, might woo the goddess of philosophy with a notion or two, or offer a word to the muse of poetry, or touch the skirt of metaphysics. But as for the Captain and Skivvy, they were not ordinary men. There is no text that touches on the mortality of dolls. This was the great question they both shared. Both wondered if a doll made into a man had a soul. Skivvy believed it to be so. "There are some feelings that are in me, Captain, that I can only believe are eternal." The Captain wasn't sure. Perhaps they would become dolls again after they died. Perhaps they didn't have all the parts of real human beings, and died into nothingness, changing again into dolls. The Captain was prepared to die in ignorance of the outcome. All that one might say on the subject was idle talk. So the friends kept company in silence, sharing their solitude and watching the heavens float westwards above them, passing into the dark sea.

But this night Skivvy had something to say. After a two-minute silence, he spoke:

"I don't think I'll be sailing with you, Captain."

The Captain removed his pipe from his lips and looked at the top of Skivvy's head.

Skivvy had been reading the Bible. Strange fears were working on him. He feared the dark figure of the Bad Sister. He feared a voyage that was prompted by a search for gold treasure, for surely there is much to be said in the Bible against any endeavour turned to that purpose alone. More than any of this, he feared himself. For the first time in his life, he had been moved to violence. Skivvy felt he might do better to be on land, out of the way of any adventure that might touch on his fallibility.

"What can be expected of a man that's been made up of dirty laundry? There's better places for men like me," Skivvy said. "I could live like a hermit in a cave and be out of harm's way, or maybe enter a monastery and live alone like a monk if they'd have me. I could pray for you, Captain, and for the voyage, for I believe that's all I'm fit for. I fear the voyage, Captain; I fear myself; and most of all I fear the gold and the greed. It's best for all if I don't sail with you, Captain. I'm not worth any help to you, and worth very little to myself."

He fell silent. The Captain drew on his pipe. He paced a few steps along the railing and back again.

"I need you, Skivvy."

Skivvy looked into the black water.

"I need you and I trust you, Skivvy, and I feel that my trust is strong enough for us both. You're not wrong about the danger we're sailing into, for I believe it myself. That's the very reason I need you. Your feelings about Captain Kimberly's sister are right. She's after the gold only. But she's made up an evil story against me, and gold is the only thing that can get rid of her. Otherwise she could have me hanged and take the ship as well."

Skivvy looked up at the Captain.

"It's the truth, Skivvy. And more than that. I haven't any proof of it and I hate slander, but I believe that Mister Cloud may be in some plot with the Bad Sister. And that means, Skivvy, that you're the only one aboard that I can trust completely, except for Amy, of course, but she's a little girl. As for the gold, it's an evil only for those who have evil uses, and who love it for itself. As to our crew —

[142]

why, you've done a wonderful thing. They'll not have a love of gold like men, for they aren't men. Their hearts will be as pure and glad as Mother Goose herself, full of wisdom and caution, eager for the joy of life itself and not for any consequence of riches."

Skivvy fixed his eyes on the dark water.

"Last of all, Skivvy, is this. There may be dangers, but I think our destiny is in the very dangers we'll face. It's a destiny we'll find no other way. It may mean the end of us, but it's going to be the right end, and maybe our only chance for it. In some way that I don't understand, the gold treasure is part of that destiny." The Captain puffed on his pipe and was quiet for a few moments.

"It's come to me strange, Skivvy, but don't you see how I'm a sort of inspiration of Amy, and yourself an inspiration of myself, and the animals you bought a sort of inspiration of yourself, and Amy herself an inspiration, and here we are all together like some inspiration greater than whatever evil might come upon us, because we all came about out of love and care and the Bible and *Mother Goose*. What can stand against that? It's all linked, Skivvy, and who knows but you're the most important link of all?" The Captain looked down on Skivvy's bowed head. "So that's it. If you leave us, perhaps we'll all fall apart. Aye, we may need a prayer on this voyage, and you may have Captain Kimberly's Bible for yourself, and pray for us all close up, where it might take better effect than if you're away at a monastery. I need you, Skivvy. You may think you're a weak link, but it might turn out you're the strongest of all."

That was all the Captain said. His pipe had gone out, but he didn't relight it. A drifting log bumped the side of the ship, sounding it like a huge drum. Voices from New Liberty came across the water. A man shouted. A woman laughed. A bell rang. A dog barked. Skivvy cleared his throat. The Captain looked down. Skivvy said nothing, but held his hand up above his head, and the Captain gripped it.

"God bless you, Skivvy," said the Captain. Then he returned to his cabin, leaving Skivvy on the cathead, staring into the dark water. Presently Skivvy quoted from the Bible: Acts 27:10.

" '... This voyage will be with hurt and much damage, not only of the lading and ship, but also of our lives.' "

Skivvy was later to make other prophecies, but none were truer than this.

CHAPTER TWENTY

Come hither, pretty cockatoo;
Come and learn your letters,
And you shall have a knife and fork
To eat with, like your betters.

The faults of the *Bad Sister*, her snarly ways and her snide pokes, were balanced somewhat in that she was a good cook, although she would not serve. When the bread was baked and the pot was ready, the vegetables cooked and the coffee perked, she stuck her head out of the galley and called out in her roostery voice the well-heeded country call, "Come and get it or I'll throw it to the hogs." Then she disappeared for a few minutes to her cabin while the three men – the Captain, Skivvy, and Mister Cloud – came to the galley and helped themselves at the stove and oven and sideboard and made small and large talk at the galley table.

Now, the small talk was of the ship's lines, and bilges, and ballast, tar pots, tarpaulins, and crosstrees. Also of winds and weather. When the Bad Sister returned to the galley and took her place at the table, newly painted with rouge and mascara, for the heat of the cooking somewhat melted her countenance, the small talk might turn to cooking and condiments, and with compliments to the cook, compliments that the Bad Sister sloughed off or scoffed at. But there was large talk also.

Very soon, if all went as planned, the *Ariel* would be

manned by a crew of toy animals. And so, sitting at the galley table sipping at their after-dinner cup of coffee, or a glass of wine, the Captain told his story from the beginning. This was to prepare for the advent, for the coming alive of the toy animals. The Captain told how he had been a doll himself and had come to life. He told how Amy had been a real girl and had come to be a doll. Also, he told about Skivvy. All secrets were out. To the Captain's astonishment, neither Mister Cloud nor the Bad Sister showed much surprise. Mister Cloud's comment was strictly practical.

"Can a goat handle a line? Can a duck tie a half hitch? Can rabbits tar a rope?"

The Captain fetched his copy of *Mother Goose* that the company might examine it.

"I believe so, Mister Cloud. As you see by the pictures in the book, the animals are quite capable. Here is a dog, for example, playing the flute. And here, a mouse at a spinning wheel. And here, look, a cat playing a bagpipe. And see here – a whole crew of mice sailing a ship, with a duck for a Captain." He passed the book to the first mate. "Yes, I should think so, Mister Cloud. I believe we'll have a crew that can hand, reef, and steer as well as any ordinary seamen. The donkey should be of brave use at the capstan. The two monkeys in the rigging should serve as well as four men. Incidentally, I'll want you to bring me whatever texts you have on ship-handling, navigation, knots – whatever you have so the crew will know their duty. I'll read it along with the poems."

The Bad Sister also had a practical comment, turning away to her stove.

"Just don't expect me to clean up after 'em, Captain."

When she retired to her cabin, Skivvy set about washing the dishes. Mister Cloud got the books the Captain wanted. Thereafter the Captain put full time into reading to the toy animals. All meals were brought to his cabin by Skivvy. He read from daybreak to kerosene light, front to back and back to front in *Mother Goose* and Mister Cloud's books. Keeping to this schedule, he calculated that he might bring the animals up to readiness in a week, or two at the most.

For the first few days, as they were anchored there in the bay, a gentle wind rounded out of the west, and the crew of the *Ariel* had little care and easy chores. The Captain took to leaving his cabin door open to catch the breeze and refresh him at his long hours of reading. Whoever passed might hear his voice reciting for the twentieth time something such as this riddle:

"I've seen you where you never were,
And where you ne'er will be,
And yet you in that very same place
May still be seen by me."

Hearing this one evening, Mister Cloud paused for a moment, then climbed to the poop deck and looked out to sea. The answer to the riddle is: your reflection in a mirror. Mister Cloud did not know this, nor did he try to think it out. He was moved by the poetry of the riddle itself, and he looked out over the shining sea. A mood was upon him, a mood that may explain the lack of dismay he showed when he was told about the coming to life of dolls and toy animals.

Mister Cloud could play music and sing to his concertina, and once, when he was but twenty years old and far out to sea on a full moon's night, he was singing to the phosphorescent wake of his ship when he saw a mermaid. She flipped her tail, raised her head in the sparkling water, flung her hair about her head, and called his name. Mister Cloud did not answer, but watched her as she rolled in the water. She called his name again, her face wrapped in the strands of her dark hair. Her eyes glowed softly like pearls. She called again and said that she loved him and would forever follow his ship. Then she dived and disappeared.

Mister Cloud had since that night stood watch in hundreds of full moons and thousands of other nights, but he never saw her again. Finally, poor man, he spoke in his heart against this vision and called it a fantasy. But now, in the light of the singular situation aboard the *Ariel*, the vision of the mermaid came to mind again. If toy animals could come to life, then might his mermaid still follow his ship?

Later that night, Mister Cloud took out his concertina from a deep corner in his sea chest and went on deck. Very softly, after long silence, he found the notes of a tune long forgotten. He put the words of the riddle to it and sang over the dark water.

> *"I've seen you where you never were,*
> *And where you ne'er will be,*
> *And yet you in that very same place*
> *May still be seen by me."*

CHAPTER TWENTY-ONE

A dog and a cat went out together
To see some friends just out of town.
Said the cat to the dog:
"What d'ye think of the weather?"
"I think, ma'am, the rain will come down,
But don't be alarmed, for I have an umbrella
That will shelter us both," said this amiable fellow.

On the sixth day that the *Ariel* was anchored in the bay, the barometer began to fall, and in New Liberty threats began to rise against the ship. The wind picked up, coming out of the northeast. Sails were furled on the ships and shutters were set on the houses. Men gathered in the taverns and women gathered in the parlours. A grey whipping rain came and the sunlit blue patches in the sky closed up. In one of the parlours, tea was served.

"A witch ship."

"Did you see her, dear?"

"My husband saw her come aboard. That morning of the drowning she came aboard. That was all part of it, starting with a drowning."

"What did she look like?"

"Dark, like the clouds a-coming, and her face like a pale moon with bright red blood spots on it."

"A moon, the colour of blood," came a whisper.

"Hand me a biscuit, dear."

"A witch ship," came another whisper.

"Would you like some jam?"

"Thank you, dear. That's a lovely shawl you're wearing. Did you make this jam yourself?"

"Sarah did. Blackberries, you know, from behind her shed ...?"

"What sort of a name is *Ariel*, anyway? It's a witch's name, sure."

The wind rattled the shutters.

"Can a witch bring a storm?"

"Witches can bring anything bad. They sit and they brew and stew, and out of it comes evil-doing."

"Three men and a witch on that ship, just sitting out there all week. What do you suppose they do, just sitting out there?"

"More tea, anyone?"

"Someone ought to sink that ship."

And the echo of the last sentiment bounded off the tea tray, the dish of jam, bounced under the door, hit a post, ducked under a fence, rode awhile in a carriage, flew out and struck a tree trunk, knocked into the side of a building, rattled along a boardwalk, glanced off a shiny boot and into the door of the Riptide Tavern, ran about the walls and found a home in the open mouth of a sailor, then reverberated without distortion:

"Someone ought to sink that ship."

The other three sailors sitting at the table looked at the speaker, all hunched over with pints in their hands. They had been talking about the strangeness aboard the *Ariel*, also.

"Naw, she'd clutter up the bay, and it wouldn't be rid of her. That's sinking bad luck in the bay."

A blast of wind hit the building. The men turned and looked towards the door.

"Storm coming on. Not likely, this time of year. It's a good one. Nor'easter."

"More tea, anyone?"

"Eh!" The three men looked at the one with his mouth open, who blinked, then banged the table and called out, "More ale here!"

"A witch ship, that's what it is."

"Cut her loose, say I, and let the next tide take her to wreck."

"Aye, easy to say."

"Aye, and I'd do it more easy."

"Hand me a biscuit, dear."

"Eh?!"

(Echoes, coming from a longer way around, were still arriving to the open-mouthed sailor.)

"*I'd* cut her loose," said this same sailor loudly and boldly to cover his last remark, which he did not quite understand himself.

"So you say."

"And so I would if someone handled the boat."

"I'll row you out there if you'll cut her loose."

"I'd do it if you'd do it."

"I'll do it. Here's my hand on it."

"Done!"

"Done! More ale here!"

"That's a lovely shawl you're wearing."

And as those two sailors in the tavern struck their bargain to cut loose the *Ariel*, low black clouds overran the town like the charge of a sable cavalry, their glistening edges outlined in flashes of lightning, and the thunder came like the rumble of giant wheels rolling cannon over New Liberty. The sky shook the hinges of heaven loose, and the rain fell on the town like a small fresh sea, beating shingles from houses and tearing gates from fences as the wind reared and struck like pounding hooves at house and ship and stable. Gutters ran like rivers, windows rattled, shop signs broke free and tumbled down the streets, where some unlucky souls, necessity calling them forth, laboured against the wind bent forward like drudging slaves, or flew before it, coat-tails flapping, erratically making their way like broken-winged gulls.

Ships broke loose from their moorings and, breasted by this great horse of a wind, piled up on to other ships. Bowsprits tangled in riggings, canvas ripped, booms swung free and raked fo'c'sle and poop, wheels smashed, binnacles toppled, rudders tore off, and sailors belowdecks heaved to and fro among their chests and bags, hammocks and small belongings flying in the darkness, all battering about with their prayers and cursing as they clamoured to reach the decks.

The *Ariel* strained at her hawser, but her anchor held, else she would have been dashed across the bay and into the docks and wreckage of the other ships. There was not enough manpower aboard to haul the second anchor, so they must ride the storm in the open bay until broken loose, or until the wind dropped. All sails were furled tight. The Captain put Amy in a cabinet for safe-keeping. He went on deck, where he joined Skivvy and Mister Cloud. The three men were in their rain gear, crouching and clutching at low handholds to keep from being washed overboard, lashing gear and taking up slack in all lines. The Bad Sister was in the galley making strong coffee in a hand-held pot, for there was no level place to set it down as the ship bucked in the froth of the charging storm.

The light cavalry of the storm passed, leaving ruin behind. Then came the heavy cavalry, leaving disaster. And then the wanton infantry, leagues deep in driving rain, searched every defence of the standing town and board by board tore at every structure. And two men, drunk enough to be two of God's fools who come to no harm, put themselves aboard a pitching boat near the Riptide Tavern. They began rowing against the wind and running tide, begging their way through the chopping sea towards the *Ariel* to cut her loose.

"We're breaking out, Captain," Skivvy yelled, grappling his way to where Mister Cloud and the Captain stood on the poop deck. "We can't hold."

The Captain nodded, the rain whipping across his face.

"We might take her to sea if we had sail, Captain," Mister Cloud yelled. "The wind's coming aback. Another point south and we could run with her and come around through the bottom, and haul for the open sea. We need a crew, Captain!"

The Captain looked leeward into the darkness, judging the distance to the shore.

"Can a dog handle a line? Can a cat set a sail?" Skivvy yelled.

The Captain looked at him. But was it time yet for the animals to come to life? The Captain faced into the storm, blasting now its cannon of thunder. The three men looked at one another, their faces flashing grim in the lightning.

The situation was this. Imagine that you are in a bay that is shaped like a large, round bottle, the neck of it being the passage to the open sea. At the bottom of the bottle are the docks of New Liberty, like fingers pointing towards the sea. The *Ariel* was near the centre of the bottle, and if she broke free without sail, the wind would drive her to a side of the bottle, or into the docks, where she would be wrecked. But if she had sail, and given just a slight change in the wind, the Captain could steer towards the bellied side of the bottle, gathering wind for steerage, and come around in a circle through the bottom of the bottle, up around the other side, dodge around the shoulder, and take the roadway to the open sea. It was a narrow way, however, and a close chance, for they could very well be blown into the docks as they came around through the bottom of the course. Again the Captain shielded his eyes and looked towards the shore, and then to the swinging lights of New Liberty. Yet they might safely ride out the storm at anchor. And such was the decision he must make. Skivvy and Mister Cloud swayed in the wind and watched his face, both in suspense, waiting for command. And then the strain of the moment was released. Not by the Captain, but by the two drunken sailors in their drunken boat bobbing like a ball at the hawser of the *Ariel*, one man at the oars and the other slashing with his knife at whatever length of the anchor line was presented near his hand. And then he cut it through.

"We're broke loose," yelled Skivvy, as a loud pluck was heard and the hawser snapped through the air like a broken bowstring. The *Ariel* heeled on its boards and fell off to port, heaving towards the wrecking shore.

"Set the jibs," yelled the Captain, already making his way down the ladder. "Stand by, Mister Cloud. I'm sending you up a crew." And with that shout into the wind, the Captain wrenched open his cabin door. He threw open a chest, plundered about and brought out an old biscuit tin and dumped the contents on his table. Taking up the biggest needle he could lay his hands on, he stumbled to his bunk where the toy animals were propped to listen to *Mother Goose*. The Captain took up the one nearest to him. It was a monkey. He held it in his hand for a second, breathed deeply, then drove the needle into the monkey's head.

"Yiiiiiii!" it screamed and jumped nearly across the room. The Captain grabbed the next animal, which was a

[154]

stuffed chicken. He plunged the needle into its head. It squawked, then fluttered to the floor and stood looking around. The Captain picked up another monkey.

"I'm the Captain," he cried over his shoulder. "Get on deck! We're adrift. Make sail, now. Lively, lads!" The monkey was at the door and out in an instant, the chicken following, and in another moment the second monkey. The cabin door banged on its hinges, and Mister Cloud shouted above the storm as the animals came out looking for orders.

"Set the topsails, brace the yards!"

And the animals poured forth from the Captain's cabin. "I'm the Captain," he cried as he stuck each in the head. "Up the ladder, lads, heed the mate. We're adrift!"

"Hands aloft!" the mate shouted. "Take the wheel, Skivvy. Let go all clews, Hard alee, Skivvy. You cats, lay back on the main sheets ..."

You must bring the image to mind. The *Ariel*, driven by the raging wind, was being expertly worked by fifteen toy animals. Fifteen, all told, fresh for duty they clambered out of the Captain's cabin and pulled themselves up the hand-rails. See them in the rigging and on the yards, clutching, pawing, clinging, clawing – the wind and rain driving at them – unfurling the sails, making fast the lines.

1 chicken,
1 turkey,
1 pig,
2 monkeys,

raising their heads into the beating rain, eyes sparkling, expressions clenched bravely against the weather and the danger aloft on the rolling, pitching ship. Then the *Ariel* took hold of the sea, the wheel became stubborn in

Skivvy's hands, and the ship ran before the wind towards the dark shore. Also, there were

> 1 goat,
> 1 donkey,
> 2 dogs,
> 2 cats,
> 2 rabbits,
> 1 squirrel,
> and a frog.

The Captain joined Mister Cloud and Skivvy on the poop deck, measured with his eye the course the mate was running, and yelled out, "It's a narrow way, Mister Cloud!"

"Aye, Captain. Ready to wear ship when you give the order."

"The ship's yours, Mister Cloud."

Mister Cloud nodded and put a hand on Skivvy's shoulder. The next manoeuvre called for fine judgment. Now they must bring the ship around through the bottom of the bay. They must come very close to the docks of New Liberty. The mate threw his eyes back and forth towards the lights of shore. And then the moment came.

"Ready to wear ship!" the mate called to the crew, and then, giving them a few moments to set themselves, he called out the order. "Wear ship! Helm alee, Skivvy!"

Skivvy spun the wheel. The head sheets were let go, the jibs were passed, the trysail was hauled aweather, and the *Ariel* was sideways to the wind, the sails luffing. The ship seemingly must come to wreck on the lee shore, and the mate yelled out again.

"Mainsail haul!"

The main yards were braced around, the jibs hauled over

and sheeted home, and the *Ariel* put her head towards the docks of New Liberty, leaning hard on her starboard boards. She was pulling hard, paying off on the port tack, the mainsails billowed out taut. The crew trimmed sails and watched the docks of New Liberty reach out like the dark fingers of a hand to clutch and crush them. It was going to be very close. The sails bloomed, and Skivvy held the wheel down hard. He said a prayer for the wind to veer a point. They drove closer to the dark docks. Half a point! prayed Skivvy. Three degrees! A few yards!

Even the Bad Sister was on deck, watching from the galley door. They could all now clearly see the first ship tied up at the first dock. They could see the very figurehead of it – the carved figure of a woman with a bunch of flowers pressed to her breast, and in a moment more they could see that the flowers were yellow. Skivvy still prayed – and then silent and dark the *Ariel* passed the first dock, missing it by a breath. You might have leaned from the bow and kissed the lady with the flowers as he passed.

Now then, a word about figureheads – and not entirely by way of a digression, for an event shortly follows that supports some interest in these wonderful carvings set at the very prow of a ship. The figurehead of a ship is the grand and final evolution of an ancient notion – the notion that a ship is a living and knowing body, and it must have eyes to see. In obscure and prehistoric times a pair of eyes painted on the prow served the purpose. The placing and painting of the eyes was the final touch and the dedication of the ship as well, bestowed in ceremony, with offerings and prayers. The notion was expanded upon, and the gods and deities, the overseeing and protecting images of a people, were painted on the bows of ships. Ravens were painted to see the way, and bears and wolves, on the cedar canoes of the Haida or Nootka Indians of Northwest

America, sea monsters and dragons for the Vikings, Olympian gods for the Greeks and Phoenicians, hawks and solar discs for the Egyptians, the Lion for the English, and the Unicorn for the Scots, and Mercury, Cupid, and Venus for the Romans. Crocodiles and fish from Indonesia, serpents from the Auckland Islands, and from the Marquesas, no eyes at all, but just the staring empty sockets of an enemy skull set atop the stempost.

Be the ship dedicated to commerce, war, exploration, or mere fancy, she must have eyes to see, and sailors counted it important. So the figurehead was the prime altarpiece of a ship, so to speak, the sacred emblem, the incarnation of her soul, her guardian angel and her omen. And a sailor knew what he knew, and he would tell you so, that only a careless, irreverent, ignorant, stupid, or utterly depressed fellow would sail on a ship that lacked a figurehead or eyes to see. It is a dangerous place, the open sea, and a sailor holds to every spirit-raising indulgence or grace he can find and believe in. Never mind his infidelity when he is ashore, his disgraceful and fallen state. It is a weekday always in port, and Sunday always at sea.

Now, the figurehead of the *Ariel* was a beautiful water spirit, half naked, and with her finger to her lips as if holding the endless secret of the horizon to herself.

As the *Ariel* drove past the second dock, the water spirit glanced at the figurehead of the ship docked foremost there, a silver-visored knight with shield and spear. The *Ariel* ticked its bowsprit to the knight's spear and they passed. The third dock loomed up, and for a moment the water spirit of the *Ariel* stared into the eyes of that ship's figurehead, a rampant and raging lion, bright yellow, with a fiery red mouth. They came to the fourth dock just at the same moment as did the two drunken sailors who had cut them loose. The *Ariel* cleaved their boat in two. The sailors were left behind clutching for ladders and pilings as the *Ariel* rounded out the bottom of her course. Now they must pass the final dock and the last ship. It was the *Locust*, Goldnose's ship.

The figurehead of the *Locust* – for this was a merchantman taken prize by Goldnose – was the carving of a man in an unbuttoned frock coat. He was portly, and had his chin pulled into his collar. His eyes glanced down towards his belly for inspection of his watch, which he held open at his waistcoat pocket. This was probably an effigy of the ship's original owner, and was no doubt meant to remind the master and crew that "time is money." Surely it was a stupid place for a figurehead to be looking, rather than straight ahead, and was likely the reason that the ship came to grief with pirates. Yet even a ship dotted all over with eyes, and watching the *Ariel* approach, could not have avoided what happened next.

A great blast of wind pressed the *Ariel*'s bow into the gully of a swell, which lowered her bowsprit so that the point of it was thrust between the stem of the *Locust* and the figurehead of the fat merchant consulting his watch. And the figurehead was plucked from the ship as neatly as a grape is plucked from the vine. Even as it fell into the water, the *Ariel*'s bowsprit tore through the bobstays, and jibstays, ripped off the dolphin striker of the *Locust*, snapped the fore royal stay; and then, hung upon her bowsprit with the wreckage of rope and splintered wood, the *Ariel* pointed out into the bay.

"Ready about!" Mister Cloud yelled.

The animals jumped to their duty. They had come through.

"Hard alee!" the mate commanded, and they were running free and safely towards the bottleneck and the open sea.

[159]

"Well done!" said the Captain. "Well done!" Skivvy spun the wheel, and the Captain clapped both him and Mister Cloud on the back.

Aboard the *Locust*, Goldnose came thundering out of his cabin in his stocking feet, clutching a blanket to himself, swathed about his middle like a great skirt and waving a cutlass in the air. He bellowed out curses, waving his sword about and looking for an explanation and an object for his wrath. But the sailor on watch was no longer on board. He had failed in his duty. He had been sleeping, and had not even seen that the *Ariel* was loose. He did not bother to take the gangway but simply jumped overboard and swam away. Goldnose, as he knew very well, would have cut him down on the spot. Other of the pirates were soon on deck. The story came clear quickly enough, even before the *Ariel* was completely out of sight in the darkness and slamming rain. Goldnose, dragging about in his sopping blanket, dispatched men to collect whoever of a crew they could find in New Liberty. The pirates aboard were breaking out whatever foul-weather gear they had, and were climbing the rigging to unfurl the sails. All the while, Goldnose slogged back and forth, hurling damnation upwind and down, slapping rails and masts with the flat of his sword.

"Plucked our nose and pinched our eyes, damn 'er to Davy Jones! Haul on that line, you son of a jakes. Make fast there, you dog's hill! Damn 'er to thunder, that pig's belly, she'll not outrun us, by my nose she won't!"

Not quite half an hour had passed when the *Locust* threw off her last line. In half an hour more she was in deep water, giving chase to the *Ariel*. Goldnose put on more sail than was prudent in such heavy weather, figuring correctly that the *Ariel* would carry only enough sail to keep her squared to the storm. By first light he hoped to spy her running before the wind. But the pirates must now depend on their own eyes to find the *Ariel*. The figurehead of the fat merchant consulting his watch washed against the docks of New Liberty, his belly upward, his hand holding the gilded watch – a reminder, as Skivvy might have said, that " 'time and chance happeneth to them all.' Ecclesiastes 9:11." And the *Locust* raced swiftly after the *Ariel* in the blowing darkness.

CHAPTER TWENTY-TWO

Peter White will ne'er go right;
Would you know the reason why?
He follows his nose wherever he goes,
And that stands all awry.

orning. The blow was over. The storm was now working far north of the *Ariel*. The *Locust* was nowhere in sight, from window, deck, or masthead.

The new crew had behaved splendidly. They were making themselves at home aboard the ship, quite jolly, talking about the adventure just passed, very smart and seamanlike, good shipmates all. During the night they had grown considerably, for work will make you grow, and all were within reach and grasp of what duty called them to put their hands to. The monkeys hung about the ratlines. They had taken for their main task to work the mainsails. The squirrel and cats took the mizzen under charge. The dogs worked the jibs, and were even now out on the bowsprit disentangling the lines that had been torn off the *Locust*. A rabbit was on lookout in the crow's nest. The frog was taking a turn at the helm. The hooved animals, Goat, Donkey, and Pig, kept to the deck mainly. Turkey and Chicken fluttered about bracing lines.

Skivvy stood amongst them. All had been awake the entire night. The Bad Sister kept the crew in strong black coffee, and this morning they had just finished breakfast.

Skivvy appointed the watches, and the animals off watch were going to turn in to the fo'c'sle for sleep.

As the turkey passed Skivvy to go below, he said, "What happened to the duck?"

"Aye, there was a duck," put in the chicken, alike being one of a feather, and having this interest.

"Hmmm," said Skivvy. "Yes, there was a duck. I'll look into it, mates."

"Some problem?" asked Mister Cloud, as Skivvy strode past him towards the Captain's cabin.

"A question about the duck," said Skivvy. "Seems he's missing. His mates asked about him. I was going to inquire."

"I'll come along. The Captain should have our new course worked out by now."

The mates knocked, and were called to enter the Captain's cabin. He was bent over a chart, plotting with divider and straightedge.

"Ah – Mister Cloud," said the Captain, "arrived at the very moment to know that our course is ... ah ... sou'sou'east." He laid aside his instruments and smiled at the men. "And good morning, Skivvy. All well on deck?"

"Aye, Captain, but for just a question to ask you."

Mister Cloud turned to leave. "Aye, Captain, sou'sou'east it is."

"But stay, Mister Cloud. Or is this something personal, Skivvy?"

"Nothing personal, Captain. Some of the men – I mean, the animals – were asking about a duck, a shipmate that didn't come up evidently."

"The duck," said the Captain thoughtfully. "Oh yes, the duck," and he moved his chair back from the table and searched the floor.

"There it is," said Skivvy, bending down and taking it

from under the table. He held the rubber duck towards the Captain.

"Yes," said the Captain. "So much excitement I'd forgotten. But the duck didn't come around like the rest. I stuck it two times in the head, but it just lay there on the deck."

"Do you mean to give up on it, Captain?" asked Skivvy.

"Indeed not. Here, Skivvy, this is the very needle I used on the others. Perhaps you'd like to try."

The Captain wiggled the needle free from a timber he had stuck it into, and handed it to Skivvy.

"What do you say?" asked the mate. "Are there special words to use?" He was cradling the duck like a child, very gently and uncertainly, like a new father.

"Everything's been said already, Skivvy. All you do now is just stick it in the head."

Mister Cloud leaned in to get a close look at this strange midwifery.

"Just ... stick it?"

"That's it, Skivvy."

And lightly, hardly enough to break the skin on a real person, he touched the pin to the duck's head.

"No, no, Skivvy, you've got to jam it in. Maybe that's the very trouble I had with it, rubber being thicker than just a cloth stuffed animal. *Push* it in there."

Skivvy swallowed, took in some breath and the nerve to do it, and shoved the pin into the duck's head. Immediately the duck cried out and leaped from Skivvy's hold. It dashed across the room and stood glaring at the three men.

"Quack, quack!" it called out. "Who's the Captain?"

"I am the Captain, my good fellow, and you are one of the crew of the *Ariel*, and most welcome. Out you go, now. Mister Cloud will give you your duty."

But the duck seemed not to recognize the information.

"Quack, quack," it said again, and demanded, "Who's the Captain?"

"Here, lad, jump to it," Mister Cloud said, "up the ladder, smartly now!"

He advanced on the duck.

But the duck avoided him, and once more called out, "Quack, quack. Who's the Captain?"

"It's a little backward," Skivvy said, "coming around so late. Not like the rest, maybe. Give it some understanding, Mister Cloud."

"I'll give it some understanding in its rear end!" The duck seemed to understand Mister Cloud's intentions. It jumped around him and out of the door. Pausing a moment, Mister Cloud said to the Captain, "Sou'sou'east."

"Aye, Mister Cloud."

The first mate went out. On deck, the duck was swaggering up to the other animals and asking over again that same question: "Quack, quack. Who's the Captain?" As Skivvy said, perhaps the duck was not quite up to standard.

"A strange one," mused the Captain, watching out of the cabin door.

"I think he needs a little extra understanding," said Skivvy.

And at that moment the rabbit at the crow's nest cried out, "Sail ho! Sail ho!" In another minute both the Captain and Skivvy crowded the rail with the other animals, the Captain with his telescope levelled at the far-distant sail just topping the horizon. Goldnose was on the deck of that ship with *his* telescope, looking right back at the *Ariel*.

"There she be, lads," said the pirate to his crew. "Floating along like a fat grape. Aye, juicy, and we'll have her under foot soon enough, and ye can dance barefoot in her blood."

CHAPTER TWENTY-THREE

St. Dunstan, as the story goes,
Once pulled the devil by his nose,
With red hot tongs, which made him roar,
That could be heard ten miles or more.

ll day the *Locust* followed in the wake of the *Ariel*, but far off. Late in the afternoon she came up closer. The Captain studied her through his telescope.

"A merchantman," he told Mister Cloud. "Only that, perhaps – we're still in the trading lanes. She may be nothing besides a trader."

"Aye, Captain, but the wind's fair and she could outsail us if she wanted. A merchantman ought to be about business. She could lay enough sail to pass us long ago."

"That's true, Mister Cloud." The Captain handed the glass to the mate. "Then what would you make of her?"

"I say it's a chase," said the mate, squinting through the glass. "She's got no colours raised and she's riding high. I say it ain't no trader. Word was out with the old crew that we were sailing for gold treasure. I say it's a chase."

The Captain took the glass back. He looked at the sky.

"I agree, Mister Cloud. An hour more and the sun sets. Hold this course, and let her mark it well. Douse all lights. No one's to smoke a pipe on deck tonight. Luck is with us, there's no moon. We'll change course after it's dark and lose that ship, whatever she is!"

"Aye, Captain." Another few minutes they watched the alien ship gaining on them. "She might overtake us anyway, Captain, and raid us at night. Mayhap that's her plan."

"Aye, Mister Cloud. Tell Skivvy to break out cutlasses from the arms cabinet. Arm the crew all round. I'll make up our new course."

"Aye, Captain." The men parted.

Going below, the Captain took Amy out of the cabinet and propped her up in a chair. "That's a lovely bedroom, isn't it, Sis? All mahogany with brass fittings." He smiled at Amy and worked at his chart.

"Sis, we're in trouble. Pirates, I believe. They know we're going for gold treasure, and it's just as well you're not come back to your real self if they board us. Being a doll could save your life in that case. And as to that, Sis, you've been wonderful patient. There's a reason I haven't brought you around to your real self with the rest of the dolls, now that we're at sea and safe from authority. It's important, Sis, and it will make you the hero of the whole voyage."

He scratched some numbers on a paper, and sat down facing Amy.

"You see, Sis, the gold treasure is at the bottom of the sea, such as that treasure map said. *'Captain Cowl all hands.'* That means we've got to find Cowl's ship, lying down there on the bottom, filled with gold. So how can we do that? And that's a good question. You're the whole answer to it. See, now, here's how I figure. When we get to the place, and you're still just a doll, we snip your eyes off and put them in a bottle and lower it overboard, way down to the bottom. You can look around and search for the ship..."

Someone knocked.

"Aye?"

The Bad Sister entered. She was carrying a large frying pan in one hand, and a long French carving knife in the other.

"Cloud says there's trouble coming after us."

"That's right, madam. We're being followed. We hope to lose them in the dark."

"They're after the gold, I guess."

"I should think so, madam."

She stood for a moment longer, looking at Amy, and her curiosity put a civil question in her mouth.

"Do you talk to that thing?" she asked. "I heard you talking through the door."

"Aye, madam, and she hears me."

"You mean she's well enough even if she's a doll?"

"Quite well. By the way, madam, you won't be able to cook in that frying pan you're carrying. Nor can we even have coffee tonight. The slightest spark flying from the cookstove could give us away."

"Don't worry, Captain. The pan's for use as a hat on some pirate's head if we're boarded. The knife's to cut another hole in his belt." She hesitated a moment more. "All right, cold grub. But speaking of tomorrow, Captain, if I may stoke up the stove again when it comes light, did you notice how plump that pig is, and that's a fine-looking turkey, drumsticks as big as ..."

At that moment, Mister Cloud appeared at the door. "Excuse me – Captain, madam." Then he reported, "All lamps are down on the ship, Captain."

"Very good." He handed Mister Cloud the slip of paper. "Here's our course."

The Captain snuffed his lamp and joined them at the door. "Madam, let's hear no more on that line of talk about the pig and the turkey. These animals are our shipmates and will be treated with all courtesy."

[168]

When it was dark, the Captain studied the lights of the *Locust*, glinting like bright planets near the horizon. The first mate shouted orders and the ship veered to her new course. A paddle of feet came alongside the Captain.

"Good evening, Captain."

It was the duck. He had a pipe in his bill, stuck there in his fixed smirk. The duck was also a sneak. He had found a place aft of the ship where he could lurk and listen in on the Captain at a window casement, and spy into his cabin.

"Good evening, Duck," said the Captain.

"Davy, ye might call me, sir. It's a name I give myself."

"Very well, Davy." He noticed the pipe. "You've heard the order there'll be no smoking tonight, Davy?"

"Aye, sir," said Davy, holding the pipe out and giving a disbelieving look at its existence. "Now, what was I thinking, being almost ready to light it? Now, ain't that shameful? Yes, sir, and I knew that was an order and I'm a duck to obey orders. It's the Captain what knows best, sir, and you're the Captain, sir. Yes, sir, ye are. You're the Captain, sir, indeed ye are, sir, you're the Captain…"

And as Davy Duck continued this repetition, he paddled softly away. The Captain watched him for a moment, shook his head, and looked out towards the *Locust*. The lights of the pirate ship had moved off a point to port. Then, as the Captain watched, they blinked out entirely. He put the glass to his eye again, but it was too dark now to find any shape on the horizon. The Captain supposed that they had lost the pirate ship. But it was not so. Goldnose had ordered that all lamps on the *Locust* be extinguished. He had worried about this part of the chase, and had hoped for the light of moon or stars to keep the *Ariel* in sight. But now he had another light to steer by.

On the afterdeck, over the taffrail, Davy Duck had taken up his station for the night. He was smoking his pipe. Now and then he drew deeply, then pointed the red, glowing bowl of his pipe towards the dark horizon.

"Aye," said Goldnose, seeing the faint red glow in the distance. "We've got a friend aboard that ship. Tie your eye to that light, helmsman, they ain't getting away from us this night. Aye, there's someone aboard that ship with a love for pirates, bless his nose."

CHAPTER TWENTY-FOUR

> *A cat came fiddling out of a barn,*
> *With a pair of bagpipes under her arm;*
> *She could sing nothing but "Fiddle cum fee,*
> *The mouse has married the bumble bee."*
> *Pipe Cat, dance Mouse;*
> *We'll have a wedding at our good house.*

S o *in the morning,* having followed the glow of Davy Duck's pipe all night, there stood the *Locust,* in full sight and closer now.

"Damnation!" said the Captain. "That devil must see in the dark. Bring her around to course again, Mister Cloud."

"Aye, Captain. Do we make directly for the island, then?"

"She can overtake us whenever she wants, Mister Cloud, but it appears that's not her plan. Whoever's master of that ship knows we're sailing for treasure, and knows we have a map. He supposes we'd destroy the map if he ever came around to board us. So we're safe there. No — what he's after is for us to lead him to the island. Then they'll take their chances. And that puts time in our favour, Mister Cloud. Whoever's sailing that ship must have got our course while there was still a touch of light, and held it as steady as ourselves. We'll give them another try at it tonight. This time I'll have several course changes for you. Keep the crew busy, Mister Cloud. I'm going below."

In his cabin, the Captain worked at his charts and talked

with Amy, who sat in her chair and listened, for she could hear and attend in her dreamy way. The Captain talked some more about snipping off her eyes and sending them down in a bottle to hunt for Cowl's sunken ship. He rambled on about the old days, then, at St. Anne's Home for Girls. He remembered Mrs. Hill, and the good Miss Eclair and the awful Miss Quince.

"Well, I do wonder about Miss Eclair. Perhaps we should have visited her after all, before sailing. Like a mother to you, wasn't she, Sis? When we're rich with gold, maybe she can travel with us. Perhaps she could adopt you, if there's nothing in the way of that. But wouldn't she have to be married so you'd have a father, too? Now, it's Mrs. Hill that would know all about that. Thank heaven that Miss Quince is out of the way. It chills me every time I think of how nearly she caught me. And that dog — I thought he was going to tear me to pieces. Hmmmm. Someday you'll have to tell me what went wrong with that plan to have the dog locked up."

The Captain walked his dividers across the chart.

"How wonderful to have a mother. And you will, Sis. And a father? Well, I think about our father every day, Sis, and wonder what became of him. That's only natural, I guess, since he created me."

The Captain paused in his work and put a finger to scratch his jaw. "Yes, that's true. I suppose the person that creates someone else thinks about them a lot. So here we are, Sis, maybe thousands of miles apart from each other, our father and us, and maybe both thinking about each other. Well, if he's alive, that is."

The Captain had been staring vacantly off. Now he looked at Amy. He picked her up, looking closely into her button eyes.

"But I believe he is alive, Sis. One time I said to Skivvy

that this voyage wasn't all for the gold alone, but for something else, like there was some sort of destiny to it all. And maybe, Sis, just maybe I'm right. Maybe..."

Someone knocked at the door. "Captain!"

"Come in, Skivvy." The Captain put Amy in the chair again.

"Something important, Captain," said Skivvy, closing the door behind himself. "I waited to tell you when we wouldn't be interrupted. Mister Cloud and the Bad Sister are in their cabins. It's something about them."

"Mister Cloud and the Bad Sister? Well then, let's have it. I've suspected something between them all along, you know. Sit down, Skivvy. Now – what is this all about?"

"It was late in the first watch last night," Skivvy began, "as I was up and about, waiting to take the middle watch, somewhere near midnight it was. The ship was uncommonly alive, what with the excitement about the pirates and the warning that we might be boarded and have to fight them. Some of the crew was amidships, swaggering about and clanging their cutlasses together, practising as it were, boasting about how vicious they could be in case of a fight. But I've got no study of war and fighting, Captain, so I went forward and sat myself down on the port cathead, wishing I could smoke a pipe. After a few minutes of sitting there, I heard a voice right nearby. I peeked over the railing to have a look..." Skivvy paused, and cast a glance at the door.

"Well, well?" urged the Captain.

"Well, Captain, it was the Bad Sister, maybe come out to take the air. And there with her, sitting on the hatch right next to her, was Mister Cloud. Now, I couldn't make out the few words he said, but he had a squeeze box with him, which I'd never seen him play before – a concertina, you know. And he began playing it, and right well, too, if I can judge. Then he began singing to the Bad Sister."

"In the middle of the night, Skivvy? Mister Cloud out on deck entertaining the Bad Sister with singing?"

"That's the most peculiar thing, Captain. Because it wasn't so much like an entertainment, but like he was *wooing* her."

"Oh no, Skivvy," exclaimed the Captain. "It's possible they may be in some plot together, as I've suspected, but surely not ... not lovers, or any such thing as that."

"Captain, I know something of love affairs out of the Bible. There's some strange pairing up when love gets into the story, as you must recall. Aye, and strange doings. Solomon and Sheba, for example, or Samson and Delilah, not to mention the Book of Esther. Bloody business, Captain, and all because of love. Aye, strange and bloody. But it's not that I'm calling out murder or mutiny on Mister Cloud and the Bad Sister. Not yet. Listen, here's what I heard last night, sitting there on the cathead with my ear poked up when Mister Cloud sat down beside the Bad Sister."

The Captain scooted his chair closer. "What, Skivvy, for God's sake, what did he say? What did she say?"

Skivvy leaned back, glanced at the door, and then leaned forward towards the Captain.

"Nothing, Captain. Nothing at all."

"Dammit, Skivvy!" said the Captain, thumping the table. "Are you trying to tie my ears in a knot? What do you mean – nothing?"

" 'Greensleeves'," Skivvy said.

" 'Greensleeves'?"

"I mean that Mister Cloud didn't say anything," said Skivvy, "but he did sing a song, and that song was called 'Greensleeves.' Do you know it, Captain?"

The Captain sat back. " 'Greensleeves', aye. Yes, I know it. Let's see now, how does it go ... ?"

"Alas, my love, you do me wrong," said Skivvy.

"I beg your pardon," said the Captain.

"To cast me off discourteously," Skivvy continued.

"Ahem, oh yes. Ah — *For I have loved you, oh, so long* ..."

"Delighting in your company," recited Skivvy, completing the rhyme.

"Of course," said the Captain. "Yes, I remember it now. Well, then, and so Mister Cloud sang 'Greensleeves' to the Bad Sister. So then, what of that?"

"Right prettily he sang it, too, like he was wooing her. But it didn't seem to take. He finished it up and she didn't say a word. I peeked up then. She was just sitting there, sort of watching Mister Cloud out of the corner of her eye. And then he said something."

"About the mutiny," said the Captain, "about their plot together?"

"No," said Skivvy. "What he said was, 'A sailing ship is a beautiful thing, madam, and it ought to have a beautiful name.' That's exactly all he said."

"And she said ... ?"

"Nothing. Just turned her head to look at him. I couldn't see her eyes."

The Captain rubbed his hand on his head. "A code. It's a secret code, Skivvy. Here, pen and paper. Let's see now." The Captain pulled his chair around, dipped the pen and began some figuring on the paper. "Let's see. 'Greensleeves.' Now, what's in that? It's a code, Skivvy, depend on it. They're clever, those two." The Captain worked at the paper for a few minutes, Skivvy looking on with interest. "There, Skivvy. See? If we arrange the letters of 'Greensleeves' we can get the words 'veer' and 'lee' out of it, which could mean that they mean to take the ship and veer to the lee."

"The lee of what?" asked Skivvy.

"Well, here we have more letters left. G, N, S, E, and another S. These could be compass points to sail. We could get NE, or SE, or SSE out of these. Maybe it means we're to veer to the lee, SSE. That's it, Skivvy, and meet up with another ship, perhaps."

Skivvy twisted his head to read. "But even making that SSE, that leaves a G and an N left over," he remarked.

"True," said the Captain, touching the pen to his tongue. "Ah, here we have it." He scratched at the paper. "We take all the leftovers and spell out S-N-E-G-S. So then we have 'Veer to the Lee of the Snegs.' That's the message, Skivvy. That's what Greensleeves means, letter by letter."

"What's a Sneg, Captain?"

"Indeed," said the Captain, tapping his pen on his teeth. "They're clever, Skivvy. Possibly it's a number code. Let's see, now. Greensleeves. Take it a letter at a time and count it out by numbers. G is seven, and R is ... ah ..." The Captain began counting on his fingers.

"Eighteen," said Skivvy.

"Right, and E is five, and another E is five, and N is ... ah ..."

"Fourteen, Captain, but I don't know," said Skivvy doubtfully. "The Bad Sister didn't seem to get it. She didn't say anything back to Mister Cloud, and he had to sing the song to her all over again."

"He sang it again, you say?"

"Aye, and waited for her to say something, is how it seemed to me, but she didn't. And then he said, Mister Cloud did, 'The *Ariel* is a beautiful name for a sailing ship, don't you think?' But she didn't give an opinion on that."

The Captain threw his pen down. "Huh! It's a code, Skivvy. Otherwise it doesn't make any sense."

"Well, a code or a wooing, that's all I have of it, Captain.

I leaned back listening for more, and dozed off a bit, and when I heard eight bells I looked over the rail and they were gone. Then I took the watch. So that's all I know about it, and that's what I had to tell you."

"And well done, Skivvy. Now we know they're plotting together for certain. Aye, so keep an ear turned towards them when you can. What I wonder is how the crew would fall out in case they start a mutiny. She's a woman, that's the danger there, as Mother Goose was also a woman, and they were raised on her poetry. It's all good-hearted poetry, but she might be able to turn it to a bad use. They might follow her just because she's a woman, same as Mother Goose. Sex is stronger than poetry, Skivvy."

"Aye, Captain."

"But I think they'll not make their move so long as those pirates are close to us. If the Bad Sister and Cloud take over the ship and get the gold, they'll still need everyone of us to fight those villains off."

"Aye, Captain. I'll keep a weather eye on 'em."

When Skivvy left, the Captain thought awhile on the possibility that Mister Cloud had been singing "Greensleeves" as a wooing song, and might be in love with the Bad Sister. It was barely possible. If this were so, then there might be an opportunity to work his love to the favour of all. Yes. He would broach the subject to Mister Cloud. He would find a convenient time to make compliments about the Bad Sister. He would draw the first mate out. That was the way. Yes. Those in love need understanding. The Captain would find a way to approve of the romance. This would be the Captain's way to win Mister Cloud away from any plan of mutiny.

Actually, the Captain was entirely wrong about his suspicions of Mister Cloud, even from the very first. Mister

Cloud bore the Captain no ill will, nor any ill wishes, and in fact his mind was set at the very opposite pole.

Old Captain Kimberly and the first mate had sailed together many years, and the men were almost like brothers. It was true that Captain Kimberly had intended to give the *Ariel* to Mister Cloud when he died, before the Captain had come aboard the ship. Yet the first mate was provided for quite well otherwise, for he did not put a foot on land for years at a time, and he quite agreed that the young Captain – the somewhat adopted son of the old man – should receive the ship. The men had discussed this. Furthermore, Mister Cloud promised Captain Kimberly that he would watch over the young man as best he could. Therefore he stayed aboard when the rest of the crew deserted the ship. So he followed the fortunes of the ship, not out of love for gold, but out of love for the old man, and out of loyalty.

As to the story between Mister Cloud and the Bad Sister, it was no love story. Mister Cloud had sung "Greensleeves" to discover for certain that the woman was an impostor. In the many years he had sailed with Captain Kimberly, the first mate had never heard him speak of a sister, or any remaining family whatsoever. Mister Cloud now had his proof that the ugly woman was no relative of Captain Kimberly.

Before owning the *Ariel*, Captain Kimberly had owned another ship. It was named the *Greensleeves*. Mister Cloud was first mate on that ship also. He sang "Greensleeves" to the Bad Sister so that she might make some recognition of the name, for surely if she had followed her brother's career with such jealousy she would have known the name of his former ship. But she gave no sign at all, even with prompting and the singing of the song twice. Therefore Mister Cloud was convinced that the woman was no sister to

[178]

Captain Kimberly. After the second singing of the song, the Bad Sister – so-called – got up and left Mister Cloud alone on the hatch. Presently he himself got up and strode aft. He hummed quietly for a while, looking into the wake for his mermaid.

Then Mister Cloud went to bed, determining that at some convenient moment on the morrow he would inform the Captain of his proof that the Bad Sister was no relative to good Captain Kimberly, and had no rights but to the fortune she brought upon herself, and to no other.

CHAPTER TWENTY-FIVE

Hey diddle diddle,
The cat and the fiddle,
The cow jumped over the moon.
The little dog laughed
To see such sport,
And the dish ran away with the spoon.

S hortly after his interview with Skivvy, the Captain went on deck with Amy in his arms. It was a lovely day, the sea running in long, low swells, the sky bunched with a few friendly cumulus clouds, and a firm wind driving the *Ariel.* The *Locust* was following a league or so off. The Captain had meant to bring his copy of *Mother Goose* on deck and to entertain Amy with some reading of the poems she knew so well. But the book was missing. The Captain had searched the cabin diligently, but could not find it. He now leaned on a rail and watched Mister Cloud, who was instructing a half-dozen of the animals in the use of the cutlass. If Mister Cloud and the Bad Sister meant to take over the ship in a mutiny, the book would constitute a sort of symbol of authority to the animals. The Captain could not keep the suspicion out of his face as he watched Mister Cloud. But the first mate glanced openly at him, gave over the tutorship of his class to his best swordsman, one of the dogs, and joined the Captain at the railing.

"A fair sailing day, Captain."

"Aye, Mister Cloud. Will we have a fighting crew, do you think?"

"If it comes to that, Captain, we may put a cut or two on 'em. But we'd be fighting real men, not toys and dolls."

The Captain felt the thrust of the insult, for he was, to begin with, a doll. Or at least he had been, and Skivvy, too, for that matter. They were at least not "real men", as Mister Cloud had put it. Here was a prejudice to be sure. And could it be—the Captain wondered—could this be rankling the first mate? But the next moment after Mister Cloud made this remark contrasting real men with dolls, he looked candidly and innocently into the Captain's eyes. Taking the telescope from his belt, he handed it to the Captain.

"It may be she can't overtake us, Captain. Her bow stays are ripped through and her jibs are torn away."

The Captain set the glass on the *Locust* and saw that it was true.

"A good observation, Mister Cloud. We'll make use of it if we can." He closed the telescope upon itself and assumed a casual tone of voice. "Oh, by the way, Mister Cloud, have you seen my copy of *Mother Goose*?"

"*Mother Goose*? No, Captain, not I."

"Very good," said the Captain, frowning and turning away.

"Oh, Captain ... if you've got a few minutes. There's something I'd like to talk with you about, something private. It's about that woman –"

The Captain turned his head and raised his eyebrows. "Indeed, Mister Cloud, indeed. Let us talk about that woman. Nothing would please me more. First, however, let me take care of some ship's business. I'll be back to you directly, Mister Cloud. Yes indeed, and we'll talk about that woman." He gave a slight salute to Mister Cloud and walked away.

Mister Cloud went back to directing his cutlass students. Propping Amy up on a hatch, the Captain bade her enjoy the sun. Then he made an inspection of the ship. He found the crew to be in high spirits, all talking about the defence they would make when the pirates overtook them. The Captain had been pondering the problem himself. There were several powder kegs in the hold and about a half-thousand shot for the small swivel gun on deck. Otherwise, there were only six muskets, the Captain's own pistol and one other, and of course cutlasses to go around for the crew. The Captain ordered the powder kegs and lead shot brought to hand near the swivel gun.

As this was being done, the cats and rabbits turning themselves to the labour, the Captain spied the Bad Sister standing at the stern of the ship looking off towards the *Locust*. How interesting, he thought. The first mate asked to speak to *him* about the woman. Perhaps Mister Cloud was ready with his confession that he loved the Bad Sister. Perhaps he wanted the Captain to perform the marriage service. Astounding! He made a bow towards the Bad Sister. She whipped her cloak about herself and turned away. The Captain chuckled to himself. Ah yes, the blushing bride. Well now, where was Mister Cloud? The Captain strode off, attending to business as he passed the crew.

"Fetch a small tarpaulin for that powder," the Captain said to one of the cats in passing.

"Aye sir."

"Haul that shot box nearer the gun, there, Rabbit, and secure that lid."

"Aye sir."

Mister Cloud was standing aside from his cutlass class, amidships, watching the Captain. The Captain beckoned to him, and the two men stood privately near the mainmast.

"After you've worked the crew out on the cutlasses, Mister Cloud, turn all hands out for gunnery drill."

"Aye, Captain," Mister Cloud followed the Captain's glance towards the Bad Sister, who stood with her arms folded looking off at the pirate ship, her black cape blowing about her. The Captain turned his head to look at Mister Cloud, then looked back at the dark figure.

"Now, as to that woman –" Mister Cloud began.

"Yes," the Captain interrupted, "and a handsome woman, wouldn't you say, Mister Cloud?"

"Ah ... well, Captain as you must know, I've been all my life a bachelor man ... ah ..." The Captain's question seemed to have taken him by surprise. "But as I was going to say, Captain ... there's more to her than meets the eye –"

"Yes, yes," the Captain interrupted again. "It's very true. Not just another pretty face with nothing behind it. The woman definitely has character. And it does well for a man to look past the obvious charms and graces. Beneath that mask she puts on and her harsh manner, the Bad Sister is still a woman, Mister Cloud, and has once been young and perhaps known love."

"Well, Captain, those were not my speculations. As I was going to say –"

But the Captain put in again. "A ship at sea away from the fair sex is a lonely place, a lonely place. A man wants company with a woman by and by. It's easy to understand. And given our present situation, the dangers we may soon be facing, dangers to pursue us, perhaps, even to our deaths ... I mean to say, Mister Cloud, that a man may seek to find some last comfort, a sweet word, a gentle touch."

"Is ... is that a fact, Captain? Well, sir, I ... I didn't realise ..." Mister Cloud was looking at the Captain most curiously.

"Oh yes, Mister Cloud. Perhaps it was inevitable that someone should find a true and tender heart beating in the Bad Sister's breast. Inevitable." He turned and smiled at the first mate.

"Ah ... aye, Captain ... inevitable. Well, sir, if you say so, sir."

"Indeed I do, Mister Cloud. And do you agree with me, sir, that love is to be approved of wherever it arises?"

"I ... I do agree, Captain, of course."

The Captain turned to look at the Bad Sister. The first mate stood with his mouth open.

"Good. And let me say that I entirely agree with *you*. As an object of one's love, given the circumstances, I find that I can easily approve of the Bad Sister herself."

Such amiable compliments, thought the Captain, should soon bring Mister Cloud to confess his love for the woman. Then, in a magnanimous and forgiving aspect, the Captain would open the subject of their plot, and hush the evil affair forever under the wing of a mild pardon. Forgive and forget. The Captain smiled upon Mister Cloud in approbation.

"Easily approve," the Captain repeated.

"You can, sir? Aye, sir. Well, sir –"

"Not at all," said the Captain, turning again to the first mate and putting a hand on his shoulder. "It seems to me the most natural thing in the world. For when all is said and done, a woman is still a woman, if you take my meaning, sir."

"Aye, Captain," said the mate, swallowing and taking on a peculiar twist to his features. The Captain waited for some further comment, but none came. He could find nothing else to say on the subject to encourage Mister Cloud. He clapped the mate on the shoulder.

"Well, Mister Cloud, I believe we understand each other, then."

"Aye, Captain. A woman is ... ah ... is a woman, sir."

The Captain waited a few moments. Evidently Mister Cloud needed more time to digest the conversation. The Captain smiled and clapped Mister Cloud on the shoulder again, winked, and walked away. Mister Cloud could hardly believe what he had just heard. "Good God," he whispered to himself. "He's fallen in love with the woman!" He searched his fingers through his beard as he watched the Captain approach the Bad Sister, hands clasped behind his back. He observed him turn his head to the woman and speak to her. Perhaps, thought the mate, he should immediately call the Captain away and inform him that the Bad Sister was an impostor. He had been too stunned to speak when the Captain was praising her. But no, thought Mister Cloud. No, he would say nothing of what he knew. As long as love was working the stage, his own discovery could bide in the wings and await some other cue. He shook his head, turned, and called some animals away from their swordplay. Then he began setting up for gunnery drill.

"Good day, madam," said the Captain, upon that little stage, the afterdeck of the ship.

"Pirate pigs, are they?" she said, looking off towards the *Locust*.

"We have every reason to believe so, madam." The Captain looked closely at the woman in the good light of the day. How Mister Cloud could be at all attracted to her he could not imagine; for although her form was in all womanly ways comely enough, the grotesque mask of powder and paint upon her face seemed to the Captain sufficient to repel a very considerable loneliness.

But the Captain had not come up to her to judge of her beauty. He was disappointed that Mister Cloud had not responded with a confession of his love for the Bad Sister. He did not expect that the woman would admit to any such thing. Yet he thought it a good idea to put her on notice that he himself knew she was having private meetings with Mister Cloud, and to let her guess that he knew of their plotting against the ship. This could serve to deter or muddle any immediate plans they might have for mutiny — delay or confusion to the enemy being always a wise engagement. So the Captain cleared his throat, hummed a note for pitch, and sang.

> "Alas, my love, you do me wrong,
> To cast me off discourteously,
> For I have loved you, oh, so long,
> Delighting in your company.
> Greensleeves was all my joy,
> Greensleeves was my delight,
> Greensleeves was my heart of gold,
> And who but my Lady Greensleeves?"

Now the Captain was not a *very* good singer, but he thought he was carrying the tune well enough not to deserve the criticism the Bad Sister put in.

"Garbage," she said.

"Ahem. Well, madam, it was not so much the tune itself I was seeking to inform you of, but rather ..."

The Bad Sister spat over the side.

"I say we ought to slop the pig with the garbage, but his shipmates won't have it. They say it would hurt his feelings, if you can imagine hurting a pig's feelings."

Then the Captain saw the object of her comment. The frog, who had been assigned duty as her messboy in the galley, had just dumped a pot of garbage over the side of the ship. The mess now floated off in the wake.

[186]

"Well," the Bad Sister continued, watching the garbage trailing behind them towards the *Locust*, "those pig pirates might hang by their heels and slop it up themselves as it goes by."

And at that moment the Captain had an inspiration.

"Madam!" he exclaimed, barely keeping himself from grasping her arm in appreciation. "Madam, I thank you for the suggestion. You have just given me an idea of how we might deal with those pirates."

The Captain turned and called out to Mister Cloud.

"Belay that drill, Mister Cloud. Bring the swivel gun to the aft post here. You there, Goat and Donkey, haul that powder keg and shot box up here."

In a few minutes the small cannon was set up on the swivel piling of the afterdeck, primed, loaded, and made ready to fire.

"Mister Cloud, are you a marksman, sir?"

"As a matter of fact, Captain, I was a gunnery mate in the Royal Navy many long years ago."

"Excellent, Mister Cloud. And do you mark that little flotilla of garbage off there?" The Captain pointed towards the patch now floating in the *Ariel*'s wake.

"Aye, Captain," said Mister Cloud, clearing the animals aside to take his place at the gun.

"Please put a shot in the centre of it, Mister Cloud."

All stood back while the first mate raised the muzzle of the gun, turned his head towards the mainsail to take his windage, and at his command the primer was touched off and a lead ball was exploded out of the cannon. A quick eye could see the shot arc through the air, and all of the crew gathered there saw the splash as it hit in the middle of the jetsam of garbage. Cheering and backclapping all around was given animal to animal. The Captain shook hands with the mate.

"Well done, Mister Cloud. Gunnery practice will commence immediately. I judge that distance to be about half a cable's length. Use for your target an empty keg secured to a line. When you have your drill well under way, please come to my cabin."

And then, doffing his hat, he bowed towards the Bad Sister.

"Madam, my compliments."

To which pleasantry she sneered and turned away.

The Captain left the group to their gunnery drill and strode to where he had left Amy on the hatch enjoying the sun. Nearby, crowded close to the mainmast, Davy Duck was whispering into the ear of the chicken. As the Captain approached, he broke away and spoke out loudly.

"Aye, shipmate. Thanks for the use of the tobacco."

The chicken, throwing a nervous glance at the Captain, hurried off. Davy Duck turned towards the Captain, affecting a look of surprise.

"Oh! Good day, Captain."

Unlike the other animals, Davy Duck was now dressed in a jacket. He had made it himself out of a lightweight canvas material carried aboard ships called "duck." He was quite proud of his jacket and felt himself to be suited the most suitably of anyone on board the ship.

"Good day, Davy," said the Captain, taking up Amy from the hatch. "Seems you're handy with a needle. That looks to be a workmanlike piece of sewing. We might put you to work on some sailmaking, by and by."

"Aye, sir. It just came sort of natural. A sailor's got to find something to keep him busy and out of trouble. Sailmaking? Aye, sir, it's the sort of thing that keeps ye out of trouble, sailmaking does, and that's a duck's fact. And a sailmaker I'll be, sir, if ye say so, sir, for you're the Captain, sir. And a Captain is what gives all the orders aboard a ship,

sir, if I may make the observation, sir. And it's the Captain
what knows best. And you're the Captain, sir, indeed ye
are, sir. As I always say, sir, it's the Captain that gives
the —"

"Yes, yes, Davy. Now up the ladderway aft. Mister
Cloud's giving gunnery drill."

Trailing more "Yes, sirs" behind him, Davy paddled off
to join the drill. The Captain watched after him for a few
moments. With Amy cradled in his arms, he strolled to his
cabin, speaking to her.

"I shouldn't be too familiar with that duck, Sis, when
time comes and I bring you around. He puts a loose hand to
his work, and there's some grudge working on his mind for
all his 'Yes, sirs.' He's beating into some wind, Sis. Aye, it's
not all secure with that duck."

CHAPTER TWENTY-SIX

I sent a letter to my love
And on the way I dropped it,
A little puppy picked it up
And put in in his pocket.
It isn't for you, it isn't you,
But it is you!

The day passed under the fair, thrusting breeze on a line directly towards Vulcan Island. Gunnery drill continued. The Captain told Mister Cloud and Skivvy his particular intent for the practice, other than the mere practical reason that the crew should be able to handle the ship's weapons. The Captain figured rightly that in close quarters the *Ariel* should be able to outmanoeuvre the *Locust*, for the reason that she was a smaller ship and could be handled more smartly. Also for the reason that the *Locust* was lacking her jib sails. Therefore, reasoned the Captain, if the *Ariel* trailed behind her some kegs of gunpowder somehow secured on a floating platform, it might be possible to place her in a position to drag this target into the hull of the pirate ship, whereupon a good marksman might put a shot into the kegs and blow the *Locust* into splinters. Gunnery practice continued. Skivvy would set to work building the platform to float the gunpowder kegs.

Skivvy set about his work. The Captain set about making and checking the course changes for the night, when again all lights on the *Ariel* would be shut down in hope of losing the pirates. Now and again a shot from the swivel gun would boom out. Sometimes it would be followed by a cheer when the gunner made a close hit on the target, an empty barrel dragged behind the ship.

Goldnose stood on the deck of the *Locust*, following about a mile off, trying to figure out what this puny display of firepower was all about. A swivel gun was no match for his eight-pounders. He shrugged and scratched his nose, then set a man to keep an eye on the exercise and let him know if they brought a larger cannon to bear. In his cabin, Goldnose stood with his large belly half flopped on his chart table. He studied the position of the ship. A large expanse of ocean opened before them, if they should continue on this course. Several hundred miles away there was a group of small islands. Some had names, some did not.

"Tanner Island," Goldnose muttered. "Hmm. Dorsal Island. Hmm. Vulcan Island. Hmm. No name, no name. Hmm. One o'those. Aye, that's where he's making for. Hmm."

But the islands were as much as ten or twenty miles from one another. If Goldnose lost the *Ariel* it might take him days of scouting about to find which island she was anchored at. And if she got the gold before he arrived, she might scoot off to the south and escape.

"Hmmm," Goldnose muttered again. "But there's a light on that bucket of a ship. And a light in the dark means a friend, if it weren't no accidental light. Tonight we'll know about that. Hmm."

When the sun was low, Goldnose went on deck and spied through his glass at the *Ariel*. To the delight of sailors always, the sun set in a red sky. The hue of it passed through the spectrum from pink to crimson to magenta to burgundy, then faded into a brilliant cobalt blue. Then it was dark, with the diamond-bright point of Venus in the west. Goldnose watched the stern of the *Ariel*. Then he spied a faint orange glow.

"Mark that light," Goldnose said to the pirate at the wheel. "They's some Jack-tar on that ship that's got a love for smoking, or a love for blood. Well, he shall have both smoke and blood if he leads us to the gold."

After it was dark, the Bad Sister came on deck in her great cloak. She walked the port side, then sat down on a locker box. At the other end of the ship, the watchman rang the ship's bell to tell the time. "Ding-ding," it rang out. "Ding-ding —" and the Bad Sister watched the rising evening star.

She was sitting there in a study when presently she heard voices. She pulled her legs up onto the box and wrapped the cloak completely around herself. It was Donkey and Goat approaching. They stopped at the railing nearby. Goat looked both ways. His eye fell on the Bad Sister's form. Nothing but a dark object there on the locker box. He turned to Donkey.

"So ye don't think anyone ought to speak out to the Captain?"

"It ain't needed. It's all just talk. Your word against his. Get messed up in that? Not me, thank'ee."

"But look, Donkey, what if others go in with him?"

"I ain't heard of it yet. It ain't going to come to nothing, that's how I think."

"Chicken said a good word about him. You heard it. Chicken said he was smart."

"He *told* Chicken he was smart. That's why Chicken said he was smart. Chicken — I tell ye — and not meaning to run down a shipmate — Chicken ain't got much brains."

Goat thought this over.

"That's true. It ain't smart to join up with a mutiny."

"That's what I mean," said Donkey. "He can't get any of us on his side, I say. Except Chicken, maybe. And maybe Turkey. Turkey don't think too much for hisself."

"I saw him reading to Turkey out of the book," said the goat.

"He did that to me, too. Well, that's his authority, the book is. Aye, reading it and thumping on it like he was some sort of preacher. Not that I say the book ain't right. Don't get me wrong. I don't say that. I just say you can't use it to get your own way about a thing. Ye see, he reads ye something and gives his own meaning to it. Why — devil chase it, man — that's a complicated book. Ye can make it mean just about anything ye want to. And he just sticks his own meaning to it. That don't seem right to me. Ye take the book for just what it says, ye don't go sticking your own meanings into it to please yourself."

Goat nodded.

"Did ye bring any tabakky?" asked Donkey.

Goat shook his head. "That's right. He was telling me things out of it — about who ought to be the Captain of the ship."

"That's what bothers me most of anything," interrupted Donkey, "him using the book like that, to make himself look important. It kind of goes against me, so I just stubborned it out with him and he left me alone."

"Aye, best to say nothing. That's right. There ain't nothing going to come of it."

"That's right," said the Donkey. "No tabakky? Well, we got to go below to smoke, anyway." And they walked away.

The Bad Sister put her feet to the deck, swept the cloak about herself, and vanished down a ladderway in the darkness.

All was dark and quiet again on the deck of the *Ariel*.

The Captain slept soundly. Then he heard a voice, calling to him. He recognized it at once. It was Amy.

"Caaaaap-tain. Oh, Caaap-tain."

It was Amy, to be sure. She was sitting in the crow's nest at the very top of the mainmast, the flesh-and-blood Amy, calling down to the sleeping Captain. It was a dream. It was the rare sort of dream that twins have sometimes, the sharing of the very same dream. Both Amy and the Captain dreamed it, she in a chair next to his bed, and the Captain stretched out asleep.

"Caaaaaap-tain," she called again. In the dream it was a bright day. The ship was sitting on an ocean as still and clear as a mirror.

The Captain dreamed that he woke up. He went on deck, noticing how very quiet the ship was. He called out, "Mister Cloud! Skivvy!" No one answered. Not another soul seemed to be aboard the ship.

"Captain!"

"Amy!" said the Captain, looking up. "Come down from there before you get hurt."

But Amy only stepped out of the crow's nest and walked along a yardarm, laughing.

"Amy!" yelled the Captain. "You'll kill yourself!"

"No I won't," said Amy. "Everything's fine, Captain. Miss Eclair is taking care of me. Oh, how far away and small you look down there. Did I ever tell you about the time Miss Eclair took me to the tower at St. Anne's? It was beautiful, Captain. She'll take care of us, Captain. She's on board, you know." Amy sat down on the yardarm. "Now guess where she is, Captain."

"Amy, come down from there!" The Captain started to climb up to her, but all at once she was gone. She called out to him again.

"Captain, I'm over here!"

She was now sitting at the top of the mizzenmast.

"We'll play a game, Captain. You try and find out where Miss Eclair is, and I'll tell you if you're hot or cold."

"Then you'll come down?"

"Then I'll come down."

The Captain began searching the ship, going up and down ladderways from place to place, finding nothing but empty rooms, while Amy laughed and called out "Hot" and "Cold" and "Warmer" and "Colder."

At last the Captain tired of the game.

"Amy, come down!"

"Over here, Captain."

She was now out on the bowsprit.

"Do you give up, Captain? All right, then I'll give you a hint. Miss Eclair is right where I can see her."

The Captain began crawling out on the bowsprit to rescue Amy before she fell into the water. When he got to within arm's reach of her, she told him to stop.

"Right there, Captain, Now turn around."

He did so, and looked over the empty length of the ship.

"Don't you see, Captain? Couldn't you feel it all along? There she is ... there!"

The Captain looked to where Amy was pointing. It was the figurehead of the water spirit she pointed at, the woman holding her finger to her lips. And at this moment both the Captain and Amy woke up.

The Captain sat on the edge of his bed and reached out for Amy.

"Sis, don't worry. Somehow this will be all right. You'll be with Miss Eclair again. I promise you."

How pleasant it is to sail upon the sea. Our hearts beat expansively, our breath draws deeper, our limbs are graced with the rolling of the ship, and we are guided to our destination by the bright-lit mind of man set upon clear and starlit proofs. So if a deed is to be done, or a mission is to be accomplished, what better man to entrust the matter to than the Captain of a sailing ship, who takes his course by the very motion and inspiration of the heavens?

Amy was lucky to have such a brother. The years of his confinement in a shoe box may have somewhat touched his character with brooding, and caused him to mistake his fellow man at times, but his heart was true and he was set upon a duty and a destination. And a man should have a duty and a destination, that he may know his worth. And so we sail along, trusting to the Captain's path. He may seem at times to be simple, and sometimes ignorant. Nevertheless, the Captain is particularly endowed and, even when stumbling, falls in the right direction. He shall mistake his footing and stumble some more, going forward with a passion that is no less a sort of blindness than being in love.

The sea swells, and the wind and water season us with salt. The outcome of our story is uplifted by Amy's dream and the Captain's promise, as the Ariel is uplifted by the sea. Yet we should beware anticipating the weather or any certain conclusion. Dreaming, we may die. And very soon an innocent will die, as innocents sometimes die, with their thoughts set upon the horizon, the curve of the earth, spherical things, and the roundabout ways of God.

Book Two

Book Two

CHAPTER TWENTY-SEVEN

Birds of a feather flock together,
And so will pigs and swine;
Rats and mice will have their choice,
And so will I have mine.

 ive times the *Ariel* changed course during the night. In the morning the *Locust* was on the horizon. The three men stood on the poop deck.

"We must be showing a light," said Mister Cloud. "There's no other answer for it, Captain – some light needs dousing."

"Aye," said Skivvy. "'The light of the wicked shall be put out, and the spark of his fire shall not shine.' Job 18:5."

The Captain nodded to them both.

"Right you are, mates. Make for Vulcan Island, Mister Cloud. If they're following by some light, they'll have no beacon tonight. Incidentally, Skivvy, have you seen my copy of *Mother Goose*?"

"*Mother Goose*? No, Captain. Did you lose it?"

"Maybe," said the Captain. He turned into the galley for some coffee, Skivvy following him. Mister Cloud made towards the helm with the course change.

As they poured coffee for themselves, the Bad Sister peered into her oven and barked at her messboy, the frog.

"You call that dough punched down? I've punched frogs down more than that. You understand?"

She had the frog cowed. The poor creature stood in a

corner wringing a dishcloth in his hands. He warily accepted the bread pans she handed to him, dumped the dough out, and began his chore anew. The Captain sat down at the galley table.

"I was going to read to Amy last night," he said. "But I couldn't find my copy of *Mother Goose*. I don't suppose you've seen it about, have you, madam?"

"I've got no interest in *Mother Goose*," she said, watching over the shoulder of the frog as he punched at the bread dough, "if this is the kind of help comes from it. *Punch* that bread, you green pig, *punch* it!"

So saying, she smacked the frog on the side of the head with a ladle. He whined and fell to his task again. The poor frog was leading a fearful life. He had complained to his shipmates and had tried to get out of his galley duty, but the Bad Sister would have no animals in her kitchen with feathers or fur. "Nasty beasts," she said, in what might pass as friendly confidence to the frog. "Do you know what goes on underneath fur? And feathers are worse." She did have the virtue of cleanliness. She liked the frog because he rinsed off so nicely.

"Not I," continued the Bad Sister, keeping a stern eye on the frog. "Mother Goose and a Christmas goose is all the same to me, Captain. But thinking about thieves, Captain, I've lost a bead necklace. You wouldn't know of that? No? Well, so we've got a thief on board."

She smacked the frog with the ladle again.

"*Punch* that dough, you lizard!"

Then, turning back to the Captain, "I never did trust an amphibian, Captain. You've got to watch 'em every minute. I count 'em all double-dealing, two-faced turnabouts. But I keep him on for his plump legs. He can sing, too, Captain, this one can, in his croaky sort of way. Aye, and I taught him a song to sing to you."

She gave a kick to the frog. "Sing, you green noodle, sing that pretty song for the Captain."

The frog stopped punching down the dough, took up his dishcloth, and turned to face the Captain and Skivvy at the table. And in a rich though nervous and wavering baritone voice, he began singing, while the Bad Sister stood with her ladle in her hand, arms akimbo, smiling at the Captain. Oh, and the sight of the frog might bring a tear to a hard man's eye as the pitiful beast stood there, broken by intimidation, nearly sobbing the words out, wringing the dishcloth as if it were his wounded heart twisted by a lost lover. He sang:

> *"Greensleeves was all my joy,*
> *Greensleeves was my delight,*
> *Greensleeves was my heart of gold . . ."*

The song had a withering effect on the Captain. Here now, the Captain had considered that he might have got a foot in front of the Bad Sister, perhaps to trip her up, when he found out that she and Mister Cloud were meeting secretly. And now the woman was flinging the very proof of it back at him. He met her eye, then looked at his cup, his jaw clenched. The boldness of the woman! Well, he would not stay to hear any more. Let her plot. Skivvy and he would stand alone if need be. There was more to this voyage than plotting for gold treasure. There was destiny to it, and let them all – Bad Sister, mutinous crew, and pirates – look into the face of that when the time came. The Captain got up without a word and left the galley. Skivvy followed him. They heard the Bad Sister laughing at their backs as they shut the door.

Out on the deck it was a wide and bright, lovely and lolling day. The monkeys were swinging limb and tail among the sails for pure joy, and the cats sported on the bowsprit. Goat and Donkey rested near the capstan, chatting away about hooved matters. A rabbit was at the masthead on lookout, and both dogs, the other rabbit, and the squirrel stood about the swivel gun bracing themselves up like soldiers. They were making manly talk and wide boasts about their courage and readiness for a battle with the pirates.

The pig lay in the shade under the poop ladderway, for he liked to be out of the way of any chance encounter with the Bad Sister, who looked at him, he thought, with the eye of a butcher, which is indeed a distressing way to have your character judged. At intervals, Mister Cloud called them together in small groups for sword or gunnery practice. All hands occasionally turned their heads to watch the progress of the pirate ship.

The animals now were fully out of their doll stage, cloth turned to fur, stuffings to bones and innards, rubber to feather, paint to skin, twists of yarn to flicking tails; and the embroidered noses of the dogs were now moist and cold. In fact, all were in good health, except that the frog had a worried mind and sang a worried song, and Davy Duck ... Well, Davy Duck would shortly expose his ambitions to Amy herself.

It was early afternoon when the Captain mounted the afterdeck for a look through his telescope. Skivvy had informed him that the pirates had approached close enough that the wake of the *Ariel* broke in small waves on their bow. They were almost within reach of a shot from the swivel gun but Skivvy had not yet finished his work on the platform that would float the six kegs of gunpowder. There was no hope of blowing the pirates up on this approach. Goldnose had brought his ship up to take a look at what the gunners had been shooting at. The Captain put his telescope to his eye and studied the *Locust*.

Clambering along the rails and in the ratlines, the pirates turned their faces towards their enemy. All the children of Mother Goose gathered on the aft parts of their ship and gazed back. There they were, the pirates, the dirty and damned visages of Goldnose's scummy crew, hairy and hairless alike, scarred and broken faces, hatchet-toothed and toothless, ragged and wretched, the dregs and dumpings of ports from the East Indies to Gibraltar, Madagascar to the Pribilofs, of all colours and abandoned creeds, fallen from hateful cradles, spoiled rooms, forbidden doorways, and worlds without hope, all with unholy secrets and unmentionable deeds in their hearts and bad dreams in the place of conscience. The *Ariel*'s animals stared in fascination. These were the men, these men now howling from the decks of the *Locust*, whom they might have to meet in mortal combat. And they, the darling animals of the nursery, looked back at them, innocent of expression. Always running through their Mother Goose minds like a current of consolation bearing them on were such rhymes as:

> *Cuckoo, cuckoo, cherry tree,*
> *Catch a bird, and give it me;*
> *Let the tree be high or low,*
> *Let it hail or rain or snow.*

Compare that with a chant that was popular among the pirates:

> *Take a prize and kill the crew.*
> *Kill the women, children, too,*
> *Hang 'em up and run 'em through.*
> *Dead men never tell no tale,*
> *Drink your grog and go to hell.*

Even the stout hearts of the dogs at the swivel gun wallowed at the sight of the pirates, but the Captain was not dismayed. He stood firmly, looking them back face to face. Then for a second he started, tightened his grip on the telescope for a steady look, and after a moment's study handed the instrument to Mister Cloud.

"It's Goldnose," said the Captain. "You'll find him by that forward cannon. Aye, and so that's the pirate Goldnose, or else someone who's had his face in a mustard pot."

Mister Cloud brought the telescope to bear on the man, and then handed the glass to Skivvy.

"So it is, Captain. Aye, second only to the bloody Captain Cowl in the damned trade, and now pirating Cowl's waters and chasing us for Cowl's treasure. A fat rascal, ain't he, blast his nose. Huh! Seems I've seen him before, but can't raise the memory of it."

Skivvy had focused in on the pirate ship. Now he let out a gasp.

"The *Locust*!"

"What's that, Skivvy?" said the Captain.

"She's called the *Locust*." Skivvy lowered the glass, slowly, and seemed to be staring without seeing towards the pirate ship.

The Captain took the telescope and again spied at the ship.

"Aye, the *Locust* it is. And a good name for the vermin on it, I should say."

Skivvy had turned away. He made his way towards his cabin. A sickness seemed to have suddenly overcome him. And on his unsteady way to his cabin, Skivvy interrupted a scene amidships.

Now, the Captain had been entirely right in cautioning Amy to avoid acquaintance with Davy Duck, for Davy Duck was planning a mutiny. When the right moment arose, Davy intended to rise up with his men and challenge the Captain, and if need be to engage his mutinous crew in a battle to see who would be master of the ship. These matters were the gist of the conversation between Donkey and Goat that the Bad Sister had overheard, sitting and listening the night before. But so far the only mutineers Davy Duck could raise were the turkey and the chicken. Amy had again been left on the hatch to enjoy the sun. She was lying there thinking slow thoughts when Davy approached her, crawling around the corner of the hatch and raising his head near hers. Glancing this way and that, he whispered to Amy.

"Pssst. Davy Duck here, miss. D'ye hear me, miss? Supposing ye do, I'm happy to make your acquaintance, having seen ye about these few days. Aye, miss, and I been taking notice of ye, and of certain other things aboard this here ship, I have. Now, give a fair hearing to me and I'll say a few words about how things is falling out for the future of this ship, so ye may set your course as best suits your fortune."

The duck paused in his speech to take another close look about that no one should be overhearing him. The chicken was crouched near the mainmast on lookout in case anyone should come that way.

"Ain't it lovely weather now, miss? Aye, and there they are, all the rest of the crew worrying about those pirates. But we needn't worry about pirates, yourself and me, miss, if we come to see eye to eye as regards the business I want to talk to ye about. Aye, there's reason we might have pirate friends because of a certain favour I'm doing for them. But leave that be for now. It's something else confidential I want to say." Again the duck glanced carefully about. "Chicken's on the watch — he'll give a whistle if anyone pokes nearby, so ye can listen freely, miss, and make your right judgement on what I say.

"Ye see, there's some sort of thing between us that needs speaking, miss, something I seen right off, that brings us close together like this, and I'm the sort of forward duck that dares to say it. I mean to say, I seen right off ye was my kind of people, miss, someone I could talk to and get an understanding about how it is with ducks, having no lips yourself."

Amy stared at him with her blue button eyes. It was true, she had no lips, just a stitched line of thread for a mouth. Davy Duck continued his talk, the very same recruitment speech he had given Turkey and Chicken, and which convinced them to throw in with the duck for a mutiny.

"Aye," said the duck. "That's the trouble with the world, that's exactly what it is, and I can see a fellow creature what knows it. It's those with lips that cause all the trouble in the world. Now tell me if that's not so."

He paused and looked closely at Amy for a reply, cocking his head, but of course she could not speak. But she listened.

"Aye, those with lips, that's where the misery comes from. Us without lips has got to stick together. Oh, I know 'em. I seen the Captain come out of his cabin after a meal, smacking his lips together as he passes by, pretending like I'm not there, just lording it over me 'cause he got lips to smack together and I ain't. Aye, ye see 'em, puckering up their big fat lips – aye, all of 'em, sucking on apples, blowing out blubbering sounds smacking 'em together and making kissing sounds, aye, like they was the very gods of the earth. Aye, thinking like I care a penny about their confounded lips! Arghhhhh . . . !"

Davy Duck had been steadily raising his voice, his exasperation quickening. Now he caught the noise of it and dropped to a whisper again, but still spoke with passionate intensity.

"And I ask ye, how's an order best given on a ship – with a quack, clear and sharp, or rather come rubbering out of a pair of fat lips? But I don't mean ye got to be able to quack to be of any worth, miss, and I take ye like ye are. Mainly it's lips I'm speaking of, and I tell ye straight that the Captain's going to come down a step or two before this voyage is done, and be not so high and mighty, I tell ye."

Again the duck looked around fore and aft.

"But here now, ye says, who's to be Captain of this ship if it ain't the Captain himself? Well, it's a question I can answer, miss, and satisfy ye with the answer. And I tell ye this to your relief, miss, it's someone who won't be talking about snipping off your eyes. Aye, ye hear that well, don't ye? Don't ye worry, there's more that Davy Duck knows about what goes on in this here ship than he says. If it wasn't on account of not having lips, ye just might want to fall in with me because of wanting to save your eyes, now ain't that reasonable?"

Amy listened.

"But here now, we was talking about the next Captain for this ship. D'ye like poetry? That's where the truth is, ye know. Aye, when ye want the real bones of what's what, and what's really right and true in the world, where do ye go to find it? In a navigation book, or one about latitudes and longitudes, or moons and tides and such? Not likely! But ye snatch out a poetry book to get the true bearings about your course, and then ye lay sail on that line."

Davy Duck then reached under his jacket and pulled out the Captain's copy of *Mother Goose*. He riffled through to find a place.

"Now, I ask ye," he continued, laying a wingtip across a page, "who would know more about sailing a ship, a duck or a man? Straight now, with no prejudice, who would ye think knows the most about the wind and the water, a duck or a man?" Amy said nothing. "Aye, it's a question a thinking creature might ask and consider carefully. But here now, don't take my authority on it. Here's the gospel on that subject."

So saying, he held the book for Amy to see.

"Mother Goose," he exclaimed, "who never told a lie in her life. But listen, and hear it for yourself."

The duck looked to his text, then read this poem to Amy. He looked up now and then when he came to a place that he thought particularly emphatic and significant in the verse.

> "I saw a ship a-sailing,
> A-sailing on the sea,
> And oh, but it was laden
> With pretty things for thee.
>
> "There were comfits in the cabin,
> And apples in the hold;
> The sails were made of silk,
> And the masts were all of gold.
>
> "The four-and-twenty sailors,
> That stood between the decks,
> Were four-and-twenty white mice
> With chains about their necks.
>
> "The Captain was a duck
> With a jacket on his back,
> And when the ship began to move,
> The Captain said, Quack! Quack!"

Davy slapped the book shut.

"Hah! There! D'ye see? That's the word of the wisest

person what ever lived, Mother Goose herself. The Captain of the ship ought to be a duck, and that's how it's going to be, miss. Just fall in with us and we'll treat ye right. It may be we'll find some little matter ye may help us with by and by, seeing as how ye can't handle a sword, but there's others what can. And say, miss, maybe ye can give me an opinion on a thing. Would ye say, miss, that a frog has lips?"

At this moment Skivvy interrupted the scene at his approach. The chicken came running around the side of the hatch.

"Someone's coming, someone's coming!" the chicken cried in a whisper.

Davy Duck crammed the book into his jacket and took the chicken angrily by the throat.

"Ye was to *whistle* a warning," he snarled.

"No lips, no lips," said the chicken pitifully.

The duck looked at the chicken for a moment with a puzzled expression, then said:

"Right!"

They crept off around the other side of the hatch and disappeared into the fo'c'sle. But they need not have worried. Skivvy passed that way with an unseeing, glazed look. He headed directly to his cabin without even a word of greeting to Amy as he passed.

Amy lay there slowly thinking about what she had heard. She decided she would have to inform the Captain of Davy Duck's intentions as soon as she could speak. But that was for the future. For now the sun shone and warmed her, and the ship rocked with the comfort of a cradle. Actually, Davy Duck's talk had made her think how nice it would be to have lips again, how nice to whistle, and smack them together, and how nice to kiss. She then fell to thinking about Miss Eclair and how good it would be to be held by her again, of good Mrs. Hill also. Then her thoughts turned to Miss Quince. Even the sunshine failed for a moment to warm her in those thoughts.

But her dear brother the Captain would find the gold treasure. They would return to land, and somehow everything would turn out all right. Such is the charming and optimistic mood of a doll.

CHAPTER TWENTY-EIGHT

Multiplication is vexation,
Division is as bad;
The Rule of Three doth puzzle me,
And Practice drives me mad.

Skivvy sat in his cabin with Captain Kimberly's great black Bible open in front of him. His fears of the voyage had been growing. He had no joy in the thought of the gold treasure. It brought to Skivvy's mind only thoughts of death and destruction. Skivvy turned the pages of the Bible. "Locusts," said Skivvy to himself. It was the name of the pirate ship that had alarmed him. He turned to the last book of the Bible, the Book of Revelation. He had been reading in that book only the evening before, and locusts are spoken of therein, and not to the happiness of those who encounter them. Skivvy put his finger to the page where he found again the verses he had read the day before:

And he opened the bottomless pit; and there arose a
smoke out of the pit, as the smoke of a great furnace;
and the sun and the air were darkened by reason of the
smoke of the pit.
*   And there came out of the smoke locusts upon the*
earth: and unto them was given power, as the scor-
pions of the earth have power...
*   And the shapes of the locusts were like unto horses*

prepared into battle; and on their heads were as it were crowns like gold, and their faces were as the faces of men.

There it was, the dreadful locusts with a sting of death, crowned with gold. Skivvy, his hands still on the Bible, leaned back in his chair. "Locusts," he whispered, "Crowns of gold. Goldnose. Locusts with the faces of men." And in making this connection between the pirates and this mention of locusts in the Bible, Skivvy took a step on a path so betwined and beset by thorn and bush that no mind of man has ever cleaved free and clear through the tangle of it.

The Book of Revelation announces and describes the end of the world in the most satisfying and dismaying display of metaphor that has ever been given to the mouth of man, as if it had been inspired by a dreaming God, and man is not equal to know the dreams of God. The book is a challenge to even a steadfast mind. It is not a book to be entertained by a troubled mind such as Skivvy's, for he worried about his soul a lot, did Skivvy.

There is also a great temptation in the Book of Revelation, for a puzzle is given, and if a man can solve this puzzle he may be fairly sure he has saved his soul. The puzzle is this. In the unlucky Chapter 13 in Revelation, it is said that a Beast will come upon the earth out of the sea. Many men will worship that Beast, and with that worship comes the end of the worship and the love of God. Moreover, when the Beast appears it is very near the end of the world. And they who worship the Beast will receive his mark on the forehead or hand, and by that mark they will be doomed. There is a great mystery in this mark of the Beast, for this mark is his number, and his number tells who he is, that men may beware, and the number of the Beast is 666. That is the puzzle – a number puzzle. The writer of Revelation leaves it at that. The wisdom of Solomon would be needed to solve it.

And so poor Skivvy, intent to know his soul and the very mind of God, which is maybe much the same thing, being not satisfied to know merely the goodness of his heart, advanced himself into a great and teeming wilderness where many men become lost, or return with a babbling of dreams.

Skivvy's eyes unlocked out of his stare. He moved the Bible aside and took up paper and pen. At the top of a fresh piece of paper he wrote out the alphabet. Underneath he matched up numbers for each letter, like this:

A	B	C	D	E	F	G	H	I	J	K	L	M
1	2	3	4	5	6	7	8	9	10	11	12	13

N	O	P	Q	R	S	T	U	V	W	X	Y	Z
14	15	16	17	18	19	20	21	22	23	24	25	26

Now, there is a Queen of all science, and her name is Mathematics. She is the Mother of Numbers, and when man puzzles over the world, it is one of his methods to turn to her that she will enfold and comfort him in her immense array, and instruct him out of his confusion. The mystery of God and creation, and of every small and large part of the universe, and every movement therein from the past to the future, is thought by some men to be made up of many numbers. The men who are content that this is so lie upon the bosom of the Queen and count towards the great mystery. There is justification in this, for she is a great and elegant lady, and she does not lie. Yet she is subtle and requires labour and devotion to search her truths, and much of the truth comes slowly.

Now the Queen has a Wayward Daughter. Men seek her for consolation also, for she is easy of access and prompt in her favours, and makes promises that the Mother of Numbers never makes. Her name is Numerology, and she is a wanton. She goes her way by magic and divination and casts herself about promiscuously. She gives the lucky numbers of 3 and 7, and the unlucky one of 13. She gives reasons for the numbers on playing cards and dice so that you may read them as in a book that tells the future. One of her practices is to make numbers out of plain language, also thereby to lead men to her worship, for she promises to reveal hidden things by the right application of her gifts. She has a peculiar jealousy of the alphabet, and she lures men to lay numbers to the names of things, therefore to find rare secrets and to get knowledge even of things unknown to the angels. And so in his puzzlement, beset upon him by the Book of Revelation, Skivvy turned to find ease with this quick lady and to write up solutions to save his soul out of her endless alphabet. Perhaps he might even solve the mystery of the Beast, the mystery of his number – 666.

Skivvy wrote down the word "locust" on his paper and below it, according to the ancient practice, he gave each of the letters of the word its proper number, according to its station in the alphabet, like this:

L O C U S T
12 15 3 21 19 20

He totalled the numbers up and wrote the total down. The number was 90. That was the number of the *Locust*, Goldnose's ship.

"Of course," said Skivvy, looking to the open Bible. "Drop the zero, and that's Chapter 9, Revelation."

And it just so happens that it is Chapter 9 in the Book of Revelation wherein locusts are particularly mentioned, and in no other chapter of that book are they mentioned. Surely this could not be mere coincidence, thought Skivvy. He was excited that the first truth had been found so quickly. Make no mistake, the daughter of the Queen is a Princess. She has the imperial touch, and men are led by her hand. Poor Skivvy had taken a step inside her chambers. He then added up the sum of the letters of the *Ariel*. It came to 45, exactly half the number of the *Locust*. Surely this was not mere chance.

We leave Skivvy to his wanderings. The next time we meet he will not be the same man, for a shade is falling across his heart, which comes of searching into the shadows at the end of time and the vast dimensions of prophecy as given in the Book of Revelation, and which comes of flirting with the Wayward Daughter of the Great Queen.

CHAPTER TWENTY-NINE

Who comes here?
A Grenadier.
What do you want?
A pot of beer.
Where is your money?
I've forgot.
Get you gone,
You drunken sot.

The Ariel rolled on the swelling sea, and the earth rolled into the great bowl of the night. All hands were on deck watching the *Locust* until the thread that separates night from day was lost in the black web of sky and sea. The Captain had shortened sail earlier in the day, hoping that the *Locust* would do likewise so as not to overrun them. And so she had. Now he called out to a dog and a squirrel on the mainmast yard.

"Set the mainsail!"

He turned to the goat.

"West-sou'west, helmsman." The goat peered into the dimly lit binnacle and spun the wheel down to the new course.

The Captain then spoke to the first mate.

"Take over, Mister Cloud."

"Aye, Captain. Heave there, you cats!" bellowed out the first mate. "Haul on those lines, you pussies! And can't ye sing! Heave ho! Sing out and haul!"

"Hey, *heave*, and the boys do leave!" sang out the cats. "Hey, *haul*, and the girls do bawl!" The mainsail bellied out and the *Ariel* lost the *Locust* in the darkness.

The Captain turned his attention aft, bracing his hands on the stern railing. The *Ariel* was towing her boat. Two monkeys sat in the thwarts and watched towards the looming shape of their mother ship.

"Do we show a light, mates?" the Captain called to the monkeys.

"Dark as the dead, Captain," called back one of the monkeys.

"Give slack," the Captain ordered the donkey, who let out more line and took a turn on a cleat. The boat dragged farther behind the *Ariel*.

"And *do* we show a light, mates?" shouted the Captain, this time cupping his mouth with his hands.

"Dead as the dark," called back the other monkey, which was the same expression but back ways around. But he did not correct himself, and the call was understood at any rate. The other monkey slugged him. Knowing they would be out all night in the open boat, the monkeys had supplied themselves with a good ration of rum to warm and cheer themselves. They had been sipping at it already. Yet their watch was true. No light showed from *Ariel*. Davy would not lead the *Locust* with his pipe this night.

"Make fast that line," said the Captain to the donkey. "Helmsman, give the middle watch due east to steer. We'll hold that course till morning watch, then take our true course. Mister Cloud, I believe that's your watch. Call me out at four bells or at the first peek of light or sail following us."

"Aye, Captain."

The Captain retired to his cabin. Behind the *Ariel*, straining at a fifty-yard tug of rope, the boat bobbed in the darkness. The monkeys were enjoying their distance from their mother ship and the crowded fo'c'sle. It was somewhat like leaving home for the first time. They were chatting and pulling drinks from one of the bottles of rum they had cheated away from ship stores.

"So what did ye say to him, then?" asked one monkey of the other.

"I told him to ship out, that's what I said. 'Ship out,' I said, and off he went, and best he did, too, or I would have given him a clout."

"That's what I told him," said the first monkey. "Lemme have that bottle. That's exactly what I told him. But he'll make trouble yet, and ye can lay to that."

"Well, I wouldn't blab on a shipmate, but I got me eye on that there Davy Duck."

"Chicken and Turkey is in on it with him, that's what he said."

"I never took to him anyway," said the other monkey. "He talks smart and sassy enough in the fo'c'sle, but ye see how he scuttles around when the Captain's on deck, like he can't scrape low enough with his 'Yes, sirs,' and 'You're the Captain, sir,' and all a' that slavish muck. Do your duty, I say, and ye can stand fast to God or man."

"Aye. Are ye going to keep that bottle for yourself? Aye, but he made some sense talking about tails, ye know. There was something to that after all. Like he said, and its something to think about – it's those without tails that make all the trouble in the world, keeping in mind them pirates chasing us."

"Hmmmm. Well, there may be something in that. But look, d'ye call that a tail a duck has? Or Chicken or Turkey? Would ye say those are tails, I mean when ye get right down to the bottom of it? More like fat noses with feathers stuck in 'em."

"Aye, they ain't true tails, not like the dogs' or the cats', or Donkey, or even Goat or Pig, come to that. Aye, that's what I told him. 'Shove off,' says I, come up to me in his fancy jacket talking about how us with tails has got to stick together. Then he turned around and wagged at me with that little nose in his rump."

The monkeys had a good laugh and more rum, handing the bottle back and forth with their tails.

"Now, if he was talking about a *working* tail . . ."

"That's it, that's it!" said the other monkey. "That's when ye can begin talking about tails, when ye can hang on a yardarm with it. Not that I mean to say anything low about the dogs or anything, good shipmates that they are."

"Aye, they got good tails, though they don't do much with 'em but wag 'em back and forth. Ye may say that ain't much, but it gives me a sort of good feeling to see it, ye know."

"Aye, they's fine boys, them dogs. Disposition, that's what they got. Them cats is all right, too. They don't talk much, but they got a way of letting ye know how they feel by flicking their tails around."

"Expressive, that's the word for it. Is that a bottle ye got there?"

For a while the monkeys drank silently.

"But I got an eye on that Davy Duck."

"And I got the other eye on him, mate."

Taking a long drink at the bottle, one of the monkeys broke into a song out of *Mother Goose*, and the other monkey joined in.

"Over the water and over the lea,
And over the water to Charlie,
Charlie loves good ale and wine,
And Charlie loves good brandy,

And Charlie loves a pretty girl
As sweet as sugar candy."

Their voices came up to the poop deck. Mister Cloud considered for a moment to call at them to pipe it down, but the *Locust* was far off and the singing was cheery.

The voices of the monkeys barely reached below decks. Down there in the bowels of the ship, a figure crept along a dark and low passageway, pushed through a small door, closed it behind himself, and lit a candle. It was a small storeroom, the magazine locker where was stored cannon shot and the gunpowder kegs, also spare iron fittings, brackets, braces, bolts, hooks and hawser eyes. It was Davy Duck lighting the candle and setting it on top of a nail keg. He had lost his chance to guide the *Locust* that night, yet he had reason to think he wouldn't need the help of pirates to make his mutiny and take over the ship.

"Shhhhhhhh," he whispered. "Shhhhhhhhhh." So cautioning himself, he slid aside a crate, bent down, and lifted a fold of sailcloth in the corner of the small room. And lying there peacefully in their dreamy time were a dozen small ducks, sewn out of "duck" cloth, stuffed with shreds of old sail, and with beads for eyes. It was Davy who had stolen the Bad Sister's necklace. He bent over the toy ducks like a father over his brood.

"Aye, it's me, shipmates – the Captain. Quack, quack! Are ye resting easy? Quiet and comfortable down here, ain't it? But I see you're full of action, and the time's coming, shipmates, when ye can get up and stretch your wings and follow your Captain. Look here now, I brung your swords for ye, just like I said I would."

Davy took some small wooden cutlasses out of his pocket and one by one slipped them into loops he had sewn onto the waists of the ducks.

"And I've plenty extra for your shipmates," said Davy, now taking out scissors and needle and thread from his sewing box, a biscuit tin. He sat down and applied himself to a piece of cloth already cut to pattern,, and sewed at the seam of a new duck.

"Shipmates, it's us ducks against the world," said Davy, making himself at ease with his work. "Quack, quack, mates. Ye know the call when ye hear it, don't ye, and don't it raise your hearts! And who are we against, ye asks, and who's the enemy? Well, I'll tell ye, mates. It's those with tails, that's who. And the reason why is because it's those with tails that makes all the trouble in the world, and that's a duck's fact, and the word of your Captain. Quack, quack! Aye, you'll know 'em when ye see 'em, dragging and wagging those things behind themselves. It's a disgusting thing to see, mates, a sort of moral inferiority, if ye take my meaning. Look here, why would an animal *want* a tail, lying about and getting in the way, all in danger of getting stepped on or slammed in a door, unless he was trying to hide something? Ye see, it's distraction they want, them with tails, 'cause they don't know how to be honest or straightforward with their shipmates, and they flap those tails about to catch your attention because they can't look ye in the eye."

Davy stitched, turned a knot, and clipped his thread, thinking bitter thoughts about the monkeys, telling him to "shove off" and "ship out." He continued his lecture.

"And monkeys, shipmates, monkeys are the worst of the lot. They'd make ye sick, watching them at mess, a biscuit in one hand, a knife in the other, and drinking out of a cup held by their tails. Ugh! Can ye picture it?"

Davy paused in his work a moment and mused.

"What it is, mates," he said, pointing the needle at his brood, "is a sort of perversity of the backbone, a tail is.

Aye, that's it, like a backbone gone wild, not knowing its proper bounds, and there we get back to the question about morality, shipmates, and discipline, and it's discipline that's wanted aboard a ship. And that's a duck's fact. Quack, quack!"

After stuffing the duck he was working on, Davy neatly sewed on two of the Bad Sister's stolen beads for the eyes, and snatched up the final seam. He held the new duck up to the flickering candlelight to approve his work. The first consciousness floated into the duck's head, as if the small candle flame was the first rising of the sun bringing life to the first creature on the first day of a new world.

"Ahoy, mate, you're a duck," said Davy. "Quack, quack. And I'm the Captain. Here, now, join your shipmates and learn a lesson. Poetry is what we teach first in this school. Ah, almost forgot, here's your sword, and you'll be needing it. Poetry is mightier than the sword, that's true, but ye got to keep a sword for the critics, and I believe we'll have some critics when we come up on deck. Aye, there's many without a love of beauty and truth, and that's a duck's fact. Quack, quack." Davy set the new duck down with the others and fumbled behind a gunpowder keg to find the copy of *Mother Goose* he had stolen from the Captain.

"Well," he said, "I know you've all been waiting to hear me recite, so just gather around your new shipmate and open your hearts, for here's a poem done by Mother Goose herself, and it ain't got a fault in it."

Opening the book and propping it against the keg, Davy commenced drawing out a new pattern on a square of cloth, and with a glance now and then at the book, he recited:

"I saw a ship a-sailing,
  A-sailing on the sea,

And oh, but it was laden
With pretty things for thee...

    "The Captain was a duck(that's me, mates)
    With a jacket on his back,
    And when the ship began to move,
    The Captain said, Quack! Quack!"

Davy smiled down on the ducks.

"Aye, shipmates, quack, quack! That's the command. Then it's out with your swords and stand up for your Captain. And then it's death to immorality and perversity! I mean to say them with tails. And death to them with lips!"

Davy Duck took thought for a second.

"Ah, but I haven't told ye about lips, have I? Well, mates, and then I will, and ye may lay it to your hearts. It's them with lips that causes all the trouble in the world..."

And in the small light of the candle, Davy Duck sewed at his ducks and condemned those with lips, while above deck all was quiet and dark, and the *Locust* sailed confounded on her path over the horizon. The *Ariel* had finally lost her.

CHAPTER THIRTY

> *"I went up one pair of stairs."*
>   *"Just like me."*
> *"I went up two pairs of stairs."*
>   *"Just like me."*
> *"I went into a room."*
>   *"Just like me."*
> *"I looked out of a window."*
>   *"Just like me."*
> *"And there I saw a monkey."*
>   *"Just like me."*

Daylight. The sun rose a brilliant white disc as if lifted out of a silver cauldron. The Captain stood with Mister Cloud and studied the circling line of the sea. Mister Cloud grappled a hand in the white bush of his beard.

"She's gone, Captain, devil take 'er. But I fear that she's got our scent. Pirates have a way of following on where there's gold to smell after." Mister Cloud's eyes roved the sky. "Fine day for sailing," he observed. "Now, take Captain Cowl," he said, looking at the Captain. "There was a bloody buccaneer if ever there was one, and you wouldn't expect he'd get any luck from any sort of Providence. But they say he used to spin a bottle and take a course to his next battle from the way it pointed. Many ships went down from that piece of sniffing out. But I mean to say, Captain, that I wouldn't put much faith in thinking

I had a pirate fooled." Mister Cloud settled a long, steady glance on the horizon. "She's back there somewhere, Captain. We've given that fat pirate a fair look at our true course these last days. It's all open sea on this line except for that group of islands we're sailing for. Aye, and that Goldnose isn't a fool. That's where he'd make to. By and by he'll come up on us, I'm afraid."

"That's as may be," said the Captain, "but there's just one of those islands we'll visit – Vulcan Island. He's got a half-dozen to choose from, so the chance of it falls on our side, Mister Cloud."

The Captain saw that this might be a time to open the subject of the conspiracy between Mister Cloud and the Bad Sister, since they now stood as shipmates facing a common danger. He hoped that the clear and bright openness of the heavens might prompt Mister Cloud to make a confession of any mutiny or secret business he had set afoot in partnership with the Bad Sister. Yet he decided not to accuse Mister Cloud outright, but to open the subject artfully. But artfulness cannot serve every occasion, and it failed miserably this time. Taking up a metaphor from Mister Cloud's reference to Cowl's bottle-spinning, the Captain spoke, tuning his voice, so he hoped, to an urging, confidential and forgiving note.

"Aye, and concerning bottles, Mister Cloud, there's things, as it were, bottled up on board the *Ariel* that might best be spoken of, for as it's a danger sometimes to take a cork from a bottle, sometimes again it's a worse danger to keep the cork in." The Captain, seeing a chance to extend the metaphor, and having had little practice in the matter of letters, pressed onwards in hopes of enforcing his plea with some elegant rhetoric. "For as the nearness of the enemy lends a certain heat to the atmosphere, so therefore in that case is a contained fermentation liable to produce an explosion, the best relief for which is to have it out with it entirely."

The Captain considered in his mind what he had just said, and decided to give up a career in that direction. But yet Mister Cloud dug a hand in his beard and seemed to understand, for he nodded his head. The first mate, in fact, understood something entirely different. He understood by the reference to bottles that the Captain had found out that the monkeys had stolen some bottles of rum and had been taken aboard the *Ariel* that morning in a drunken condition. Mister Cloud had decided not to report the incident, but perhaps last night their drunken singing had reached the Captain's ears, he thought. Yet otherwise the monkeys were blameless in their duty. So now Mister Cloud essayed to make a defence in their behalf. And the gods of confusion, if they inspire scripture, might have given a verse to this next exchange between Mister Cloud and the Captain.

"Well, Captain, it's lonely in a boat, and that's to be understood," said Mister Cloud, thinking of the two monkeys sitting alone in their small boat the past night.

"Yes, Mister Cloud, and I do understand that," said the Captain, thinking of Mister Cloud sitting and singing love songs to the Bad Sister. "Yes, indeed, sir, and let me say that I respect a man who can make an honest confession of a thing. But you have my understanding. A boat is a lonely place."

"And especially at night, Captain."

"Say no more, Mister Cloud, I understand that perfectly. A certain time at sea does turn a sailor's attention to such things as – ah, sitting close to someone, and singing ..."

"Captain, I was thinking of piping that down, but it wasn't so loud, I thought, to carry very far, so I supposed there was no danger in it."

"No danger at all, I should think. In fact, singing seems to me quite suitable to the – ah, occasion. No, no danger at all, but quite in favour, I should think, if the song were to express the sentiment that was wanted."

"Sentiment, Captain? Well, as to that, Captain, being under the influence and all . . ." Mister Cloud began, thinking again of the drunken monkeys.

"Precisely what I would expect," said the Captain. "No – I have no objection at all to the singing. But since you mention the particular *influence*, Mister Cloud, I must say I am somewhat puzzled as to that. But I make no judgment there. There is, as they say, no accounting for taste."

"Oh, I don't think it was taste that had anything to do with it, Captain. Mainly, I believe it was the *novelty* of the experience that was the temptation, having had very little previous experience at all . . ."

"Ahem! Mister Cloud," the Captain interrupted, for he was not seeking to know the intimacies of Mister Cloud's affair with the Bad Sister. "Let us settle this out. Believe me, I am in the utmost sympathy with whatever reasons you might put forth along those lines. The important matter now is how we are going to resolve the affair. Let us turn to that."

"Well, Captain," said Mister Cloud with an imploring gesture, intending to make a plea for the monkeys because of their tender age, "I would have reported the whole of it to you sooner except for thinking on the punishment, which is surely deserved, but I was thinking it might be overlooked, considering the age – "

"Indeed, Mister Cloud!" the Captain said with an enthusiastic sympathy, believing that the first mate was now asking for leniency because of his own age, which years upon his back would not well support a flogging. "Indeed, Mister Cloud!" the Captain repeated wholeheartedly. "I promise that there will be no punishment at all, nor even that a record of the offence be entered into the ship's log, since no harm has come to us because of it. We might say our voyage is begun afresh and anew from this moment if only a clean breast be made of the fault and the air cleared once and for all."

"Aye, Captain," said Mister Cloud gratefully. "Good clear air. That's the idea. Best thing for a hangover. Good clear, clean, fresh air should get those monkeys on their feet again. I'll have 'em holystoning the deck first thing after breakfast, Captain, and I thank you, Captain." Touching his forehead in salute, the first mate walked away. The Captain stood looking dumbly at his back, wondering what at all had passed between them that had anything whatsoever to do with monkeys.

And the gods of confusion might have enjoyed another touch of their influence that morning, for the *Locust*, chasing the *Ariel*, was now sailing out in front of her. When Goldnose discovered that he would have no light to lead him that past night, he held his course and again studied his charts. Now, after three days of determined running towards that same group of islands, and being just as clever as Mister Cloud supposed he was, Goldnose determined to go straight to the island group. Once arrived there, he would set up a path of investigation, cruising around each island to discover the *Ariel* where she was anchored. There would be time. It takes hard work to dig up gold treasure or to raise it from the bottom of the sea. Yes, give them some time, thought Goldnose. Let them have the treasure on board. Pirates would rather swing cutlasses than shovels and picks. Now, which of the islands should be the first to sail for? Goldnose, who disdained the gift of intuition, feeling that the vaporous mode of it was unmanly, shut his eyes and made a thick-fingered stab at the chart. He opened his eyes.

"Tanner Island it is," he said, and plotted at his chart. Then he pushed open his skylight and shouted the new course up to the helmsman.

The weather held fair and the *Ariel* cut her way through the soft seas. The figurehead of the woman with her finger to her lips gazed steadily at the turning world. They sailed without incident for two more days. Skivvy, relieved of other duties, had gathered the carpenter's tools into the main hold. There he was building the platform that would float the gunpowder kegs that might – or might not – blow up the *Locust*. Half the hatch cover was removed. Bold, straight shadows enclosed Skivvy in his hammering and pounding and sawing. When he finished his work, the platform was hoisted onto the main deck. Six gunpowder kegs were placed inside the super-structure of board casing, which was painted a bright red. The device was let out on lines and floated alongside the ship for proof of its seaworthiness. It was good work. Skivvy received a cheer from the crew, which he acknowledged not at all, but only frowned on his invention. Then the bomb was taken on board again and lashed to the railings. Gunnery practice commenced anew at a mock target, with heightened enthusiasm now that the true target was in sight, its flaming red casing promising an explosion worth aiming at.

CHAPTER THIRTY-ONE

> *"Flying-man, Flying-man,*
> *Up in the sky,*
> *Where are you going to,*
> *Flying so high?"*

> *"Over the mountains*
> *And over the sea."*
> *"Flying-man, Flying-man,*
> *Can't you take me?"*

Many miles to the south, on the third day after the *Ariel* lost the *Locust*, an old black woman got out of bed when the uprising sun was announced at her open window by a great white bird. She opened her eyes at once, threw a leg over the side, and heaved herself up to sit on the edge of the bed.

"Oh yes, oh yes," she said to the bird, who was sitting on her windowsill. "Blessed be the day. Blessed be the house, and blessed be the hill. Bless you too, and bless old Mama Dah-dah. Ain't it the truth. You come back again, eh?"

She sat on the edge of the bed, which was sturdily supported by several driftwood posts, brushing her large black hands at the white nightgown that covered her knees. She looked around and spoke to the bird. "Always hungry, huh? Yes, you are. Maybe best I oughtn't to raised you up. Huh! Some poor little bird you are. Huh! Where you been these two days? Now you get hungry you come home. Huh!"

The bird was a pure white albatross, a giant of birds, a sea-wandering cruiser with a twelve-foot wingspan, an ocean-crossing bird who could lock his wings and sleep on the air and fly in a dream, who could soar over thunderheads and fly faster than the fastest sailing ship. He sat in the open window, taking up the whole height of it, as bright as white paper to the eyes in the early-morning sunlight. The woman was called Mama Dah-dah. She had married three husbands, and all of them had died. One of them, the one named Anthony, she had not expected to be of much account as a husband, but he had surprised her mightily, and she had loved him very much. But then he died, too. Anyway, when Mama Dah-dah found the small wounded bird that was to be the albatross, she thought he was a sea gull. She nursed him back to health and kept him. The bird grew to be a giant albatross, which was a mighty surprise to her, and he would not fly away. She named him Anthony.

"Big help you are," she said to the bird. She stuck her feet into her slippers and rather more slid than walked over to her little stove. "Where you been? Out all night with the ladies? Anthony, the way you carry on does surprise me, indeed it does. Ain't it the truth. Here, you look me in the eye so I can see what you been up to." She turned and looked at the bird. "Breakfast? Well, we got no breakfast, how do you like that?" She shook a stick of kindling at the bird, who turned his head this way and that and said, "Errrrrrr," in his throat.

She lived in a one-room shack on a small hill overlooking the little fishing village below. After dressing in a bright blue dress, she went to the open door, there to look down on the small boats tied closely at the fringe of ocean, as if held by strings to the apron of the village. "Early fishes been brought in," she declared, and reached for a crocheted shawl. Anthony was waiting outside the door for her. He walked along behind Mama Dah-dah down the path to the village, where she would buy a fish and maybe some eggs. Down the hill they went. She sang to herself as they walked, "Dah dah daaaah, dah dah daaaah ..."

The woman was old in love and experience, and also she was thought to be wise. Perhaps she was, and one of her wisdoms was to get up early in the morning and start the day out without complaining. Mama Dah-dah's door was open to everyone. Almost every day she had a visitor, either from her own village or from some neighbouring village, and even, on a rare day, someone from another island would visit her. For she was a healer, Mama Dah-dah was. She had the wonderful gift of being able to get in touch with sick people in such a way that they always went away feeling better. Sometimes they went away and were cured for good. How it came about that she could do this, she didn't know. Yet she *could* cure people, that was certain. Perhaps only a fool would ask into the way and reason of it.

Mama Dah-dah was always busy around her little house. When someone came to see her, she did not stop in her business for very long. And her business, if one were to watch her at it for a while, was more ritual than actual employment. She rearranged things. With a feather duster in hand, she made her way around the single room, talking all the time to the visitor, who sat at the central table. She would take up a jar from this shelf and set it on the table, dusting where the jar had been, into which place she would then place a nautilus shell. Then perhaps she would move a blouse from a peg, fold it into a drawer, take a picture from its place, hang it on that peg, and put another picture where the first had been. Then she might sweep, moving the matted rug to the other end of the room. Then go to her spice shelf, take everything down, wipe off the bottles and little tins, and replace all onto a different shelf. Yes, and pick up that jar from the table and place it on the spice shelf. All the while she talked to her visitor, who had come for the cure of some illness.

"You'll be all right. Look at that cobweb. I showed that spider out yesterday. Yes, yes, it was the same one. I know him. Here, now, you sit on the end of this stick, and if I see you in here tomorrow, maybe I'll smash you. Never can get the bugs out entirely. You know how that is, dear? But you got to keep working at it, ain't it the truth. Do you hurt much? Here now, let me look at you." Then she would sit down and look the person in the eye for a minute or so, holding hands. Up she would get then, and go about her work.

Since the place was so small, Mama Dah-dah often put a hand on the person's shoulder as she moved around the chair. If the person wanted to talk about the illness, she would sit down at the table also, but not for more than a few minutes. Then she was up again and rearranging things. Sometimes her visitors were not hurt in their bodies, but suffered in their minds, or their hearts.

"That *is* a hard story. Indeed it is," Mama Dah-dah would say, getting up. "That reminds me about my second husband. Oh, that man. Never mind him. He's dead now. Ain't it the truth. Why, look at that dust there. I just dusted that place. Didn't you see me dust that place? You got to keep moving all the time, ain't it the truth. Everything's going to catch up with you if you don't keep moving. You see that bird? Look now, you see that white bird there in the window? You just look at him and see how much he helps me. Now, what's that candle doing over there?

Didn't I put that candle on the table? Excuse me while I get around you here. Oh, you got nice soft hair. You'll feel better. That's right. Now, why don't that door stay open? Wind is changing, that's it. Everything changing all the time. Got to keep moving. Ain't it the truth. Dah, dah, dah . . ."

That was the way of it. Nothing more. But it was said by many people for many years that Mama Dah-dah was a great healer.

On this morning, when she got back to her home with a fish, she cleaned it and threw the guts out of the window for Anthony as usual. As the fish cooked, she watched the albatross eat.

"You eat like that in front of your lady friends? Don't know how they can stand you. Ain't it the truth. You come up here now and let me see where you've been!"

The bird jumped to the windowsill. Mama Dah-dah looked into his eyes. The bird stared steadily back at her.

Mama Dah-dah could look into the eyes of the albatross as if looking into a crystal ball. She could see what the great white bird had seen and she could search through his travels to discover many things that happened beyond her hill. She could see the earth from high above, ships sailing on the sea, strange islands, and the continent far to the north. When the bird landed near people, she could hear in her mind what they said. Now she spoke.

"That woman again! Anthony, why you go visit her at all? She's no good, that one! She feed you better than I do? You like her because she got a big house? I can't understand you. What do she do, except be young? Nothing. Looks in that mirror, smiles at her teeth. I got better things to do. Now, just listen what you missed, being off to see her. Yesterday a man come to see me with only one leg. You hear? And when he left he had two legs. That's right," said Mama Dah-dah, pointing and looking out the door. "Yes, he did – he walked right out of here and down the hill, skipping like a child. What do you think of that?"

She looked at Anthony to see what he thought of that. But he had his eyes closed. When Anthony wanted to end the talk, or when he didn't want to show what he was thinking or feeling, he closed his eyes. He didn't believe about the man coming with one leg and going off with two legs.

"Open your eyes, Anthony. Where else you been? Forget that woman. That's all right. You'll find out about her. Where else you been now?"

The albatross opened his eyes. Mama Dah-dah looked closely.

"Ah, you been visiting that poor man again. Oh, yes, there he is, poor man. I see him. Don't know how he can live so long all alone on that island. Feeling mighty bad, but he just *will* go on living, won't he. Maybe because he's so rich – you think so? All that gold lying around? No? Don't blink now, – I can't see what he's doing. Oh yes, talking to that thing again. What is that? – just an old head bone stuck up on a stick. Mighty lonesome when you get to talking to head bones. There he is, poor man. Nothing to do for him, Anthony. So far away."

Mama Dah-dah then looked past the albatross out over the sea. "Errrrr," said the bird. She glanced at him and nodded.

"Oh yes, I see. He gets down on his knees and prays. I see that, don't worry. Something happen, maybe. Can't waste a prayer. Ain't it the truth."

CHAPTER THIRTY-TWO

If all the seas were one sea,
*What a **great** sea that would be!*
If all the trees were one tree,
*What a **great** tree that would be!*
And if all the axes were one axe,
*What a **great** axe that would be!*
And if all men were one man,
*What a **great** man that would be!*
*And if the **great** man took the **great** axe,*
*And cut down the **great** tree,*
*And let it fall into the **great** sea,*
What a splish-splash that would be!

O n the third day after they lost the *Locust*, a tragedy happened aboard the *Ariel*. One of the rabbits fell out of the rigging and was killed. He was to be buried at sea, and was laid out on the galley table. The Captain and Skivvy stood looking down at him, watching him very closely. Here at least was one answer to the question of their mortality. There was no indication at all that the rabbit might turn back into the stuffed toy that he had been. He remained a true fur and flesh animal.

The Captain and Skivvy did not have to speak of this. They looked at each other solemnly, each knowing the thoughts of the other. They were truly men, and they would never be dolls again. Never again would they enter that faraway and comfortable limbo of dolls. What happened to men when they died would happen to them. The Captain ventured a smile. Skivvy looked back at the body of the rabbit. He reached out and smoothed its fur. So it was certain. Now they were truly men with all the parts of a man. They had souls.

The Bad Sister came into the galley with needle and thread. Behind her followed Mister Cloud with a piece of canvas and a cannonball.

"Seems we're short of canvas, Captain. Davy said this was about all he could find." The mate lifted the rabbit and laid the small piece of canvas underneath him. The Captain reached out to the Bad Sister for the needle and thread.

"I'll do that," she said. "You'd only poke him full of holes doing it yourself." She wrapped the rabbit in the canvas and began sewing the shroud together. Mister Cloud put the cannonball in for weight. Just before the shroud was closed, the Captain spoke up.

"Wait, I almost forgot. Mister Cloud, Skivvy — have either of you a gold coin? No? Wait then, please, madam — I've one in my cabin."

"Never mind," said the Bad Sister, "I know the stupid custom. King Neptune's payment, ain't it? Here." She plunged into a deep pocket of her dress and brought out a golden ring set with a small diamond.

The Captain received it in his hand. "Oh no, not a memento. No doubt this is of some meaning to you."

"I've remembered it enough," said the Bad Sister. "Maybe it's time it went to the bottom of the sea to be forgotten."

The Captain placed the ring in with the rabbit. The Bad Sister finished sewing up the shroud. Mister Cloud carried the small bundle out on deck.

A smooth board had been brought out, one end set upon the railing of the ship, the other resting on the donkey's back. Mister Cloud set the rabbit on the board. A cat and a dog took places on either side. The frog came forward with a folded white tablecloth, which he draped over the bundle. The crew stood all about. It was a beautifully clear day, not a cloud in the sky. The squirrel at the masthead watched from above. The other rabbit stepped to the head of the board, a piece of paper in his hand to read from.

"I don't know what to say, except that he was a good friend, and I'll miss him. You all know how he loved to sing, and how he loved *Mother Goose*. Here's one of his favourite poems. It's a riddle about an egg, you know. I'll just read it for him this one last time. He . . . he was looking forward to Easter. He wanted so much to see an Easter egg." The rabbit then cleared his throat and read.

> *"In marble halls as white as milk,*
> *Lined with a skin as soft as silk,*
> *Within a fountain crystal-clear,*
> *A golden apple doth appear.*
> *No doors there are to this stronghold*
> *Yet thieves break in and steal the gold."*

The rabbit stepped back. The Captain moved forward and said the very simple and stout service for burial at sea. Then at last:

"We commit this rabbit to the sea. He was a good sailor, and a friend. May he rest in peace."

The cat and dog tilted the board. The bundle slid down underneath the tablecloth and off the end of it into the sea. It made a very small splash. The crew stood about with bowed heads. And in that quiet moment, the squirrel at the masthead sang out.

"Sail ho! Sail ho!"

"Where away?" the Captain cried, running to his cabin to fetch his telescope.

[238]

"Dead away! Dead away!" the squirrel cried down to him. In a few moments the Captain was atop a railing, arm looped tightly in a line, training his glass on the horizon. It would be a few minutes before those on deck would be able to see what the squirrel at the masthead had seen. Some took to the rigging to get the sooner view. But before the sight of it came to the Captain, the squirrel called down to him.

"Belay that, Captain. Only a cloud. Sorry, Captain. No sail in sight. Excusing the mistake, but ye might understand, it being the only cloud in the sky."

"Um," grunted the Captain, jumping down to the deck and closing his telescope. Skivvy was standing next to him, his Bible under his arm.

"Captain, if I may have a word with you. In private."

"Certainly, Skivvy," said the Captain. He led the way to his cabin, grumbling at the squirrel's mistake. He glanced at Amy, where he had left her in a chair – not to depress her with the burial of the rabbit. The Captain walked to a rack circling a post. He lifted out a musket from among the half-dozen standing there. "Just a word on duty first, Skivvy, as I suppose you're the armourer, having made that bomb for us. These pieces need cleaning. Looks as if no one has touched the priming for years, and the barrels are like ratholes." He thrust the musket towards Skivvy and indicated a drawer. "You'll find a pistol in there you might look at also. Aye, if that had been the sail of the *Locust* and she'd found us after all, we might have been close on to a fight, and we wouldn't want our own muskets blowing up in our faces."

Skivvy took the musket in his free hand. "'They that take the sword shall perish with the sword.' Matthew 26:52," he said, laying the weapon on the table with the great Bible. "But there's a greater danger than that, Captain. I've said it from the first. There's something wrong about the voyage, something cursed. Mainly I believed it only for myself. That's all right. You said you needed me, and I shipped on. But it's worse that that, Captain." The second mate placed his fingertips on the Bible. "It's all in here, and I've found it out. A doom is coming upon us all. But it's not too late to save ourselves."

Skivvy opened the Bible to a marked place. "Look here, Captain. It was the name of that pirate ship that put me onto this. The *Locust*. It all begins with locusts. See, for the number of the *Locust* is 90." Skivvy produced a few sheaves of crumpled paper from inside his jacket and laid them aside the Bible. "See – the letters number up to 90. Now that means Chapter 9, Revelation. Listen. 'And there came out of the smoke locusts upon the earth ... and their faces were as the faces of men.' That's the beginning of it, Captain, the beginning of the end. And now take the *Ariel*. Our number is 45 – exactly half that of the *Locust*. So take half of that again, which is twenty-two and a half, so round that out to 23. That means the twenty-third book of the Bible. That's Isaiah. We go to Isaiah, then. He was a great prophet, Captain. Here. But what chapter do we read, that's the question? Chapter 29, Captain. We find that by adding the number of letters in Isaiah to 23, giving us the chapter to read. Chapter 29, Isaiah. Now there! Read it for yourself. The second verse. I'll read it. 'Yet I will distress Ariel, and there shall be heaviness and sorrow...'"

Skivvy looked up at the Captain. "That's us, Captain. The *Ariel*. Don't you see? This is our warning. First come the locusts, then the end of the world! It's perfectly clear! It means our doom, Captain. The voyage is all wrong. Turn away, Captain, it isn't too late."

The Captain turned the Bible and sat down at the table. He thumbed through the papers. Names and numbers were scratched all over them, many additions and subtractions, scribbles and blottings marking the anguish of a man condemned. The agony and confusion written into the pages were obvious. The Captain glanced at Skivvy, who reached out and tapped a finger on the Bible.

"Then here, Captain. Let me find it. Here in Revelation again. Smoke, Captain, smoke ..." Skivvy flipped at the pages. "And then there's the Beast and his number ... out of the sea, crowned with gold ... so we subtract – "

"There now, Skivvy," the Captain put in, moving away from the table. "Here now, lad, let's have a tot of brandy and talk this over. That's it, and a quiet smoke ..."

"Smoke, Captain. Listen, here it is. 'Out of the smoke ... and ... and as it were a great mountain burning with fire was cast into the sea: and the third part of the sea became blood.' That's the great heaviness spoken of in Isaiah, Captain. A mountain is in it somehow, and then the sea turns to blood ... and ... and ... we must save the ship!" Skivvy was now thumping the Bible with his hand. "Don't you understand, Captain? Goldnose is 91 and Cowl is 53. That's 144. It's all in the Bible. And the Beast, that's the worst of it. I've got to find out who the Beast is, that number: 666. I'm working on it. If you divide 666 by 144, that gives us the fourth chapter, sixth verse ... Look, here it is. No, here it is. We subtract, then ... and ... and ... Captain – don't you understand? IT'S THE END OF THE WORLD!"

"Here! Belay that, Skivvy. Here now," said the Captain sternly. He had taken a moment aside to fetch the bottle of brandy. Now he put a glass into Skivvy's hand and poured a stiff measure. "Now drink this, man, and put a steady hand on yourself. How do you mean me to understand anything, coming at me with all this arithmetic and talk about the end of the world? You've been working too hard, and looking into that Bible too much. By heaven, you could use a little bit of *Mother Goose*, and I'd put it in your hands if I could find it..."

"*Mother Goose*," Skivvy whispered to himself. He had by now become quick at mental arithmetic. "That's 79 and 61, which is 140. That's almost the same as Goldnose and Cowl added together! Then we add 4 because of, because of, of ... the Four Horsemen of the Apocalypse ... and that's 144 exactly! Can't you see it, Captain? Everything's falling into place. It's the end! We've got to turn back, or we're doomed! It's in the Bible!"

The Captain laid a hand on his shoulder and shook him. "Skivvy, belay that! The *Locust* is a plain ship manned by plain men, sea dogs, maybe, but no locusts. We don't need a prophet to tell us we're on a dangerous voyage. No more of that. Forget your smoke and mountains. Toss that brandy down. We're men, Skivvy, not numbers, and I believe we can die as men without the company of the whole world dying with us. There are no locusts on that pirate ship, but only men. We may have cannon to fear, but no burning mountain. Blood, aye, there may be blood, but I daresay we can stand the sight of some blood. Put a grip on the wheel, Skivvy. Mind your helm, shipmate! Come now, drink down that brandy and we'll light our pipes and talk this over. And as to the Bible, we'll have it into the conversation with us, but let us turn to hope, Skivvy, and not despair."

The Captain turned the pages of the Bible. "The Psalms, Skivvy, that's where we'll get our lesson, I believe. Here now, Psalm number 11, this is the sort of text we follow on. 'In the Lord put I my trust ...'"

Just at that moment, the squirrel again called out from the masthead.

"Land ho! Land ho!"

Skivvy stared listlessly at the Bible as if he had not heard. The Captain jumped up, took his telescope in hand, and paused for a moment to give Skivvy's shoulder a steady grip. Then he hurried out on deck. The squirrel had been watching that single cloud that he had mistaken for a sail. Now at last he saw that it was not a cloud, but a great pillar of smoke rising from a mountain just visible on the horizon.

"Vulcan Island!" said Mister Cloud, handing the Captain the glass. "Vulcan Island, Captain. We might have known it. A volcano, by gad! A volcanic island named after Vulcan, the god of fire."

"Right you are, Mister Cloud," said the Captain, again looking towards the island through the glass. He was silent for a moment as his thoughts measured back to what Skivvy had just read to him from the Bible: "... and as it were a great mountain burning with fire was cast into the sea..." He roved his sight along the horizon, then shook his head and thumped the telescope shut.

"But no locusts in sight," he muttered.

"Pardon, Captain?"

"What? Oh, give out the news, Mister Cloud, that we are near the gold," said the Captain, sticking the telescope in his belt. "And a ration of rum all around. And you might raise a cheer for the voyage, a cheer for the crew, and a cheer for the gold treasure."

The crew cheered lustily when the measure of rum was given all around. The Captain saw the Bad Sister forward near the bow of the ship. He caught her eye for a moment, and she seemed to nod at him, as if in reminder of their bargain, for one half of the gold treasure was hers.

Below, in the Captain's cabin, Skivvy had put down his glass of brandy and moved to the port window. For a minute he stared at the great pillar of smoke. Then he

[243]

walked to the drawer the Captain had indicated and took out the pistol. Finding also powder and shot, he loaded and primed the weapon. All was coming about: the prophecy was correct and his numbering was true. First the locusts, and now the great mountain burning with fire. Next would come a third of the sea turned to blood. But Skivvy was going to step in before that doom came upon them. The pistol was loaded and ready. Skivvy was determined to go on deck and forcefully take over the ship in order to save it. They must turn the *Ariel* away from the search for the gold treasure before it was too late. Soon the *Locust* would be upon them, and then the Beast would arise out of the sea, and then they would be doomed. He took a step towards the door. He heard the shout of the crew as they received their rum, and the three cheers, and then a cheer for Vulcan Island.

Skivvy stopped. "Vulcan Island," he said to himself. "That's 73 and then 59. That's 132. Hmmmm." he lowered the pistol and stood there musing. "Or subtract 59 from 73 and that's 14. Twice 7, that's lucky." He looked down at the gun in his hand. "'They that take the sword shall perish with the sword,'" he said. Nonetheless, he stuck the pistol in his belt and took up his Bible and papers, mumbling to himself as he walked out on deck. "Or divide 79 by 53. Is that it? No, but multiply, I mean." Attempting the mental arithmetic to find that product, he walked past the Captain without comment and went to his own cabin. The Captain followed Skivvy with a worried look, but he was upon business that needed his attention.

The product of 53 times 79 is 4187, Skivvy found out as soon as he could get a pen in hand. So therefore, upon a doubtful logic, and blind to other errors, he then subracted 41 from 87, which is 46. There is no chapter 46 in the Book of Revelation, so upon memory of the Captain's mention of

the Book of Psalms, Skivvy turned to the Forty-sixth Psalm
and read aloud:

"*God is our refuge and strength, a very present help
in trouble.*
"*Therefore will not we fear, though the earth be
removed, and though the mountains be carried into
the midst of the sea.*"

Skivvy looked up for a minute, puzzled.
"The mountain – not to be feared? But – the locusts . . .?"
He took a fresh sheet of paper. This would take some
study. He took up his pen again, touched his lip in thought,
then wrote down the number of Vulcan Island at the top of
the page, 132. He added the numbers of the *Ariel* and the
Locust. Skivvy had spent the previous night in company
with the Wayward Daughter. He would spend this night
with her also.

Now, there was a witness to the scene between the
Captain and Skivvy when they sat at the table with the
Bible between them. Davy Duck, who took close notice of
all that happened aboard the *Ariel*, had seen Skivvy
approach the Captain. When the two men went to the
Captain's cabin, Davy had slipped over the afterdeck
railing unnoticed and taken up a place beside the stern
windows, which were both pegged open. He had heard the
entirety of Skivvy's worried calculations. Now he slipped
back onto the deck and paced up and down, whittling out a
small wooden sword, pondering how he might use Skivvy's
fears to his own advantage. If the second mate's mind could
be turned against his Captain . . .? Davy Duck walked and
pondered. Perhaps, Davy thought, he should do some
reading in the Bible. But he never got around to it.

CHAPTER THIRTY-THREE

> *Blind man, blind man,*
> *Sure you can't see?*
> *Turn around three times,*
> *And try to catch me.*
> *Turn east, turn west,*
> *Catch as you can,*
> *Did you think you'd caught me?*
> *Blind, blind man!*

T he sure and steady wind that had blown for days now quitted the *Ariel*. Her sails slacked, and by middle afternoon hardly a ghost of wind moved the ship. The *Ariel* could not expect to reach Vulcan Island that afternoon. As night approached, the Captain decided to lay well off from the island, as a caution against unknown rocks or reefs. The ship was brought around. Her sails were pressed aback, and her spare anchor was loosed from the cathead and let fall. Sails were furled to the yards and the quiet night threw its drape over the sea.

Below decks, Skivvy was passionately engaged with the Wayward Daughter. His swaying lamp cast circling shadows about his cabin. Outside could be heard the lapping of water on the ship's hull, the ringing of the ship's bell each half hour, calling out the time. His table was disordered with sheaves of paper scribbled upon. The dipping of his quill pen into his inkpot was like the quick drinking nod of a bird's beak into a black-water well. Captain Kimberly's great Bible was open before him. Skivvy's face was of keen aspect, his eyes narrowed like to some David regarding a Goliath with a fearful yet calculating wonder. The greatest deceit of the Wayward Daughter was yet to come upon him.

All hands were on deck until late. The crew marched up and down, talking and bending their backs to look up at the great cloud of steam and smoke that welled straight up out of the mountain in the still air. It was like a tall white pillar of a temple so gigantic that the next pillar was out of sight. And as if they were on the doorstep of a temple, the animals tended to whisper out of reverence and awe.

More so, it was eerie and strange that the volcano did not rumble, but poured forth its wondrous plume all in silence. Nor was there a brim of fire at the high mouth of the volcano.

At last the crew retired. A single watchman was set and the decks of the *Ariel* were otherwise abandoned, except for the Captain, who could not sleep and had just come awake from a troubled dream. Earlier, he had rapped on Skivvy's door out of worry over his friend's agitated behaviour, but Skivvy had not answered. Now again he went to Skivvy's door and knocked. No answer. Quietly, he spoke Skivvy's name, but the second mate did not answer, as if by silence protecting his hermitage from intrusion, no doubt advancing himself in his thoughts of doom. So the Captain gained the deck again and paced up and down, considering the day to come.

The Captain now remembered the strange dream that had brought him awake. He dreamed he was in a long, green corridor. It was narrow and slippery underfoot, so that he had trouble keeping his step. Yet he continued along, for behind he heard a crashing sound, as if the corridor were breaking up and caving in behind him. Presently he passed an arm, a detached arm. He recognized it as belonging to Skivvy. It was a long underwear arm. He picked it up and continued along. Then he came upon the leg of a doll. It was Amy's leg. He picked this up also, increasingly concerned, for he must find the parts to which these members attached. Yet behind him the crashing became louder and closer. He hurried on. Far in the distance he could see a golden glow. The crashing behind him came closer, and he started to walk faster, then to trot. Next he came upon another leg of Skivvy. He stooped to pick it up, and saw also that there were arms, legs, and torsos of toy animals strewn all about. He was going to pick them all up to mend them to their owners, but directly behind him the corridor crashed in.

He started running in panic, dropping even the arm and leg he carried, his eye on the far end of the corridor where the golden light shone. He was certain that if he could reach that place, everything would be all right. But the corridor was falling in behind him. He ran faster. Then, in his way, he saw Amy's eyes lying before him. Yet if he stopped running he would be destroyed. He ran past Amy's eyes towards the golden light. It was closer, and closer still, and at the very nip of his heels the corridor fell and crumbled. Then he woke up.

What could it mean? The Captain thought of the word he had used when he had convinced Skivvy to take the voyage. Destiny. He did feel that. The voyage seemed to him a fulfilment, the absolutely necessary and right thing to undertake. The recovery of the golden treasure, all of it: that might have been the golden light of the dream. But following in his track was there destruction, the destruction of Amy, Skivvy, and the crew, as in the dream? Destiny it might be, but was it drawing him on to destroy the *Ariel*? Was the golden glow an evil that was making him forget the safety of those he loved? Was he tainted, as true men were — for he was a true man now — was he tainted with love for gold? But yet that golden light had seemed so promising.

For an hour the Captain walked, carrying his anxiety alone as he strolled the deck, alone as only a commander can be alone. Was the treasure worth the risk? Goldnose was nearby, perhaps even now sailing towards Vulcan Island. Every soul on the ship might be lost in that encounter. Was the dream telling him this — everyone hacked to pieces by the pirates? And what if he should lose Amy's eyes, for he had no other plan than to let them down in a bottle to search for the treasure? Was the treasure worth any risk at all? Why not sail away immediately? Let Mister Cloud and the Bad Sister have the ship. He and Amy could run for it when they got to land. Skivvy's fears — could there be anything in that at all? Was Vulcan Island the mountain in Revelation? Would a Beast rise out of the sea? The sea turn to blood? The end of the world? Maybe, anyway, the world of the *Ariel*?

The Captain stood alone with his troubles, staring at the quiet, dark water. At last he jerked his head erect and shook himself. Away with doubt! He was not made a Captain without cause. He knew how to make a decision. He slapped both hands on the railing. So be it that Mister Cloud sang love songs to the Bad Sister and had some secret plot! So be it that the crew might be mutinous if called to it by that pair! So be it that Skivvy seemed to be losing the sound use of his mind! So be it that the *Locust* might be on the morning's horizon! So be it ... even had the Captain known that at that very minute Davy Duck was raising a mutinous crew below decks. So be it! They had come for gold treasure. This was the heart of the voyage. And gold treasure they would search for, come reef

[249]

or wave, mountain or mutiny. That was his destiny. He would search it out no matter what the dangers.

The Captain straightened his back and settled his hands on the railing, looking off towards Vulcan Island. Two bells sounded. It was 1 A.M. of the middle watch. The Captain leaned his head back, measuring upward the great pillar of smoke reaching into the dark sky. Yet what was it that Skivvy had said? ". . . a great mountain burning with fire . . . and the third part of the sea became blood"? No! The Captain shook his head. He would examine it no further.

As he looked down again, his eyes caught a motion forward of the main mast. Someone on deck. Was that Skivvy? The Captain pushed himself away from the rail and walked leisurely towards where the figure had disappeared around the galley. Well, if not Skivvy – someone. The Captain felt in need of company, and here was someone to say a word to, someone with whom to share at least a word on the weather, a familiar topic of common interest to all men of every station, the very cradle of converse, a topic having the familiar comfort of generalities with reputations that go back to the flood, with pedigrees from the very stables and rooms of Noah's Ark itself. Talk about the weather makes a bond of fellowship even between king and beggar. So the Captain approached the figure. And then he saw it fully, standing near the rail forward of the main hold. It was a figure, seen dimly but surely, of someone in a cloak with the hood pulled forward on the head, looking off towards Vulcan Island.

The Captain paused in half step, and the chambers of his memory flung open three doors. Inside the first door the Captain saw the hooded figure that had followed him in the streets of New Liberty when he had first docked the *Ariel*. Inside the second door he saw this same hooded figure on horseback, the one who had followed the Bad Sister in the charge past the carriage. Inside the third door the Captain saw the figure standing nearby in the Riptide Tavern as the Captain was forced to the duty of carrying the Bad Sister aboard the ship. The Captain put a hand to his pistol, the other to his sword, and let his foot fall to complete his step, thumping it against a cleat. The hooded figure started, and in a flow of robe ducked low and ran behind the galley. The Captain cried out, stumbling forward.

"Ho! Stand, there!"

But the figure was out of sight. The Captain drew his sword and ran to the corner of the galley around which the hooded figure had disappeared. He awaited the encounter. No one. He then chased completely around the galley, paused, then chased around in the opposite direction. Nothing. He searched the ship fore and aft with his eyes, looked to the fo'c'sle companionway, and in his exasperation, anger, apprehension, and confusion made directly down the ladderway and pounded with his pistol on the door of the Bad Sister's cabin.

"Open!" he cried. "Open, or by heaven I'll break down the door!"

A bustle and a bang came from inside, and a curse of a general nature. The door gave noises of latches and locks. It was opened slightly, but the Captain put a foot on it and kicked it fully back so that the Bad Sister was almost knocked off her feet as she avoided the swing of it. Clutching her long French knife, she stood trembling, wrapped about in a blue robe. The Captain stood facing her with sword and pistol in hand.

"Ah-ha!" cried the Bad Sister boldly, but with nervousness in her voice. "I should have known. It's the way of you seagoing swine. If love songs don't do the trick, you come for a lady's favours at swordpoint. Well, if you think I've no virtue to defend, you're wrong, Captain." She stood there swinging her long knife from side to side. She hadn't her black wig on, but her hair fell forward to mask her face. The Captain ignored her. In a very short time he had made a complete round of the small cabin, kicking, poking, and making discovery into every nook that might contain a person. Satisfied that they were alone in the room, the Captain turned his attention to the woman.

"Yes, what is it now, Captain?" she said. "Have you come to sing me another pretty song after all? Hang me if I don't get more attention than a real lady aboard this ship."

"Just so, madam, and a hanging it may come to," said the Captain. He was high-blooded at the moment, and he put the case to the Bad Sister without smoothing it out. "I've better reason to instruct you to contemplate the gallows than ever you had to ask the same of me, in point of a hanging offence. I believe I know your plot, madam, and I know the person you are plotting with, and I tell you as plainly as the matter can be put – I am the Captain of this ship, and I will brook no rebellion. If you but raise a hand to mutiny, I will have you confined in chains, woman or not, until we put into port again, and I will see you through trial and even to dock where they will hang you."

The Bad Sister had lowered her knife. Only her narrowed eyes were visible to the Captain, peering out from the strands of her hair stringing across her face. It passed the Captain's mind very quickly that somehow she did not look like the same woman as the Bad Sister – a notion that was so quickly gone that the Captain did not reflect on it at that moment. He sheathed his sword and stuck his pistol in his belt.

"Furthermore, madam, raise no hope that your villainous 'shadow,' as you once called it, will find another day's stowaway aboard this ship. And if you have discourse with that shadow before daylight, you might say that every room and closet, barrel and pot, crate and canister, will be searched with bare blades point foremost on the morrow, and if that shadow bleeds real blood it will suffer grievously to be found at the end of my sword, that I assure you. Therefore, surrender it up before the sun rises or blame yourself for whatever may follow."

With that, the Captain strode out of the door. Above decks, the hooded figure, the shadow, had since scrambled down the ratlines leading to the foremast, into which rigging it had leaped and climbed when the Captain had made his surprise upon it, and had lain pressed against the mast as the Captain wheeled his search around the galley. Now all was again quiet on deck. The Captain passed to his cabin, fairly growling. The hooded figure then dropped to the deck, and in a few minutes went below.

CHAPTER THIRTY-FOUR

Arise, arise, pull out your eyes,
And hear what time of day;
And when you have done, pull out your tongue,
And see what you can say.

hen morning came, the Captain gave orders that raised the ship into an eruption such that every inner part of it was thrown up or thrust aside from its place as the entire crew was turned out to discover the stowaway, swords in hands and instructed to strike down any resistance.

Davy Duck contrived to find his duty near the magazine locker where he kept his ducks. He entered there alone while a cat stood at the small doorway holding a lantern.

"Just room for one of us in here, shipmate," Davy advised, entering the place. Davy jammed his sword about into the corners, overturning kegs and kicking at crates, while with one foot he carefully shoved the sailcloth nest of his ducks out of sight. "Heyyyy!" he yelled, at the same time swinging wildly with his cutlass and taking a chunk of wood from an overhead beam. Then putting his sword on guard again, he commented to the cat, "Only a rat, mate, but I thought I had the lubber's head. No, he can't be in here. But crowd yourself in if ye want to take a swing at a rat. I'll hold the lantern."

But the cat was convinced that the job had been done, and they made their way back to larger parts of the ship.

The other animals, sweating from their exertions on the search into every small part of the ship, and even into the Bad Sister's oven and bread box, were assembling again on deck and enjoying a cool breeze that promised another vast and blue day. They gave the Captain their answers to the search in such round certainty that the Captain must be satisfied that no hiding place was left to the hooded figure unless it was indeed as flat as a shadow and could be folded like a towel and stuck under a mattress, or hung on a peg in disguise during the daylight hours.

During the search, the Captain had found reason to stay close to Mister Cloud, engaging him in conversation even though the mate wanted to go below to help ferret out this mysterious figure the Captain had described to him and the crew.

"Mister Cloud, I believe I haven't told you how I intend to find that treasure. Yes, I'll be wanting you to instruct the crew. You see, Amy's eyes are able to see even when they're detached from her body. Yes, you may look surprised, but it's the truth. This is basic to the whole plan. First I'll snip them off and put them in a bottle. Then ..." As he spoke, the Captain kept an eye on the Bad Sister, who took up her place forward. With arms folded inside her great cloak, she kept watch towards Vulcan Island that morning, and the great tower of smoke that rose from it. The Captain studied her. Now – what was that fleeting notion he'd had about her the night before in her cabin? He narrowed his eyes and bit his lip, but he couldn't remember.

Before noon, the *Ariel* had been so closely pried into that pin or button, if either had been the object of the search, might not have found a private place to hide but that it would have been found. When the crew returned to their proper duties, the anchor was hauled to the cathead and the *Ariel* approached Vulcan Island. Both monkeys were aloft with keen eyes watching for rock or reef.

Before they had sailed fully around the island, it was obvious to a near certainty that they would find no harbour. Every shore was pitched steeply with volcanic out-croppings. Past that surrounding rock wall, the island for a mile or two inland was covered with scrubby trees and a dense front of bush. Beyond that, the mountain itself rose steeply to a height of some three thousand feet. The island itself was approximately circular in shape, perhaps some five or six miles in diameter. One might suppose a ship-wrecked man could not live long in such a place, for surely there would be no large game on the island, although birds were in profusion. Yet otherwise they saw no sign of life. The Captain stood with the treasure map in hand, glancing from it to the shores. He called Mister Cloud's attention to the X marked on the map, below which was the writing, "Captain Cowl all hands." The *Ariel* was now at about that place where the X was marked. A hundred yards or so away there jutted up a large rock, the size of a manor house, peaked at the top and supporting a great colony of gulls and other seabirds that milled about it, abandoning and again reclaiming a place on the rock in a fit of restlessness, while the chorus of their crying and screeching fairly drove a wind out from their fortress.

"This could be the place, Mister Cloud. There, that rock. You see that the X is marked here, in the sea itself. Cowl might well have struck that very rock. The prevailing winds would argue for that. If he were looking for harbourage in a storm, he would have sailed to the lee of the island, to this place. Possibly he broke up on that bird rock and sank with all hands. Do you like the opinion?"

"Aye, that *could* be the story, Captain," said the first mate, leaning over the map. He then looked towards the island and the rock indicated. "One of the crew might have got to the island and sent out that bottle. Yes, that's possible. I wonder if the chap's still alive."

"Not likely," said the Captain, scanning the island. "It's been ten years and more since Cowl disappeared. No, I wouldn't say it would be likely that a man could live on the side of that teapot for long. However, if there's a spring of fresh water ... But I wouldn't know, and we've got no sign of him in any case." Slowly, the *Ariel* approached the bird rock.

"In the South Seas I knew such an island that had a volcano," said the first mate. "The natives had lived under it for generations. They called the mountain a god, they did, and they prayed to it and threw sacrifices into it. Now, I was a young man when I first saw that island, and it came about that I was there again in my middle years. Aye, we came up on that same island for water, twenty years later, it was. Well, the Captain of that ship was a fine navigator. He had a sextant with nine jewels in it, and I'd swear to the Big Dipper that we crossed that exact place two or three times, but never found that island. So there's another one of the lost gods, you may say. Finally, I suppose, it blew itself away, or maybe sank into the sea again."

The Captain frowned and nodded, looking at the great spout of the mountain. "I don't mind saying, Mister Cloud, that it makes me somewhat uncomfortable being this close to it. I suppose we'd hear some rumblings if it was collecting itself for an explosion."

"Aye, Captain," said Mister Cloud. He looked off towards the bird rock. "I'd suggest, sir, that we shouldn't lay in any closer to that rock."

"Right, Mister Cloud," said the Captain. "The rest of the work will be done with the ship's boat. Drop anchor, then, lower the ship's boat, and take a sounding for depth. I'll be on deck presently."

"Aye, Captain."

While Mister Cloud handled this business, the Captain went to his cabin and propped Amy up on his table.

"Now, Sis, you've got to relax and trust me," said the Captain, as he rummaged through a drawer and tossed some clothes out onto the deck of the cabin. "Ah, here it is. See, Sis, this is the very bottle that had the treasure map inside of it." He held the green bottle up for Amy to look at. Then he took a coil of thin line and sat down. He talked as he wove and knotted a sturdy harness for the bottle. "Plenty of line here, Sis, since we don't know how deep you'll have to go down. We'll take no chances the bottle will come loose, be sure of that. This is all going to work fine, and the credit is all yours. If you hadn't dropped my ear on the floor when I came to life back at St. Anne's, I wouldn't have thought of this. But remember how I heard that mouse sniffing around by that ear? The same thing with your eyes, I'm sure. With your eyes in the bottle you'll be able to see, and since your body will be with me, you'll be able to tell me when you find the gold treasure."

The Captain pulled at his knots, finished the harness, and dangled the bottle to test it. "We'll fill the bottle with water so it'll sink, Sis. Whatever you see down there on the bottom might be a bit watery, but gold gleams bright no matter how long it's been in the sea, and a sunken ship is a large sight to see, all the timbers and ribs of it like the gigantic skeleton of a fish. That's what you'll see if we have the luck of it. That's the plan, Sis. Then we'll fix up some way to dive down for the gold and scoop it up."

The Captain smiled at Amy, and got a pitcher of water. He filled up the bottle and set a cork aside to stop it up with. He then drew his sword and cupped Amy's head in his hands.

"Time's come, Sis. First I snip off your eyes, and then stick you in the head with this needle. Then you'll be yourself again, at least so much that you'll be able to talk. Oh yes, still a doll, but a real person in just a short while. Of course, we'll have your eyes sewn back on when that happens, or otherwise you wouldn't have any eyes. But there'll be time for that. Those animals came around out of being dolls very quickly, almost right away, but real people take longer."

The Captain slipped the blade of his sword behind one of Amy's button eyes, then the other, and they fell into his hand. Then out of his palm he took each blue eye and dropped each into the bottle, and they settled to the bottom. Taking up his needle, then, he put the point of it to Amy's temple and quickly darted it in and out of her head. She gave a cry of pain, and spoke.

"Captain! I'm here again. I can feel! I can talk!"

The Captain hugged her, and the affection of reunion was settled out in a few minutes. He set the cork and thumped it in place, and then held the bottle up close to his face.

"This is very strange, Captain," said Amy. "There you are, dear brother, and there I am in your arms. I can even see my mouth talking. It *is* peculiar, you know."

"You'll get used to it, Sis. The mind wanders miles and miles away sometimes, but then comes back home, so what's a few yards away for your eyes in a bottle?"

"Captain," said Amy, remembering some urgent business. "I must tell you something. There's a mutiny being planned against the ship. The other day when I was lying on the hatch ..."

"Listen," said the Captain, raising a hand and looking

upwards. One of the animals had sent a weighted line to the bottom to find the depth and called out, "Three fathoms on the mark." A pause. "Four fathoms on the mark." Another pause. "Full fathom five."

"Yes, Sis, I know all about that," said the Captain. He took Amy under one arm with his bottle, and coiled the line about his wrist. "There's nothing for it now, Sis. That mutiny has been brewing for some time. Up on deck, there's our business now, and onward to the gold treasure."

And so the Captain missed his chance to hear about Davy Duck's plans for mutiny, for he supposed that Amy was going to tell him about the plot between Mister Cloud and the Bad Sister. As for Amy, she supposed that the Captain must already know about Davy Duck's plans, and she did not mention it again.

Mister Cloud had told the crew what the Captain was going to attempt. They stood about with interest in the project. Skivvy was there, also, looking very worried. The Bad Sister was out and nearby the main place of action, too. She seemed to be made up with powder and rouge over-much this morning. The Captain glanced at her for a second, trying to call up the notion of the night before when he burst into her room. Something about her eyes, was it? Yes, now he had it. It was her eyes that were different. And her hair, of course, since she was wearing no wig then. And why should she, since she had a full head of long auburn hair? That was it. She was not a woman as old as the Bad Sister appeared to be, but much younger.

"What a stupid thing to do with a pair of button eyes," she said to the Captain, putting him off his reflections. "I volunteer Greensleeves for the job. I mean this worthless frog. Stuff him full of small shot and let him over on a hook."

The frog, standing beside her, grinned foolishly and nodded his head, ready with heart and hand to do her bidding. He hadn't his dishcloth in hand to wring, so almost unconsciously he reached out for her skirt to employ his hands, and the Bad Sister socked him on the top of his head with her ladle for his forwardness.

"Do you hear, Captain?" she continued. "That's a terrible risk. There must be another way." The woman sounded quite anxious, her voice softened in her pleas. But the Captain ignored her. He was looking at the green bottle in his hands. It flashed through his mind that this was the narrow green corridor of his dream. Yes, a corridor with rounded sides. Now it came to him. And wet underfoot, of course. And at the end, the golden light. His destiny! The Captain gripped the bottle tightly. He had no more doubts. This was the way. The dream was true. He must go past his fears towards the golden glow, and all would be made right. His destiny!

The Captain put a leg over the ship's railing and steadied himself on the first step of the Jacob's ladder leading down to the ship's boat. The dogs were at the oars, one of them half standing to aid the Captain into the boat.

"Five fathoms," said Mister Cloud.

"Very good, Mister Cloud," said the Captain, handing the bottle and doll to a reaching dog. He had a fifty-foot coil of line around his wrist. Five fathoms is thirty feet only.

"The bottom seems fair level, Captain, but I think the lead was hanging up on rocks now and then."

"Or perhaps on the timbers of Cowl's ship, Mister Cloud," said the Captain brightly.

"Whatever, Captain, I'd drag along slowly, as it wouldn't do to foul up. There's a strong current down there also. I'm thinking you could lose the bottle, Captain.

Thirty feet is a deep dive for a man. I can't say I've got the wind for it anymore."

"That's good advice," replied the Captain. "I'll go slowly. If we find the treasure, I'll hold the boat in place and we'll anchor the ship over the spot. Watch for my signal. We'll search this side of the bird rock first, then make a slow circuit around it."

So saying, the Captain set his foot in the small boat and seated himself at the stern, taking the tiller in hand. The dogs let go the painter and pushed off from the *Ariel* with a boat hook. The animals at the railings got off a cheer for the adventure.

The Bad Sister did not cheer, but said aloud, "What a stupid thing to do. What a stupid chance to take with Amy's ..." She stopped talking, noticing Skivvy standing nearby. She said to him. "Amy — that's the little girl's name, isn't it?"

Skivvy said nothing. He was shaking his head and muttering to himself. "And a Beast will arise from the sea ..." The Bad Sister looked away.

"He must be mad," she said, looking at the boat pulling away from the ship. "What a stupid thing to do with Amy's eyes."

"A Beast crowned with gold will arise from the sea," muttered Skivvy. "A Golden Beast."

"What are you doing, you green wad?" said the Bad Sister to the frog, giving him a kick. "Make yourself useful. Wait! Yes. Go and tie some string around your middle. Then eat about a pound of nuts and bolts." The frog bobbed his head and started to run off. "No! Forget that," said the Bad Sister, looking away at the boat again. "It's too late. He's just put the bottle over the side. Oh, that stupid man!"

The dogs at the oars skilfully rowed the boat around the

bird rock. The Captain dragged the bottle across the bottom, but sounded out no sunken ship. Holding Amy cradled in one arm he slipped the line through his hands, letting the bottle run the bottom with the delicate touch of a fisherman. Amy reported all the while.

"It's mostly all flat down here, Captain. And it *is* dark looking through this green bottle. Maybe a jam jar would be better. There, now, a big fish just swam by and looked in at me. There he goes. Oh, there's a rock in our way. Oop! Well, we bounced off it. And now – oh, how lovely. A whole cloud of silver fishes is passing all around me, like hundreds of tiny mirrors. There they go. My eyes do tumble around in here, Captain, and I can't always look where I want to look. Now it's like a light green sky above me. That dark shape must be the boat I'm in. My, what a strange thing to say."

"Now, Sis, you've got to keep looking at the bottom. What you're looking for is timber, or cannon, or maybe the bones of pirates, or most of all the sight of gold. If the ship held together there would be no mistaking it at all, but watch closely because we wouldn't want the line to get tangled in its ribs."

"Yes, Captain. Oh, look, now here we are among some sea flowers. Sea anomalies, I think they're called. And there's kelp, too. Now I'm in a sort of weedy place and I can't see anything. Bring me up a bit, Captain."

The Captain took in some line. "Let me know when you've passed over that kelp bed, Sis."

The bottle twisted in the current, tumbling Amy's eyes about. And then came the call that men have destroyed their bodies and sold their souls to hear, the call that has presumption even to rise above the call of God's name, the call that crowns the kings of the world and saves all but the dead.

"Gold!" Amy cried. "Gold! It's the treasure, Captain, I've found it!"

"Where, Amy, where?" the Captain cried. "Shall I let go the line? Are you directly over it? Is it the ship? Amy!"

"Oh no. It's gone, Captain. But was it up or down? I'm getting dizzy. My eyes are tumbling all about. This is so confusing. But it was something golden, Captain. It was above me, I think. Yes, the light was above it."

"Ah, Amy, it was a fish."

"No, Captain, not a fish. It was real gold. I could see it flashing by. But now I'm looking down again. Oh, now there's a great crack in the ocean floor. Hold me, Captain, don't let me fall now, I'm right above a deep canyon!"

"Hold there," said the Captain to the dogs. "Backwater oars. We're close to something, mates. Amy, tell me about this gold thing again ..."

But there was no need to tell. Because at that moment there came two hands over the bow of the boat, two golden hands, all beringed on every finger with golden rings, set with brilliant jewel stones of ruby, sapphire, diamond, and emerald.

The dogs gave a shout of alarm. The Captain gaped at the sight. Next was seen the golden crown of a golden head, then golden arms with bracelets of gold, gold biceps and gold shoulder, as a man pulled himself out of the sea and into the boat. He sat on the bow thwart taking his breath in heaving gulps and staring with an expression of alarm at the two dogs at the oars.

On board the *Ariel*, all the animals stood at the railing in silent wonder. The Bad Sister was also speechless, looking on with her mouth open. Only Skivvy said a word.

"Out of the sea! The Beast! 'Yet I will distress Ariel, and there shall be heaviness and sorrow.' The Golden Beast!"

CHAPTER THIRTY-FIVE

There was once a fish.
  (What more could you wish?)
He lived in the sea.
  (Where else would he be?)
He was caught on a line.
  (Whose line if not mine?)
So I brought him to you.
  (What else could I do?)

H e was a man in his middle years, a man of flesh and blood to be sure, with golden hair and a golden beard. His skin was tanned golden by the sun. He glistened in the sunlight in his golden rings and bracelets. Golden necklaces, and a golden girdle about his waist. And the image of him rising out of the sea, sparkling in the sunlight, thereafter caused him to be called the Golden Man when the animals discussed him among themselves. He was otherwise wearing only a loose pair of shorts, evidently made from a scrap of old sailcloth. He now looked to the Captain, getting his wind, and, eye to eye, mouths wide open, he and the Captain stared at each other with a wild surmise.

Then the Golden Man glanced at the *Ariel* and spied the gathered animals all crowding the railings, all looking in equal wonder back at him. At last he beat the side of his head to bang the water from his ears, and as if the pounding brought him out of his thrall, he spoke.

"Well, bless me! Ten years I've been alone on that island, and I tell you straight, mate," said he, addressing the Captain over the heads of the dogs, "I tell you straight, mate, my imagination must have improved with the solitude." The Golden Man looked back and forth at the dogs, then addressed himself to the Captain again. "Are you the Captain of that ship, for you do have the look of a Captain? Aye? Then you'll excuse me, sir, in saying that our mates here at the oars look to me like dogs, and that there gang at the railings like a seagoing barnyard. No offence, no offence," he quickly added, raising his hand. "I take it for my own fault, some delirium that's come out of my loneliness mayhap. But even if it's so – and those are real dogs at the oars – I'd sail with you to leave this place, and I've got payment for the passage. Ten years, Captain, ten long years! Aye, day by day every week and month of it, I been shipwrecked on that island. Aye, and I'd put off in the belly of a whale to leave it, I would, and get my foot on a true shore again. But look here, maybe there's been another flood and you're like as to some Noah with his Ark looking to start a new world. No?"

He left very little room for the Captain to express his own astonishment, but most of his questions were answered as the Golden Man continued upon his history. During the narration, he began slipping off and unfixing himself of rings, bracelets, golden belt, and every golden ornament that hung on him, except for his golden earrings.

"Aye, Captain, I'll pay for my passage and be happy for it. If animals have come along these past ten years to be like human beings, I'm game for it. Ten years, Captain! I'd share the same plate with a pig and drink out of the same cup as a goat, for I'm sick of the look of my own footprints and the sound of my own voice, and I'm sick of the sight of gold, as there's not one minute of loneliness that it cures."

The Golden Man had been throwing his gold jewellery into the bottom of the boat. Now the Captain got in a question.

"Then you're one of Cowl's men? It was you who put out the map in the bottle?"

"So it is, Captain, the famous and bloody Cowl, and I was his sailmaker. On first raising sight of you this morning, I figured you for pirates. That's why I came dressed in gold. See, then you wouldn't kill me straightaway, but wait to know if I had any more of it hid away. Aye, and that I do. But I see you're not pirates." The Golden Man kicked a bare foot at the pile of gold at his feet. "I've got gold enough on that island to fill this boat, Captain. That's to pay my way on your ship. You're a clever map reader, that's the truth. Right now you're drifting over the very place where Cowl and all hands went down. Aye, we smashed on that rock in a storm and sank in minutes. It was all yelling and drowning after that. I was the only one to reach the island. But there's no gold left down there, Captain, none you could hook or haul up with that line you're fishing with."

"Then you've got the treasure?" asked the Captain. "You've brought it up by yourself?"

"Not all. Ten years I've been swimming out here, taking it back to the island little by little, and now and then a skull to keep me company, you know, to set up on a stick to pass the time of day talking with. That's so I wouldn't forget my own language, 'cause I've heard that can happen. And there's comfort in a human skull that even gold can't give you." The Golden Man leaned over and spat into the water. "Aye, gone to bones, every one of 'em. Not a shipmate lived, but only me. But you see that mountain? It's not easy living under a volcano. It could blow up your whole world at any minute, maybe. It's nothing you'd want to spend any time thinking about, so I collected gold to take my mind off it. Aye, gold's a bright thing to take your mind off the time that your lights go out forever. And see that mountain again, Captain – it's come alive. Aye, just these past weeks there's been rumblings and earthquakes. The ocean floor right below us is split open. Down into that hole went every post and plank of Cowl's ship, and all the gold that was left. But never mind, for you shall have this boat full of gold. And never mind for myself, as I wouldn't argue for an ounce of it. Take it all and only give me passage on your ship. I'll sleep on deck and eat bread and water to get back to the real world, for I've got family business that's long overdue."

This said, the Golden Man was content to be quiet and suffer the Captain's judgment on the case. But the Captain's first attention was to Amy.

"Did you hear it all, Sis? It's one of Cowl's men. He says there's no more gold down there. I'm bringing you up." Then, looking at the ex-pirate, the Captain indicated the doll. "Oh, you should know that this is my sister, who is at the moment a doll, as you see. Her eyes are in a bottle down there looking for the gold treasure. But it seems we've found it, so up she comes."

"Oh, for God's sake, Captain," said the Golden Man, "spare me somewhat." He put his hands over his eyes and leaned back against the bows. "Don't tell me all at once how the world is nowadays. Try to suppose like I'm an innocent baby come new into the world. You'll want to give me some milky news to think on before telling me that dolls are coming to life. Be kindly, Captain, as I'm just getting used to the dogs, you understand."

The Captain nodded sympathetically and said, "Of course, I'll explain everything later." Then he shifted Amy beneath his arm to take a better grip on the line. In doing so, his fingers let slip the line and the bottle fell. The Captain grabbed at the line with his free hand, missed it, fumbled, and when at last he caught it, he felt a shock on the other end. Then it became weightless in his hand. At that moment Amy cried out.

"Captain, the bottle's fallen on a rock. It's broken!"

The Captain immediately dropped Amy into the bottom of the boat and hauled hand over hand on the line. In a dozen long hauls he had the end of the line out of the water. He stared at the limp netting that had cradled the bottle. Not a portion of the bottle remained. All the glass had dropped through and now lay on the bottom of the ocean floor with Amy's eyes.

"Amy!" the Captain cried out. He dropped the line and began tearing off his jacket.

"My eyes are lying in the sand, Captain. Pieces of the bottle are lying all around me. There's that big fish again, Captain, and he's looking at me. Oh, Captain ... and I'm right near the edge of that deep canyon!"

The Golden Man had risen out of his seat, and now, as the Captain threw his jacket aside and kicked off his boots, the Golden Man put his foot between the two dogs and crossed amidships to the Captain's end of the boat. He put a hand down to touch the doll. "Hand me that rope there under the thwart," said the Captain. "If I give two strong jerks, pull me up." The Captain then stripped off his shirt. "The rope, man, the rope!" But the Golden Man could only stare at him in perplexity for a second. Recovering himself, he threw the rope about his own waist and knotted it.

"Right you are, Captain. Two quick tugs, and pull me up. You'd never make it down there. Strong currents. I know 'em, and I'm strong from swimming after all that gold. Now, what is it, two eyes I'm diving after?"

"Button doll eyes, blue buttons," said the Captain, eager to be over the side himself, but seeing the wisdom in what the Golden Man said, and grateful that he should go instead. He took up the rope and let some loops fall free.

The Golden Man put a hand and a foot on the gunwale of the boat, took a deep breath, nodded at the Captain, and leaped into the water headfirst in a sprawling dive. Down he went, eyes open as he swam, fighting for depth. At about three fathoms he came upon the shear of a current, a layer of cold that swept at him and demanded double strength to stay in place below the boat on the surface. He turned his head to look upwards. He could see the dark shape of the boat as if it sailed in a light blue sky. He struggled with great sweeping breaststrokes to the very bottom of the ocean floor, and half swam, half crawled with grips on rocks and seaweed looking for the bottle and Amy's eyes. Then he saw the bottle, a few glints of bright green. In a few strokes, clutching at rocks and kelp, he was over the broken shards of glass. Then his face was above that ruin of glass. There in the centre were Amy's eyes, looking straight upwards. The Golden Man put out a hand to enclose them, and looked straight into Amy's eyes.

Above, the Captain felt a tug on the rope. A moment later there arose a great surge of bubbles. The Captain leaned back and hauled.

"Give a hand here," he shouted to the dogs. "Something's gone wrong. I'm pulling dead weight." And below, the Golden Man tumbled helplessly along the ocean floor, all breath gone out of him, unconscious and drowning.

All three hauled at the rope, pulling the Golden Man out of the depths. All were too busy to answer Amy, who called out, "What was that, Captain? Was that the Golden Man? He reached out for me, opened his mouth wide, and then he was gone. What happened, Captain? Oh, and there's that big fish again! That fish is looking at me, Captain!"

The Golden Man's head broke the surface of the water. One of the dogs grabbed him by his hair. The Captain took him by the arm, and between the three of them they hoisted the man over the side of the boat. He flopped and rolled onto his back and lay in the bottom of the boat without breathing. The golden colour of his face was turned pale yellow. The Captain quickly turned him over onto his stomach and began to pump at his ribs, but hardly before that situation could be improved on, Amy cried out again.

"Captain, that big fish has eaten my eyes! Captain, it's all dark! Captain, I'm inside the belly of a fish!"

CHAPTER THIRTY-SIX

For want of a nail, the shoe was lost,
For want of a shoe, the horse was lost,
For want of a horse, the rider was lost,
For want of a rider, the battle was lost,
For want of a battle, the kingdom was lost,
And all for the want of a horseshoe nail.

rowning *is a sort of drifting off*, a sort of comfort and ease, a sort of going gently to sleep, so say those who have nearly drowned but come back to speak of it. The pain of it is the coming back, when you must vomit up water and cough as if your lungs would split. Your bones chill and your head shoots thunder and lightning and your ears bang like kettledrums. The Golden Man was alive and suffering the pain of it. He was brought back to the ship alive, but with very little breath left in him. He now lay in Mister Cloud's cabin to recover, for it had the best access to the galley. The Bad Sister was keeping a brew of thin soup potioned with healing herbs to serve him. Every hour or two she looked in on the Golden Man, and ladled a spoonful of the broth into his mouth. Once, while he was sleeping, she stood beside the bed for a long while, studying him. Certain that his sleep was deep, she touched his cheek. Then she smoothed his hair. Outside his door, she took out her handkerchief and blew her nose.

The Golden Man opened his eyes once to look up at his

nurse, but the rawness of his throat prevented him from speaking. Now and then he retched into a pan at his bedside, which the frog attended to as his duty. The frog spoke to him as he dabbed the Golden Man's mouth with a clean cloth and settled his blanket.

"Oh, aren't you lucky? She's a wonderful nurse, isn't she? And a good cook. I'm her helper. Yes, and you'll be all right soon. They call her the Bad Sister, but she isn't, really. It's only her way. I go with her everywhere. We're just good friends, actually. She likes me."

The Golden Man closed his eyes on the frog and waited for further revelations. He remembered Mister Cloud, who had carried him down the ladderway. "You're welcome to the cabin," the first mate told him. "I'll bunk with the Captain. You'll get a nice breeze this side of the ship. Just give a call if you need anything."

The Captain, too, came in while the Golden Man was in a half waking state. He expressed his gratitude for the man's actions, which had nearly drowned him. Also, he told the Golden Man that Amy's eyes had been eaten by a fish, and that ... but the Golden Man seemed to be weak yet. The Captain promised to come back later with a full report of the ship's business.

On the deck of the *Ariel*, the ship was all commotion, for every small line aboard was tossed over the side with a baited hook on it, to fish for the fish that had swallowed Amy's eyes. Every caught fish was tossed on the main hatch cover, where the cats, grimed all over with blood and entrails, were cutting open the caught fish, extracting their stomachs, and carefully opening them, therein to search for Amy's eyes. The Captain stood with Amy in his arms, overseeing this process. He talked to her all the while.

"Any light, Sis? You'll see some light when we cut open the right fish, so watch close and sing out. We've got a hundred lines down, Sis, and we'll catch that fish if he can be caught. Is there no light at all?"

"Oh, Captain, I can't see a thing. It's just all darkness in here. I don't know what the fish is doing or where he is, so I can't be of any help. It was a big fish, Captain, a sort of green colour, I think. I just saw his big eyes looking at me, and then his mouth opened ... It was terrible, Captain."

"Yes, Sis, it must have been. But we'll have him caught before long. Don't you worry."

But the Captain was considerably worried. He left Amy in his cabin when later in the day he expressed his chief concern to Mister Cloud. They were drinking coffee in the galley. The Bad Sister was looking into the simmering brew she fed to the Golden Man. She hunched over the pot with the appearance of a real witch, humming to herself and now and then pinching up some herbs to add to the brew. Then, hubbly-bubbly, she would stir the mixture with her ladle. The frog stood nearby, watching her every move and awaiting his orders.

The Captain was sharing his troubled thoughts with the first mate. Amy was coming into some fullness of life. Even now, the Captain could feel her growing when he held her in his arms. Soon she would begin to take on the nature of a real girl. And she had no eyes. That was the Captain's woe. Mister Cloud saw the easy solution to the problem. Get two other buttons and sew them onto Amy. Simple. The answer was as easy as buttons. The Captain nodded his head. He had already considered this, and he found the implications of that solution both doubtful and alarming. For understand, a new pair of eyes would not be *Amy's* eyes. The new eyes would be innocent of all that Amy had ever seen. They would not know a familiar face. She would not even recognize the Captain. And after all, was it reasonable to think that a strange pair of eyes could even *see?* For a person cannot have a double set of eyes. Amy might yet be blind except for what her *real* eyes could see, deposited perhaps finally on some ocean floor, or washed up on some lonely beach, forever and ever to be crawled over by crabs, pecked at by birds, swallowed again and again by fish after fish, or lost forever in the mud of some river bar, curled about as a prize by worms, or taken into the clamped houses of clams, never to be relieved of the torment of being a possessed thing.

And so although Amy might become a real girl, her eyes would forever be playthings of the tides and all the creatures of the deep. Therefore Amy might grow up in a way removed from all other people, suffering as it were some remote and constant injury, some troubling and distracting pain inflicted without by nature, heartless and witless of its abuse.

The Captain sat staring into his coffee cup. He supposed his company to be his enemies, but he shrugged at it. Nothing mattered to him but Amy's eyes, let them have everything else. He spoke out his feelings.

"I was a fool, a fool!"

"That was my opinion," said the Bad Sister.

"It was the dream, the dream! I had a dream. Everything was going to be all right. A golden dream. But Skivvy was right, then. I was blinded. He said the chief danger was the gold. I didn't see it. The gold treasure is nothing. I thought it was my destiny. The dream—it seemed so clear, so different. I was a fool."

Mister Cloud put a hand on the Captain's shoulder as he sank his head nearly to the table. The Bad Sister looked at the Captain silently, not further pressing her opinion of his stupidity.

The sound of the fishing crew was all about the galley: the hauling of lines, the call for fresh bait, the sullen flopping of the fish upon the deck, even the merry call of the crew, who had never fished before and had made a competition for bringing in the largest fish. The Captain's mood, however, was not raised. He sat in a depression as dark as the fish's guts wherein rested Amy's eyes. Greensleeves the frog left for a few minutes and returned with the report that there was no luck yet. He stood by the table for a moment, then reached out, touched some spilled salt and brought it to his tongue. The Bad Sister banged her ladle loudly on the rim of her pot. The frog started, expecting a blow on his head. But he was actually the cause of a bright idea she'd just had, and might have received a compliment if it was the Bad Sister's nature to make compliments.

"Salt!" she said. The frog jumped to the table to get the salt cellar for her. "Not that," she said, *now* banging the frog on the head with her ladle. She repeated again, "Salt. Salt's the word." She faced the two men, who looked blankly at her. "Salt, or are you too dumb to understand? How do you keep beef and pork from spoiling? Salt, don't you see? It's a preservative. It keeps meat from turning, don't it? That's the treatment. And Amy's meat, ain't she, or soon will be. But see, she could be kept off from changing by packing her in salt. It'll give more time to get her eyes back. That's my opinion, anyway. You can take it or leave it, for all I care. All I want is for that Golden Man to get well so he can lead you off to where he's got that gold hid away. When I get my half of it, you can all go to the fishes for all I care — eyes, ears, teeth, and toenails."

As usual, whenever the slightest bit of goodness came out of the woman, she covered it immediately with some foul wish that upheld her bad name. And it was a good suggestion. The Bad Sister complained that since she was the cook and it was her galley and her salt, you might say, then she supposed she'd have to help with the job, although she let the Captain know what sort of stupidity it was to bring a little girl on a treasure-hunting voyage anyway. As the Captain went off to fetch Amy, and Mister Cloud returned to the deck, she found a proper container and poured it half full of salt. Returning to the galley with Amy in his arms, the Captain approached the galley table. He stopped and frowned.

"What's that?" he asked, pointing to the container.

"A bread box, Captain. Just the thing for a doll to sleep in, don't you think?"

"I've bad memories of bread boxes," the Captain said. However, time was short and the Captain did not further his objections. Reluctantly he laid Amy down on the salt bed. The Bad Sister put her hand in to press and snuggle Amy down, caressing her gently into place. Soon there was a layer of salt over her as undisturbed as a sandy beach. Before her mouth disappeared beneath the salt, the Captain exchanged good-byes with her. He assured her that he would uncover her head a few times every day and talk with her.

So the salt was smoothed over her and the Bad Sister put the lid on the bread box. The Captain stood watching with an expression suitable for a burial. The Bad Sister tapped her fingers on the lid and spoke.

"My opinion, Captain, is that you should let me keep the box here. Nothing worse could happen than if water should get mixed in with the salt and dissolve it. That would soak her up completely with salt water. Salt poisoning's a hard way to die, Captain, not that it makes any difference to me. Think now, with all those fish flopping about on deck, and the slippery guts all over and sloshing about, and there's the danger of rain, too. Well, I won't guarantee this lid will keep a tight fit. It's up to you and none of my affair, you understand, but I wouldn't want you to lose Amy and break your heart enough to forget about the gold treasure. You've got your duties, Captain. You can't be watching over this box all the time."

The Captain declined the offer, of course. The woman was hardly a good trust. With Amy for her captive, the Bad Sister could direct the Captain with her little finger. The Captain thanked her for her attentions and, taking up the bread box, he left the galley.

When the Captain closed the door, the Bad Sister turned to the frog and made a kick at him. He had been standing at her side cowing at her every motion and wringing out a dishcloth long since wrung dry. "Here now, Green-sleeves," she charged him. "Get yourself out of here and do some soft business on those long toes. Find where the Captain keeps that box, and if he finds you snooping, I'll have your legs for breakfast."

"Yes'm, yes'm," said the frog. He turned to go, but she slapped him on the back of the head with her ladle.

"Wait! Give me your report."

"Report? Oh, yes'm, report. Ah, nothing, mum."

"Then *report* it, you green curd."

"Yes'm. Ah, Mister Cloud, he does his duty, and he doesn't do anything else. So that's the report on Mister Cloud, mum."

"All right, so that's nothing. Good. No secret meetings or anything with anybody?"

"No, mum. Just does his duty, mum."

"All right. And Skivvy, then."

"Does his duty also. But seems a little strange the last day or so, like I said. Sort of dreamy like. Spends a lot of time in his cabin."

"Hmmm. And you don't know why? Hmmm. Did you put yourself in front of him again like I said to, in a private place?"

"Yes'm. In a place where we were alone together."

"And still he said nothing to you? Didn't talk to you about religion, or say anything out of the Bible or anything? Or talk about a mutiny?"

"No, mum."

"Hmmmn. Then who were Donkey and Goat talking about?" The Bad Sister sat down at the table and mused aloud while the frog waited for orders. "Someone's raising a mutiny and using a book for authority. Hmmm. Maybe someone else has a Bible." She noticed the frog. "Well, you lump, what are you standing about for? Get your eye on that bread box. And keep up your spying on Cloud and Skivvy. Out! Out!"

"Yes'm, yes'm," whined the frog, holding for a moment an imploring eye up to the Bad Sister, torturing his dishcloth and smiling pitifully. Then he, too, went out, devoted as a lover set upon a labour to prove his worth. For the most amazing thing had happened. The poor frog, punched about, kicked at, and managed by the Bad Sister in the most belittling and degrading ways, treated by her in such lowly form that it might be offensive even to the dignity of a cockroach – even so, he had fallen in love with the awful woman.

Here is one of the great curiosities of nature. How is it possible that love might take up life out of such an abusive environment? And yet, in its way of being so curious, it may be perfectly suited to an amphibian, which double-natured creatures can live in both the water and the open air, and who take their breath of life out of the continuum of oxygen wherever it might be found, in the thickness of water or the thinness of air. And so it might be with a frog in love. Let us consider that there is in love a continuum also; it also has both its thickness and thinness. There are creatures perhaps capable of discerning the slightest breath of love's presence even in the atmosphere of kicks and blows and insults and cold regard. Perhaps they take this thinnest distillation of love into their hearts by some amphibious curiosity and can thrive in love while we more single-natured of God's creatures – who seek love in its thick and warm aspect – have long ago closed the door on such a miserable existence.

Or perhaps the frog loved the Bad Sister out of pity. One night when the frog had been up late scraping a pot he had burned some beans in, he went to her cabin door hoping to see a light so that he might report to her that his job was done. He heard her voice inside and listened. She seemed to be talking with someone.

"I know who you are," she said. "You can't fool me." The frog listened, but heard no reply. For a minute or two all was quiet. Then the Bad Sister began crying, and she spoke again. "No, no. I'm sorry. Please – please forgive me. I didn't mean to do it. Oh – I'm sorry." She wept loudly for a minute, then all was quiet again. The frog looked under the door. No light.

"Poor dear," he said. "A bad dream. Oh – I wish I could comfort her. Oh, the poor, dear lady." And the frog went to his bunk.

There was one other incident, also, that the frog held close to his heart. He was napping late one afternoon on the bench in the galley when the Bad Sister came in to draw some water. He opened an eye and lay still, certain he would get a good cuffing if she discovered him. Then she did a most peculiar thing. Over the sink was a small mirror. After drawing her water, she paused and moved her face close to the mirror and spoke.

"Who are you?" she said. Then again, after a long pause, "Who *are* you?"

She left then. Greensleeves lay with his eyes open, wondering. "What a mysterious woman. The poor woman doesn't know who she is. The poor, dear lady."

So these might be the reasons the frog loved the Bad Sister – out of pity, and because of the mystery of her so deep that even she didn't understand it. But the opinion is strictly aside. Who knows why the frog loved the Bad Sister? Perhaps he had ambitions to be kissed, for frogs have a reputation of wanting to be kissed by women, perhaps upon the speculation put forward by fabulists that they will be promoted thereby. Poor fool frog. He peeked around the galley corner. There went the Captain aft. Greensleeves skipped after him, ducking behind a mast. He watched and hummed to himself, and quietly took up the words:

> "Alas, my love, you do me wrong,
> To cast me off discourteously ..."

Poor benighted, delighted frog. He thought of it as "our song." He watched. Ah, the Captain was going to visit the Golden Man, the bread box under his arm. Greensleeves followed and watched until the Captain entered the cabin where the Golden Man lay. He would report it at once to the Bad Sister. It seemed to him ages that he'd been away from her. Off he went.

CHAPTER THIRTY-SEVEN

The boughs do shake and the bells do ring,
So merrily comes our harvest in,
Our harvest in, our harvest in,
So merrily comes our harvest in.

We've ploughed, we've sowed,
We've reaped, we've mowed,
We've got our harvest in.

T he Golden Man's door had been left open to receive the full freshness of the breeze, much needed for a man who had almost entirely emptied himself of air and must put in a new supply. Seeing that the man was awake, half sitting up in bed and staring at the ceiling in concentrated thought, the Captain rapped his knuckles on the doorjamb.

"Ah, come in, Captain," said the Golden Man, motioning with his hand and shifting himself up farther in bed.

"You're feeling better, I trust," said the Captain, setting down the bread box and pulling a chair up near the bed.

"Much better. And I've many questions I've been thinking on, if you're not holding secrets to yourself."

"Not I," said the Captain, "and I hope to satisfy you, for I'm much in your debt. You nearly drowned, you know, and for what you must think to be a trifle — for two buttons."

"That's exactly one of the questions," said the Golden Man. "That and other things."

"Precisely the reason I've come around to see you," said the Captain, taking out his pipe. He cast his eye about for Mister Cloud's tobacco. "Yes, and you'll want to know about the crew," the Captain said, as he got up to fetch the tobacco from a shelf. "Oh, no, it's not your imagination. They are real animals, straight out of *Mother Goose*. And you shall have that story. Now, where's a taper? Oh, here." The Captain touched a light to the taper and lit his pipe, blowing out a great cloud of smoke. He settled and crossed his legs, studying the Golden Man, who had now pushed himself erect in bed.

The Captain's intention was to bind the Golden Man to some honourable promise, if a pirate can thus be bound, for he feared that the Bad Sister might seek to enlist him in her mutiny. Then there was the *Locust*. A pirate, after all, is a pirate to the heart. The Captain feared that the Golden Man might take the pirates' side when it came to a fight, and the *Ariel* would need every fighting man they had to resist that onslaught. What the Captain could offer to the Golden Man was his help and protection if they should ever again reach land, for no doubt the authorities would be eager to hang a member of Cowl's old crew. Also, he meant to lay over to the Golden Man's account whatever part of the treasure he should name, even unto the last token if that was needed to buy his loyalty. All must be turned to sacrifice now, for the only important thing in the Captain's mind was to find Amy's eyes. The Captain blew out a thin line of smoke. Perhaps he could touch off some sympathy in the Golden Man by telling him Amy's story from the first.

"There is a danger of mutiny aboard the ship," said the Captain, taking the pipe from his mouth, "and a danger of pirates also, who even at this moment are searching for us in these waters. But for the questions you have, I'll begin the story much further back than yesterday, or last week, or last month – as far back as the time you've spent on Vulcan Island, back a full ten years ago."

The Golden Man nodded and leaned back, raising a hand to stroke his mouth, assuming the attitude of a most thoughtful and receptive audience. The Captain took a puff on his pipe. He smiled. All at once he felt a great relief. Here was someone he could tell the entire story to. He could begin at the beginning and tell it all, including all his fears and suspicions and the doubtings of his mind. He would unburden himself of everything. The Captain was exhausted with command. The Golden Man tugged at a moustache. The Captain was relieved that at last he could talk everything out, and perhaps find some understanding with this stranger. The man smiled back at the Captain, his eyes branching wrinkles across his temples. The Captain let out a deep breath, and began his story.

"You see," said the Captain, "Amy is my sister." He pointed the stem of his pipe at the bread box. "She is in that bread box now, packed in salt, and she'll become alive again soon, as a real girl, and that's the reason it's so important that we find her eyes. It's a story that began ten years ago. And now I'll tell you how that is." The Captain took another large puff from his pipe. For a few moments he watched the cloud of it rise, and then began. "Once upon a time ..."

"Once upon a time," interrupted the Golden Man, "when Amy was just a baby, the story begins."

"Yes," said the Captain. "Well, of course. All girls begin as babies. And so it was. At the beginning of the story she was just a baby, and now she is a doll. You may find that hard to believe, but here is something more difficult. At that time I was just a doll."

"Your father was a tailor," said the Golden Man.

"Hum," said the Captain, for any storyteller hates to be successfully guessed at before his surprises. "Very good. Yes, and it's true. Well, whoever might make a doll might be a tailor, just as you guessed."

"And after he made you, he gave you a tattoo," said the Golden Man.

The Captain plucked the pipe from his mouth. "Now, how could you guess that?"

"He might have," said the Golden Man, shrugging. "You were a sailor doll after all, and sailors have tattoos. Besides that, I saw the tattoo when you took off your shirt to dive after Amy's eyes. Very nicely done, too. I don't think there's another one like it in the world. Could I have another look at it?"

The Captain pushed back his sleeve.

"You see, it's a needle and thread. It was done just about the time Amy was born. And, I am sad to say, it was also about that time that Amy's mother died."

The Golden Man had put a finger out to touch the tattoo. Now he withdrew it and bowed his head. "Her name was Amy, too," he said softly.

The Captain coughed, and held the bowl of his pipe up to study it. "Oh, it might have been," he said, putting the taper to the lamp and lighting his pipe afresh. "I never heard him say, really, but if you want to guess at a name, that's fine." Then, puffing smoke out, he continued. "Anyway, there we were on the road, for Amy's father was going to sea, and Amy and myself – I was only a doll then, you understand – were riding in a basket . . ."

"With a loaf of bread, also," said the Golden Man, looking up.

[285]

"Aha!" said the Captain. "You've struck the mark again! There *was* also a loaf of bread in the basket. I suppose that's easy enough. Yes. But it wasn't for Amy to eat, and it wasn't for me to eat, and our father didn't eat it. No. It was a gift."

"For the Ladies at St. Anne's," said the Golden Man.

"Right," said the Captain. "It was just getting dark when we got there, and he set the basket down near the gate..."

And then, with his pipe halfway to his lips, the Captain stopped so still it was almost as if he had become a doll again. He stared without blinking as the Golden Man continued the story.

"And the sea not being so far away," said the Golden Man, looking out of the window, "Amy's father left the basket at St. Anne's with a note saying that he would be back, but not knowing a pirate from a poop deck, he put to sea with buccaneers on Captain Cowl's own ship..." Hearing the pipe fall from the Captain's fingers, the Golden Man turned back to look into the amazed face of the Captain.

The light of the day suddenly filled the room, giving to all objects a golden face and a golden aura, and the Captain's mind was illuminated with the knowledge that his quest had found its ending, for sitting before him was the golden treasure he had been seeking – Amy's father and his maker. This had been the golden and soulful attraction to the island and his yearning to be there, the destiny he followed upon and the fulfilment of himself. No words are left to complete the scene. The Golden Man reached out, and father and son embraced.

CHAPTER THIRTY-EIGHT

Here comes I,
*   Little David Doubt;*
If you don't give me money,
*   I'll sweep you all out.*
Money I want,
*   And money I crave;*
If you don't give me money,
*   I'll sweep you all to the grave*

t that moment, fifty miles to the north, Goldnose was standing over his chart.

Within an area of several hundred square miles, there were a half dozen islands. That day Goldnose had wrapped his wake around Tanner Island without finding a sign of the *Ariel*. His blind, finger-poking stab at the chart had been wrong. Now he stood with his hands flat on the table studying out his next move. His first mate stood at the cabin door, awaiting orders, a stringy, black-bearded scoundrel with his nose bent half sideways on his face, a tall, lean man as hard as chain links, who stood slightly hunched like a curved cutlass.

"They's impatient, Captain, and they's got doubts, Captain," he said. "They's wondering we ought to get back to the trading lanes and take a ship. They's looking for prizes, Captain."

Goldnose gave him a sour look. The man made a thin smile as if it were no fault of his own, but secretly, as all strong and bold pirates make a fantasy about, the first mate was ready to take over the ship if the crew would come to his side and he could get behind Goldnose with a drawn sword. Which wasn't likely. The sound of metal touching metal, or any click or snap of gear, caught the fat pirate's attention as if someone had tapped him on the nose with a spoon. In a dodging crouch he would turn and come up with pistol and sword in hand and rake everyone behind himself with a killing glare. One dared hardly approach him from behind without calling out while a few paces away. It was his gold nose, possibly, that set this impulse in action, for it acted as a sort of bell to the clapper of a metallic vibration, and sent an alarm straight up between his eyes, through his sinuses, and into the frontal lobe of his brain, clanging out a warning to him like the brazen call of a signal buoy.

His mate had more to say. He shrugged it out casually as if he were no part of this report, either.

"They also says they don't like the looks of that crew they seen. They been talking it out together, and they say they can't see it any other way except that a bunch of animals is handling that ship. It's getting on their nerves thinking about boarding such a ship, Captain. They says it ain't natural. And there's talk about a witch aboard that ship. So they was wondering about having answers to that, Captain, and reasons."

Goldnose gave up his patience at last and banged both fists on the table. "Answers! Answers is it they want? And reasons? Maybe we ought to have brought a school-teacher along and set 'em up a little schoolroom to give 'em their answers and reasons. Well, damme, when we next put in we'll find a little nursie maid for 'em, and we'll bring a parson along so they can go to church on Sundays, aye, Dimlid? And I can go down to the fo'c'sle come night-times and fold their hands for 'em to say their prayers and sing lullabies to 'em. Hah! Well, kiss my nose, Dimlid, ain't that a lovely pudding of a pirate crew to be sailing with, all nervous and wanting their nappies changed when it comes to a fight. Well, well, sugar and spice and everything nice, that's how to call 'em out, and play patty-cake with 'em. Next thing you'll be coming to tell me about their bad dreams, and I'll have to go and pat their heads and spoon 'em warm milk to keep out the goblins."

Goldnose rolled his belly around the corner of the table and walked up close to his mate.

"Here's answers and reasons for 'em, Dimlid, and ye can carry it off straight, mister. The answer they get from me is a pig's satchel and a donkey's rump, a duck's haircut and a cat's meow, aye, and a goat's handle and a dog's bladder. Give 'em that for answers and reasons, and wipe their noses for 'em."

Goldnose lowered his voice and threw an arm around Dimlid, leaning at least a hundred pounds' weight on the man. "But as for yourself and me, shipmate, seeing as I wouldn't have a first mate that didn't have a pole up his backbone and was intelligent, I can give ye the reason. Aye, confidential like, as between officers of this here ship. Never mind them scum on deck. It befits officers to stay lofty and keep mum, for that's how ye get discipline and respect, and ye lay a knotted rope across their backs for the reason why. But look here, Dimlid, as I respect an intelligent man, I'll lay out the true answers and reasons as between men of education and rank. Aye, and I'll just spell it out for ye."

Goldnose cast a look towards the door in an attitude of caution. He leaned a few more pounds onto his first mate, coming close to his ear.

The first mate winced. He knew what was coming. He

himself could not read or write. Goldnose knew this of him, yet played as if he thought otherwise. Goldnose also knew that somehow or other, although it was a rare case among pirates, Dimlid's lack of education was a great shame to himself. He would nearly rather hang than admit that he could not read or write. Now he must again endure the reminder of his ignorance in this respect. He sweated and smiled and bit his lip as if he had been caught up and exposed for a grievous fault. Goldnose tightened his arm about the man in a confidential hug.

"Aye, Dimlid, as between men with some polish put on 'em by schooling, I'll spell out the answer for ye. Our real reason, shipmate, is b-e-c-a-u-s-e. Aye, and now ye see why we can't pass that on to those ignorant, uneducated swine."

Dimlid had heard this spelling before. He now attempted to remember the sound of it, as a parrot remembers sounds without knowing the reason of it. He nodded his head and took a quick look at the captain, trying to put a glint of comprehension into his eye, but he failed at that and let his aimless glance fall to the deck, and laughed nervously.

"Aye, Captain. B-e-c . . . and the rest of it, Captain. Heh, heh."

Dimlid wanted terribly to escape. Goldnose let his arm fall and clapped him on the back.

"Good. Now that ye understand, get out of here. I've some calculations to be done. Take the helm. I'll shout up the new course."

Dimlid gladly left the cabin. Goldnose rolled around the corner of his table again and stared at the chart. He closed his eyes to poke a finger at the group of islands, but then had a better idea. Rounding his glance past the windows and door, he put both hands over his great belly to pull it in somewhat, closed his eyes, and leaned down towards the chart until his nose touched it. He opened his eyes.

"Vulcan Island," he said to himself. He shoved up the skylight stick and shouted up to the poop deck.

"Mister Dimlid! Our course is west-sou'west. We steer for Vulcan Island. And ye know the reason, don't ye, mate?"

"Aye, Captain," yelled back Dimlid, putting the wheel down to the new course.

A small delegation of pirates had gathered on the poop. The spokesman put up a question to Dimlid.

"Answers and reasons, Mister Dimlid, that's what we're waiting for. We ain't chasing any zoo with a witch aboard unless we get some satisfaction."

Dimlid pulled a man over to take his place at the wheel. He faced the lead pirate. He breathed deeply, stared hard into the face of the man for a second, and then relaxed. Taking the man by the arm in a friendly manner, he led him aside from the other pirates, walking over by the railing, and spoke softly to him.

"Look, now, mate," said Dimlid, stealing a quick look at the half-dozen pirates over by the wheel. "The Captain's got some answers, but he thinks how it's best that not everyone on board the ship be in on the reasons and such. But he says he'll pass the word on to yourself, sort of in secret like. There now, I'll just stand here and twiddle my thumbs sort of nonchy-lanchy-like, while yourself leans over the railing where the Captain's going to stick his head out the windee and give ye what's what in a whisper so as all these bilge rats won't know except upon your considered judgment. There now, I'll just whistle a little tune while ye lean over. That's the way, shipmate."

When the man leaned over the railing, Dimlid took him by the seat of the pants and with a whistle flipped him over the side into the dark water. The man sank almost immediately. Goldnose saw him fall past his window. He came out of his cabin and looked upward to the poop.

"What's that man overboard?"

"He was looking for some answers, Captain," Dimlid said, "and I was just spelling things out for him, as it was, until we can get that schoolteacher on board."

"Ah," said Goldnose, "right ye are, Dimlid. That's a good lad – send 'em to school with the fishes." He returned to his cabin.

The rest of the disputing pirates tucked their chins down and fairly crawled towards the fo'c'sle. They put up no more questions about the animal crew aboard the *Ariel*, yet they still worried it about among themselves.

CHAPTER THIRTY-NINE

One, two, three, four, five, six, seven,
All good children go to heaven,
Some fly east,
Some fly west,
Some fly over the cuckoo's nest.

B y damn, that was strange!" the Golden Man was saying, fifty miles to the south. "When you tossed off your shirt ready to dive into the sea after Amy's eyes, there it was, the very same tattoo I made ten years ago. Then when you called that doll 'Amy' ... Well, there wasn't any time to find out if I was crazy or not. Maybe I'd been talking to skeletons too long, that's what I thought. But then when I got down on the bottom and found that broken bottle, and I reached out my hand and looked right at those buttons, right into Amy's eyes, I *knew* her. I could *see* it was her, and I shouted out, 'Amy!' Lost all my breath, and I would have drowned for sure if that rope hadn't been on me."

"And maybe if the dogs weren't there to help pull you up."

"Son," said the Golden Man, "that's all a mighty strange story about the animals. But don't worry, I'm used to it already. No problem. Our problem is with Goldnose and the Bad Sister most of all, you say?"

"The Bad Sister and Mister Cloud at the moment. She wants the gold and he wants the ship. They're in this together. As to Skivvy, he's not much help these days, but he can be trusted. The animals — well, I don't know whose side they'd go to."

"Hmmm," said the Golden Man, laying his head back and looking at the ceiling. "Somehow, I can't believe that about Cloud. He seemed a good man. But I'm new here. Anyway, there's no danger until we get the gold on board. It seems to me we can make some bargain out of that. See it this way. What do ye want — myself and you and Amy? I'm a tailor still, and you're a sailor. We can begin our lives all new and shake all of this behind us. That's our best part. We'll let them have it all. Now, that puts us at their mercy, to be sure. I can't believe Mister Cloud would turn us over to the sharks, and the Bad Sister — well, she's been good to me." The Golden Man touched his cheek. "Yes, she has a nice touch. . ."

"A touch to keep you alive only so you'll lead us to get the treasure," said the Captain.

"That could be," admitted the man.

"And then there's that hooded friend of hers that creeps about deck," said the Captain. "Who's that — and what's the plan there? But last of all, there's Goldnose. If he finds us with that gold aboard, we'll get no mercy, and you can tell me that from your own experience with pirates."

"True," said the Golden Man. He breathed deeply and let his arms fall along his sides. "Well, Son, I'm tired. Tomorrow we'll get the gold on board, and then we'll see." He closed his eyes. The Captain sat looking at him for a minute, then his eyes went over to the bread box. He touched the Golden Man on the arm.

"We're forgetting Amy," said the Captain. The Golden Man opened his eyes. "We must let her know you've been found." The Captain set the bread box upon the bed. The Golden Man folded his legs and sat upright. He ran a hand through his hair and made some attempt to comb his beard with his fingers.

"How do I look?" he asked.

"She can't see you, of course," said the Captain. "Ah, but she'll be thrilled to know you're here with us."

The Captain took the top off the bread box. He put a hand in to uncover Amy's face, but the Golden Man stopped him.

"No," he said. "No, not now. Wait. Let's think, now. There's danger coming upon us and there's no telling what may happen. What if Goldnose finds us? Then there'll be a battle for sure. I might be killed. It's best we wait. It would be terribly cruel if Amy should know I'm alive this evening and tomorrow must know that I'm dead. No, we can't tell her anything yet."

"Yes," said the Captain. "That's true." He replaced the lid on the bread box. "But all will be well. You'll be together again."

The Golden Man smiled. "Well, it's good to have a prophet aboard the ship," he said. "I'll sleep, then."

Again he closed his eyes. The Captain took up the bread box and left the cabin. He went onto the deck, where he watched the catching of fish for a few minutes. Mister Cloud came to his side and sniffed loudly at the air. "Change in the weather, Captain," he observed. The Captain nodded, looking at the plume of smoke rising from Vulcan Island. Then he went to his cabin and lay down on his bunk, his hand over the side resting on the top of the bread box. He would nap before supper. He closed his eyes and wondered what might be done about Amy's eyes. He listened to the sound of the fishing crew on deck. But no luck would come of that. The fish that had swallowed Amy's eyes was now many miles to the south, swimming low, looking for other bright things to snatch up.

There was indeed a prophet aboard the *Ariel*, but a prophet that the Golden Man would not care to meet. Skivvy came up on deck and passed among the fishing crew, who saluted him in greeting but Skivvy did not answer. He walked to the bow of the ship and stared into the water. "And a Beast shall come out of the sea," he said to himself. "A Beast crowned with gold. A Golden Beast." He turned to glance at the ladderway leading down to Mister Cloud's cabin, where the Golden Man lay. He touched the butt of the pistol stuck in his belt. Skivvy now supposed that he had identified the Beast for certain, the terrible Beast of the number 666 that would lead men to its worship thereby to destroy them. Behold – out of the sea had come a Golden Man, and of all things in the world, it is gold that is most worshipped by men in contention with the worship of God. Skivvy had pondered this forward to its dreadful conclusion. When the Golden Man arose from his bed, the danger of the eternal end was come upon the *Ariel*, for the Golden Man would then walk the decks and employ himself in miraculous ways that would lead everyone to worship him, for so it is written. Yet more than that for the proof of it. Skivvy was content at last in his numbering. Several hours earlier, he had found the Golden Man to fit exactly the number of the Beast – 666. Here is Skivvy's proof, that you may understand his madness, for he was now set upon the murder of the Golden Man.

The number of Vulcan is 73, and the number of Island is 59. The sum is 132. After adding up many other numbers and getting little gain on the large number 666, Skivvy at last took the number 5, for it was out of five fathoms of water that the Golden Man arose, and he multiplied the number of Vulcan Island (132) by the number of the rising up of the Golden Man (5). The sum of that is 660. Skivvy was much excited to find this out. Only 6 numbers were needed to bring the total to 666, the very *perfect* proof of his fears. When one dallies with the Wayward Daughter, she is flattered, and will give her favours out of the very air. And it was out of the very air that Skivvy found these 6 numbers, for in the minute of his final multiplication, the ship's bell was struck 6 times. The total was brought to 666. It was sealed in Skivvy's mind that he had the truth. The Golden Man was surely the Beast of the number 666. Living upon the cusp of a dream given him out of that almanac of disaster, that festival of destruction and wrath that comes in the book of Revelation, Skivvy now felt himself pressed to an act of violence that would save the ship. A bell called him to it. He checked his arithmetic several times over. He prayed and meditated on the matter, yet still he had doubts. He lay on his bunk and napped on his conclusion. He dreamed of being a monk in a monastery, walking the peaceful cloisters in his cowled cloak. He reached for his prayer beads in this dream, to pray for the salvation of the *Ariel* from the Beast, and came up with a pistol in his hand. He awoke with a start and saw the whole affair alight with a great clarity. The question was closed. He must kill the Golden Man. Why else should God give him such a dream?

Skivvy looked to see that his passageway was clear. The animals were pulling up fish now and then, not nearly so many as earlier, and were lounging at the rails looking towards Vulcan Island, wondering about the coming day. In a moment, Skivvy was out of sight and down the ladder-way, and then standing in the doorway of Mister Cloud's cabin. He looked in. There he lay, the Golden Man, the Beast, apparently asleep, near enough so that Skivvy need not step inside the door to make his assassination. Quietly he took the pistol from his belt. With the palm of his left hand he pulled the cocking piece back to its lock. Every addition of the act had been given its sum, every subtraction taken away its part, every multiplication awarded its increase, and at the last the very voice of time had called him to this place, the six clear notes of the ship's bell that had identified the Beast beyond every doubt, and marked him for his death, completing the number 660 to 666, the mark of the Beast.

Skivvy pointed the pistol at the Golden Man's chest. His finger printed itself upon the cold brass trigger. He steadied his hand, braced his feet apart against the rolling of the ship, looked down the barrel of the pistol to kill the Beast, and slowly tightened his grip.

And then, just as the Golden Man had been condemned out of the tolling of the ship's bell, it now seemed that he would be killed out of double proof, for the ship's bell began striking. How neat, thought Skivvy, how precisely and admirably does God touch even swiftly flying time in His appointments. For upon hearing the first ringing call of the bell, Skivvy saw the special Providence that commended him to the murder, for he supposed that it was six bells, or 7 P.M. of the afternoon watch. At the sounding of the sixth bell he would pull the trigger, the moment of execution echoing the moment of condemnation. "Ding-ding," the bell rang in its couplets, and then a pause. "Ding-ding," it rang again. And then, "ding ..." But the sixth bell was not sounded. The time was only five bells, or 6:30 of the afternoon watch. Five bells only? thought Skivvy. But it should have been six. The exactness of it would then have been the final, perfect, and compounded proof of the rightness of the deed. But why only five bells? Skivvy, in this small moment, was still looking down the barrel of his pistol, where it pointed at the Golden Man's chest. His every nerve was alert at the ringing of that fifth bell, now faintly dying. But where was the sixth bell? Why only five? And then it came to Skivvy, as certain as if the number 5 were carved on stone and set before his eyes. The Fifth Commandment. That was the tolling of the bell, tolling the number 5, the Fifth Commandment, whereof God forbids without metaphor to mar the matter: "Thou shalt not kill." Skivvy lowered his arm, trembling. He leaned his shoulder to the doorjamb and stared at the pistol. He put a hand up to cover his eyes. "My God," he said to himself, "what am I doing?" Silently he turned out of the doorway and returned to his cabin.

The Golden Man had awoken at the sound of the ship's bell, just in time to see Skivvy lower the pistol. He now opened his eyes wide, breathed deeply out of relief, and wondered why the Captain had not known enough to warn him of this strange man made out of underwear. Well, he would keep mum; perhaps there was more to discover that the Captain didn't know about. He was still a pirate to the rest of the crew, and a pirate is useful for dirty work. The Golden Man would play the part. He would lie awake and watch how the night developed.

His next visitor was the Bad Sister, bringing his dinner. He had his eyes closed. He listened to her set the tray down, and next expected that she would speak to him to wake him up. But she was silent. He opened his eyes. She was looking at him. She sniffed and turned away quickly, saying in a gruff voice, "Supper." Then she hurried out of the door. But in that moment when he opened his eyes, before she could look away, the Golden Man saw nothing harsh or mean in the woman at all. It was in fact a soft look, a wistful faraway sort of gaze. He took the tray onto his lap and stirred the broth. Was this a woman who was plotting a mutiny? wondered the Golden Man. She hadn't the look of it. No. And Mister Cloud seemed a good and honest man, no mutineer himself. A strange story there.

Blowing upon the broth, he took a sip. He felt well enough to get out of bed. Yet he would wait and watch some more.

It was a most wonderful fish supper that evening. All hands said so. It was garnished with a white sauce the savour of which nearly touched the soul with its delicacy. Of course, the Bad Sister would take no credit for the goodness of it.

"The best I could do with the bilge in this kitchen," she said. And when the frog doted on her with compliments, she said, "Yes, and wouldn't I love to see your legs dancing around in that sauce." Which comment made the frog nearly galvanic with ecstasy. When she retired to her cabin, he hopped around the galley mopping away with his dishcloth, muttering to himself.

"What a dear lady, what a dear lady. It's only her way, and she's not to blame. And she does like my legs. Didn't she say so? Oh, she may have them for soupbones. She may have my heart on a biscuit. What a joy she is, what a good woman. And she is good, I know it. Let her hit me and scorn me. What matter is that? It's just her way. Mysterious – that's her. She likes me, yes she does. What a delight! What is she doing now? I'll go to her door. Maybe she has an errand for me. What a woman, what a woman!"

All lines had been hauled aboard, and all fishing gear and tackle secured. After supper the crew took their rest. Some went below, and some hung at the railings or sat atop the hatch covers, looking towards Vulcan Island, smoking their pipes and watching the overtowering cloud of smoke and steam rising from some deep forge within the earth. The sun set behind a bank of clouds far to the west. Patches of cold air blew across the deck.

Donkey sniffed the air. "Rain," he said.

"Gunpowder," said the goat, likewise sniffing.

"Trouble," said the pig, putting his snout up and snorting out with a grunt.

"Gold," said the monkey.

"Fire," said a cat.

But all of them turned to the dogs, both of whom were sitting on a hatch, both smoking their pipes. As to what was on the wind, in the matter of smelling, the dogs were the authorities. The larboard dog took his pipe from his mouth and looked towards the western clouds, nearly lost in the darkness now. He turned his head to the north for a few moments, then looked at the faint outline of Vulcan Island, all the time with eyes squinted and nostrils flared. Then, tapping the ashes from his pipe, he slipped off the hatch.

"Blood," said the dog, and walked off.

The other dog mimicked every move of the larboard dog, and left the deck with a single word behind him as well.

"Death," he said, and followed his partner below.

Soon it was dark, and all animals were below in their hammocks, swinging gently to a lullaby a cat was softly singing.

> *"Hush-a-bye, baby, on the tree top,*
> *When the wind blows the cradle will rock;*
> *When the bough breaks the cradle will fall,*
> *Down will come baby, cradle and all."*

CHAPTER FORTY

Sing a song of sixpence,
A pocket full of rye,
Four and twenty
Naughty boys,
Baked in a pie.

I *t was dark.* A heavy swell was running. A hooded figure sat on a yardarm high above the deck of the *Ariel*, rocking as if the yardarm were the very bough of the lullaby. The figure saw Davy Duck descend the companionway towards the cabin where the Golden Man lay. When again the deck was deserted, the hooded figure scooted out to the end of the yard, hush-a-bye, careful not to fall, while the cradle of the ship rocked far below.

The Golden Man was drowsing.

"Evening, mate," said Davy Duck. The Golden Man roused himself in bed. "Glad to see you're feeling better, and that's a duck's fact."

Davy Duck had come to discuss current events aboard the *Ariel*. He was invited in, and obligingly lit the lamp afresh. He settled in a chair pulled up near the bed, looked at the doorway, cocked his head for any sound, then quickly got to business.

"Davy Duck's the name, shipmate. Quack, quack. And I tell ye, it's good to be in the company of a fellow creature that's got a heart like myself. Aye, and so ye was a member of Cowl's crew, and a great man he was, so I hear, and I'm one of a kind that likes such company as a pirate what sailed with Cowl, for I'm one of the breed myself." Davy winked and stole a look towards the doorway. In a lower voice he spoke again. "I'm speaking of us who follow the bony flag, mate. Aye, that's the poetry of it, and the plain words is the skull and crossbones, the black flag of us pirates."

The Golden Man nodded, not knowing what to make of this duck with his wry and tricky expression, who was now sitting back smiling smugly. "So you're a pirate? Huh, that's good, and who've ye sailed with?"

"Oh, not with a man such as Cowl," said Davy, "but when it comes to being a true pirate in the chambers of your heart and the length of your whole guts, I'm your duck. Look here, I've got pirate friends. Have ye heard of Goldnose? It's him I'm talking about, him and his whole pirate crew, him and the *Locust*, all of which owe old Davy Duck a favour for being a sort of lighthouse to 'em on a couple of dark nights. Right now they're searching for us, no mistake about that, and if they find us, it's only Davy Duck that escapes alive, aye, and his friends that come over to his side. For I'll tell it to ye straight, shipmate, I mean to take over this ship and be the proper Captain, quack, quack."

"So," said the Golden Man, "and then you've raised a crew for yourself." He scratched his chin as if figuring the odds of the adventure, and gave his opinion. "All right, and so it's yourself and that woman and Mister Cloud I suppose, and maybe that Skivvy –"

"Argghhhh," growled Davy. "Nah. Look, man, I'm talking about my *own* crew, not those blubber-lipped, sop-livered – Oh, well," Davy said in amendment, touching the Golden Man's leg. "I don't mean to say there's anything

[303]

wrong with having lips. Live and let live, that's my motto. If ye got lips — well, have 'em, I say, and welcome, too... But never mind Cloud and that woman. We don't need 'em for the mutiny. And Skivvy? Skivvy's got his own mutiny going on, mate. Up here," said Davy, tapping his head.

"All right, but look here," said the Golden Man. "What's your name? Davy? Then look, Davy, one thing I know is that it takes a fighting crew to take over a ship, and a good many of 'em, and a crew to sail the ship after you've got it in hand. It's a matter of having your own loyals behind you. So who can ye count on? Are the dogs with us, then, and the monkeys?"

Davy laughed quietly and moved his chair closer to the bed. "Mate, I've got my own crew, a secret crew all waiting belowdecks, just waiting to get blood on their swords. Aye, and they know me for the Captain."

"A secret crew. Now, that's good," said the Golden Man. "That's what I like to hear. That's something I could throw in for." He gave a gruff nod of encouragement to Davy, who was now proud to tell the story of his ducks belowdecks, and how he had made them and got them ready for the mutiny. The Golden Man smiled and nodded, with expressions of admiration at the duck's cleverness. Then he leaned back and appeared thoughtful. At last he came forward to Davy again and made his pledge. "Shipmates, I'll go in it with ye. Two dozen, ye say, and ready for battle? Yes, that could be enough. Could be, depending on the ducks, and there's a point. I'd like to put an eye on 'em, for I've an eye for pirates." He threw a leg out of bed. "See here, now, I'm well enough to get about. Could we take a look in on these here pirates? I'm a judge of pirates, ye know, and if ye can understand and hand me that there pair of trousers, we might take a look at this crew."

Davy handed the Golden Man a pair of Mister Cloud's

trousers that were laid out, and also a shirt. "Pirates?" Davy was saying quietly. "I'll show ye pirates. Aye, ye want to see pirates, I've got pirates." Davy looked both ways at the door. "The way's clear. Come. It's a small place. Watch your head. Out we go now."

Stealthily they crept down the passageway, through a hatch, down a ladderway, through another narrow passage, and at last they crowded into Davy's sewing parlour, the magazine locker. Davy lit a candle and proudly unfolded the sailcloth. There lay his two dozen ducks.

"Um," said the Golden Man, taking up a duck and examining the seam. "Um." He put it down and took up another, yet making no other comment. Davy looked at him with agitation. He had expected immediate approval. Taking up and laying down another duck or two, the Golden Man made his appraisal.

"Davy," he said, "they're mean-looking ducks, and that's a fact, and there's enough of 'em. The work is good. It's a tight stitch, and what I'm thinking about is how they'll hold together in a real battle. And maybe even we'll have a pirate battle on our hands, for I don't take no trust in pirates even if ye say they owe ye a favour. It may come to that at last. And let me tell ye, Davy, you've never seen such a riot as a pirate battle. It wouldn't do to have your own pirates falling apart or getting weak in their arms or sides. Aye, but that's a good tight stitch. And these little splinters of wood, ye say, they'll be real swords? Hum ... But look, here's another thing. Ye hear about pirates coming at a ship and swinging half-naked on board and cutting a storm through the enemy? Well, so they do, some of them, but they're the ones without any brains. For the smart pirates don't go about half-naked, not any of that for them, because if you've got a real battle going, it's like jumping about in a brush of brambles, and the brambles you're in aren't just thorns, but the points and edges of swords. There now," he said, taking a handful of Davy's jacket front. "Here's right what I mean. Maybe ye came on it in inspiration, being a natural Captain, but that's protection in a battle, a good stout jacket is. And ye could call it a uniform if all your ducks had the same. Then the crew would save their own blood, and not be striking at a mate in all the confusion if they all had the same sort of jackets. For a battle is all thunder and lightning and confusion."

Davy smoothed out the front of his jacket. He looked at his ducks, then to the Golden Man. "I see how you're right, but I didn't make them jackets. No time, mate. Tomorrow's the day, I'm thinking. No, we'll have to make do — not that I don't appreciate the idea, you understand, and the use of your experience."

"Look," said the Golden Man, picking up a scrap of canvas. "Here's my idea of it."

The Golden Man flattened out a piece of cloth, put the candle nearby, and with his thumbnail traced out a pattern of a tiny jacket. Davy stood looking over his shoulder. He liked the idea of a uniform. He moved the biscuit tin towards the Golden Man. In only a few minutes, the Golden Man had very expertly cut the pattern out and fashioned a small jacket. He slipped it onto one of the ducks and held it up for Davy's approval.

"No trouble for me," said the Golden Man. "I was Cowl's sailmaker. Let's see, now. That took me maybe ten minutes to tailor. That means, give me four or five hours, and I'll have 'em all outfitted, and all the better for us. All day long I been sleeping and sipping soup, so a night's work is nothing to me. I could have these ducks in uniform by morning."

"Do ye like it, shipmate?" said Davy, taking the duck

into his hands and smiling at it, for he was most charming-ly taken with the idea himself. "Aye, it's me, the Captain. Quack, quack, and always looking out for your welfare, ain't I? That's the way of a Captain, and you'll know me by the very same uniform, for what's good enough for the Captain is good enough for his crew, and that's a duck's fact. Quack, quack."

"Good," said the Golden Man. "Now, first off, I'll get back to the cabin and fix up a sort of dummy in the bunk so anyone come looking in will think I'm sleeping. I'll make it back here on my own. Can ye have enough canvas laid out for me?"

"Mate," said Davy, setting down the duck and putting out a hand, "ye shall have it, and let's put our hands on the bargain!" The Golden Man put his hand out. "There's just one thing so we'll be clear on it, shipmate. Quack, quack, who's the Captain?"

"Him whose uniform you're wearing," said the Golden Man, shaking on the bargain. Davy took thought for a moment, and then beamed his approval of the answer. He spoke out to his brood.

"Shipmates, do ye hear? You'll be wearing the Captain's uniform, like regular troops. Hark to that, mates. Him whose uniform you're wearing, that's your Captain."

Then the two of them departed the magazine locker, the Golden Man for his cabin, and Davy on his way to secure more material for the jackets.

CHAPTER FORTY-ONE

Old Abram Brown is dead and gone,
You'll never see him more;
He used to wear a long brown coat
That buttoned down before.

L ater that evening, Greensleeves came into Mister
Cloud's cabin with broth and bread for the
Golden Man. Seeing that he was asleep, and the
cover turned over his head, the frog set the tray on a chair
beside his bed and took a shuffling step towards the door.
But then he noticed that the Golden Man's covers lay very
still. Fearing that the man might be smothering himself, his
lungs being in poor and weak condition from the near
drowning, the frog turned back the blanket and found no
man there at all, but only bunched-up covers.

"Oh, ah," said Greensleeves to himself. "Good, good,
something to report. This is unusual, yes, and she'll want to
hear about it. Alert frog, that's what she'll think. Bright and
smart, that's me." Off he went to the Bad Sister's cabin. She
came out of bed at his knocking and put her eye to peek out
of the crack of her door. Greensleeves gave his report.

"Now is that certain, you green turnip?" she asked, and
the frog bobbed his head. The Bad Sister mused for a
moment. "The Golden Man up and about and playing at
some dirty pirate game, no doubt." She rubbed a finger
over her chin, thinking. "Things are starting to come out.
Now the question is, who's in on what with whom? It's

quiet tonight. Yes, the lull before the storm. All right, then," she said, crooking a finger outside the crack of the door and using it expressively as she gave her instructions to her menial. "We *must* find out who the Golden Man has fallen in with. Go out now and listen at all doors. A plot's brewing to take over this ship. We've got to protect ourselves. Anyway, it's not good for us that the Golden Man is running around the ship on some secret. Most of all, I believe Mister Cloud's a danger. Also, that Skivvy." The frog stood looking at her eyes, nearly hypnotised. She settled her gaze on him. "Well, go!" she said. "And look here, you green dumpling, if you get caught, I'll have you replaced with a toad."

"Yes'm. Yes'm," said the frog, saluting her, and off he ran. "Oh, how clever she is," he muttered to himself. "What a wonderful woman. Oh my, and I was admitted to her boudoir, wasn't I? Very nearly, anyway. What did she call me? A green dumpling. Oh, sweet insult. Delightful, delightful. All plump and juicy, that's what she thinks of me. Oh, that's good, that's good. She trusts me, too. Yes, yes, and she sends me on secret errands. Intimate, that's our relationship. Here now is Mister Skivvy's door. I'll listen. Shhhhh ... No. Very quiet. Nothing. Where now? Mister Cloud is in the Captain's cabin. That's next."

At the top of the ladderway, Greensleeves halted and pulled his head down. The Captain was strolling on deck, worrying to himself and pacing the dark ship. The frog waited for him to pass. He then went to the door of the Captain's cabin and listened. He could hear Mister Cloud snoring. After that he went to the fo'c'sle. He then made a round of the other large and likely meeting places for a secret rendezvous, but of course he did not go deep into the ship and squeeze into the magazine locker, Davy Duck's sewing parlour. Then he hurried back to the Bad Sister's cabin and made his report. She said:

"The Captain's on deck, is he, and did he have the bread box with him?"

Greensleeves stuck the tip of his tongue out of the side of his mouth, thinking back. "No. The last I saw of it was in the Captain's cabin."

"All right," said the Bad Sister. "It's bad work that we don't know what the Golden Man is up to, but I suppose it's probably to get the whole treasure to himself somehow. But let that be. There's other dangers. What we want now is that bread box, Greensleeves. What we want now is that doll. That's an important doll, Greensleeves. No telling what the Captain might do next. We need that bread box. Now, there's a slippery sort of business suited to a long-legged slyboots like yourself." The frog folded his hands and blinked his great eyes in admiration as the Bad Sister gave him further instructions to carry out, and off he went to kidnap Amy.

That night, the first blood of life ran on the deck of the *Ariel*. It was just at the striking of six bells of the first watch (that is to say, 11:00 P.M.) that the Captain looked over the port and starboard bows, hoping to find Skivvy sitting on a cathead, so that the two friends might smoke a pipe together and share a silent watch into the darkness. But Skivvy was not on a cathead that night. Thinking he must be in his cabin, and perhaps fretting over the Bible, the Captain decided to go below and lead him away from his fears if he could. Yes, thought the Captain, he had been neglecting Skivvy, so much else had been on his mind. As he turned away from the bow, the entire ship, sails furled up, was open to his sight. The masts and spars of the ship appeared like a winter's naked forest of elm – and then he saw a figure just coming down the rigging leading to the main mast. The Captain had not set a masthead watch, so he thought that this was curious. Then the Captain saw who it was. It was again the figure in the dark cloak and hood.

The Captain immediately drew his sword and advanced, but the figure heard the sound of it, jumped from the railing, and ran around the side of the galley. The *Ariel* was rolling slightly in the swell. With his free hand touching the starboard railing, the Captain ran towards where the figure had disappeared. He stopped at the corner of the galley. Banging his sword on the starboard side of the low building and stomping his feet as if he were charging around that way, the Captain instead ran in the opposite direction, to port, sword foremost. And rounding the next corner, he came head on to the mysterious figure.

The Captain could not make out a face inside the hood thrown forward on the figure's head. His glance did not hesitate there but caught upon the glint of the knife that flashed out from under the folds of the cloak. The Captain had just time enough to raise the point of his sword. It ran into the folds of the cloak and pierced into living flesh. The figure grunted and fell backwards. At the same time the Captain fell sideways to avoid the knife that had caught his eye, thus catching his foot in a coil of rope, whereupon he pitched onto the deck and cracked his head at the scuppers.

For a few seconds he was dazed entirely. Realising his disadvantage, he pulled himself up, put his back to the railing, sword ready, and looked into the darkness. All was quiet. Carefully the Captain stood up and approached the galley. Slowly he walked around it. Cautiously he opened the door and entered, sweeping his sword ahead of him in the darkness. He lit a lamp, searching the corners, and looked under the table. Going outside again, the lantern in hand, he went to the place of the collision and set the lamp on the deck. A dark stain marked the spot. The Captain took the test of it between his fingers. He smelled at it, and felt the stickiness of it. Blood. A few spots of it led off halfway around the galley. Then no more.

Returning to the galley, the Captain wiped the blood from the point of his sword with a towel. After soaking the towel in water, he took his careful way onto the deck again. With the wet cloth he wiped up the blood spilled there. No reason to alarm the morning watch. The Captain would use this information how and when he chose to. He walked to the rail and threw the bloody towel over the side into the sea. For a minute he watched as it drifted. Then it slowly sank into the darkness. Looking upward into the rigging, wondering what the man had been doing aloft, he saw through the forest of spar and mast and rope the great white plume of Vulcan Island. Skivvy's voice sounded in his memory: "'. . . and as it were a great mountain burning with fire was cast into the sea: and the third part of the sea became blood'!"

The Captain looked down to where the bloodied cloth had disappeared. Could Skivvy be right? The Captain stared at the volcano. It seemed to grow larger as he watched, as if the *Ariel* were drifting towards it. The Captain gripped the railing and shook his head. No! No, and no again! What is to happen God alone knows, and it is said that even the angels are ignorant of tomorrow. He opened his eyes on the mountain again. It had regained its distance. The Captain put a stern face towards it. There are many mountains in the world, and much blood, and seven seas. The Captain's job was to command his ship and save Amy's eyes, to take the golden treasure on board and return his crew safely to land. There was enough business in that without worrying about the end of the world.

"'Sufficient unto the day is the evil thereof,'" quoted the Captain aloud. "Matthew 6:34."

The Captain then returned to his cabin, where Mister Cloud snored and slept without dreaming. The Captain lay down with his clothes on. He put a hand over the side of the bed to touch the top of the bread box wherein lay Amy buried in her salt bed. He closed his eyes.

A shadow appeared at the Captain's stern window. After a few minutes, the Captain stirred. The shadow watched. The Captain turned slightly. His hand fell away from the bread box. The figure at the window quietly opened the window a few inches. The Captain stirred again. He moved his hand to rest atop the bread box again. The shadow at the window hesitated a moment, then quietly closed the window and continued watching all through the night.

Belowdecks in the magazine locker, the Golden Man sewed jackets for the ducks, now and then talking to them.

"Mates, I'll tell ye again. You'll have to be brave soon and fight for your Captain. Aye, mates, we're in dangerous waters, but just follow your Captain when the time comes. That's what I want to put next to your hearts. It's the jackets you're wearing that gives ye the sign of your Captain."

The Golden Man slipped a jacket on a duck. "Here, now, is that snug on your back? A fine fit, and a fine duck ye are. There's a good lad." He picked up another duck and sat it in the cradle of his crossed legs. "Have ye been listening, shipmate? 'Hurrah for the Captain,' that's what ye sing out when ye know him, and you'll know him by this here jacket I'm making up bright and new for ye. Aye, that's the sign. Hear my voice now, and remember it. You'll hear it again in a desperate time, and ye must heed to it. Time's coming, mates, time's coming, but don't think on that. Take heart, for that's where the sign is. Listen now, all shipmates, your Captain is he whose uniform you're wearing. Aye, that's what to remember, aye, and the Captain of your hearts, and then stand up for your Captain."

And so forth, with other encouraging talk to the ducks, the Golden Man sewed through the night. And down the dark passageway outside the magazine locker, up a ladder and around a corner, Skivvy's door swung open back and forth on its hinges as the ship rolled on the sea. Anyone who passed might see him sitting at his table. He was writing. His head nodded as if he were on the verge of sleep. Now and then he put his shaking hand towards the inkpot. Then, in a slow and laborious signature, he wrote some more. His left arm rested in his lap, pressing into his stomach. Blood ran between his fingers and dripped onto the floor.

CHAPTER FORTY-TWO

Whether it's cold, or whether it's hot,
There's going to be weather, whether or not.

Very early in the morning a blanket of low grey clouds pulled over the sleeping ship, and a drizzle of rain lightly settled like an undersheet upon the *Ariel*, and covered the sea as it tucked into the horizons. The figure at the Captain's window, being a frog, did not much mind the rain, but the grey morning light might give him away. He climbed up and over the taffrail to rouse the Bad Sister and make his report. He found her already up and in the galley. She cuffed his head with her ladle and endeared his affection to her with other abusive treatment and reproaching words for not having the doll with him. He quickly returned to his station outside the Captain's casement, there to perch and drench in the rain the whole day if need be and wait on his chance to kidnap Amy, for the Bad Sister said that it must be done.

Mister Cloud was out of bed before the Captain was. He made his way bareheaded to the galley. He returned to the cabin with coffee for both himself and the Captain, his white hair and beard glistening with droplets of water. Setting the coffee down, he combed his hand through his beard and studied the barometer mounted on the bulk-head. Then he sat down and sipped his coffee loudly and watched the sleeping Captain, whose hand still rested atop the bread box. The frog at the window watched them both.

Now and then the wind threw the rain against the window, making the sound of tin drums, far away. Presently, before the Captain's coffee had cooled, and using no art in the matter, Mister Cloud resettled his chair, sliding and bumping it on the deck. The Captain awoke. He turned his head towards Mister Cloud, then sat up and looked towards the stern window.

"Low and wet," said Mister Cloud. "Here's coffee, Captain." Motioning towards the barometer with his head, he reported, "The glass is steady, just the wet tail of something farther north."

The Captain grunted, pulling himself from the bunk. He took up the bread box and sat at the table. He took a long drink of the coffee and commented, "She's got some use, that woman." Mister Cloud nodded his head solemnly, still believing that the Captain was in love with her. Perhaps he had been up late courting her, thus to come to bed worn out from romancing, to sleep in his clothes. A knock came at the cabin door. "Come in," said the Captain, and Davy Duck opened the door. He stood there sleek with the rain, and nodded his head in a sort of deferential bow to both the Captain and the first mate.

"Davy Duck here, Captain. Lovely weather, sir, if ye have the right point of view on it. I mean to say if you're a duck, sir. No offence intended to the gentlemen."

This was a rather bold piece of amiability from the duck, but he had that morning inspected his crew in the magazine locker, all dressed out in their new jackets. It seemed to him that a light rain and a wet deck was just the weather for his takeover of the ship, for a duck is cheerful in such weather and has an advantage in footing. This he had discussed with the Golden Man. The mutiny would begin, so they decided, just as soon as Cowl's treasure was on board the *Ariel*.

"I come to pass along word from that there Golden Man, like I heard him called, and he's up and about, Captain, feeling much better. Anyway, that Golden Man says to me — myself being on this watch and all — he says to me, seeing as I'm a sort of shipmate that can carry a message and make a good account of a simple matter — he says to me, 'Tell the Captain, Davy —' And right there I breaks in on him and says something myself, knowing he's got a pirate's background and can't be trusted entirely — I says to him, 'Aye, the Captain, and you keep it in mind. He's the Captain, mate, and best you remember it, and the Captain of a ship is the one who gives the orders, and that's a duck's fact, for it's the Captain who knows best always, and . . .'"

The Captain threw an appealing glance at Mister Cloud, who returned the look with a slight smile under his beard, and looked down at the deck.

"All right, all right, Davy," said the Captain. "So what did the man say?"

"Ah, that's it, that's it," said Davy. "What he says is that if we was to get the gold off the island we'd best do it right away, since he says that the last time it was weather like this, the mountain started grumbling and the earthquake came. So he says he's ready to push off and needs a crew in the ship's boat to help get that gold off the island and onto the ship."

"Right," said the Captain. "Here's orders, Davy. The dogs are to help with the treasure. They're good with the boat, and strong for the work. Swing out the boat and get the rest of the crew fishing soon as they finish breakfast. I'll be on deck presently."

"Aye, sir," said Davy. "If those are the orders, then that's what's to be done, for you're the Captain, sir, yes indeed, sir, you are, and the Captain of a ship —"

"On your way," growled Mister Cloud, "on your way, lad." Davy made an apologetic bow and went out. "I'll get my rain gear and take the deck," said the first mate. The Captain nodded, and was left alone in the cabin. The frog, who had heard the voices but not the words of the conversation, now in the lull peeked a big eye around the casement of the window again. The Captain opened the bread box, uncovered Amy's face, and spoke to her.

"Good morning, Sis, and how is it with you today?"

"Oh, Captain," said Amy, and her voice was broken with a sob. "It's all the same, Captain. It's all dark, Captain, and I don't know where I am at all except still inside the fish."

"Steady now, Sis. We're fishing again, and I've hopes that we'll get your eyes back today." The Captain tried to think of some cheery matter, but resisted telling Amy that her father had been found, for the good reason that soon enough there might be fighting and dying aboard the *Ariel*. It would be cruel indeed if Amy should have to know that her father was killed shortly after he was found. "Sis," said the Captain, "today we get the gold treasure! Think of it, just like we set out to do, just like I told you about when we were in the carriage riding away from St. Anne's. Yes, today we'll have it. Then we'll go off wherever we please and retire somewhere and just have a boat for pleasure cruising."

"And Miss Eclair? Can't we find Miss Eclair again?"

"Aye, Sis, of course Miss Eclair. She can come, too. We'll visit St. Anne's and visit Mrs. Hill and tell her the whole adventure. And you'll be dressed in a blue satin dress with silver slippers if you want, and wearing golden earrings. We'll drive up in a fine sparkling carriage with four horses. We'll be so elegant and bright that everyone's eyes will pop out when they see ..."

At this unfortunate turn of phrase, Amy began crying.

"Oh ... oh, Captain," she said. "Oh, Captain, will I be blind? Will I ever have my eyes again? What if you never catch this fish?"

"Sis," said the Captain sternly, brushing her yarn hair, "I won't hear such talk. You *will* have your very own eyes back. That's all there is to that." For a few moments more he sat with his hand on Amy's head, and then said, "I've got to go now, Sis. You just remember that we're fishing every line on the ship. Think about that gold treasure, and Miss Eclair, and how wonderful things are going to be. I'll talk with you later. Be brave, Sis. Good-bye for a while, now."

"Good-bye, Captain. Please don't let me be alone too long. Good-bye, Captain."

It was spoken in a brave voice, but now the Captain blinked back his tears as he smoothed the salt over her face. Standing up and taking the bread box under his arm, the Captain looked around the cabin. He opened a tall cabinet drawer and put in the bread box. Slipping into his rain gear, he left the cabin. Outside, he turned a brass key in the door's lock, tried the latch, and went on deck.

"Oh, happy, happy, happy," Greensleeves said to himself, looking in. He tried the window. It was still unlatched. The frog was in pure delight. "Oh, happy, happy, happy, she'll be. And with me. Oh, the dear woman. Oh, my darling, she shall have all she wants. But I'll bide my time. Yes, yes, I'll bide my time. I'll go to her again and say how hard it is and how dangerous sitting out here. I'll say I'm getting pneumonia and cramps. I'll say my lumbago is giving me pain. But I'll say it doesn't matter. How she'll weep for me. Oh no, she won't show it, and that's why she'll kick me and yell at me, because she doesn't want to show how tenderhearted she is. Complex, that's how she is. But then I'll bring her the doll and fall down shivering like I'm sick to death ... and she'll kiss me and tell me she loves me... Oh, happy, happy, happy. Oh, secret love, oh, lovely rain, lovely tears of joy."

He settled himself as comfortably as he could, crossed his arms, tucked in his head and sang a song out of *Mother Goose*, biding his time.

> "A frog he would a-wooing go,
> Heigh ho! says Rowley,
> Whether his mother would let him or no,
> With a rowley, powley, gammon and spinach,
> Heigh ho! says Anthony Rowley."

The crew on deck, soaking in their fur and feathers, baited their lines abstractly, paying attention to the ship's boat as it was lowered. The Golden Man took the tiller. The dogs took the oars and pushed off from the *Ariel*. The rain and running tide washed them towards Vulcan Island, a grey boat with a grey crew on a grey sea on a grey day. Yet soon enough there would be brightness upon the day – the brightness of blood and gold, and the brightness of fire, and the last brightness of the eye before death puts out the light of the world.

CHAPTER FORTY-THREE

O that I were where I would be,
Then would I be where I am not;
But where I am there I must be,
And where I would be I can not.

Many miles to the south the sun was shining, and Mama Dah-dah trudged up her hill with a breakfast fish in her woven basket. Her great white albatross followed behind. Coming into her home, she spoke out as she always did.

"Hello, house, how you doing? You feeling all right? You miss me? Here I am. Got a big fish. How you doing, stove? Getting hot?"

She then cleaned the fish and threw the guts out the window to Anthony. After she had laid the fish fillets in her frying pan to cook, she moved to the window, wiping her hands on a cloth. She watched the albatross plucking at the fish guts. And then out from the fish's stomach into the bright sunshine fell two bright blue buttons.

Far away to the north, the light burst in on Amy's darkness and she cried out.

"Captain, Captain! I'm out of the fish. Wait, wait, I can't see yet, it's so bright. There, there! Now. Yes, I'm on dry land, Captain. Oh my – there's a big white bird standing right over me. And a black woman is standing in a window looking at me. Captain, I'm out, I'm free! Captain, Captain!"

But no one heard Amy's cry, for she was in her burial of salt and the lid was closed tight on the bread box. The Captain was on deck watching the caught fish being opened up in search for Amy's eyes. Now and then he turned and looked through the drizzling greyness towards Vulcan Island, where the steaming mountain itself was lost in the low grey clouds. The Golden Man had been gone with the dogs for an hour or more. The Captain did not expect them to return soon, for if what Amy's father said was true, there was a whole boatload of gold treasure to load.

Mama Dah-dah recovered Amy's eyes from where they lay on the ground and brought them inside. She set the blue buttons on her table and admired them, for they were brighter than ever, having been polished inside the stomach of the fish. Mama Dah-dah sat and smiled at them. She wondered how she might use them, for every pretty thing must have a use. Amy looked back at her, and spoke again in the salt of the bread box.

"Captain, an old black woman has found my eyes. She has black hair with lots of white hair in it, and with a bunch of pink flowers stuck in it. She seems to be kind, for she's smiling at me. I'd like to smile back, and I am, but only with my eyes. We're in a small room. Oh, Captain, can't you hear me? Someone caught the fish, and a big white bird — oh, there he is now, standing in the window. That's what to look for, Captain. Where I am is in a small room in a small house. You'll see a big white bird sitting in the window. And inside lives an old black woman who's wearing a blue dress. But most of all, look for that bird. Now the woman is reaching down to pick up my eyes. Now I'm in her hand, my eyes, I mean. Captain? Captain, can't you hear me?"

Mama Dah-dah had decided what to do with the blue buttons. She moved a chair nearer the window and got a needle and thread out of an old cigar box. Then she took an embroidered blouse from a drawer. It was all encircled about the neck with tiny flowers, a piece of work that was a gift from someone she had helped. She spoke to the albatross, who stood in the window watching her.

"See, Anthony," she said, holding out her hand to show the buttons to the bird again, "you did good today. Pearly blue buttons for Mama Dah-dah. How sweet you are. Just like my good man, Anthony. Oh, how he used to bring me presents. Come home sometimes, sometimes not. Now, there was a man you could learn migrations from, bird. But he gone into the spirit some time ago. Ain't it the truth. Look, now, how pretty this will be. Dah, dah, dah . . ."

After Mama Dah-dah had sewed the buttons onto the blouse, she hung the garment up on a wall so she could admire it as she moved about. Shortly after that a woman came to the door who had struggled up Mama Dah-dah's hill. She was thin and hunched over, pale as a ghost, with ugly lines at her mouth. But she was not so very old, only her attitude would make it seem so. She kicked at the pebbles beneath her feet, as if they were at fault for being on the pathway. Most of all her back hurt her, and her neck. It gave her great pain to lift her head, so mainly she looked at what was underfoot, and kicked at it. She had not been able to stand up straight for a long time.

She somewhat believed in Mama Dah-dah, but not much. It was a forced visit she was making. She lived in the village below and was kept by relatives even though she complained much because of her pain and could never be happy. But at last the relatives had lost their patience, and told her she must visit Mama Dah-dah or be cast off. So she stumbled up the hill with a step and attitude as if the gentle morning breeze were lashing cruelly at her. She fairly limped to Mama Dah-dah's door.

The old woman took her in. The painful woman didn't

have anything to say. She grunted and sat. Mama Dah-dah touched her hands. The woman turned her eyes away. Then Mama Dah-dah got up and went about her business.

"Drat that thing," she said, taking up her broom, "Drat it! Out the door now, and take your family with you." She swept some ants out the door. "That's life for you, everybody wanting to eat. Can't eat food, they eat somebody else. Everybody hurting about something. Ain't it the truth." For a while she rearranged some things and dusted, while the woman sat bent over at the table. "That's right. Man came up here with one leg, cussing sharks. Not the shark's fault, I tell him. He says he knows that. Not God's fault, I say. He says he knows that. Then why you cussing, I say. He don't know. Nobody knows. Round and round it goes. Everybody having troubles. Everybody hurt about something. Got to keep moving. Look now, you want to see something pretty?"

The woman turned her head around sideways, painfully. Mama Dah-dah pointed to her blouse.

"See that? Now, isn't that a pretty thing? That white bird helped me with it. Pretty blue buttons he brought me. You ought to see how nice that is."

The woman angled her head around to look towards the blouse. For a few minutes she was silent, while Mama Dah-dah moved about dusting. Then the woman got up and made her way over to the blouse, as if she had seen something that needed closer inspection. Painfully she tried to raise her head to look up. Amy saw her and cried out.

"Lady! Oh lady, can you help me? I'm buried, and no one knows where my eyes are. Can't you hear me? Oh, please, hear me! I'm lost. The Captain doesn't know where my eyes are. Oh, please, I think I'm dying. Lady, please help me, I can't move. Oh, don't leave me alone. Please help me!"

The lady could not hear her, of course, since Amy's mouth was not there. Then Amy began weeping. The buttons glistened, and the woman raised her head in wonder. Then a tear fell from one of the buttons. The woman straightened her back to stand taller and see better. She reached up a hand, touched the button, tasted the salt tear on it, and looked with alarm to Mama Dah-dah, who was dusting with her back turned. Now the woman was standing straight up, not heeding her pain. Now she spoke out in wonder.

"They're crying! They're hurt!"

"That's right," said Mama Dah-dah without turning around. "Everybody's got something to cry about. Everybody's got some hurt. Ain't it the truth. Got to keep moving, that's all. Oh, now, look at you. Up and about. You feeling better? Ain't that wonderful. You feel like taking up that broom? Sweep some sand out of here. You'll be all right. Better life coming up now."

The woman kissed Mama Dah-dah when she left. She walked down the hill with her head up, her back straight, looking around at the colour of the sky and the ocean as she had not for a long time.

Mama Dah-dah sat at the table silently after the woman had left, looking into the bowl she made with her hands, and she was quiet in her thoughts. Then, in a quick movement, she laid her hands flat on the table and looked up and out of the door, as if hearing a sharp noise. Then she looked quickly at the window, where Anthony was dozing. Quietly she got up, quietly she took hold of her broom, and lifting her feet quietly she went to the open door. Then, with an outburst of a cry – "Hooooooooooooo!" – she jumped outside and in a second had whacked on either side of the door with her broom and stood ready to whack some more at anything that moved. But she stood alone. Only

[325]

Anthony was a witness. He flopped around the corner, wakened from his nap, cocked his head and growled "Errrrrr?" as if in question.

"Huh!" said Mama Dah-dah "Huh! Somebody try to fool with this old lady, they get whopped. What you see, Anthony? You been sleeping again? Somebody been looking in on this old lady, Anthony. You stand for that? You always sleeping when I need you? Huh! Ain't it the truth."

Then, after walking once around her shack, she made a final "Huh!" and went inside again, shaking her head and mumbling to herself that someone had been looking in on her, but she could not understand how the fellow had got away. And as her great bird jumped again into the window, she frowned towards him and a flash of light from his wing shot across the buttons freshly sewn onto her blouse so that they blinked like a pair of blue eyes.

Mama Dah-dah laid the blouse on her table and looked steadily into the buttons with her own eyes deepening as it were into dark wells in her searching concentration and Mama Dah-dah made a full discovery of the matter within a few minutes.

"Ohhhhhhh," she said, leaning back. "Look, Anthony! Little girl eyes. My, my, now isn't that something? Little girl eyes changed into blue buttons. Look, Anthony!"

Immediately she clipped them from the blouse and took them in her hand to show to her white bird. He put his beak down nearly to touch them, but Mama Dah-dah pulled her hand away. "No, no, Anthony. Not to eat. My, my, how strange. But where is the little girl? That's the question, Anthony. Better look at this some more."

So saying, she set the buttons on the table and sat down before them. Clasping her hands together, she leaned close and stared into Amy's eyes until her own were almost closed in concentration on the wonder. Presently she began humming softly to herself, and presently she saw in her mind a large stone building with children playing around about it. Then she saw a doll dressed like a sailor, being carried about by a little golden-headed girl. Mama Dah-dah sat in her clean little room with the sunlight coming in at the door and the white albatross standing in the window. She looked into Amy's eyes and saw the near wrecking of a carriage on a roadway, and a fight in a tavern, and a ship manned by animals, and all else that was in Amy's eyes, and now and then Mama Dah-dah exclaimed lowly, "Ain't it the truth, ain't it the truth."

CHAPTER FORTY-FOUR

Speak of a person, and he will appear,
Then talk of the devil, and he'll draw near.

N ow, *aboard* the *Ariel*, those many miles away
from Mama Dah-dah's sunlit hill where the old
black woman was learning Amy's story, the
Captain paced the wet decks with an increasing depression
of heart and mind, as if the very greyness of the day and the
drizzling rain sopped into him and anointed his spirit with
despair. Mister Cloud kept the crew busy at their fishing,
even though he himself much doubted the chance of bringing up the very fish they desired to find out of a whole
ocean of fishes. The crew found no joy or sport in the
occupation any longer, but were suffering it merely as
duty, and they were catching very few fish out of the rain-
spattered ocean. The Bad Sister, wrapped in her great
cloak, now and then came out of the galley and stared
towards Vulcan Island as if to establish her claim to the
gold by showing herself, and to indicate her watchfulness
that no cheating in the division of the treasure would
escape her attention.

Skivvy was below. He had at last come to his final con-
clusions out of the Bible. After he had nearly killed the
Golden Man in his bed, he had returned in great remorse to
his studies, and by mere chance had discovered at last the
true identity of the Beast of the number 666. It was not,
after all, the Golden Man. He was taking some pains to

explain his discovery to the Captain in writing, for blood came to his throat when he tried to speak. Skivvy wanted the Captain to understand certain actions that he had taken, for he had reason to suppose he would not live out the day.

Belowdecks, Davy Duck found privacy now and then to visit his ducks. He patted them and admired their new jackets. He had them lined up in rows, each laid with its head turned aside, ready for the plunge of the needle that would give them life and make them full of sense. When the Golden Man returned with the treasure, Davy was going to take over the ship. The weather held good for ducks, and the Captain was distracted by his worry over Amy. It was a good time to strike, thought Davy.

The morning passed. The Captain took no report to Amy, for he had no good report to make. He decided to let her lie peacefully in her bread box beneath her salt cover. In some ways he envied her. He was in more torment than ever. The crew had not caught a fish for the last hour. He almost wished he had never become a real person. A doll can't know the hurt of it. It seemed to him that most of his life had been made up of separation, pain, loss, deceit, and betrayal. Was worse to come yet? The Captain could not stir his small cold hope enough to give even a candle's warmth to his dampened mood. Not only was it heavy upon him that some second-best solution must be sought out concerning Amy's eyes – for he was beginning to think that she would never have her very own eyes back again – but also he knew that it was only a matter of time before the *Locust* searched them out. If Goldnose suspected the truth of the situation, that the *Ariel* had found the gold treasure, the fat pirate would surely attack them. The Captain could not see any outcome of that except that they would go down to death whether they surrendered the gold or not. Also, he thought it very likely that the entire crew was by now won over to the Bad Sister, all of them by now charmed under her dark wing by the authority of *Mother Goose*. He supposed that she would brandish the book like a flag, or emblem, when the time came for her uprising.

Bearing the wet weather, the Captain walked about the deck with his hands behind his back. And at last he came upon the proof that a mutiny was brewing. He had paused in his walking up and down to lean on the red-painted casement of Skivvy's bomb, the better to steady himself as he raised his dripping telescope to look towards Vulcan Island. Doing so, he heard a sound that he took to be the wind about his ears, but then recognised it for whispering, and a word out of the whispering came to him, clearly heard, and the word was "mutiny." The Captain looked over the top and around the corner of the bomb. He caught Turkey's eye. The bird started with alarm and silenced Chicken by sticking a pipe in that bird's mouth. They had been sitting fast against the lee side of the red structure, smoking a pipe and speculating on Davy's mutiny. Now both of them were aware of the Captain. They quickly got up, not certain that they had been discovered at their plotting. The turkey tried to brave it out, fearing that the word "mutiny" had been heard. He touched his forehead in a salute and made to pass the Captain.

"Scrutiny, Captain, we was saying. Meaning to say, sir, that we was talking about keeping our eyes on a close lookout for that pirate ship. Routine scrutiny, that's the word — routiny scrutiny, Captain, as that's our duty. Routiny scrutiny, sir, as we was saying. Right, Chicken?"

Chicken caught on, and took up the game.

"Absolutiny. No disputiny. Routiny scrutiny, Captain."

The Captain made them all the more nervous with his silent, wry demeanour, so they were not at all certain if he had heard them pronounce the word "mutiny." They fumbled some more as they worked their way around him and towards the crew.

"Just en routiny," said Turkey, going past the Captain.

"Dutiny calls," said Chicken.

And they were gone. The Captain watched after them for a minute, and then turned his telescope towards Vulcan Island again. The shore was barely visible. No sign yet of the boat.

In the early afternoon the rain slackened and the sky showed patches of blue. Presently the low weather moved north and presented a dark curtain in that direction. The decks of the *Ariel* steamed in the warm sunlight, and the volcano came fully in sight again, sending up its enormous plume. It had been some full six hours since the departure of the small boat for the island. Then at last a monkey in the yards shouted out that the boat was in sight. All hands crowded to the railings.

In the distance came on the Golden Man in a golden boat, so laden with treasure heaped above the gunwales that it looked like a pat of butter on the dark sea. It was heavy with gold, loaded nearly in danger of swamping, so that the dogs at the oars pulled carefully through the swelling sea. All were on deck. The Bad Sister, still wrapped in her great cloak, stood next to the Captain and Mister Cloud on the poop deck. Skivvy at last had finished his letter to the Captain and laid it inside the Bible. A slight trail of blood showed the way he had stumbled onto the deck from his cabin. He stood on the poop deck with his arm encircled around a shroud. Davy Duck put his head out of the fo'c'sle ladderway and watched the approach of the golden boat. He stroked the point of a sailmaker's needle stuck in the lapel of his jacket. He surveyed the deck. The humans were all on the poop deck, the animals amidships at the railings. The Golden Man, after coming aboard, would work his way to stand behind the Captain on the poop deck, as he and Davy had agreed. He was to strike down the Captain when the word was given. Davy and his ducks would cut through the animal crew easily, since they were not armed at the moment. Then the ship would be Davy's. He would be the Captain at last. Quack, quack.

The Captain fixed his telescope on the approaching boat, heavily and slowly coming towards the *Ariel*, and even so shipping water over the gunwales. The Golden Man was obliged to handle the tiller with one hand and scoop seawater from the boat with a large golden bowl. The Captain smiled to himself, looking upon this small hill of gold making its way towards them, for he had come upon an idea that might put off the Bad Sister's mutiny and save the ship. Since her motive was greed and her interest was gold – for the Captain could not think of any other interest she might have – then it was the very gold treasure that could be used against her. There might yet be a chance to save the *Ariel*. There might yet be a chance that the Captain could sail free with the ship under his command, thereby to find some solution to Amy's problem.

"There it is, Mister Cloud," said the Captain, "Cowl's treasure, or whatever remains of it." He handed the telescope to the first mate. Looking to the Bad Sister, he remarked, "So now, madam, it appears that we're near an end to our bargain – if I made a bargain with an honest woman. Yet I've reason to doubt that, and I'll not suffer any surprise for what you may have to say to me now, for I believe that you intend to Mother Goose me out of the entire gold treasure and the ship as well, and I don't put it beyond your miserable estate that you might have plans to kill me at this spot or maroon me on the island."

Mister Cloud paused at his study through the telescope. He turned towards the Captain with a look of puzzlement and concern. He hadn't, of course, an inkling of this side of the Captain's mind. Had there been a falling out between them? Were they no longer lovers? Talk of killing and marooning?

The Captain continued. "So have your say, madam, and gather your mutineers. Your time has come. But give a thought first." The Captain pointed to the returning boat, it now having covered half the distance to the *Ariel*. "See that Golden Man? He's a pirate, and is pledged to my service, for reasons he deems fit, and he cannot be won over with gold. And now you see how he sits in a place where he might easily sink that boat and send Cowl's gold back to the bottom of the sea. And upon my order and my signal, he will do so. Consider, madam — consider once again. Your interest in the voyage is the gold, and I swear by God that I will send every ounce of it back to the sea if you do not on this moment reveal yourself entirely to me and pledge yourself and your fellow mutineers away from your designs and come under my authority — including also your shadow that creeps the deck by night, if he is not now crawled away to some rathole to die."

The Captain drew his sword and stepped back and away from the Bad Sister and Mister Cloud. "There is the situation, madam, latitude and longitude. So set your course. I intend to be master of this ship or to die on this deck, here and now."

The Bad Sister, her face streaked with the recent rain so that rivulets of mascara ran down her cheeks, seemed for once to be without a word or malediction. She put a hand forward as if to touch the Captain, and he tensed. She threw a glance at Mister Cloud, who raised his eyebrows at her. Then, imploringly, she held out both hands to the Captain.

"The mutiny, Captain. It's not me. I'm no danger to you."

The Captain blinked. Her face seemed to change as he looked at her, the mask melting away in the rain. Her eyes seemed changed, also. They looked softer, and worried. The Captain blinked again. This was her manner in defeat, he thought. The woman was discovered and confronted at last. She was surrendering to him.

For a brief moment only, the Captain considered that he had won the day away from her. Then that brief moment was broken by Mister Cloud's voice. He had taken the telescope to his eye again, and now he spoke out.

"Whatever the matter is you're speaking about, Captain – it looks like we all might soon be dead on these decks. There! Off she comes! Off the port bow, out of that bank of cloud! It's the *Locust*!"

The Captain reached for the telescope with his free hand. He clenched his teeth as he studied the pirate ship through the steam and quivering atmosphere. To be sure, it was the *Locust*. He put the glass on the *Ariel*'s own boat laden with treasure, and made a calculation of time and distance. Thrusting the telescope back to Mister Cloud, he spoke to the Bad Sister again.

"Madam – unless you think you can handle a mutiny and a shipload of pirates at the same time, you'd best put off your plans for now. We must all stand together in this or we'll surely be taken. Later, if we live through the day, you will have my pardon, and amity as well if you stand with the ship, and half the gold as well, as was our original bargain. I take your word of honour loosely, madam, but this is a loose moment and I'll take a simple 'yea' for security. Then we shall take the gold on board and revert to our original bargain. You shall raise no mutiny. Do I have your word? Quickly!"

"I shall raise no mutiny," said the Bad Sister.

The Captain nodded curtly and gave orders, first calling out to the Golden Man.

"Lay those dogs to the oars! Goldnose is upon us! The *Locust* is in sight! Mister Cloud, lift our bomb overboard and put your best marksman to the swivel gun. Arm the crew immediately and keep them smart. With a lucky wind and running space, we can blow that bum barge back to New Liberty's gutters. Madam, if I were you I would take a safer place to stand on deck, but that's up to you. Skivvy . . ."

But the Captain broke off his order to Skivvy, observing that his second mate hung limply to his shroud with a vacant look in his eye.

Mister Cloud descended and was among the crew. As the bomb platform was settled alongside the ship, the Golden Man approached with his golden boat and put his tiller over nicely to nestle against the side of the *Ariel*. Lines were fastened, and nets, buckets, and ropes were let over the side to bring up the golden treasure. It was freely dumped in a pile on the deck, a heap of glistening gold sparkling with precious gems.

If the animals had been men, and had they had the love of gold that afflicts the mind and heart of man, there would have been a delay of pure awe in gasping at the richness, magnificence, and variety of the treasure, and in the loving and caressing care and delight of the touch of the individual pieces of it. But the animals handled it like so much hardware. They tossed doubloons and pieces of eight around like tap washers. They crammed golden figurines into buckets as if they were plumbing tools. There was coin of ancient and modern vintage, stamped in a dozen languages and of a hundred sizes and shapes. There were golden tools of the dining table and the battlefield; dinner plates of pure gold, and decanters, goblets, all service to eat with and all service to wage war with; golden hilted swords there were, finely worked daggers with jewelled sheaths, gold-mounted pistols, and a golden horn. There was a golden crown, also, and a golden breastplate, necklaces, rings by the score with sparkling gemstones set in them, and small chests so heavy with golden chain and coin and craft that they could hardly be hoisted aboard. All this was thrown to the deck with barely a comment as the crew strained at the work and cast worrying glances at the approaching pirate ship, which was taking a straight course towards them on a fair wind. The Captain, during this while, took his chance to go to his cabin and take up the bread box so that Amy should be under his own protective care. If his last moment came, there would perhaps be time to say good-bye to her. He took no time to uncover Amy and speak to her, but came directly onto the deck again, just as the last of Cowl's gold was tossed aboard. Then, the gold treasure all loosely piled upon the deck and underfoot, the Captain ordered the crew to jump to the shrouds and climb the rigging. The Golden Man and the dogs secured the boat and climbed up and over the side of the *Ariel*. All the animals were armed with cutlasses now. The *Locust* was fast approaching.

"Stand by for my command, Mister Cloud. We'll set the last shirt-tail on her just as the *Locust* shortens sail to run up to us. Helmsman, make ready to run with the wind. Donkey! At the capstan, lad, and prepare to haul anchor!"

It was a scene that would have seemed to be all in terrible confusion to a landsman, but to a sailor it was all a picture of grace and coordination the way the animals scrambled to take their places, even though, stumbling over the pile of gold, the crew kicked several fortunes through the scuppers and into the sea. But no attention could be taken of that. Monkeys, Cats, and Squirrel were dancing out on the yards while the animals below put their hands to the lines that would let free the sails and bind them to use. Once they were under sail and clear to manoeuvre, the Captain intended to let the bomb platform out on the long line and attempt to place it close enough to the pirate ship so that the dog at the swivel gun might make a fair shot at it.

The Captain stood near the wheel, his legs braced apart, bread box under his arm. He appeared just as he was made to be by Amy's father, every stitch a Captain and worthy of a sailor's last confidence. He commanded all attention as the crew waited for his order. He watched the *Locust* with a straight face. At a thousand yards off, she drew up her royals. More slowly she approached, and then drew up her upper topgallant sails, and her bow settled as she lost speed still more. The crew of the *Ariel* watched and waited. Then finally the mainmast topgallant and upper topsail were drawn up as the *Locust* prepared to ease in broadside upon the *Ariel*. The Captain looked on a moment longer, then returned to Mister Cloud and spoke quietly.

"Set the sails, Mister Cloud, and clear the decks for action!"

CHAPTER FORTY-FIVE

Simple Simon went to look
If plums grew on a thistle;
He pricked his fingers very much,
Which made poor Simon whistle.

He went for water in a sieve,
But soon it all ran through;
And now poor Simple Simon
Bids you all adieu.

T he *Golden Man* was standing behind the
Captain. The Bad Sister stood near the railing,
Greensleeves at her side. Skivvy was hanging on
his line next to the frog. Before the order to set sail could be
passed on by Mister Cloud, Skivvy cried out as loudly as he
could force his breath from his pierced body, spitting blood
onto the deck as he did so:

"'And there came out of the smoke locusts upon the
earth: and unto them was given power ... and ... and their
faces were as the faces of men'!" And so shouting, gasping
out his little reserve of life's strength in his breath and
blood, Skivvy let go the shroud he was hanging on to and
fell to the deck, yet trying to speak with the feeble breath he
had left to him. The Captain ran to where he lay crumpled
and turned Skivvy's coat aside. There, above the butt of
the pistol he carried in his belt, the second mate's shirt was
cut through, frayed, and clogged with dark blood. Fresh

bright blood now ran onto the deck from the sword wound in his stomach.

"Skivvy!" cried the Captain. "Then it was *you* last night. Good heavens, man, what were you doing ...?" The Captain was fumbling with Skivvy's shirt to staunch the flow of blood. Skivvy took him by the arm and tried to pull himself up, speaking.

"A Beast ..." the second mate whispered brokenly. "A Beast, Captain, shall arise out of the sea ... 'The Golden Man and Mister Cloud had come up behind the Captain. Skivvy looked with glazed eyes at Amy's father, who now tore a patch of his shirt off for a compress to the wound. Skivvy braced himself as he reached out, held himself rigid from the touch, and implored the Captain in a voice rising with alarm and delirium. "Gold, Captain! The *Bible*! Revelation! A Beast shall arise out of the sea ... 'and the number of the Beast ...'!"

"Quiet there," said the Golden Man, putting the compress in place. "Every word you say is pumping blood out of this hole. You there, Bad Sister, or whoever you are, give me a strip off your petticoats."

The Bad Sister, without a word, turned her back, lifted her greatskirt, and in a moment handed the Golden Man a wide and long piece of clean linen. All the while the Golden Man continued to talk to Skivvy, hoping to soothe his outbursts.

"I am no Beast, man, and before you pass out or die you might as well know who I really am. No, and no pirate either, but we are relatives, my good fellow, although I think no one has yet invented the connection. I am the man who made the Captain when he was made into a doll – the maker of the man who made you. I am Amy's father."

Mister Cloud had at last turned away from this bloody

scene to pass on the Captain's orders, which he shouted out over the Golden Man's revelation.

"Set the mizzen sails!" he called out.

The cats jumped to the task, loosening lines, and the lower-course mizzen sail fell from the yards, covering Skivvy and his tending group. As the Captain struggled out from beneath the weight of canvas, the ruin come upon the ship became evident. Other sails were falling to the decks of the *Ariel* as the crew ran from line to line. The animals aloft scrambled port to starboard on the yards, but on each mast and every yard the worth was the same. Someone had cut through clewlines and buntlines, brails and sheets – so that the running lines and securing ropes of every sail were so badly hacked apart that even those sails that yet hung on the yards drooped and flapped as uselessly as towels flung over a clothesline. It was Skivvy's work, he in the dark-hooded cloak prowling about this last night with a knife in his hand. It was Skivvy's work, out on the dark deck, not meaning to be any imitation of the Bad Sister's shadow whom the Captain had seen in New Liberty and on the roadway, but only Skivvy. He was dressed in cloak and hood as he imagined a proper monk might be attired, in anticipation of a vow he had made – a vow to enter forever into a monastery if God would deliver the *Ariel* from her doom and let her sail again to a civilized port. This was one of the things explained to the Captain in the letter he left in his Bible.

When Amy's father uncovered Skivvy, and when the Bad Sister threw off the folds of canvas, Skivvy confessed the deed and attempted to explain further the path he had been set on.

"I did it, Captain ... The reason ... was the gold ... The pirates must take it, Captain ... to save us ..." He caught and gripped the Captain's arm with a dying strength. "First

King ... uh ... Kings ... 10:14 ... the Beast ... I wrote it all down ... uh ..." And he fainted.

As Amy's father lowered Skivvy's head to the deck, a whistling sound came overhead. A cannonball tore through a hanging sail and plunged into the sea beyond the *Ariel*, splashing into the water at about the same time that the thunder of the cannon was heard. Another shot followed, as Goldnose, now but two hundred yards off, sought to cripple his prey by taking off one of her masts. But then he perceived the distressed state of the *Ariel*, her sails uselessly fallen on the deck, and ceased firing.

The Captain was on his feet. He turned to watch towards the *Locust*. The Golden Man said, "Take care of that man," to the Bad Sister, leaving Skivvy's side. The Captain shouted the crew down from the rigging to take their stations on the deck. Mister Cloud was among them, making sure every man was armed. The Golden Man took a cutlass for himself and swung it about, testing its balance. He stood beside the Captain near the wheel.

"Is he alive?" the Captain asked, looking towards Skivvy.

"Only a little," said the Golden Man. "So he thinks I'm a beast of some sort? That explains it. Last night he came to my door with a pistol, possibly with intention to kill me. I woke up just as he turned away."

"It's all out of the Bible," said the Captain, pacing to the railing. He shouted down to the crew. "Clear that sail from the deck and make room for a fight, lads. Mister Cloud, put your crew to the swivel gun. A gold nose is the target this time." Then he spoke to the Golden Man again. "Skivvy's seen doom in the voyage from the beginning, all having to do with greed and gold and the end of the world. Aye, Father – poor Skivvy – his brains are all practically chapter and verse out of the Bible. The nearer we got to the gold treasure, the worse it came on him and tormented his mind,

for he thought that gold was the chief evil in the world."
The Captain grunted and smiled. "Humph. And maybe he
was right. Yes, and he thought that you were the Beast out
of Revelation. That's what he meant by that. What did he
say – that he'd explained it all in writing for me? Too bad
there won't ever be a chance to read it, but no matter,
probably."

"Well, I might agree about the end of the world, Son.
Here comes the *Locust*. I knew Cowl, and I know pirates. I
guarantee they aren't thinking much about *our* futures."
He looked among the animals below on the deck. He spied
Davy Duck off to one side, shirking his duty and edging
towards the fo'c'sle companionway. "Yet there's still a
chance, Son . . ."

"Wait," said the Captain. "Wait. Maybe Skivvy was
right. I believe he meant to say that he cut the sails so the
pirates could take the treasure. Well, then, let them have it.
Can't we bargain with it? Let them have the gold, in
exchange for our lives."

The Golden Man shook his head. "Oh, they'd make the
bargain all right, just like Cowl would. And after they got
the gold, they'd blow us to the bottom. That would be the
easy end to it. More likely they'd have some fun with us,
such as walking us over the side to the sharks, or using us
for cutlass practice. No, Son. It's a matter of fighting to the
death or getting drowned like cats in a bag. That's small
choice there. Is Amy safe?"

The Captain tapped the hilt of his sword on the bread
box still clutched under his arm. "Aye, she's safe, Father,
safe as in her coffin, I'm afraid. Maybe it doesn't matter
that she has no eyes any more. I think we've seen the last of
what's pretty in this world." He looked at the *Locust*, now
only a few score yards away. "But I'll be dead myself before
they get to Amy, Father, you may be certain of that."

[342]

Goldnose had taken up more sail. The *Locust* now came around heavily and slowly to put her bow upwind and abreast of the *Ariel*. Along the tops of the railings a half-dozen pirates were standing upright, their shipmates holding their legs for support. They swung iron grappling hooks in their hands, judging heft and throw that would set their hooks onto the *Ariel* and draw the ships together for their boarding. The *Locust* dropped her anchor.

A fair judge of pirate flesh would have found a strange element in the scene, or, rather, strange that the scene lacked an element. The pirates numbered some fifty or so against the *Ariel*'s crew of less than twenty, but yet the buccaneers were strangely quiet. The air should have been filled with their shouting of oaths, their jeering, their cries for blood and death and fire, their growling and spitting, their taste for the coming battle heightened by the sight in plain view of the gold treasure dumped on the deck of the *Ariel*. Yet instead there was a quiet and wary watch in the eyes of the pirates. The whispers from the fo'c'sle continued to pass among themselves as they crowded the railing looking over to the animal crew of the *Ariel*.

"Not natural, Billy, and that's what I say."

"Old Johnny, he says they ain't real animals. He says they's dressed up that way, like in a masquerade ball."

"Hah! That's easy said from a cable's length away. But look ye – are those true animals or not?"

"Hi! Look over there! That's the witch, ain't it?"

"Looks like one, don't it. See, she's got a frog with her. Witches fool with frogs is my remembering of it."

"Once I read a book ..."

"Ye didn't!"

"Once I read a book which said that an enchantment comes upon ye on the day of your dying."

"Huh! That's not healthy."

"Let 'em keep the gold, say I."

"Old Tom don't like it. He says it's against religion."

"Well, Tom was a preacher before he was a pirate. I don't see any sermon in that."

So this was their talk, and not the shouting out of butchery war cries. But there was no loss of heart aboard the *Ariel*.

"There's good lads," Mister Cloud said, passing among the animal crew. "Cut the grappling hooks free as they throw them over. If they get onto us, thrust into their bellies like I showed you. Then get back to your balance. Hack their legs as they swing across. Stand back to back in the thick of the fighting. Keep an eye out for your shipmates." Commanding in his strong, confident voice, he belied his own opinion of how the battle must end, but he continued his march back and forth, now and then glancing towards the Captain on the poop deck.

Goldnose was upon his own poop deck. He was directing ship's business, calling out orders to his gunners, who now had their six port cannon snugged into place, rolled forward so that their ugly black snouts levelled across the decks of the *Ariel*. Perhaps the pirates would not board, but merely charge the cannon with scrap iron and canister shot so that the cannon would act like giant shotguns to tear up the *Ariel*'s crew like hamburger and leave the ship afloat for plundering. Mister Cloud looked over the side to where the bomb platform with its six kegs of gunpowder was tied up alongside between the two ships. There was no use in that any longer. Worse yet, a stray shot into those kegs would blow them both out of the water. Nothing to do about it now. He turned his head, as did all of both crews, towards Goldnose. His preparations were now complete. He bespoke the *Ariel*'s captain across the water of the matched poop decks.

CHAPTER FORTY-SIX

> *Bow-wow, says the dog,*
> *Mew, mew, says the cat,*
> *Grunt, grunt, goes the hog,*
> *And squeak goes the rat.*
> *Tu-whu, says the owl,*
> *Caw, caw, says the crow,*
> *Quack, quack, says the duck,*
> *And what cuckoos say you know.*

A hoy there, Captain!"

"Ahoy there, for a bloody, black-hearted villain!" the Captain called back.

"Hah, hah, hah," the fat pirate laughed, now looking at the heap of gold treasure, counting to himself the richness of it with a practised eye, all in obvious delight and anticipation, for he saw that he would have it by blood or bargain. He looked back to the Captain.

"Aye, Captain, bloody and black-hearted ye may think, but with a nose for gold, and ye may lay to that. Aye, and it may be you've got a keen-nosed rat among that zoo ye call your sailors, one with a nose for gold like myself, aye, and with keen teeth, eh, matey? How'd your sails get clipped, Captain? Aye, it looks like a rat's been gnawing your lines, for I do believe you've got some sort of rat aboard. What? Did ye find him out already, and hang him? A pity — as I was looking to give my compliments and thank him for showing us the way to these islands."

The Captain spoke low to the Golden Man. "Some one of the crew showed a light during some nights past when we were running to escape in the dark."

"That I know," said the Golden Man. "And I know who it was, Son. It was Davy Duck. I've had no chance to say all I know, but he'll soon be on deck again if I'm not mistaken. There'll be a change of wind in that if I'm not wrong. Listen quick, now – last night he came to me –"

But the Golden Man had no time to speak further. Goldnose spoke out again. "Captain, I'm a reasonable man, and I trust you're the same. Don't ye love to see the sun come up in the morning, and don't ye love to breathe deep, and look at the lovely clouds and feel the breeze on your face? And ain't it reasonable, Captain, to want to keep breathing and feeling that nice breeze and see some more sunrises? I know ye thinks so, and ye may have the pleasure of it until your hair turns white for all I care if ye only remove that there gold from your deck to my deck. Ain't it reasonable, Captain? Don't ye see how agreeable that would make us, Captain? Ah, but ye may not trust me entire. Look ye, then – I take me hat off right here under heaven and swear to God as he knows the number of hairs on me head not to kill ye off if ye just pass the gold on over to us."

Goldnose held his hat out at arm's length, imploringly, eyes cast upward, as if for a moment waiting for God to count the hairs on his head. The Captain looked at the Golden Man, who shook his head slowly. The pirate, seeing no gain in his mockery, stuck his hat back on.

"See here, Captain, ye call me black-hearted, but here's a bargain. I've got some polite chaps on board ye ain't seen yet, all washed up clean with clipped fingernails and scrubbed ears. I keep 'em for special occasions like this, as I get respectful when I see a woman on board, like as that woman over there kneeling down. Now these here diplomats that I'll send over to get the gold won't have cutlasses or pistols with 'em. They'll not molest the smallest liver among ye, in respect for the woman's feelings. Now, what do ye say, Captain, can we make a brotherly bargain and sail away from each other like friends of the sea? Say it's so, Captain. Throw your cutlass over the side now and beg your crew to do the same, for it's a lovely crew indeed, and as much as I don't mind killing a few of me own kind, cruelty to animals is something me dear mother taught me against."

Although he did not let on, Goldnose was himself touched with doubt about the strange crew of the *Ariel*. He would rather have made a clean, unbloodied confiscation of the treasure. All sailors have superstitions. And now that he had come to look closely at the *Ariel*'s crew, the fat pirate thought about enchantments and unknown powers. Yet spitting into the face of the holy was his way. He would attack if he had to. Goldnose looked to his pirates at the railings. They would swing across also, with himself and Dimlid behind them to cut them down if they did not. But they were not singing for blood and beating their chests for the onset, nor cursing or spitting as was their custom, but their mouths were dry and their liquids all collected in their bladders.

The reply that Goldnose was waiting for never got to him. The Captain was framing his defiant answer within a curse when there came from the fo'c'sle ladderway what sounded at first like a great rattling and clapping of flat sticks together, or, again, like a whole orchestra playing castanets out of rhythm with one another. The sound took firm shape as Davy Duck came on board waving a cutlass and shouting out behind him for order and smartn   in the ranks. For up from the belowdecks passagewa   ed

[347]

two dozen ducks all quacking loudly, all dressed in bright new sailcloth jackets, all flourishing their cutlasses and crowding about Davy, who was the tallest of them all and obviously their master. When the last of them was on deck, Davy waved his sword in a circle, conducting his clattering band to silence. As the last of the quacking died away, he ordered them to stand at attention. They all stiffened up, and Davy called out.

"Quack, quack! Who's the Captain?"

At this, the ducks, who had come to some semblance of military order, now began paddling about and set off a quacking loud enough to dent the ears, running about in small circles, bumping into one another in a turmoil of new life and high spirits. Davy was pressed to shouting and whacking about among them, smacking them with the flat of his sword on head and tail to bring them to silence again. The silence also covered the whole ship ... also the *Locust*, as man and beast alike looked with awe at the smartly jacketed company of ducks, all with bright, sharp swords.

It was Davy Duck's moment. He held the stage alone. It was a prince's moment, all beset with wonder and perfect silence, a hushed moment pregnant with expectation and dismay. Davy Duck gazed regally about. Slowly, then, he made his way through the throng of ducks towards the poop deck, towards where the Captain was standing. It was a great moment – Davy could not have got more attention or rapt curiosity had he been walking towards his coronation or to the gallows. He climbed the poop ladderway with magnificent aplomb and stood before the Captain. Slowly and confidently he sheathed his cutlass, taking every last use of the pause, his heart filling with triumph. Then he spoke.

"A good day to ye, Captain," he said, touching his forehead in a salute, doing also the same towards Goldnose. "And a good day to ye, also, Captain Goldnose, and I might add a good night or two into the bargain – and that's a favour from a duck that likes to keep a glowing pipe lit up to keep him company on a dark night, if ye take my meaning. And a good day to all of ye," he said, waving his hand in largesse towards both the crews at the railings of their ships. "Aye, and another good day to both the Captains. And being a Captain myself, a good day to me as well. Come to think on it, and by the looks on your faces, it may be that I'm to have the best day of all."

Davy smiled all around and gave a look to the Golden Man, who was standing behind the Captain. Davy dared a slight wink. The Golden Man nodded ever so slightly in return. The situation looked well to Davy. Mister Cloud was amidships below. Skivvy, the Bad Sister, and the unarmed frog were aside. Davy took a deep breath, cocked his head upward, and made his account.

"Now, you may all wonder why I've gathered you here together. Oh yes, and it was me that done it, however ye may think ye had your own way about it, for a true Captain long beforehand knows the outcome of a thing. All that needs to fall out is the time and place of it. And here's the time and place of it, Captain. Now, can ye guess the outcome of it?"

Davy took two steps back and gripped his sword. "Can ye guess, Captain, the one single thing I need to be a true Captain? Aye, and it's a question ye must answer yourself, so all may hear. It's the command of this ship I'm talking about. Who's the Captain? Quack, quack!"

The Captain took on a grim aspect. He crossed his arm to touch the hilt of his own sword. Davy looked at the Golden Man, who then grasped the handle of *his* sword.

"Now, move slowly, Captain," said Davy. "It's only the

ship I want. Ye needn't die for it, as ye will for certain if ye choose to fight, for see here, there's more in on this mutiny than you've given credit for, perhaps." He turned and shouted towards the deck. "Chicken, Turkey, fall in with the ducks." He looked back to the Captain. "There's more of us to carry on the fight if you're foolish, Captain, which ye may take as a duck's fact. Give up the ship, Captain, or I'll take it by blood and death. Ye may live safe and alive on that island with your bread box and whatever else interests ye. But here's my claim. Ye may speak out now if it ain't so."

Davy drew his sword. He raised it towards his troop of ducks and shouted out, "Who's the Captain? Quack, quack!"

The ducks at the other end of the ship clamoured in response to Davy's shout and shuffled in eagerness for the command to battle. The Captain was struck with hesitation. If he should strike at Davy, his crew must fight the ducks. Outnumbered as they were, they could well lose the battle. Even winning, and weakened after fighting the ducks, they must then fight Goldnose and the pirates. The Captain could only clutch tighter to the bread box. Davy sensed he had won the day. He called over to Goldnose.

"Captain Goldnose! I'll be pleased to end my first pirating adventure with the prize of a good ship. Ye may save your men and have all the gold if only ye give us clear room and passage to do our business. Hold off peacefully. We'll later find some way for ye to take the treasure while I sail off free and clear." Davy had advanced a step towards the Captain, sure of his victory. He extended his sword. He grinned and touched the point of it to the Captain's lapel, flipping it playfully, delighting himself with one last insult. "There's just that one thing, Captain, that I'd like to hear from your own lips. And speaking of your blasted lips —

[350]

but never mind that. Something I think it might be good for all to hear, just to know how things has finally settled out. Aye, just that same question to put to ye, Captain. I want your own crew to hear ye say the answer."

Then, in a louder voice that rang out over both ships, Davy called out again, "Who's the Captain? Quack, quack!"

The Captain gripped his sword. He glanced at the Golden Man, then at Goldnose and the pirates, at his own small crew, and at the throng of ducks, now set to shouting again. Davy grew bold and impatient and prodded the Captain with the point of his sword.

"Answer, or by Mother Goose I'll pin ye! Who's the Captain? Quack, quack!" So saying, he made a sharp thrust of his sword at the bread box. Before Davy could draw back, the Captain took a moment to adjust the sprung lid of the bread box. Davy jumped to the railing and called out to his ducks.

"Now, lads! Now's the time! Quack, quack! Cut a path to your Captain!"

At the moment of the Captain's action, Mister Cloud had immediately brought his crew around and athwart amidships to face the ducks. Now the lines of the animals stepped forward for the clash. But before the first cutlass was raised to strike, the Golden Man came to the foremost stage of the poop deck and cried out in a great voice.

"Ho, there! Ducks, hold yourselves! Hold, I say, and ye know my voice. Hold!"

The ducks did know his voice. They stopped in their advance. All looked up at the Golden Man, who continued to speak without pause enough for Davy to put in another word. The mutinous duck looked on dumbly, letting the moment of his command go past without recall, for the Golden Man now made a speech that entirely won the ducks away from Davy. And there was no returning to that former loyalty. Here is what he said:

"Ducks, hold and hear me! Who's the Captain, ye are asked, and that's a proper question, for some of ye must die on the answer. And the answer is that the Captain is he who owns the thread that put ye together, aye, and who owns the stuffing that made your innards, and who owns the needle that gave ye life. It's the same Captain who outfitted ye for duty and whose uniform ye wear on your backs, for why should ye wear any other than the uniform of your Captain?"

The Golden Man spoke over his shoulder to the Captain in a lower voice. "*Quickly, Captain, stand beside me here at the rail.*" Then he spoke again to the ducks. "And so the Captain is he who has the responsibility of your making and your coming to life, no matter that I helped along the way, and no matter that Davy Duck did his part – but the lord of this little world and the heart of this voyage, this ship, and the master of your obedience is he who rightfully claims your allegiance and duty to the death, and is he whose uniform ye wear. Most of all that. And so ye should know him and not be deceived, the sign of your Captain is put on ye like the sign of God is the conscience in a man. Here's your Captain standing beside me. *Roll up your sleeve, Son – hold your arm out.* There, shipmates, as ye trust my voice and my craft to clothe ye and help ye into the world to find your true Captain, so it is that I bring him before ye – and there's the sign for ye all to see!"

So saying, the Golden Man took the Captain's arm and held it high for the ducks to see the tattoo printed there, the sign of the needle and the thread.

"Aye, shipmates, ye ducks, here's your true Captain. As he's imprinted in his flesh, so are ye all wearing next to your hearts this very sign of your making and your maker, born with yourselves and the reason of your lives. So turn out your jackets. Look to your hearts and the badge of your creation – the uniform of your Captain!"

This the ducks did, each turning his jacket aside to look to the inner part of it. They looked in amazement to one another, each finding next to his heart the sign that the Golden Man had roughly sewn there, but which now in the fullness and magnificence of coming to life was an emblazonment of embroidery in red and black and gold thread, the sign of the Captain as it was tattooed on his upraised arm:

Out of the stunned silence of the discovery of this, at last a duck cried out.

"It's the Captain's sign! It's the Captain's uniform! There! There is the true Captain!" pointing his sword to the Captain, who still held his arm high in the air for all to see the tattoo. Then this duck dropped his sword and turned his jacket inside out so that the colourful sign showed sparkling in new silken thread in the sunlight. Slipping it on again, he picked up his sword and gave a shout for the Captain, whence arose a joyous clamouring as the other ducks did the same. Amid cheers for the Captain, the *Ariel*'s crew fell in among the ducks and helped them into their turned out jackets, clapping them on the backs and greeting them as shipmates. The poor chicken and turkey had nowhere to go, nor any cheer to make. They had lost on both sides. They dropped their swords and sat down on the deck in black dejection to await mercy or a hanging.

Up on the poop deck, Davy Duck himself might just as well have given up, but he saw a desperate chance and he took it. The Captain had lost his firm grip on the bread box, one arm raised in the air and the other gripping his sword, the bread box therefore tucked but lightly under his arm. With a leap and a dash, Davy was at the side of the Captain. He snatched the bread box. In another second he had leaped back to the top of the railing. Grasping the same shroud that Skivvy had hung on before he fell, Davy faced the advancing Captain with a warning shout.

"One step farther, Captain, and your precious doll goes into the sea!"

Both the Captain and the Golden Man were making quickly towards him to strike, but they now stopped at the toe of their next step.

"That's right, shipmates!" cried Davy. "Now stand fast."

Davy stood there, swaying upon his shroud, relishing his position of power, now as fresh and complete as it had been with the whole two dozen ducks behind him. More than that, for now he incorporated this power all alone, bread box under his arm. He was the very god of events, the very king. For now he grasped the Captain by his heart. Davy leisurely swayed by his rope hold, calculating how he might best direct his command towards the several elements of the strife. Goldnose also came under his command. With the bread box under his arm, he could direct the *Ariel*'s crew as if they were pawns. He could have the entire gold treasure thrown overboard if it was his whim, so the fat pirate must bow to him also. All because of a mere eyeless doll and the salvation of it. Davy Duck smiled to think of it.

Skivvy lay against the railing directly below Davy's feet. The Bad Sister knelt close to one side of the wounded man.

On the other side was Greensleeves. The Bad Sister caught the frog's eye and directed it to Davy's cutlass, where it had fallen to the deck when the Captain swept it from him. Greensleeves looked at the cutlass, then back to the Bad Sister. She then directed his eye to the place where Davy Duck's supporting rope was fastened. While Davy was yet savouring his great victory, the frog snatched up the sword and struck through the rope where it was anchored. Davy Duck fell backwards. He lost his grip on the loose end of the line and pitched headfirst into the sea, still gripping the bread box.

Even as the Captain ran to the railing, he was tearing off his coat. Amy's father was judging the distance in his run to make a one-footed touch on the railing and then his dive. But the Bad Sister came between them. She stopped them both with a swing of her cape upwards in front of them. In a second flourish she drew from the inner folds of her great cloak – Amy!

"You don't suppose I'd let a *man* take care of a little girl in times like this, do you, Captain?" she said.

CHAPTER FORTY-SEVEN

There were once two cats of Kilkenny.
Each thought there was one cat too many;
So they fought and they fit,
And they scratched and they bit,
*   Till, excepting their nails,*
*   And the tips of their tails,*
Instead of two cats, there weren't any.

This wonderful moment of good fortune might have been cheered and complimented upon. The frog might have received his due congratulations for the kidnapping job, nicely done and in the nick of time. Goldnose, however, in the long meanwhile since he had a word or a hand in affairs, had completely lost the drift of the drama aboard the *Ariel*, what with the needle-and-thread emblems, the ducks' changing loyalty, the mysterious bread box, and something about a doll. He now devised the next act to suit himself. He swept his cutlass through the air, bellowed out, "Hook their guts!" and the first grappling hook was thrown from the *Locust*.

It caught onto the railing of the *Ariel*. Another was thrown, and another. The crew of animals, now including the ducks, turned to throw them off and cut them free. Pirates in the rigging of the *Locust* fired their muskets. They killed the first who were to die in the coming battle. Enough hooks stayed secure that the pirates leaned back on their lines and drew the *Locust* and the *Ariel* together for boarding.

The Captain, upon hearing the first grappling hook clatter onto the deck, turned to the action. With a motion to the Bad Sister to stay well aft on the poop deck, he took his station at the port ladderway. Greensleeves took his stand at the starboard ladderway. The Golden Man descended to be among the ducks, to command the battle amidships with Mister Cloud. The two men, one bearded, the other golden, shook hands upon their meeting. They commanded their forces to the railing to take on boarders just as the ships finally closed. The first pirates began to swing aboard and crawl across to the *Ariel* on planks, a swarm of pirate humanity at least as ugly as locusts and as deadly in rampage. Then the battle was joined.

The confusion of a hand-to-hand pirate fight is too much to sort out, for all is shouting and screaming, dodging and running, blood and panic, shock and intense strife, the relief for another second of life snuffed out in the terror of sure death at the next instant. Neither word nor rhyme can rightly frame the whole of it. But let the eye of the narrative fall upon a single combatant. Magnify it in your imagination by the number of every animal and every pirate engaged in the fury of the encounter. Set alive the past before your mind's eye – let the scene become fresh with blood, give it the breath of life in screams and pain and the moaning of the dying, and make it quick with terror and death. Magnify it a hundredfold.

There! That cat at the railing – the tabby, just in that place where one of the pirates came across on a rope's end, his sword clamped in his teeth. The cat swung at the man's legs, but he lifted them and the cut missed. The cat fell to one side just as that pirate struck downward with his cutlass, taking a chunk of railing out. But in the effort he tumbled onto the deck, and the cat brought his own cutlass down on the back of the man's head, cleaving it open. At the moment the cat was struck between the shoulders by the feet of another pirate swinging across from the *Locust*. He was knocked head foremost, striking his face against a hatch cover, breaking out several of his teeth. He lay there stunned and was trampled on several times, but luckily was thought to be dead and was not hacked at. When he could get his feet underneath himself, he could not find his cutlass.

He crawled to where a dead monkey lay, took the sword from his hand, and turned to raise himself just as a pirate, struck down by Mister Cloud, fell on him. Bloodied still more by that encounter, his legs trembling from the blow he had taken, the cat joined three ducks who were back to back and parrying their swords with several pirates. The cat swung wildly with hardly sight in his eyes. He felt his sword hit once or twice, but so quickly was he striking out that he could not tell if his blows were taking effect to kill or wound. Then in a startled moment he found himself alone again. He stumbled over a dead duck to escape from two pirates hard upon him. He heard one of them scream. Turning, he saw a cutlass thrust completely through the man's stomach, yet no one was at the handle of it, but a duck was falling away from that pirate with his head nearly taken off.

Putting his back to the galley, the cat parried the sword of a pirate high above his head. To his surprise, the cat found that he had a belaying pin in his free hand. He smashed it into the pirate's face. The pirate fell back, giving the cat room to plunge his sword into the man's chest, whereupon it naturally drew itself out as the man fell back dead.

He heard a shout near at hand. The Golden Man was

crowded with pirates. The cat hacked one across the back. The goat joined in with him, freeing the Golden Man to attend to one of the pirates in single combat. Then a sharp pain pierced through the cat's upper arm. He dropped his sword and sank to his knees. A sharp-shooter in the *Locust*'s rigging had put a musket ball into him. The cat crawled out of the way underneath the poop ladderway. The shot had severed an artery. The cat tried to stop the pumping blood. He ripped the sleeve from a dead pirate near him and wrapped it for a tourniquet about his arm. Then he fainted.

Now, that is the battle as it happened to only one of the combatants. Multiply it nearly a hundredfold for every man and animal who fought that battle. Add as much noise to it as can sound in the imagination. Add also terror and horror and pain. Most of all, fill the picture with confusion, and you have something of the notion of those few minutes on the deck of the *Ariel*.

Yet one other fight must be noted. During the battle, the Captain stood at the port ladderway, receiving boarders at the rail and by ladder. He had received only a small cut to his thigh when at last Goldnose himself boarded by way of a plank. He advanced to fight the *Ariel*'s master, Captain to Captain. Greensleeves was defending the starboard ladderway. Upon seeing Goldnose ascending the deck, he cried out to the Captain, who was thrusting at a dangling pirate. He cut the rope the man swung on, and the pirate dropped into the sea. Then the Captain turned to face Goldnose, who had taken the deck. The two men faced each other. Goldnose took full advantage of his great size. His style was to make a step-by-step advance, matching each step with an overhead blow of his cutlass, the graceless sweeps coming down like the blades of a windmill. The Captain had lost the best use of his legs, and the sheer weight of the fat pirate's blows could not long be borne by parry alone, yet the Captain could not escape from him. He was staggering beneath the powerful onslaught, each blow striking him nearly to his knees.

The clang and clash of the battle had brought Skivvy to consciousness again. He saw through his wavering vision that the Captain was falling under the heavy attack of Goldnose. In a half-crouching crawl he made his way across the poop deck. He put out a hand to grasp from behind the fat pirate's great leather belt just as a blow struck through the Captain's defences. The cutlass of Goldnose cut into the Captain's head even to the bone, laying open a deep wound from jaw to his temple. Goldnose would have finished him with the next blow, but as the Captain fell to the deck, the pirate turned to see who nagged him from behind. Grasping Skivvy's wrist as he wheeled around, he swung the second mate completely off the deck and flung him over the railing. Skivvy bounded off a stretched rope and fell between the two ships, where the water below was now cluttered with the bodies of dead pirates and animals.

Glancing at the fallen Captain, who lay perfectly still, Goldnose supposed him to be dead. He found himself alone on the poop, save for the Bad Sister, who crouched against the taffrail hugging her cloak to herself. The frog was no longer in sight. The fat pirate swept a tactical eye over the battle, measuring his loss. Both the Golden Man and Mister Cloud still stood. They were fighting furiously. The pirates looked to be getting the worst of it. Goldnose made a quick decision to take the losses and carry out the rest of the battle with cannon and musket. He cupped his hands and shouted out loudly for a retreat to the *Locust*. The cry was heard even above the din. His men began falling back to the railings, grasping ropes and pushing off wildly to swing back to their ship. The *Ariel*'s crew did not press them too closely, but let them make their rout as they would, for they too had lost much in the battle already. Most of the standing animals were wounded at least slightly. Goldnose himself took a rope near at hand and swung over to his own poop deck. In another minute it was as if a great thunderstorm had subsided, or a tornado had passed over the deck of the *Ariel*. All those left alive sat dazed and exhausted among the wreckage and the dead. Goldnose called out another command. The pirates cut loose all lines attached to the *Ariel*, and the ships floated apart.

CHAPTER FORTY-EIGHT

There was a little man, and he had a little gun,
And his bullets were made of lead, lead, lead;
He went to the brook, and shot a little duck,
Right through the middle of the head, head, head.

The Ariel had won the victory, but there was no cheering for it. Many were badly wounded. At least half the animals were dead or dying on deck, ducks and others. Again that many pirates were dead upon the deck. More yet had been cut down to die in the water. Blood and gore and gold were strewn all about. Much of the gold treasure went underfoot and over the side in the battle. The animals who could yet get to their feet looked about themselves in a dumb wondering, hardly believing the awful sight, hardly believing they were alive. Just as Amy's father looked towards the poop deck, the Bad Sister called out for help. Mister Cloud and the Golden Man found her beside the Captain, his head in her lap. His wound to the head was deep, cut even through the skull. The Bad Sister had torn more of her petticoat. She was gently touching the blood from the wound. The Captain was conscious, but he spoke very weakly as the Golden Man took his hand.

"Father, I'm sorry. I don't think I can do more ..."

The Golden Man gripped his hand tightly.

"Amy," said the Captain. "Is she all right?"

"Here," said the Bad Sister, taking the doll from her

cloak and putting it under the Captain's hand. "She's fine, Captain. You've won the battle, and Amy's alive."

"But with no eyes. I'm sorry, Father. I kept her the best I could..." His eyes dimmed for a moment, and his head fell back more heavily into the Bad Sister's cradled arm.

"You did fine, Son. I could not have made a better ... man."

"Is Skivvy ..?"

The Bad Sister looked at the Golden Man and shook her head.

"I'm afraid he's gone, Son."

"He was good. Too much worry about his soul. He only wanted to save us. A friend."

"Captain?" said Amy, who could not see the woeful scene.

"Hush, dear," said the Bad Sister, laying a hand on Amy's head. "The Captain can't talk now."

The glaze then left the Captain's eyes. As he looked into the blue sky, his eyes became clear. "Amy ... Amy ... I wish you could see. There's a white bird ... a white ... bird ..."

The two men and the Bad Sister looked at one another. The woman put a hand alongside the Captain's cheek. "Yes, Captain, a white bird, a beautiful white bird."

"No, no," said the Captain. "Look!" He half raised his hand to point upward with a finger.

Above the ruin and carnage aboard the *Ariel*, Mama Dah-dah's great white albatross was circling without the movement of a wing, descending in smaller and steeper circles. He was watched in wonder until he at last flared his wings and touched in a gentle alighting in the centre of the poop deck. Folding his wings, he walked over to where the Captain lay. He then put his head to the deck and opened his long beak. Out fell two blue buttons.

"Amy!" cried the Golden Man, recognizing the eyes immediately. "Amy's eyes!"

"Quickly," said the Bad Sister, "give them here!" She reached into her cloak and unslipped a needle. Then unravelling a thread from her petticoat, she threaded the needle. In half a minute she sewed Amy's eyes back into place so that Amy could see. As if she had been sleeping, and had just come awake, Amy looked up into the streaked face of the Bad Sister and into her eyes, and spoke.

"Miss Eclair!"

"Oh yes, dear, it's Miss Eclair. And look, Amy, here's the Captain." She gave Amy into the Captain's hand again and cautioned her. "He's hurt, dear, and very tired."

"Amy," said the Captain, holding her close to his face. "You've got your eyes again. And soon you'll be yourself. The golden treasure, Amy, it was our father. Now ... now we're all together again. Miss Eclair ... Yes ... Of course. I should have known, I should have known. Do I have my earring on, Sis? Because I'll need it soon. Remember? Oh, I'd like to see King Neptune's palace. How beautiful that will be."

"Captain!" Amy cried and put her head on his chest.

"Don't worry, Sis. I won't be alone. The crew will be with me: Skivvy, too. Good-bye, Sis."

He looked to Mister Cloud, who put his head down close. The Captain said some words to him.

"Aye, sir," said Mister Cloud. "You may count on me, Captain. First Corinthians, chapter thirteen." He stood up again. The Captain closed his eyes and became very still. He slowly brought a hand up to rest on Amy's head.

"Good-bye, Sis. Everything seems ... so far away. Almost like being a doll. Don't worry, Sis, because ... being a doll, you know ... it never hurt."

Miss Eclair received the gentle fall of the Captain's head

in her hands. He let out one last, long breath, and was dead. Amy cried out for him. Miss Eclair took her up and held her closely. The Golden Man touched Amy's head over the hand of Miss Eclair. Then he passed his hand over the Captain's eyes. Mama Dah-dah's great white albatross hopped to a railing, dropped into the air, then swooped upwards, flying to float above the two ships and to watch what next would happen. What next happened was that Goldnose called out across the water from the *Locust*. Mister Cloud stood up to face him, but the fat pirate was looking for no conversation. He was only taking the joy of announcing his murderous intentions.

"If you're the new Captain," he yelled, "grab ahold of your gold and kiss it good-bye and farewell. Aye, and dive overboard with a pound of it about your neck, for that's an easier way to die than what's coming now, Captain." He then called to his men. "Gunners, rake that deck till the blood paints the hull red. Aye, Captain. Canister shot. If there's a leg left fastened to a body after a few rounds of scrap iron, I've never shot a cannon, by thunder. And if there's an ounce of gold left or none, I'll take it as good payment just to see the ocean coloured red with what's left of ye. Gunner! Ready and prime! Ready and aim! Ready—"

But the slaughter was delayed, for up between the ships amid the wreckage and bodies popped Davy Duck. He called out to the fat pirate.

"Captain Goldnose! Captain, sir, it's me, Captain, bless your nose, Captain, it's me, who lit your way, your good shipmate, Captain. It's me, Davy Duck!"

Goldnose held his command to fire the cannon. He looked down into the water. And there, bobbing alongside a dead pirate and making his way toward the *Locust*, was Davy. With his most engaging manner he called up to Goldnose to observe him for his worth.

"It's me, Captain Goldnose! Davy Duck. Aye, me Captain, and one of your very own kind. For it's the like of us that have got to stick together, Captain, for we are alike. I seen it right off – and didn't ye recognise it yourself. Look, now" – and the duck turned his head in profile and stuck his beak into the air. "See, Captain – it's us with gold noses that have got to stick together, Captain. And that's a duck's fact. Quack, quack! Just give me a hand aboard, now, shipmate – I mean to say Captain, yes, sir, indeed ye are, sir, and the Captain's in command, yes, sir, indeed he is, sir –"

Davy, studying the pirate's face for a sign of hope, but getting nothing except a killing look, had reverted to a lesser tack than equality, but Goldnose was not taken by the manner. He grabbed the arm of a man next to him, who held a musket. He pointed at Davy.

"Blast him," he ordered. "Flush that duck."

The musketeer raised his weapon, but Davy's luck held for a minute longer. He now saw something that none of the pirates had noticed. During the battle aboard the *Ariel*, the line holding the *Ariel*'s bomb platform had been cut away. In those several minutes of the encounter, the platform, floating freely between the two ships, had found its way bumping along the hull to be directly under the poop deck when Goldnose flung Skivvy over the side. The second mate had landed upon the six kegs of gunpowder closed within the red casing. Then, when the ships parted, the loose lines and wreckage falling between them, a grappling hook from the *Locust* fell into the water and bit into the underside of the bomb platform as the pirate ship pulled away. As if the hook were an iron hand of a dreadful iron mother, the bomb platform and Skivvy were dragged away from the *Ariel* to nestle at the side of the *Locust*.

Since that time, Skivvy had come to his senses again. He

heard Goldnose call out for the destruction of the *Ariel*. He reached for the pistol stuck in his belt, but it was gone. But there, down between the kegs, he saw it. He lay flat on the gunpowder kegs and reached to touch the butt of it, blood running down his arms, making the pistol slippery to bring up in his groping fingers. At last, with a nearly life-taking final lunge, he had the pistol in hand. Now he lay sprawled across the bomb, fumbling to cock the piece. This is when Davy saw him. He cried out to Goldnose.

"Captain Goldnose! Don't fire, Captain! Look – it's our bomb. That's a bomb, Captain. Six kegs of gunpowder, Captain Goldnose. Don't move! Don't move! Don't move! That man on the bomb has a pistol! I know him. I'll talk to him. Don't move!"

Goldnose looked over the side. No doubt about it. The fat pirate knew a gunpowder keg from any angle. There lay that pesky seaman who had grabbed him from behind – now with a pistol in hand. Goldnose saw that there was no shaking off the man or shooting him from above lest they shoot into the kegs of gunpowder. The crews of both the *Locust* and the *Ariel* stood at the railings of their ships, as if they were on high stages watching a play in the orchestra pit. Goldnose looked at Davy Duck helplessly, for it was Davy who once again seemed to have the fate of the day in his hand. The duck made an upraised motion towards Goldnose, a sign for perfect silence. Then he slowly paddled towards the bomb platform, giving out soothing words in front of his advance.

"Skivvy," he said. "Well, it's my old shipmate, Skivvy. Aye, and a Bible reader like myself, and it's us Bible readers that have got to stick together, ain't it Skivvy lad?"

As Davy paddled towards the platform, he pushed a dead pirate aside, at the same time drawing a long knife from the man's belt. He held it underneath the water as he approached. Skivvy lifted his head by nods. One of his eyes was bruised and closed. The other saw but a blur of the duck. With a grunt of pain, he finally succeeded in cocking the pistol, whereupon the effort nearly thrust it from his hand. He held it dangling by the trigger guard. Slowly he raised it up and placed his other hand around it.

"Aye, Skivvy," said Davy, seeing that Skivvy's condition was almost totally befuddled by pain. He played for confusion to get within reach of the man, now only a few yards away. "Now, don't be fast to shoot that pistol, Skivvy, for ye know what it says in the Bible – ah, Lamentations 9:20, and ... ah ... Proverbs 32:14 ... *Mother Goose*, too 6:17 and 15:2 ..." Yet the cunning was not good enough. There remained with Skivvy just enough sense to know that there *were* no Bible chapters of those sorts. "Listen, Skivvy," the duck cried out, just as Skivvy turned the muzzle of the pistol inward towards the powder kegs. Goldnose could not help but cry out also, a yell for his salvation, the yell of a single word:

"Gold! Gold! All the gold ye want!"

Davy Duck yelled out more loudly, just as he touched the platform. "Listen Skivvy. Don't! That's an order! *It's me*, Skivvy – GOD!"

Then Skivvy pulled the trigger.

The explosion killed everyone aboard the *Locust*. It separated nearly every plank of it from its neighbour plank, ruptured every nail hole, and split every spar and mast, so that what remained was kindling floating in a red sea, for Skivvy's bomb had set off the several kegs of gunpowder in the *Locust*'s magazine locker. Not that the *Ariel* was uninjured by the explosion. The force of the blast rocked her on her beams. Large sections of the railing were blown away. Also, windows were blasted out and two yardarms torn away. Golden bowls and cups and rings rolled across the deck and fell into the sea, but no one was killed. The *Ariel* regained her keel as the cloud of the explosion settled to the sea and blew slowly away like a heavy fog.

CHAPTER FORTY-NINE

One for sorrow, two for joy,
Three for a girl, four for a boy,
Five for silver, six for gold,
Seven for a secret ne'er to be told.

T he dead pirates aboard the *Ariel* were put overboard without ceremony. The dead animals were
laid out and sewn into canvas shrouds each with a
cannon ball at his feet. A golden coin was also entered into
each shroud, payment for King Neptune. Of the original
crew, only one dog was left and one cat and one monkey, the
squirrel, the donkey, and the goat. The rest were ducks, ten
of them only out of the twenty-four who had fought the
battle. The Golden Man pressed Amy to the Captain one last
time, then turned her crying face as he was also sewn into his
buried shroud. Skivvy was represented in the burial too.
Mister Cloud folded his monk's cloak over a cannon ball.

Four planks were set up at the railing. Mister Cloud had
old Captain Kimberly's Bible in hand. He was ready to
make a last word and bury the dead at sea. He looked
about the gathered company. Miss Eclair could not be
found. The Golden Man gave Amy to Mister Cloud's
keeping and went off to seek her.

She was forward on the ship, facing the bow in the
setting sun, sitting with her back to the wall of the galley.
In her arms, cradled in her lap, she held the dead frog. She
was singing softly.

> *"Alas, my love you do me wrong,*
> *To cast me off discourteously ..."*

She sobbed, wiped her eyes, and sang some more.

> *"Greensleeves was all my joy,*
> *Greensleeves was my delight,*
> *Greensleeves was my heart of gold ..."*

When she noticed Amy's father standing nearby, she broke down and wept without holding herself. He sat down beside her, and put an arm around her shoulders. Her tears fell on the frog. She brought his face up and kissed him. "I loved him," she said. "He believed in me – he was all I had. He believed in me."

The Golden Man pressed her close. She laid her head on his shoulder. "Come," he said. "We're ready for the service."

Amy's father took Miss Eclair by the arm as they walked to where the others were waiting. Miss Eclair sewed up Greensleeves' shroud. She selected from the treasure a golden ladle to put in with him.

Mister Cloud stood the part of the clergy. He hefted Captain Kimberly's great Bible in one arm, and made a simple service.

"We've all lost friends here. They were good shipmates, and I'm proud to have sailed with them. The Captain wanted me to read some verses out of the Bible. Amy, I think he wanted you especially to hear this, because of ... the way everything began."

The Golden Man was holding Amy, who was yet hardly bigger than a doll. He took a step nearer. Mister Cloud cleared his throat and read.

*"When I was a child, I spake as a child, I understood
as a child, I thought as a child: but when I became a
man, I put away childish things.*

*"For now we see through a glass, darkly; but then
face to face; now I know in part; but then shall I know
even as also I am known."*

Mister Cloud closed the Bible and bowed his head. All
the others did the same, and only Amy's sobbing could be
heard. Mister Cloud spoke.

"We commend this man and these animals to the sea.
May God have mercy on their souls."

The boards were then raised, and the shrouded bodies
slid down and into the sea. In a few minutes it was done.
The Captain went with the last group, sharing the board
with Skivvy's robe. And high above the *Ariel* the great
white albatross glided in a wide circle, looking down as the
crew broke up to assess the damage to the *Ariel*, to make
the repair of their ship, their wounds, and their spirits.

Mister Cloud allotted the crew a liberal ration of rum
that evening, that they might somewhat blunt the worst
memories of the day and gather the best of it to make a
joke and a laugh now and again in the natural joy of being
alive and knowing they had fought well and won.

The monkey was at the main masthead, drunk to his
tail's end, singing in lamentation for his lost comrade. The
animals on deck had passed through many cups of rum and
several songs. All had their griefs, and they soon brought
the monkey down with a rousing song out of *Mother
Goose*.

> *"I have four sisters beyond the sea,*
> *Perrie, Merrie, Dixie, Dominie;*
> *And they each sent a present to me,*

Petrum, Patrum, Paradisi, Temporie,
Perrie, Merrie, Dixie, Dominie...."

Miss Eclair was sitting at her cabin table with Amy, sewing some larger clothes for her, for even now she was growing. In another day she would be flesh and blood, and in a very short while a full-sized ten-year-old. Amy was writing on a sheet of paper. It was a calm, warm night. Mama Dah-dah's albatross was sitting in the open window.

"I'm going to be a poet, I believe," Amy announced.

"That's nice, dear. Did you write a poem?"

"I've just finished one. You can't expect too much, since this is only my first. I'll read it to you. It's called 'How Miss Eclair Caught Miss Quince in Her Disguise on the Docks and Killed Her Dead'"

"Amy!" exclaimed Miss Eclair. "That's a terrible thing to say!"

"But you did kill her, didn't you, after you left the Riptide Tavern?"

"Not at all, and you know it very well. I recognized Miss Quince for certain when she was talking with the Captain. After I followed her out, she jumped at me when I told her that I knew who she was. She tried to throw me off the dock, I think. But she went off the dock instead. I think she broke her neck or something. That's not at all the same as if I'd killed her."

"Well," said Amy thoughtfully, "then maybe the title should be changed. All right. Now listen ... the beginning is very exciting.

"Miss Quince is dead, ding, dong, bell,
She broke her neck and went to hell..."

[373]

"Amy! You mustn't say a thing like that. Nobody but God knows such a thing."

"I bet I'm right anyway. But I can change it. I can say, 'She broke her neck, and just as well.' You see, that rhymes also."

"That's better, dear, but it's not the way I feel at all. I was sorry for what happened."

"I put that in," said Amy. "Listen:

*"Miss Eclair was sad Miss Quince was dead,
And robbed her purse and slept in her bed."*

Miss Eclair reached across the table and snatched up the paper.

"Amy, that isn't the story at all. If you're going to be a poet, you're going to have to learn to tell the truth."

"But it is true. You told me you took her purse off the dock and used the key to her rooms and slept there, and afterwards dressed up in her clothing to fool us all."

"That was only to look out over you and the Captain. It was because Miss Quince lied about having a partner aboard the ship. I had to find out who that was, whom she was plotting with. I wouldn't call that robbery at all. Here, now, you could say instead, 'Miss Eclair was sad Miss Quince was dead. Fears and suspicions troubled her head.' Or something like that."

Amy took the paper back. "Can I say that Miss Quince's ghost haunted you?"

"That's not exactly what I said, but I suppose you could say that. Sometimes I was so worried, I could hardly tell who I was. Sometimes I even enjoyed being nasty. And sometimes it seemed as if Miss Quince was alive after all, alive somehow inside me. That came from being so much alone and having no one to talk with. Yes, I suppose you

[374]

might say I felt haunted. Here, now. Do those lines again. And you must be careful of your language, dear, if you're going to be a lady poet."

"Oh my," Amy said, crossing out the offending lines. "Rewriting is such a bore."

Amy worked silently for a while, and then said, "All right, then. Here's the next line:

> *"The* Ariel *sailed with a good crew on it;*
> *The* Locust's *crew would make you vomit."*

"Yes, dear," said Miss Eclair, biting her thread. "And the scummy pigs got just what they deserved."

The albatross quitted the sill and flew aft to take a position on the sill of the Captain's cabin.

"My congratulations," said Amy's father. He raised his glass. "To the new master of the *Ariel*, Captain Cloud." He drank and sat down at the chart table.

"Thank you," said Cloud. He folded the Captain's Last Will and Testament, wherein Mister Cloud was bequeathed the ship, and set it aside, chuckling. "All duly witnessed by a dog and a cat. It's not something I'd want to defend in court, but I think I'll not be touching too many ports in the future." He paused, looked to the window and to the floor, and said, "I'm very sorry it turned out this way, sorry that you lost your son."

"But found my daughter," said Amy's father.

"Yes, that's true," said Captain Cloud, smiling upon Amy's father. "What will you do?"

"Oh, I'll be a tailor. It's what I know. A bit of gold should set me up in a nice little shop."

"Ah yes, speaking of the gold," said Captain Cloud. He opened the large Bible and took out a mess of papers left behind by Skivvy. They were crumpled and blood-stained, covered with confused markings and uneven writing, the labour of a dying man. "I've not been able to understand this entirely. Perhaps you can help. It's something about the Beast out of Revelation, and the worship of gold."

The two men handled the papers for a while trying to make some discovery into Skivvy's troubled mind.

"It's that number 666 he was after," said Amy's father. "That's in Revelation 13:18. And here – you see. He found it in one other place in the Bible. First Kings 10:14. Here it says that 666 talents of gold were paid to Solomon every year."

"Yes, that's it," said Cloud. "And here Skivvy says that the number 666 is used in no other place in the Bible except to number the Beast and to number gold. Well now, that's interesting. I wonder if it's true."

"I wouldn't know," said Amy's father. "But the mark of the Beast, you recall, will be on the forehead or the hand of those who worship him. Skivvy writes down here that the mark of the Beast on the forehead means those who have their minds and thoughts set on gold, and the mark of the Beast on the hand means those who clutch and grasp after gold."

"Ah, I see it now," said Cloud. "That's why he wanted the pirates to have the gold. He thought that the Beast was gold itself. He thought it would destroy us, as it's said in Revelation."

"Gold has that power, yes, for those who worship it," said Amy's father. "I've seen it happen."

Both men looked towards the door, where just outside a large crate had been filled with the gold that had not gone overboard during the battle. Captain Cloud poured some more wine. The men drank, and the great white albatross flew away to circle above the ship.

On the next day, Amy took the albatross under her instruction while the ship was being repaired. In the early afternoon they set sail for New Liberty. Amy sat on a hatch and read to the great white bird out of *Mother Goose*.

"Seeing that you are at the moment a bird," said Amy, "you'll be most interested in the bird poems, I suppose. Let us see now. Shall we begin with a nightingale? That's a nice one. Or maybe you'd like something about a partridge. Or perhaps an owl, or swan, or raven. Oh, here's a very nice one. See, it's about a wren and a robin. It's a romance. It's particularly nice because the wren was a good cook. They ate well. Here they are dining on cherry pie and currant wine. They get married, of course. Now listen carefully.

> *"It was a merry time,*
> *When Jenny Wren was young,*
> *So neatly as she danced,*
> *And so sweetly as she sung...*

"Isn't that nice?" Amy interrupted herself.

The albatross looked at her in complete agreement.

Amy's father and Miss Eclair strolled by. They greeted Amy and passed on. Amy smiled after them. She looked at the albatross.

"What do you think?" she asked him. "How do people act when they fall in love? Tell me something about love. How do people know when to get married? What do they do next? Look me in the eyes and show me."

"Errrrrrr," said the bird, and discreetly closed his eyes. Amy was, perhaps, too young to be looking into such things.

Captain Cloud stood on the afterdeck looking into the wake of the *Ariel*. He intended to sail the seas to watch for his mermaid with his own family of ducks and other animals. He counted it good luck and good company — especially if he should ever find his mermaid and she was shy of too much humanity.

On the next day, Amy was completely flesh and blood.

Together, she and Miss Eclair investigated a mystery that had happened the night before. Someone had thrown most all of the gold overboard. There was enough left for Captain Cloud to sail the seas for the remainder of his days, and enough left for Amy's father to set up a nice tailor shop, but not enough to worship.

"But look," said Miss Eclair, leaning over the craft that had held the gold and had been nearly emptied of it. "There's a very nice gold ring. I believe I might save that before it goes overboard, also."

"Those golden earrings are what I want," said Amy. "It's something the Captain promised me."

And the *Ariel* sailed through the beautiful blue day towards New Liberty. The great white bird quit the ship that day, swooping out of the sky and making a low pass in front of the ship, turning his head to look into the eyes of the figurehead, the water spirit with her fingers to her lips, her secret still kept. Then he swept into the brilliant blue sky again and was gone.

All of this story that the albatross saw and heard was taken from his eyes by Mama Dah-dah when he returned. The great white bird stood beside her table and looked steadily and unblinkingly at her. Sometimes she smiled at the story, and sometimes she put her hands solemnly together, sometimes shaking her head for the folly of it, and sometimes shaking her shoulders in mirth. And so at last she knew of it all, the entire story. At the very last, she saw in the white bird's eyes the figurehead of the *Ariel*. She nodded her head slowly, and said, "Ain't it the truth, ain't it the truth."

Mama Dah-dah walked to the window and leaned on the sill. She looked out over the sea, which matched almost blue for blue with the sky. Far down the hill they could hear the children singing at their play in the little fishing village. A jump-rope rhyme came up to them. The white bird had heard it before, from Amy.

"Errrrrrr?" he questioned.

"What's that, Anthony?" the old black woman said, turning and looking into his eyes. "Huh? Mother Goose? Of course I know who Mother Goose is? Huh! Sometimes you think I'm just a dumb old woman, don't you, 'cause I don't get out and mess about the world like you?" She turned away.

"Mother Goose. Huh! I'll tell you about Mother Goose, Anthony. Mother Goose is my *sister*! What do you think of that?"

She turned to look back at the giant white bird, to see what he thought of that.

But Anthony's eyes were closed.

THE END

THE PRIME MINISTER'S BRAIN
Gillian Cross

Everyone at school is playing the new computer game Octopus Dare – but only Dinah is good enough to beat it. Then she realizes that the Octopus is trying to control her and the other Brains in the Junior Computer Brain of the Year Competition and that the Demon Headmaster is involved . . .

GOING BACK
Penelope Lively

A thoughtful book about a remembered childhood. Jane and Edward come bursting off the page with their jokes and secrets, their joys and fears, and the atmosphere of an English village in the Second World War is almost tangible.

SEASONS OF SPLENDOUR
Madhur Jaffrey

A beautiful introduction to India, lavishly illustrated by Michael Foreman, with anecdotes from the author's childhood preceding each retelling of these mythological tales from the Hindu epics.

SLADE
John Tully

Slade has a mission – to investigate life on Earth. When Eddie discovers the truth about Slade he gets a whole lot more adventure than he bargained for.

TOM TIDDLER'S GROUND
John Rowe Townsend

Vic and Brain are given an old rowing boat, which leads to the unravelling of a mystery and a happy reunion.

COME SING, JIMMY JO
Katherine Paterson

Absorbing story of eleven-year-old James's rise to stardom, and the problems of coping with the fans.

THE PRIESTS OF FERRIS
Maurice Gee

Susan Ferris and her cousin Nick return to the world of O, which they had saved from the evil Halfmen, only to discover that a hundred years later O is now ruled by cruel and ruthless priests. Susan is inspired by the dreams and prophecies related to her to face the most dreadful dangers and free the inhabitants of O from tyranny.

DRAGON DANCE
John Christopher

Two and a half years have elapsed since Brad and Simon went through the fireball. Now, captured by Chinese slavers, they are taken from California to China, where they find a nation torn apart by civil war. They learn about the power of the Mind, with its creation of illusions, and finally discover the secret of the fireball itself. Faced with a decision which will affect their whole lives, what will they do? Will they return to their own world? Or will they venture on into the unknown?

ELEANOR, ELIZABETH
Libby Gleeson

Eleanor has been wary of her new home so far: the landscape is strange and the faces in the classroom unfriendly. Then her new life changes with the discovery of her grandmother's old diary, and with a bush fire rampaging just behind her she needs help – and only her grandmother, sixty-five years away, can give it to her.

SCREAMING HIGH
David Line

Ratbag could make that trumpet laugh and cry – he was aston-
ishing – although it took a lot of Nick's coaxing to get the
seemingly half-mad loner to demonstrate this fact to their
school band leader.

DOLPHIN ISLAND
Arthur C. Clarke

Johnny Clifton had never been happy living with Aunt Martha
and her family for the twelve years since his parents had died,
when he was four. So when an inter-continental hovership
breaks down outside his house, he stows away on it.

THE AMAZING MR BLUNDEN
Antonia Barber

A ghostly adventure in which two present-day children become
involved with children from the past who died in a dreadful
fire.